After breathing new life into WWII historical fiction for the past few years, Tricia Goyer turns her keen eye to vistas of the Spanish Civil War. Goyer is a painter of words, creating memorable scenes and characters, educating while entertaining. And, at the heart of this story, she reminds us that God can bring beauty from the darkest places, that each of us have gifts that can be used to God's glory. This is a fantastic new series, not to be missed.

—Eric Wilson, author of *The Best of Evil*,
Expiration Date, and *Dark to Mortal Eyes*

Tricia Goyer has done it again . . . this time by setting her latest novel during the Spanish Civil War, a regional conflict that was a warm-up to the main event—World War II. Highly interesting and highly readable.

—Mike Yorkey, coauthor of the
Every Man's Battle series

The real heroes of war aren't the soldiers but the character of its people. *A Valley of Betrayal* speaks to the heart when deceit threatens truth.

—DiAnn Mills, author of the Nebraska
Legacy novels and Leather and Lace novels

This "wow" novel will delight Tricia Goyer's fans. She takes an unfamiliar, murky war and paints vivid portraits of individuals caught in the contradictory conflict. Tricia addresses the desperation and horror redemptively, allowing the reader a hard-fought hope. Prepare for a surprising adventure.

—Dr. Rebecca Price Janney, historian,
author of *Great Stories in American History*

A Valley of Betrayal is a haunting depiction of the autocracies of war and the triumph of faith. Through the power of story Tricia brings history alive so that we never forget the battles that have been fought and the brave men and women who have gone before us.

—Amy Wallace, author of *Ransomed Dreams*

Air battles of the Spanish Civil War were responsible for rapid improvement of aircraft fighters and bombers flown in World War II. Tricia Goyer, unfortunately no relation, has enriched the world of aviation history. In addition, I have always enjoyed reading a good action novel and getting a little history as a bonus.

—Norm Goyer
Aviation Editor, Author, and Historian

Chronicles
of the
SPANISH CIVIL WAR

A Valley of Betrayal

TRICIA GOYER

MOODY PUBLISHERS
CHICAGO

© 2007 by
TRICIA GOYER

All Scripture quotations are taken from the King James Version.

Cover Design: Gearbox, David Carlson
Cover Image: Walter Bibikow / Getty, Hulton-Deutsch Collection / Corbis, Veer
Interior Design: Ragont Designs
Editor: LB Norton

Library of Congress Cataloging-in-Publication Data

Goyer, Tricia.
    A valley of betrayal / Tricia Goyer.
        p. cm. — (Chronicles of the Spanish Civil War)
    ISBN-13: 978-0-8024-6767-6
        1. Women journalists—Fiction. 2. Spain—History—Civil War, 1936–1939—Fiction. I. Title.

PS3607.O94V35 2007
813'.6—dc22

                                                                2006034523

                        ISBN: 0-8024-6767-9
                        ISBN-13: 978-0-8024-6767-6

We hope you enjoy this book from Moody Publishers. Our goal is to provide high-quality, thought-provoking books and products that connect truth to your real needs and challenges. For more information on other books and products written and produced from a biblical perspective, go to www.moodypublishers.com or write to:

                        Moody Publishers
                    820 N. LaSalle Boulevard
                        Chicago, IL 60610

                        1 3 5 7 9 10 8 6 4 2

Printed in the United States of America

To John and Darlyne Goyer, my parents-in-love

Your prayers seventeen years ago pointed me to Christ.
Your prayers today strengthen me for the journey.

Thank you.

Other Books by Tricia Goyer

	ISBN-10	ISBN-13
Arms of Deliverance	0-8024-1556-3	978-0-8024-1556-1
Dawn of a Thousand Nights	0-8024-0855-9	978-0-8024-0855-6
From Dust and Ashes	0-8024-1554-7	978-0-8024-1554-7
Night Song	0-8024-1555-5	978-0-8024-1555-4

Coming in September 2007

	ISBN-10	ISBN-13
A Shadow of Treason	0-8024-6768-7	978-0-8024-6768-3

*D*ear Reader,

A few years ago when I was researching for my fourth World War II novel, I came across a unique autobiography. One B-17 crewmember I read about claimed to make it out of German-occupied Belgium after a plane crash due, in part, to the skills he picked up as a veteran of the Spanish Civil War. Reading that bit of information, I had to scratch my head. First of all, I had never heard of the war. And second, what was an American doing fighting in Spain in the late 1930s? Before I knew it, I uncovered a fascinating time in history—one that I soon discovered many people know little about. This is what I learned:

Nazi tanks rolled across the hillsides and German bombers roared overhead, dropping bombs on helpless citizens. Italian troops fought alongside the Germans, and their opponents attempted to stand strong—Americans, British, Irishmen, and others —in unison with other volunteers from many countries. And their battleground? The beautiful Spanish countryside.

From July 17, 1936–April 1, 1939, well before America was involved in World War II, another battle was fought on the hill-sides of Spain. On one side were the Spanish Republicans, joined by the Soviet Union and the *International Brigade*—men and women from all over the world who volunteered to fight Fascism. Opposing them were Franco and his Fascist military leaders, supported with troops, machinery, and weapons from Hitler and Mussolini. The Spanish Civil War, considered the "training ground" for the war to come, boasted of thousands of American volunteers who joined to fight on the Republican side, half of whom never returned home.

Unlike World War II, there is no clear line between right and wrong, good and evil. Both sides committed atrocities. Both sides had deep convictions they felt were worth fighting and dying for.

Loyalists—also know as the Republicans, were aided by the Soviet Union, the Communist movement, and the International Brigades. If not for the weapons and volunteers from these sources, their fight would have ended in weeks rather than years. While many men fought side by side, their political views included those of liberal democracy, communism, and socialism. The Catholic Basque Country also sided with the Republic, mainly because it sought independence from the central government and was promised this by Republican leaders in Madrid.

Nationalists—or Francoists, were aided mainly by Germany and Italy. The Nationalist opposed an independent Basque state. Their main supporters were those who believed in a monarchist state and Fascist interests. The Nationalists wished for Spain to continue on as it had for years, with rich landowners, the military, and the church running the country. Most of the Roman Catholic clergy supported the Nationalists, except those in the Basque region.

During the Spanish Civil War, terror tactics against civilians were common. And while history books discuss the estimated one million people who lost their lives during the conflict, we must not forget that each of those who fought, who died, had their own tales. From visitors to Spain who found themselves caught in the conflict, to the communist supporters, Basque priests, and Nazi airmen . . . each saw this war in a different light. These are their stories.

Tricia Goyer, October 2006

Prologue

MARCH 7, 1936
BERLIN, GERMANY

One Reich, One Folk, One Füehrer

Nazi motto

*A*dolf Hitler, chin set and chest forward, stepped up to the podium at the Kroll Opera House. Ritter Agler hardly cast the Führer a full glance. Instead, he riveted his eyes on the round, balding man sitting in the third row from the front and contemplated the best way to get his inheritance without resorting to murder. . . .

Keep your mind on the task at hand, Ritter told himself, straightening in his carved wooden chair. Hitler's gaze swept across the crowd, and Ritter wondered again how such a homely little man could rise to such greatness. He possessed more good looks and charisma in his small toe than Hitler had altogether. Of course, Ritter had considerably smaller goals. He wasn't concerned about ruling the world—just capturing and keeping Isanna's heart.

The ornate walls and golden columns of the opera house set the ideal stage for the puppet parliament assembled. Red velvet curtains. Pristine paintings with gilded frames. Suits, uniforms, hats, white or black gloves. Fake, all of it. A theater of little men acting as if they actually had a say in things. At least Ritter's uncle still had enough clout to get his nephew into the building under the guise of being his assistant. That should impress Isanna —or at least provide enough conversation to perk up her dull father during dinner.

Ritter ran a finger around the collar of his starched white shirt, feeling strangely uncomfortable without his military uniform. His week of leave from the air force was nearly over, yet Uncle Oswald had insisted Ritter join him for the Führer's unexpected announcement. And if he'd learned one thing, it was never to disappoint his uncle. *Soon I'll be back in the air—away from this nonsense. Just me, alone in the cockpit.*

After two minutes of drivel, Hitler's voice rose in volume, and Ritter noticed for the first time the brooding looks and thin layers of sweat on the brows of Hitler's generals. It was a simple meeting of the six hundred deputies of the Reichstag, but perhaps Ritter was in for a treat, after all.

The Führer's voice quavered slightly as he announced the dawning of the movement of three German army battalions across the Rhine, and their entry into the industrial heartland of Germany. Ritter leaned forward in his seat.

The demilitarized area included territory west of the Rhine River, extending to the French border. It also included a portion east of the river including the cities of Cologne, Düsseldorf, and Bonn. The mobilization was a flagrant violation of the Treaty of Versailles. Enough to set France and its allies on edge.

Ritter glanced down the row of men to his right. Not fear, but excitement tinged with greed gleamed from their Aryan eyes. They knew too well the benefits of Hitler's bold moves. Construction boomed in Germany. Handsome new autobahns connected the major cities. Factory smokestacks billowed. Unemployment had dropped, while national income doubled. Why argue with Hitler's motives when the results spoke for themselves?

Yet this march into forbidden territory also meant that war loomed on the horizon. To Ritter, war meant flying. Not the drills they'd performed *ad nauseam*, but real combat.

He lifted his hand to hide his slight smile, and a realization hit. Maybe it wasn't a grand inheritance that would be the final draw of Isanna's favor, but his status as a war hero. At least it would give him more time to persuade his uncle to open his purse strings.

Perfect. First the glory, then the money.

The Führer leaned into the podium, his silver tongue wooing the crowd as he offered his assurances that he'd no longer endanger the German people by keeping their border with France unprotected. France, after all, had signed a defense pact with the Soviet Union, and it was the Communists who posed the new and immediate danger. So the French, in a sense, had signed their own death warrant by joining with communist ideals. The fools. Ritter pitied the country—the people—that got on Germany's bad side.

The Führer's hands flailed and his voice rose. "I will not have the gruesome communist international dictatorship of hate descend upon the German people!"

Cheering, the deputies rose to their feet.

"In the interest of the primitive rights of its people to the security of their frontier, the German government has reestablished, as of today, the absolute and unrestricted sovereignty of the Reich in the demilitarized zone!"

By "the German government," Ritter knew the Führer spoke mainly of himself. Hitler made the decision. Hitler's hand. Hitler's troops. Despite this, the parliament leapt to their feet once more.

"Sieg Heil!"

The frenzied voices rose around Ritter. His mind filled with the images of German troops marching into forbidden lands—and soon flying over their horizons.

"Sieg Heil!" Ritter joined in, raising his voice above them all. *"Sieg Heil!"*

SUMMER

And the glorious beauty, which is on the head of the fat valley,
shall be a fading flower, and as the hasty fruit before the summer;
which when he that looketh upon it seeth,
while it is yet in his hand he eateth it up.
—Isaiah 28:4

Chapter One

JULY 18, 1936
SOMEWHERE IN FRANCE

Hoy se ven las nubes de la lluvia de mañana.
Today we see the clouds of tomorrow's rain.

Spanish proverb

*T*he man wouldn't stop staring, and every one of her mother's warnings about traveling alone in a foreign country assaulted Sophie Grace's mind like the heavy rain pelting the train window. Fumbling for her leather journal, she quickly sketched the man's image. That way, if she showed up missing, they'd at least have a clue to lead them to her abductor.

She didn't need to turn around to remember his long, narrow face. Thick sideburns and equally thick eyebrows set above two small eyes. His hat sat too low on his brow to distinguish his hairline, but his smile reminded her of Benjamin Franklin's on the statue in the courtyard of the Old City Hall in Boston. Slight, yet knowing. And unchanging as if the man were as stiff as a statue himself.

Ten minutes later, a sketch of the man's narrow face, beady eyes, and black fedora filled the page. She glanced back once more. He looked up and offered her a bigger, crooked smile over the masthead of a French newspaper.

Nice try, buddy. But I'm not biting.

Receiving complimentary looks from strangers wasn't something new, but feeling nervous to the point of hearing her heart beating in her throat was. Maybe the fact that she didn't know a soul for hundreds of miles had something to do with it? Yes, that was it.

Ginny, her dearest friend, had labeled Sophie's trek The Great Spanish Adventure. And through weeks of packing they'd discussed bullfights, gypsies, music, flamenco dancing, sunshine, and afternoon siestas. Yet what Sophie hadn't confessed to Ginny was that the journey had nothing to do with Spain and everything to do with Michael.

Sophie flipped to the first page of her journal and brushed an ink-stained fingertip over the edges of the photo she'd taped there. In fewer than twenty-four hours she would arrive in Madrid, and she'd be with him again. Michael, the international correspondent who had swept twenty-five-year old Sophie off her feet. Michael, who danced divinely and lived life with passion. Michael, who used his camera to transform everyday life into art, yet who also grew bored if there wasn't a bit of blood and guts, or politics, to capture on film. Michael, who once dared her to travel to Spain, and who would be both delighted and shocked to discover she'd gone and done it.

My trip to Europe is a kaleidoscope, and every new color shift brings a deeper understanding of him, Sophie now wrote on the page opposite Michael's photograph. She lifted the journal and read the words again, smiling—the train's rocking had added a gentle wiggle to her typically flawless penmanship.

She closed the book and focused on the luminous mountains ahead and the symmetrical clouds poised above. Both were slightly out of focus due to the film of water on the window— like an Impressionist painting, hinting of form and color without real definition.

Almost there.

In less than an hour she'd be at the Spanish border. In a day she'd be in Michael's arms. And in a few days she'd truly be his for a lifetime, which meant she'd never have to think again about men like the one behind her.

Shabby old buildings passed her window as the train began to slow for Hendaye, the last French town before the tracks entered Spain. But as she looked out the train window, Sophie realized something was terribly wrong.

CATALONIA, SPAIN

Philip Stanford flung his red-white-and-blue exercise jacket over his shoulder and strode out of the stadium onto Ramblas Avenue. He and the other members of the American track team had arrived in Barcelona two days before and had enjoyed the food, wine, and especially the flamenco dancers. As an undistinguished high school teacher from Seattle, Washington, Philip never expected to travel overseas, much less visit an exotic place like Spain. In fact, he only had two great talents. One was his ability to run fast. The second was to train others to do the same. And it was this role as trainer that had brought him to Barcelona.

"Tomorrow's the big day." Philip reached up to pat the shoulder of his companion, sprinter Attis Brody. Though Philip was six feet tall when he stood straight, he felt short and squat next to Attis's six-foot-four-inch frame. And now that the day's practice was over, it was with a slow stride that he and Attis headed back to their hotel by the globed streetlights' yellow illumination. The light danced on the slightly damp cobblestones and filtered into the breeze, which carried the scent of burning olive oil, flowers from the shrubbery they passed, and the sweat from Attis's tall, lean body.

"Tomorrow you'll be introduced to the world," Philip continued. "Did you see those other guys working out? They ran as if someone had tied twenty-pound weights to their legs."

Attis laughed and said something, but honking automobiles made it hard for Philip to hear his comeback. The noisy vehicles seemed to be moving faster through the streets than should be allowed, weaving through the throngs of people, the horse carts, and men on horseback. Philip shouldered up to Attis, nudging him closer to the edge of the buildings they passed.

From the buildings, the yellow-and-red-striped federal flags of Catalonia waved overhead, slapping in the breeze like clapping hands. The two men approached the end of the street, and Attis paused, looking up at the flags with a wide smile. Philip had sensed Attis's excitement for the recently instated government the first time they practiced in Barcelona's new stadium. But nothing moved his friend more than the scarlet colors of the United Socialist Party of Catalonia, the United Party of Communists and Socialists, the black-and-red banner of the anarchists, and in fewer places the government flags of Spain, showing both the old ways and the new Socialist ideas attempting to coexist. It was Attis's beliefs lived out. They'd stumbled upon a real place where people believed in a classless society working together in common ownership—or at the very least, a place where that was the goal, in the five months since the government, comprised mostly of Communists and Socialists, won the election.

Attis also did two things well. First was to run fast. And second was to make himself aware of the fight against Fascism all over the world, and in recent days, especially Spain. After years of living in the midst of economic depression, Attis had joined the Communist Party. He believed this equality among men was just what Spain needed—just what America needed too.

To Philip, the tension that hung in the air was just as noticeable as the symbolism behind the flapping flags. Rumors about a revolution in Spain concerned him, but there was no time for fretting. Attis had come to run, and Philip had come to make sure he won a gold medal. It's what they'd dreamed about since they were kids. Now they were both twenty-three, and this was the second dream Attis was fulfilling. Finding a good wife in Louise had been his first.

At the top of Ramblas they entered a park called the Plaza de Cataluna. It was decked out with brightly colored flowering shrubs, statues—including one of a naked woman forever kneeling down, peering at herself in the center of a pool—and fountains that displayed a formality and dignity unseen in the manufacturing district in Seattle where he lived. Moving beyond that, they reached a circular area of cafés, restaurants, the large telephone building that stretched like a skyscraper into the sky, and the American consulate.

On the upper side, Paseo de Gracia led to the newer, more spacious part of the town. Yet it was this lower side that most intrigued Philip—the shabby, congested quarters that suggest to him how Spaniards had lived and died for hundreds of years. If only he could walk through the streets for a few hours without drawing the attention of the people. His brightly colored uniform didn't allow for that, nor did his light hair and pale skin, which set him apart from even the fairer of the Spaniards. He put those thoughts aside. The race yet to be run, he reminded himself, was the important thing.

While the rest of the world was focused on the Olympics in Berlin, Attis had refused to attend.

"I won't run in the same country as Hitler. I won't run with any swastika waving over my head," he had said. "I'd cut off my legs at the knees first."

Philip glanced around as they approached their hotel. Soldiers in olive uniforms marched down the streets, weapons shouldered. Distant gunfire floated on the dusty air, and Philip wondered if Berlin would have been the better, safer choice after all.

Yet Attis had said Spain, and Spain it was. Even if he hadn't been Attis's trainer, he would have come as his protector—even though his friend had long since passed him by in height and strength. That's the way it had always been, and he'd promised Attis's wife, that's the way it would always be—whether the big guy knew it or not.

Chapter Two

The gloomy town outside the train's window matched Sophie's mood as she clutched her passport. Mere miles separated her from the border to Spain. Oh, yes, and the men who guarded those borders.

A porter in pristine uniform approached hurriedly, cap in hand. "I regret to inform you, mademoiselle," he said as he bowed, "the Spanish frontier is closed. Only Spaniards are allowed entrance."

"What do you mean, closed?" Sophie waved her passport under the man's thin pointed nose. "I have been traveling for nearly a month to get this far!"

"You must depart here at Hendaye—the last town before the border. There is a revolution in Spain." He dared to look at her eyes, then looked away again, peering over his shoulder as if hoping someone else on the train would come to his assistance.

"I don't care about foreign politics. I simply have to get to Madrid. It's a matter of life or death!" She wasn't lying, she told herself. Life without Michael would be death.

"Sorry, mademoiselle. Your baggage has already been unloaded at the platform. I have no choice but to escort you from this cabin."

Reluctantly Sophie rose from the cushioned seat and followed the porter to the exit. The cool evening air that hit her cheeks bore the heavy scent of rain. She tucked her journal and small satchel under one arm, and with the other she pulled the collar of her traveling jacket tight to her chin.

Sure enough, her trunks and crates were piled next to the train station. She could feel the tears rising behind her eyes. All around her, other passengers were hurrying away from the station.

She stopped a man who had just exited the train. "Excuse me, sir. Can you give me directions to the nearest hotel?"

He rattled off something in French and threw his arms up in the air when she didn't respond.

Sophie turned back toward her luggage. Next to her things stood the staring man from the train. He glanced at her, dropped his cigarette to the ground, and stamped it out.

She fumbled with the journal in her hands and glanced around.

"Miss, my name is Walt Block, and I'm a reporter from New York." He spoke with a crisp New York accent and stepped toward her, unhindered by her glare. "I see we're in the same bind here, and I was hoping we could help each other out?"

Sophie straightened her back. "Unless you have a cart for all my things, a hotel with a vacancy, and some magical powers that could cause me to wake up in Madrid, I really don't think you can be of any help."

"Actually, while you were arguing with the porter, I learned the name of the nearest hotel. Spain has refused entrance to foreigners. It could be weeks before the borders open. Yet why should we sit here forever? I know of a way via Port-Bou, but for that we'll have to get a car to Perpignan."

Sophie nodded as if she understood what he was talking about.

"Once we're in a safe zone, I can help you find a way to Madrid." He shifted the small suitcase he carried. He still wore that black hat, yet when she looked closer, in the light of the streetlamp, Sophie believed she saw compassion in his beady eyes. At least she hoped it was compassion.

"We can be across the border by this time tomorrow. If you trust me, that is," he added, tipping his hat.

"What choice do I have?"

Walt smiled, revealing a dimpled cheek, and Sophie quickly continued. "I mean, I appreciate your going out of your way to help me. But you have to tell me what *my* part is."

"I've been in Paris a few weeks on assignment for my syndicate, and I've been called to cover Barcelona. I heard you speaking Spanish on the train. You're fairly fluent?"

His voice was pleasant now, and he presented himself as a man of good breeding. Maybe her first impression had been wrong.

"Yes, for the most part. I've studied for the last year preparing for this trip, and took a few years of study at college before that."

The man sighed. "If you could interpret for me, talk to the officials at the border, I can help you with my credentials. I'm sure I can get you a temporary pass to get in as my interpreter. But there is one problem."

"What's that?"

He waved a hand toward the half-dozen crates and trunks. "Newspaper people travel light. If you show up with all this, they'll never believe us. Maybe we can get the local hotel to keep it for you—for a price, of course."

Sophie didn't hesitate. Her things or her man. An easy choice. She stretched out her hand and connected with his. "It's a deal. I've heard about the previous Spanish uprisings, and I don't want to wait around a few weeks until things settle down. How can I ever repay you?"

"Don't thank me yet. We're not over the border. Now, wait here while I find a place for your things." And with long strides he disappeared, heading toward what appeared to be the center of town.

Sophie looked to the sky, hoping the rain would hold off. Then she glanced around the deserted platform and shivered. *I'm*

alone, in the dark of night, in a village on the French border, commit-
ting myself to travel with a man I have exchanged fewer than ten sen-
tences with.

"And to top if off," she muttered under her breath, "I get to take only one suitcase!"

No matter how hard he tried, Philip couldn't think of one witty thing he could say to Marvin Duncan. Not one.

Marv was a high school classmate and the local reporter who'd promised Philip a front-page story when they arrived home from Spain.

We traveled for two weeks, didn't run one race, and scooted away like frightened schoolgirls at the first sign of danger. That wasn't exactly what he wanted to confess to Marv, who got whatever he wanted—including Elizabeth, the girl Philip admired but had been too shy to pursue.

Yet worse than having to face up to Marv was the idea of coming all this way without Attis having the chance to run a single race.

Just hours ago, after he and Attis had returned to the hotel and toasted their hoped-for success over dinner, they received notice that the Workers' Games were off, cancelled due to rebel uprisings all over Spain. As they prepared for bed, the swanky avenues they were scheduled to march down for the Workers' Games parade filled up with activists instead—some on horseback, others on foot. Still others lounged drowsily on the terraces of nearby cafés closed for the night, the red glow from their cigarettes spotting the black street like Christmas lights strung on a thin line down the avenue.

Now he lay in bed in the dark hotel room, considering their options. Maybe he could convince the committee to let the athletes run a few races despite the threat. So far this revolution consisted of more talk than bite.

His thoughts were interrupted by the sudden rumbling of

cannons, the sound of high-powered motorcars racing up the avenue, and the sputtering of machine guns. Seconds later, the pounding of marching feet met his ears.

Philip scrambled to the bureau for his trousers and turned to the window. Attis was already up and peering outside.

Shouts filled the air. "*Viva la Rep·blica! Viva Azana! Viva Cataluna!*"

"What's going on?" Philip's knees trembled as he buttoned his pants, and a rumbling of excitement coursed through his gut. He moved to the window and spotted groups of men marching below. A group broke off and literally began tearing up the streets, prying up cobblestones. Then came more crackling of rifles, closer.

Attis pushed the half-open shutters wider, their hinges squeaking.

"What's in their crazy heads?" Philip wiped at his tired eyes as if they were deceiving him.

"Building barricades, I believe."

"That means the Rebels are coming."

"Yeah, they're coming, all right. Fascist pigs."

As if sensing their presence in the window, a machine gun fired from somewhere, the pinging sound hitting the façade of their building.

"Get down!" Philip fell to the floor, his hands protecting his head.

When the shots died down, Attis rose from the floor. Then he quickly dressed and moved to the door.

"Where do you think you're going?"

"To find me a crowbar."

"For what?" Philip asked, but he already knew the answer. Attis's ideals had forced him to boycott Fascist Germany. Why would he be hesitant to fight the same ideology here?

Attis stormed out the door without answering, and Philip had no choice but to follow. He had to bring Attis back inside. To keep him safe. He'd promised Louise . . . but where was his jacket? Attis had slid it on by mistake, and it held Philip's passport. Now he really had to follow his friend. If he lost track of his passport, he'd never get out of this place.

The soft light of morning and a strong smell of gunpowder met Philip as he exited the building. Gunfire sounded, yet now it seemed farther down the street. A one-horse garbage cart rambled by, abandoning the filthy streets in an effort to escape. Militiamen darted cautiously back and forth, their rifles aimed and shooting toward those firing at them from the flat, parapet-lined roofs above. Most of the shutters on the buildings around them were tightly closed, yet a few had been cracked opened to allow snipers' rifles to poke through.

A sudden movement above him caught his attention. Philip quickly scanned the roof just as several militiamen, dressed in dark blue, dashed toward the rebel snipers. The militiamen reached them, pointing their guns to the back of their heads and . . .

The pounding of horses' hooves pulled his attention away. Horses carrying more armed citizens rushed through the streets —communist and socialist colors were tied to the men's arms.

"Viva la Rep blica! Viva Aẕana!"

"Viva Aẕana! Viva la Rep blica! Viva Cataluna!"

Other men's voices rose in Spanish song.

Moving beyond the front door of the hotel, Philip paused and hunkered down. Attis had already joined others piling cobblestones around two dead horses, building a barricade.

The horses are barely dead, he thought, noticing steam still rising from their backs. He watched as Attis now worked as diligently prying cobblestones as he had trained for his races. He wore a look of determination, as if this were what he'd truly come for.

Philip sprinted toward the men digging up the street, thinking back to every war novel he'd read. Every detailed battle. Every maimed fighter. Every lifeless soldier who gave his all for naught.

One of the men noticed his athletic uniform shirt and handed him a crowbar. The uniform identified Philip as part of the pro-communist workers' games, proving he was on their side.

Philip sidled up to Attis, then wedged the end of the bar under one of the bricks.

He dug in with vengeance, and despite the seriousness of the situation, a small smile played on his lips. It was a crazy thought, and one he wasn't proud of. In fact, if he truly realized the seriousness of the situation, it wasn't a thought he should let play on his mind at all. But the truth was, if he couldn't return from Spain with a medal for Attis, at least he'd return with a good story—one Marv would be forced to write, and one Philip and Attis could talk about, as old men do when talking is all they can do with vigor.

Nearly an hour after the world seemed to erupt, awakening a unified spirit of determination among the anti-fascists of Barcelona, a small-framed Spaniard with wide, bulging eyes approached the group of men still working to barricade the streets.

Philip paused, wiping the sweat from his brow with cracked and bloodied hands. Others did the same, their frenzied activity ceasing as if someone had flipped off an engine, and they all leaned close to the small man, eager for the latest report.

"The government regiments quartered in the city have rebelled," he said hurriedly in Spanish. "They left their barracks and now are in full-fledged attack, fighting for the Fascist cause. Their orders are to take control of the telephone building and city hall."

"Not today, comrades!" one man shouted. "They shall not pass!" Other joined in with words as vigorous as their movements had been for the last hour.

Philip leaned close to Attis. "Their own military is fighting against the people?"

Attis nodded his response.

The men around him spoke in Spanish, and he understood enough to know they were arguing about who should go evaluate the situation down the street.

"I'll go." Philip raised his hand like a schoolboy eager to be picked for an assignment. If he didn't, he had no doubt Attis would. He was glad he'd raised his hand first. And at least the gunfire had subsided.

The small man nodded, then hurried away, continuing to spread the news and shout orders to the others working to fortify the streets.

His heartbeat pounding in his ears, Philip scanned the road, hoping that snipers did not continue to lie in wait. Then, moving back to the shadowed sidewalk, he hurried down the street toward the mounting action. He stopped short when a fortresslike building loomed before him—a beautiful cathedral.

His jaw fell open when he noticed rifle barrels pointed from the windows. What were they doing up there?

Snipers crouched in the bell tower. Puffs of smoke erupted from their rifle barrels, and one of their bullets nicked the cobblestone inches from Philip's foot.

He cried out, and his heart pounded like a hammer against his chest as he sprinted toward a brick building. As he slammed against the wall to catch his breath, he saw a group of Socialist workers moving past, carrying cans of gasoline and torches.

One man crumbled to the ground with a cry, struck by a sniper's bullet. Gasoline splashed as the can tipped in the injured man's hands, but another caught it before losing any more precious fuel. They left the wounded man to drag himself off the road and marched forward, determination etched on their faces.

Philip didn't want to watch, yet he couldn't look away. His stomach knotted at the sight of yellow and orange tongues of fire engulfing the cross, rocks being tossed through the stained glass, the meek statue of Jesus with its pierced hands and bloodstained brow bursting into a thousand shards at the impact of shovels and picks.

There was an explosion, and a flock of sparrows that had nested in the trees alongside the church swished into the air and swooped down over the militiamen as if scolding them for their misdeeds. Flames engulfed the church.

Sucking in a breath, and urging his hands to cease their trembling, Philip turned and sprinted back to the men barricading the roads, hurriedly relating news of the snipers and the fire. Cheers rose from the men, and they returned to their efforts with renewed vigor. An ache filled Philip's gut, and he had a sudden urge to escape to the safety of the hotel.

Though he'd left his family's religion when he'd moved out on his own, he couldn't help thinking of his own father and his small parish in Washington. Surely there was another way to stop the snipers than to desecrate a holy dwelling. Tearing up the streets was one thing. Burning down the sanctuary dedicated to a holy God was something else entirely.

"Attis, let's go!" he called over the sound of the workers, waving his hand toward his friend.

Attis turned his direction, yet barely paused. Instead, he lifted his crowbar in salute.

Philip picked up a crowbar and joined him again. To leave the street would mean leaving Attis, and that wasn't even a consideration.

Chapter Three

Lloré al nacer y cada día que pasa explica por qué.
I wept when I was born, and every day explains why.

Spanish proverb

Sophie's pile of trunks and crates filled half of the quiet lobby. The bellman snoozed in a plush armchair. Walt waited in a second chair as Sophie sifted through her things, her mind racing as she tried to figure out what she needed most.

The lock of the last trunk clicked as it unsnapped, and she flipped it open. Was it just her imagination, or could she smell the lilacs outside her bedroom window in Boston and her mother's perfume? She pulled out the linens, fringed with lace, and remembered her mother folding them so lovingly. Her paints and brushes lay underneath, a gift from her father. She touched the simple frame of the self-portrait she'd painted as a wedding gift for Michael. Setting it aside, facedown, she thumbed through the new suits and dresses she'd saved months for—items that made her feel like the important newspaper photographer's wife she'd soon be. She'd packed and repacked a dozen times, and for what —to leave it all behind?

She slid a thin, black cotton garment bag from the trunk and pressed it to her chest. Inside was her most cherished possession —a stylish dress of light blue cotton, which made her feel like one of the women in Monet's idyllic park scenes every time she put it on. She'd bought it for her wedding.

Sophie rolled the garment bag as tightly as she could and tucked it into her satchel. She could find a way to send for the rest, but this dress represented the purpose for her trip—to marry the only man she'd ever loved.

She turned to Walt with a sigh. "Okay, I'm ready. This is the last of what I need."

Her things would be carted to a back storage room of this hotel, and now she had one last thing to do before heading out.

"I don't think this is the type of walking shoe you meant." Sophie lifted one leather-clad, pointy-toed foot. "Just give me a few minutes to change my clothes."

Walt extended his hand toward the satchel. "I'll watch your things."

"Thanks." She handed it to him with her journal. "I'll be right back."

As she dressed, she thought back to the first time she met Michael. She was working as a tour guide at the Museum of Fine Arts, waiting for her own art to be discovered, and he was on assignment, taking photographs for . . . for something she couldn't remember and that made no difference now.

Michael was tall, dark, lean, and exotic, with wavy brown hair and green eyes. Giving him a tour of the building, Sophie had found it unnerving the way his lips curled in a coy smile as he listened to her talk. It was almost as if he were studying the true message behind her words, one she didn't understand herself.

After the tour of the museum, he asked her to coffee, then to dinner. And afterward they walked on the Freedom Trail as Sophie shared about the historic places in Boston, and Michael talked about Spain, where he had spent every summer of his boyhood. His love for the country was evident from the beginning.

After that, they managed to see each other every day. She remembered the antique-style map he had hanging in his apartment, wooden thumbtacks marking each foreign location he'd visited—more than Sophie had even heard of. And she was moved by how her landscape paintings fascinated him. He was in awe, marveling at each one she completed.

They dated for six months before Michael invited Sophie to meet his parents. His American father and his mother, a first-generation Spanish dancer, seemed to come from different worlds. But when relaxing in Michael's embrace on the swing in the backyard, Sophie spotted Michael's mother dancing in his father's arms, and knew *that's* how she wanted to spend the rest of her life. With festive Spanish music drifting from the gramophone out the back window, Michael proposed. Without hesitation, she said yes.

Now, with the help of Walt, she hoped that *yes* would become reality.

Sophie came back to the lobby dressed in her sturdiest boots and trousers, a long-sleeved shirt, and jacket. Traveling clothes —for whatever elements they'd face.

"They're only things," she said out loud, with a backward glance at her trunks. "That stuff can be replaced, but I'm not going to wait until these civil battles settle down. Even two weeks sounds like a lifetime."

"I agree, *señorita*," Walt said with a flourish of his hat. His brown hair flopped over his high forehead as he did.

Sophie nodded, realizing he was younger than the hat and suit had led her to believe. "*Sí, Don Walterio*. The Spanish frontier awaits us."

"Oh, no." Walt wagged his finger. "No Don Walterio for me. No Don anything. It is the Dons—those with titles—who find themselves stripped of their possessions and their lives." He slid his finger across his neck, then dramatically shivered. "I'd like very much to keep my head, thank you."

Deion Clay hurriedly stacked the dirty dishes on the large bus tray, then glanced around before folding the stained copy of the *New York Times* and tucking it down the front left leg of his baggy trousers.

"You know you gonna get the boot if Bossman catch you."

Deion nodded but refused to make eye contact with the singer he knew only as Roberta. When she sang, her voice was as silky and smooth as the red satin dress that clung to her chocolate frame. And though she was one of the most popular singers in the joint, she knew—everyone knew—that Roberta, too, balanced precariously between the marquee board outside and the unemployment line down the street.

She slid into the chair directly in front of Deion, and he turned to clear off the next table. Still, the vivid flowery odor of her perfume, mixed with the thick cigarette smoke in the air, caused him to feel light-headed as memories of the last singer he'd gotten involved with flooded him. He wasn't going to let that happen again. With women, he'd decided, life had more complications than it was worth.

"Just what's in those ol' papers anyway? I mean, what can be so interesting?"

He cautiously glanced at her, wondering if she honestly cared.

Roberta leaned closer, allowing one of the straps of her dress to slide down, exposing her smooth shoulder. Yet her eyes held an inquisitive look that caused Deion to risk opening up.

"There's a war in Spain, Roberta. Fascist rebels are trying to take over the country, no matter the fact that the new leaders were voted in democratically. No matter the fact that they're fightin' 'gainst the very people that make up the heart of the country."

"Humph." Roberta righted her strap and leaned back in her seat. "Last week you talkin' about Ethiopia. Today it's Spain. What about Chicago? I don't see how that fighting overseas has anything to do with you."

"Then you don't know much at all, do ya?" Deion lifted the tray filled with other people's leftover food. Other people's dirty dishes. He was used to meddling in other folks' messes. And if no one cared about places like Ethiopia and Spain and things like injustice and Fascists, then soon enough they'd all be in a pile of trouble. Those dictators wouldn't stop until they controlled the people everywhere.

He clucked his tongue. "Listen now. If we crush Fascism there, we'll save our people in America and other parts of the world. I don't know about you, but being I'm from Mississippi, I've been insulted, segregated, abused, and Jim-Crowed enough to know a bad deal when I see one."

Roberta rose and returned to her spot on the well-worn piano bench. She lifted her fingers to play, but instead of pressing them to the keys, they hung in the air like limp spaghetti. "Still don't know what Spain gots to do with anything."

Deion opened his mouth to speak, then closed it again. As he walked toward the kitchen, Roberta launched into a lively jazz tune he couldn't remember the name of. It was no use trying to explain it to anyone who hadn't seen the sight of burning bodies, of their people hanging from trees, swinging and swaying like his mama's laundry on the clothesline. Heard the groaning of the helpless loved ones. Or seen the bitter rage that comes over a man unable to do a thing.

Of course, what was he doing about it? He asked himself the same question a dozen or two times a day. Sure, he should feel thankful to have a job when so many were without, yet Deion's shoulders still slumped.

There's nothing I can do about it in Chicago.

Spain was a long way away. And so was Ethiopia, where the Fascist Italian government did even worse to colored folk there.

He set the tray in the deep sink, the clanking of dishes reminding him of the clanking of the train wheels over the track—the ones that had carried him here, and the ones that could carry him to New York, where he'd heard people did more than just read the paper and talk. Maybe in New York he could find a better job than cleaning up other people's slop. And maybe he could talk about real matters with folks who cared, instead of just reading it secondhand from stolen, food-splattered newspapers that scratched his thigh as he walked.

Father Manuel Garcia had heard that in some towns the anti-fascists, Communists mostly, had killed their priests. And sometimes he wished they'd done that in the northern towns too. It would be easier to be dead than to carry the burden of those who died. He'd prayed for them, absolved their sins, but he couldn't save them. Of course, Jesus the Christ was the only One who could save.

Manuel made the sign of the cross as he heard footsteps nearing on the stone walkway to his front door. He rose from his high-back chair, his young body feeling old, moving like the antiquated priest he had replaced two years ago.

His fingers brushed the doorknob. After all this time, the door still didn't seem like his door. The church had sent him to this parish. Yet, instead of identifying with the Mother Church, he felt a part of the people, as many priests from the north did. That is perhaps the reason they'd been allowed to live, when so many others had died.

Manuel opened the door before the visitor could knock and extended a hand to the small boy who stood outside. Augustine, he believed his name to be. Or Rafael. He always got those young brothers' names mixed up.

"What is the matter?" Manuel knelt to the boy's height, his dark robe pulled tight, a stone biting into his knee.

"They've found another one. Fascist pig. He's been imprisoned, and he asks for the priest."

Curses and more curses. Unmentionable curses, Manuel thought to himself, rising. Words a priest would never spout, but thoughts were a different matter. A priest was a man, after all. A weary, confused, heartbroken man.

He fumbled with the thick silver cross that hung from his neck. Its weight reminded him of the burdens he chose to carry for his Lord.

He'd thought for many years that the greatest weight on his soul was to die to his flesh daily—to live a life of chastity and denial. But nothing had prepared him for the pleading eyes of the people staring up at him—one set murderers at heart, the other set victims.

He rose and turned his back to the door. "They're at the city hall, I presume?"

"Yes. Will you come?"

"I will come. Will you run ahead and tell them this?"

Without answering, the boy turned and darted back in the direction of town, and the heaviness on Manuel's heart burdened him more than his vows of chastity and poverty ever had.

Nothing he imagined could be worse than a civil war in the midst of a small town. He thought of the families who had lived all their lives together—whose mothers, grandmothers, and great-grandmothers had done the same. Yet now their friendships were split apart by ideologies that scarred their souls as well.

Yes, the priests in the north were much needed. To absolve not only the sins of the dying, but of the living.

Chapter Four

Nunca aconsejes a nadie que vaya a la guerra o que se case.

Never advise anyone to go to war or to marry.

Spanish proverb

A different Barcelona greeted Philip when he awoke in the morning. From the hotel window he watched the streets swarming with armed workers, rifles on their right shoulders. Most wore their civilian clothes with badges and insignia in red and black—matching the banners hanging outside and showing they were anarchists. A few wore dark blue militia uniforms. Yes, much had changed overnight.

He cracked opened the window and listened intently to the heavily accented voices. A young man, not more than thirteen or fourteen—the same age as his students back home—roamed the streets, proudly displaying his anarchist badge. The boy's eyes grew wide as a woman in overalls walked by, slinging a rifle over her shoulder. Philip chuckled to himself, realizing that this was the first Spanish woman he'd seen in trousers as well.

In contrast to the un-uniformed anarchists, the town's militia-men stood, feet planted at the entrances of hotels, shops, and administrative offices. They too watched the woman pass. Some men still crouched behind barricades constructed from sandbags, dead horses, and broken cobblestones, as if enemy tanks would rumble down the streets at any moment. Yet a few lifted their heads to note other trousered women joining the first.

In the days prior to the revolt, Philip had noticed men of all ages lounging on the city's benches, calling out compliments to any woman who caught their eye—which was most of them. It was good to see that the battles had not changed the landscape of the city too much.

Still, some Barcelonans didn't seem to grasp the reality of war within their streets. Unbelievably, Philip noted families with picnic baskets dotting the sidewalks. It reminded him of a history lesson he taught in junior high—about families venturing out to view battles in the early days of the American Civil War, only to be caught in the fighting. What were they thinking?

A soft knock sounded at the door. Attis answered it, and a minute later was at Philip's side.

"Well, my friend," he said. "We're leaving."

"Not a big surprise. Where to?"

Attis ran his fingers through his dark hair. "The organizer of the games doesn't know, but he said to take our things downstairs this evening. He'll have a better plan then." Attis flopped back on the bed. "I'm starving and exhausted. I must've had some pretty powerful dreams last night."

Philip slipped on his shoes. "Race you downstairs. Since it's the only race today."

He'd meant it as a joke, but Attis didn't laugh.

To come all this way for nothing.

Mostly solemn faces greeted them as they entered the lobby. Philip dug his sore hands in his pockets. "Is there someplace we can find breakfast?"

The balding clerk nodded. His starched white shirt with black tie and professional smile suggested unconcern about last night's events. Yet the thin layer of sweat upon his brow told Philip otherwise. "*Sí*, there are many places still open for business. The café next door has good breakfasts."

Philip glanced toward the door. Outside, a father, mother, and three children strolled by. The boy broke from his mother's grasp, tapped on the hotel window, and waved. The clerk waved back.

"What are they doing out?" Philip pointed his chin toward the family. "Don't they know what's going on?"

The concierge clucked his tongue and wagged his head. "The favorite outing of Barcelona folk is to go to the river on Sundays. They take the electric line. This tells you how common such revolts are. Sometimes the fighting is over on the first spurt. Not this one, though. That family, they'll be back. You watch." He tapped the phone receiver. "I've heard all exits from the city are closed. There will be no picnics in the countryside today."

It didn't take much convincing for Philip to talk Attis into taking a stroll of their own after breakfast. His stomach was full, yet tense, as they walked through the streets. Like others around them, they held white handkerchiefs high in their right hands just to be safe.

Gingerly they moved along, stepping over spent cartridges and bandoliers. A dead mule lay on the sidewalk in a puddle of its own blood. Already flies swarmed around it, and the morning sun combined with a gentle breeze to spread its stench. Philip pinched his nose, and his stomach churned as he noticed smaller, dried pools of blood on the roadway where injured men had lain. It brought to mind the faces of those Philip had worked beside last night. Did they still live? Or had they given the ultimate sacrifice after he and Attis returned to the hotel?

At least they died for a noble cause, Philip thought. To maintain the elected leaders and stand against the Fascist dictator who fought to return the burden of oppression upon the people. Their deaths, in a sense, were for all who longed for equality among men of all races and stations in life.

They rounded the corner and paused as they gazed at the smoldering church. Philip eyed the bell tower, still standing proudly over the city, where just last night snipers had perched. Centuries-old stone walls remained, but the hand-carved doors and stained glass windows lay in rubble. Inside, pew and altar alike were burned. Philip supposed the gold and silver ornaments of faith had been looted. What had the citizens of this city lost because of this "freedom fight"? He glanced at Attis, but neither said a word. Philip knew his friend, too, was thinking of Philip's father's small church back home.

As they continued on, Philip noted buildings old and new, from quaint shops to modern boutiques, pocked with bullet holes —and at the foot of one blood-smeared wall sat a small bouquet of violet irises. Philip caught his breath at the out-of-place flowers.

"Somebody's friend." Attis rubbed his forehead as if to erase a memory. "Somebody's son."

"Somebody's love," Philip muttered as he watched a young woman, tears streaking her dirt-smudged face, walk by, clutching a single iris.

By the time they'd returned to the hotel, cars and armored vehicles had parked in front of the door, and a group of armed young people stood about on the sidewalk. Their voices rose with excitement.

Philip touched the elbow of a young man, and he turned, eyes wild.

"What's happening?" Philip asked in Spanish.

"The insurgents have killed many—shooting all prisoners. Shooting our men—those who refuse to submit."

Another young man approached. "You Americans shouldn't be here. You are not safe."

"But our documents clearly state we're here as part of the Workers' Games," Attis insisted.

"Which means we're safe as long as these people maintain control." Philip leaned in closer to Attis. "But what will happen when we travel back?"

"*Sí,*" one of the young men added, butting in. "Last night I heard of many regions already occupied by the Nationalist rebels, Fascist pigs. I question if you can even get out of our country safely."

For the first time Philip noted worry in Attis's demeanor.

"We'll get out, somehow. Surely we won't be stuck here." Philip turned and watched as a shirtless man leaned a ladder up the front of the building and replaced the hotel's flags with a red one that displayed a hammer and sickle.

"Or maybe we'll choose to stay." Attis placed a heavy hand on Philip's shoulder, as he always did when sharing a big announcement. Then he turned to the two young men. "Maybe destiny brought us here."

Sophie yawned and opened her eyes as they drove into a town with a white sign that read PERPIGNAN. She glanced at Walt, and her heart pounded, remembering the previous night. She'd told herself not to fall asleep. Who knew what back road she'd find herself on with this stranger? Then again, how could she determine which road was correct in the first place? Sophie had no choice but to place her trust in the man at the wheel. Entering Spain depended on it.

She ran her fingers through her hair, tugging the ends out of her collar. She tried to act just the opposite of what she felt—that traveling with a man she hardly knew, in a foreign country, and trying to sneak their way into another, much more hostile country in the midst of a revolt was something she did every day.

"We're in Perpignan?" She attempted to brush the wrinkles out of her blouse.

"Yes, this is it. And I have to say I've never heard a lady snore quite as loudly as you do. I wish I'd had a gramophone to drown out the noise."

She shot him a glance and noticed a smile curled on his lips. "Not to worry. If things go as planned, you'll be rid of me soon."

"Too bad you slept the whole time. You missed it all. Even the holy city of Lourdes. It was quite a sight by the light of the moon. All silver and mystical."

"Too bad. We could have stopped and prayed. As my grandma says, it never hurts in tough spots."

Taking a look at the scenery around the car, Sophie sat transfixed by the towering, snowcapped mountains and the quaint town. If she had an extra hour or two she would have asked Walt to pull over and let her paint. Of course, she didn't have the extra time . . . or the materials. And actually, she wasn't even in the mood for it.

Mood, she realized, mattered as much as anything when it came to art. Sometimes the image before her gathered her attention completely. She would escape into the world on her canvas, unaware that time passed. Other times she worked even in the midst of activity, tirelessly copying the bustling streets of Boston, trying to communicate the pulse of the city with the sharp lines or areas of shade on her canvas. Then there were other times she worked feverishly, as if in response to stored-up tension inside her.

Yet today the tightness of her stomach, and even a gentle ache in the pit of it, reminded her of the last time she'd eaten bad lobster on the wharf. She wouldn't have been able to paint anything in this state, even if she had all her things.

They neared the center of town, and the place was packed with people—mostly women. They looked the same as the Frenchwomen in the museum paintings with long thin, necks and sleek bodies that moved with dignity even as they performed everyday chores.

"Is it always like this?" Sophie braced herself against the door as the newspaperman hardly slowed the automobile, weaving through the crowds. He didn't answer, but as she looked closer, she spotted foreigners.

She smiled as two women with raven hair and dark olive skin rushed across the street hand in hand. In their long skirts and white blouses, they embodied the perfect image of Spain. Her heart beat even quicker. Soon they'd be there. Soon she'd be with Michael.

"The sudden influx is most likely due to the problem in Spain," Walt finally answered, his neck craning to find a parking place. "It's an easy spot for people to flee to."

"Are things really that bad? I mean, don't these types of conflicts happen all the time?"

Walt parked the car near a cluster of small houses and then turned to her, one eyebrow cocked. "Churches and buildings are burning. Men on both sides have been dragged into the streets and shot. How do you think these types of power struggles work? You can't simply walk into a town and be handed the keys to the city. From what I've read, it's a fight, all right. A real knock-down, drag-out."

Sophie turned away, glancing at a mother hurrying three small children down the street. The woman scanned their car with sad and eager eyes as she walked past, and Sophie wondered just who she was looking for.

"I'm sorry. Of course, the struggle is bad. However, I'm still determined to get over the border." She climbed out of the car.

From somewhere beyond their vision, a church bell chimed as she snatched up her suitcase. "Are you just going to leave the car here?"

"I'll be back in a week or so; no need to worry. It's safe." He grabbed his suitcase from the backseat before locking the car and pocketing the keys.

They strolled by a beautiful cathedral with a large round fountain in the courtyard. The splashing of the water calmed her some, and she reached out her hand and let the cool drops bounce off her arm. She'd come back and paint this idyllic scene. She'd bring Michael, and he could take photographs of the people as she painted.

"Hungry?" Walt rubbed his stomach. "Let's get some breakfast, and then we're off to the border. It's a long walk."

"Can't we drive as close as possible?"

"Now *that* wouldn't be safe. Here, our vehicle will not draw attention. Near the border it would."

"I'll go with that, but I'd like to find a place to freshen up first." Sophie patted the side of her suitcase.

"Yes, of course." Walt chuckled. "You'll want to impress the border guards, after all."

Sweat dripped down Sophie's face from the long descent into Port-Bou. The mountains rose up so tall around the oceanside town that it seemed as if the whole place were nestled in the bottom of a cave. She held her aching side and urged her feet forward. *He should have warned me,* she thought as she switched the suitcase from one hand to the other. *Should have prepared me for the fifteen-kilometer walk. Just how many miles is that, anyway?*

Back home, she walked everywhere. Everything of importance in Boston was within walking distance, and the streets bloomed with interesting people and sites no matter how many times you strolled through them. But here the steep inclines caused her leg muscles to burn and her lungs to scream out in pain. She didn't let on, of course. Walt had set the pace and moved his thin frame over the pass with ease. She didn't want him to claim she slowed him down.

She finally caught her breath after the final steep descent, and within minutes Walt led her to the offices of the town committee. Two large flags waved over the small building, one Catalan and the other red with hammer and sickle. Outside, seated on a bench, a few peasant women waited patiently. Motioning her inside, a female guard with a pleasant face patted Sophie from her shirt cuffs to the hem of her trousers and even checked the lining of her shoes.

"Sit, please, *senorita*." The petite border guard studied Sophie's passport, then motioned to a chair, her face suddenly growing stern.

Sophie obliged, then winced as the woman hurriedly ran her fingers through Sophie's hair. *So much for freshening up*. She brushed her sweaty, now tangled, locks back from her face. Sun poured through the window in brilliant rays. *Spanish sun*. That small realization brought a smile to her lips.

Next the woman turned to Sophie's satchel and removed every item, placing it on the table before her. Sophie held her breath as the guard unrolled the garment bag and ran her hands over the light blue dress, but the woman paid it little attention. She returned all the items to the satchel and motioned to an adjoining waiting room.

Sophie sat on a hard wooden chair and waited for Walt, still wondering if they could pull this off. Or was she already doomed? Failure meant a trek back—which she didn't want to even think about. Or again, there might be a damp, dark prison cell. How could she have not thought of that possibility sooner?

On the desk before her, Spanish newspapers were spread out. She read the stories and studied them, realizing the reports favored the Fascist rebels—which most likely didn't put these communist-idealist border officials in a good mood.

Walt entered with a tall, black-haired man with a thin moustache.

"I am the head of the *Comité*. What is your business?" he asked in Spanish.

Sophie swept her hand to Walt. "This man is a journalist, *señor*, and I am his interpreter. We have an assignment to fulfill in Barcelona . . . and also Madrid," she quickly added.

He crossed his arms over his chest. "You should not have been allowed to pass through the border. Do you understand that you could be arrested for your attempt?" He pressed his hands on the desktop, crumpling the newspaper, and leaned toward her. "We have orders. Orders that neither your position, nationality, or sex can protect you from. You must return at once."

The man's eyes pierced hers, yet Sophie held his gaze. Seemingly impressed by her refusal to look away, he cocked one eyebrow, straightened, and turned toward the door.

Sophie's hand covered her pounding heart, and she quickly gathered up every bit of nerve she possessed. "Comrade, wait!"

He paused and turned back to her, arms crossed over his chest.

"You do not understand, *señor*. I was in Paris just yesterday, and every paper on the newsstands spoke about the success of Franco and Mola. The world expects them to have full control of your country in a matter of days. You *need* my coworker, this journalist. He is on your side. He has come to write the truth and discredit the propaganda."

The official pointed to Walt. "Let me see his identification."

She translated and handed Walt's papers over.

"And yours?"

"I'm sorry. I have only my passport. My papers . . . they are waiting for me in Barcelona." She again looked him directly in the eye.

The dark-eyed Spaniard firmly shook his head. "And you expect me to believe that nonsense? He can go, but I cannot let you through."

"But, sir, how can he write the story—know whom to interview —if he has no one who speaks the language? How will he know whom to trust?"

The man studied her face for a moment; then his expression softened. He wrote something on a piece of paper, stamped it with an official seal, and handed it to Sophie.

"This gives you permission to take the train to the news offices in Barcelona and Madrid. I will send a letter ahead to the *Comité* there, and they'll expect you. There is a train leaving tonight for Barcelona. After that, you must find your own way to Madrid. But I must warn you, many will find *your* paperwork insufficient. It is not an exaggerated truth to tell you your life is in danger. If you are accused of faking your duties, you will be shot on the spot. This is no time for games. But if you're willing to risk this, I will let you go."

"*Sí. Gracias.*" She rose and quickly shook his hand. Then Walt did the same.

"Thank you, *señor*. And if I may have one more request. May I send a telegram to Madrid? They need to know when to expect us."

"*Sí. Sí.* Then you must get out of my hair. There is enough to worry about without such as this. But promise me, will you? Promise you'll tell the world of our fight?"

"Of course." Sophie extended her hand and shook his. "We will let the world know." And once the paperwork was in her hands, she strode through the building, refusing to look back. Refusing to let her mind rest on the knowledge that it just as easily could have gone the other way.

Walking toward the train station, under guard, Sophie realized for the first time that she'd made it.

Michael's Spain.

The town sat on a small bay, and the sun reflected off the billowing white sails of fishing boats. Tall trees lined the esplanade. Shops and restaurants overflowed with handsome people dressed in colorful clothes, and Spanish music poured from the loudspeakers overhead.

As she strolled by a bakery, she breathed in the heavy, yeasty scent. Then she smiled as a small boy ran by, kicking a can down the street, its clinking sounding like change hitting the bottom of a penny jar. It was hard to believe this was a country in conflict. It was also hard not to fall in love with this place. Sophie understood even more why it held a tether to Michael's heart.

She knew Michael had enjoyed his time in Boston—with his family and her. But even during their most intimate moments of conversation, he had seemed distracted. As he had watched the setting sun, she could see in his eyes that he longed to follow it to Spain's new morning—though he would never say such a thing aloud.

This country, in a sense, was his mistress. Sophie could either love it as he did or lose a piece of Michael's heart forever. So she had come. And she pitied that poor man from the office she'd just left who'd attempted to keep her away. Pitied him because he'd just been fooled by a silly American girl who would contribute nothing for their cause, but wished only to follow her heart.

Chapter Five

Por el árbol se conoce el fruto.
By the tree the fruit is known.

Spanish proverb

Even the busyness of Port-Bou now seemed tranquil for the mere fact that Barcelona was alive with the movement of people in motion.

The train station buzzed with excited voices of the soldiers and civilians crowded on the platforms. Most of the men wore open shirts and sandals. And even the civilians clutched rifles slung over their strong shoulders. Some spoke with fervor, moving their hands with their words. Others listened, their faces tipped in serious expressions. Lips turned downward. Eyebrows furrowed.

Walt offered a hand to help Sophie off the train. He took off his hat and wiped his brow, his face appearing too plain and young without it. "Well, I suppose this is it. I have to admit that went better than planned. Then again, I should have guessed. You hardly seem a threat."

"I'm not home free yet—I still have a train ride to Madrid. Tomorrow perhaps I can grin at my good fortune."

Walt chuckled and nodded his chin toward a group of young men on the platform. They wore neither the guns nor the serious expressions of the older guards. "Don't worry; they'll keep you safe. They fight for the people, for the Socialist cause—they treat Americans well, as they are hoping our country will come to their aid."

Sophie glanced at the faces of the young soldiers. One smiled and winked as their eyes met, and she felt heat rising to her cheeks. She quickly looked away. "Yes, well, as long as they're on the right side."

"They are."

A group of men in red-and-black armbands paraded down the street just beyond the train station. "Son of the people, your chains oppress you," they sang. "This injustice cannot go on. . . ."

"Anarchists. Their views are similar enough to the Socialist and Communist causes that they've joined together to fight the Fascists, who are attempting to gain control. Of course, if they win, the next battle they fight will be among themselves."

"Worker! Worker! You shall suffer no longer . . . no longer!" The singing continued farther away.

"It's Franco's Fascists you have to watch out for. From what I overheard on the train, there's still fighting going on here in the city—and in Madrid. So get to your *Miguel* as soon as possible. He'll keep you safe."

"Overheard?" Sophie set her satchel by her feet and planted her hands on her hips. "What did you just say? *¿Habla Espanol?* Because as far as I witnessed, everyone on the train spoke Spanish."

Ignoring her rebuke with a grin, Walt motioned for a horse-cab. The dusty gray-and-white mare plodded forward, her ears perked as if picking up the excitement from the people hustling around her.

Walt tossed his small suitcase in the cab, then turned to Sophie with a grin. "*Es verdad.* What kind of communicator would I be if I couldn't converse with the people?" He cocked his brow. "Forgive me, *por favor.* I've been planning to tell you, but I didn't want to do it before we crossed the border—didn't want to hinder your acting skills. Great work in the *Comité's* office, by the way."

Sophie couldn't help but laugh. "You know, either I can't read people very well, or *you*, my friend, are a master of deception. Thanks for your help, anyway. What can I ever do to repay you?"

More singing erupted nearer. "Arise, loyal people, at the cry of social revolution!"

Walt covered his ears with his hands. He glanced toward the singers and wagged his head. "*Madre mía.* What is this noise?" Then he sighed, turning back to her. "Repay me? I only wish for one thing." He pointed to her journal. "You did a wonderful likeness of me. I think my mom would be tickled if I sent that home."

Sophie blew out a sigh. "I take that back. You are 100 percent deceptive. How did you know?"

"On the train, you glanced back and then furiously started sketching. Didn't you see me smile for the picture?"

"Fine then." Sophie flipped to the page where she'd sketched his likeness. "But since I'll never see you again, I was kind of hoping to keep this." She ripped it out and handed it to Walt.

"You never know, Miss Grace," he said with a slight bow. "You never know when we might meet again."

The train whistle stirred Sophie from her sleep, and she sat up with a start, noticing that sometime in the night a soldier's coat had been thrown over her. It smelled of cheap tobacco and body sweat, yet its warmth was appreciated as was the softness of the well-worn wool. It was a nice way to end a trip that had begun with the excited political talk of the young soldiers with whom she shared the compartment.

As the train approached Madrid, the tracks ran through an arid plain—so different from the blooming, bright port town she'd witnessed when entering Spain.

"La Mancha," said a soldier with light blond hair, pointing. "See, the blue mountains? It is Guadarrama, where they fight." The man wore a bandage on his neck, and dried blood stained his collar. She wanted to ask about the battles he'd already seen, but was discouraged by the way he self-consciously placed a hand over the gauze. She wished to know about the danger near Madrid.

"So close." She felt a slight quiver in the pit of her stomach. "Why, they could take the city any day."

Other soldiers stirred, waking; and she grinned, realizing how right Walt had been about them. These young men had seen to her every need, sharing their wine and bread. Singing their traditional songs as she clapped along. Trying to outdo each other with stories of their native regions. And besieging her with questions about America, as if it were as fanciful a place as the lost city of Atlantis.

A morning haze made it hard to distinguish the features of the city, but Sophie could tell from a wide, shadowed skyline of tall buildings that this place offered more than she imagined. She held her breath as the train pulled into the Medio Dio station.

Running her fingers through her hair, her mind raced as she wondered how to find her way to the news office where Michael worked. Would he even be there? Perhaps he'd traveled to another part of the country on assignment. Had he received her telegram, alerting him that she was coming? Who knew if it even got through?

She lugged her satchel down the train steps and scanned the line of horse carts waiting for passengers, when she heard a familiar voice.

"Sophie."

She turned, and there stood Michael. Tears sprang to her eyes, and she didn't know whether to laugh or cry. He opened his arms, and she rushed forward.

"*Divina*, you made it. I couldn't believe it when your telegram arrived. You're actually here." He kissed both her cheeks, then held her at arm's length. "My darling. Let me get a good look at you."

She laughed, taking in his strong presence and crooked smile. "Michael. Yes, I'm here. And are you a sight for sore eyes."

Michael pulled her close, and with the cadence of his heart against her cheek, tears came—tears of joy to be with him again. And tears of relief, as the fear and tension of the last few days found release within his arms.

The carriage rattled through the narrow cobblestone streets, past aged buildings that seemed to lean on each other for support.

It was too much to take in. Michael. Madrid. And the evidence of war around the city. Soon the road widened to a large plaza with a gushing fountain.

"Plaza Canovas del Castillo." Michael leaned close, whispering in her ear. "Better known as the Neptune fountain. Romantic, yes?"

The carriage stopped, and he helped her out, then led her past the fountain and swept his arm toward an elegant, five-story hotel. Above the entrance were the words *Hotel Palace* in English. "Your castle awaits, my lady."

With its neoclassical architecture, similar to the fine hotels in Paris, it looked like a home for royalty indeed.

"Honestly, Michael. I don't need something nearly this nice. There's no way I can afford it. We can just find a little apartment for me somewhere."

"Darling, did you hear me say anything about cost? I have a friend, you see, who owes me a few favors. Besides, my apartment is right around the corner from here. Don't you want to stay close to me?"

"Are you kidding?" She slid her hand into the crook of his arm. "I never want to part from you again."

After checking into a room and freshening up, she met Michael in the hotel lobby. She could tell from the expression on his face that something was troubling him.

"I'm sorry, *Divina*, but my editor called. They need me down at the office as soon as possible. I hate leaving you. You just got here, after all. . . ."

"I'll be fine." Sophie feigned a yawn, trying to hide her disappointment. "I am a bit tired. I'll rest, and maybe sketch. When will you be back?"

"How about dinner, here at the hotel?"

"Perfect." She placed a kiss on his cheek. "Now run along and make me proud."

Sophie spent the day sketching the buildings near the hotel. After settling in near the fountain, she discovered she could look every direction in bustling Madrid and find city landscape worthy of her attention.

She ate lunch at a nearby café, where the handsome waiter

was more than attentive and complimentary. But her thoughts were only on one man, and the minutes ticked by at a turtle's pace as she waited to see Michael again.

The large, square ballroom of the Hotel Palace was ornately decorated, but a thick cloud of tobacco smoke nearly caused her to choke. Michael, dressed in slacks and a suit jacket, wove through the crowd, leading her to a far corner table.

After settling in the chair across from her, he entwined his fingers in hers and pressed them to his lips. "Darling, look at you—as ravishing as the art you masterfully paint."

She chuckled. "That's interesting, since I paint landscapes."

"Yes, *Divina*, but didn't Solomon himself relate his love's beauty to the stately trees of the field and flowers of the garden?"

"I think I read something like that." She flipped her dark hair over her shoulder. "But please don't tell me my hair reminds you of a goat."

"Only a prized goat." He grinned. "State fair. Blue ribbon."

Sophie playfully slugged his shoulder, and then turned her attention to her menu. Though her stomach growled, she was even more hungry for someplace quiet where they could talk.

"After dinner, my dear, we've been invited to join my friends for flamenco in Villa Rosa in the Plaza Santa Ana. Don't forget to order coffee—sometimes flamenco sessions last until dawn."

"You're joking, right? People are still going to parties and dancing? There's a war out there. You should have seen all the guns, the soldiers on the roadway, the territories already marked off." She lowered her voice. "Michael, in one city, I saw a body lying near the railroad tracks. . . ."

"Yes, but the fighting's not in full force here. Do you think we're heartless? We're raising money for the Republican cause."

"So you'll just go on with life as usual until the fighting comes *into* Madrid? It is coming here, isn't it?"

Michael fingered his wine glass, his eyes suddenly distant. He nodded his head. "Yes, my love." He gently caressed her cheek, softly touching the edges of her curls. "The fighting will be here soon—too soon." He stared into her eyes as if trying to hold her soul in his heart. "And that's why you can't stay."

Sophie, shaking off the thrill of his touch, felt her heart sink. He couldn't mean that. Not after all she'd done to get here. She leaned back in her seat.

"But . . . we're getting married, and . . ." *And what?* She hadn't expected a war to disrupt all the plans she'd so carefully arranged in her mind. She clamped her lips tight.

Michael took a sip of his dark red wine, then reached across the table and touched her shoulder with a trembling hand. It was the first time she'd seen him anything but strong and composed.

"Sophie, you're not safe here."

"I'm safe with you." She pressed her fingers to her temples, suddenly weary. Her head throbbed and her stomach ached. "I'm sorry, but I'm not feeling too well. It's been a long couple of days. Do you mind if I go to bed? I'll meet you tomorrow at breakfast?"

Michael held her elbow as she rose. "My love, it's not that I—"

"No, really. Not now. I'm tired. I want to go to my room."

"I understand."

Sophie's hands quivered slightly as Michael escorted her back to the hotel lobby. "When we're both rested, we can talk." She attempted a smile. "I'll feel better in the morning, you'll see."

Sophie finally reached the door to her lavish room, kissed Michael good night, stepped inside, and shut the door behind her. "He's simply trying to consider what's best for me, for us," she mumbled to herself, trying to hold back tears.

Flamenco dancing and parties in the midst of war? As she unpacked her tiny satchel, she wondered if she were as prepared for this as she thought.

She hung her only other elegant garment in the closet—a black cocktail dress with a long-sleeved bolero jacket that Michael's mother had helped her pick out. Last, she pulled out her wedding dress. She put it on a hanger and shoved it to the back of her closet.

It will just take a little time, he'll see. Within a week or two things will be back where they were . . . revolt or no revolt.

Chapter Six

Father Manuel Garcia stared at his own rugged visage in the mirror and ran his fingers through dark hair that was just beginning to gray at the temples. In his mind's eye, he pictured himself wearing the blue *mono* of a soldier's uniform rather than his cassock and collar. He flexed his muscular arm, then turned and lifted his Bible from the hall table. *The fight for this truth is the battle God called me to,* he reminded himself.

Still, his mind could not help but escape back to the days he roamed the hills of the Basque countryside with his friends. Their chosen enemy changed through the years, depending on what faction controlled Spain at that moment or who most threatened their desire for an independent Basque nation. Had it been almost twenty years ago that their adolescent shoulders bore sticks as guns and they'd used root-knotted clumps of dirt for bombs?

Yet in the quiet solitude of those hills Manuel had also experienced another war—the battle within his soul. Surely an all-knowing God could not have called the son of a simple farmer to the priesthood. In the end, he discovered He had.

Manuel had found God in those mountains, and it was there he returned time and time again to pray. His confessions he had spilled out before the priest in the holy sanctuary, which smelled of candle wax, incense, and polished wood. But his pleadings for communion with the Almighty and his prayers for wisdom took place under the tall pines that reached their branches to the sky, a constant reminder of the evergreen faith of his soul. And though he'd chosen divine service over allegiance to human commanders, Manuel experienced the passion of a soldier surging through his frame as he attended daily a community not far from where he'd grown up.

After his time of spiritual training in Madrid, he'd been sent back here, mainly because outsiders weren't appreciated. Though officially part of Spain, the Basques had a distinct culture and language that few others understood. They were an independent people who believed in strong local rights. Manuel felt especially honored to serve Guernica—the symbolic capital of the three mountainous provinces.

Now he trod to his simple kitchen and sliced a thick piece of bread, delivered this morning by Alfonso, the town's baker. The old wicker of his chair complained audibly as he sat and scooted it closer to the scarred wooden table. He cocked his head to listen as he tuned the radio dial until he distinguished the voice of the Madrid broadcaster through the static. News of conflicts in Madrid and Barcelona seemed distant, as if they were war stories from another country.

A smile curled on his lips as he realized they were one step closer to the independence desired for so long. Just days ago, the government in Madrid had recognized Basque sovereignty. For the elected government of Spain, to fight for the Republicans meant fighting for an independent Basque nation.

But to him, another war waged, a greater, closer war for the seven thousand souls living a simple life in the broad valley that stretched from north to south. Mountains rose around Guernica. A river on one side snaked against a high, forested hill.

Armies battled far away, yet he worried it would not always be so distant. Vivid reports allowed Manuel to see the conflict in his mind's eye. Throughout Spain, the Republican Socialists had led the people to destroy religious objects. In every town, antifascist committee members ordered the people to deliver their images, statues, prayer books, talismans—all to be burned in public.

"*San José ha huerto*. Saint Joséph is dead!" was the cry that carried through his radio. The saints were dead. And worse, to the people, God had died too. *A dios*, "with God," was a greeting that had existed as long as the hills of Spain, but that too had been abolished.

Even worse were the Nationalists—the Fascist rebels who once again desired to oppress the people and rule them with an iron fist, keeping them in bondage to the old ways of Spanish society where most of the people lived and died in poverty.

Manuel pushed his bread to the side, no longer hungry. *Love your enemies. Bless those who curse you.* Weren't those the commands of Christ? Yet Christ had not lived in Spain, which faced more struggles for power and death and destruction than any country should.

He shoved back from the table, rose from his chair, and moved to his modest bedroom, where he fell to his knees on the wooden floor next to his bed. To pray for the people. To pray for their ultimate independence. The Rebels among them sat in prison, giving the people a false sense of security. He prayed for their souls too.

A rapid, light knock on the door stirred Father Manuel from his prayers. He quickly rose and marched to the door to find the Carmelite sister Joséfina waiting outside. She couldn't have been more than twenty years old, with pale skin, dark brown eyes, and flushed cheeks from her trek to his rectory.

"The convent." Her childlike voice pulsed with anxiety. "The government has requisitioned it as a military hospital." She wiped a bead of sweat that trickled from her temple beneath her habit. "The militia is moving us out, Padre, forcing us to a few solitary rooms to live and serve. Perhaps I speak out of turn, but don't they realize the Relifiosas Carmelitas de la Caridad is one of the oldest religious orders in Europe?"

"Yes, Sister. But your prayers for peace can be prayed in a quarter of the space, can they not?"

Sister Joséfina lowered her head. "Yes, Padre."

"In fact, it is good to be used in this way. Hasn't Christ called us to care for those in need?" He gently patted her shoulder, shut his door behind him, and led her to the gate. He could see the large, square convent ahead, one that would stand strong under the most intense gunfire. And one he'd already considered as a possible fortress for his people, should war come to their village.

"After all," he added with a smile, "if the faithful prayers of dedicated nuns can't keep us safe, what can? Come, lead me to the Sisters, and I'll make sure the brides of Christ are treated with the respect they so deserve."

The next day, Sophie attempted to forget the conversation of the previous night. Instead, she strolled with her hand tucked into the crook of Michael's arm as he led her through the streets of Madrid. The entire Castelana, from the Museum of the Prado and the blocks and blocks to follow, were lined by classical palaces and ornate public buildings.

"It's just beautiful." Sophie sighed, noting a circular plaza with trees and fountains. In the middle sat a stone statue of a man on horseback, frozen as if in the midst of running off to battle.

"It is said that the right magical words will awaken the army set in stone. Carved men like this are all over the city, just waiting for the right person to break the spell cast on them."

"Maybe you will be the one to break it." She squeezed his arm. "What do you think the phrase is?"

"Now this I know. 'For the love of a woman,'" he said with a grin.

"Hmmm . . . I like that."

Michael looked every part the photographer with his camera case hanging around his neck, the wide strap secured over his shoulder and across his body. His sleeves were rolled to his elbows and the top three buttons of his white cotton shirt were loosened, showing off the golden brown of his chest.

"So tell me, *Divina*. I want to hear everything. Just how did you cross the border?"

Michael's eyebrow rose as Sophie related her story.

"You're telling me a strange man approached you, urged you to leave your things behind, and travel with him, *lie for* him, in order to get across the border?"

Sophie's fingers stroked the bare skin of Michael's arm as she adjusted her peaked emotions to the sight of him, the sensation of his touch. "Well, it does sound bad when you say it like that, but you don't understand. I had no other choice. The risk paid off, don't you think? If I hadn't met Walt, I'd still be sitting in some hotel lobby in France, instead of being here with you." She walked her fingers down his arm and squeezed his hand. "Besides, I was the one who benefited. He was only thinking of me."

Michael scowled at her. "If you were a Spanish girl, you wouldn't even have considered such a thing. *Señoritas* aren't even allowed to walk the streets of the city without an escort. Let's just keep this story between us, shall we? I don't want my friends to get any false ideas of the type of woman you are."

"You mean the idea that I'm a *modern* woman? You sound like the bellman at the hotel. He stopped me in the lobby and urged me to remove my hat and return it to my room. He said only women of wealth wore such things, and it would not be appreciated by the people—they might get the wrong idea about me."

"A hat, that's no trouble. But traveling with a man, alone? That doesn't make me one bit comfortable. And you say he spoke and understood Spanish?"

Sophie hesitated before warily answering. "Yes."

They paused at the street corner while a tram approached, and she studied the political posters that seemed to cover every bare wall and lamppost, shouting their beliefs with shocking images.

In one, a farm laborer-turned-militiaman impaled a monstrous representation of capitalism on his rifle, tossing the monster over his shoulder like a bale of hay. *Columna de Hierro. Campesino, la revolución te dará la tierra.* "Land worker! The revolution will give you the land."

The plight of the people unnerved her, but even more worrisome was the ache that filled her chest as she noticed the children begging at cafés packed with what appeared to be journalists and state employees. They were the most beautiful children Sophie had ever seen, with round faces and dark hair and eyes. Yet their thin forms seemed to tremble, despite the lack of a breeze.

The tram passed, and Michael led her across the road without even noticing the children.

"And this Walt claimed you were his interpreter?" he continued, his thumb stroking the top of her hand. "Don't you think that shows you *he* was the one who needed a cover? Or better yet, needed you to smuggle something inside for him."

She laughed nervously. "You're joking, right? That's not possible. I would have known. I kept a close watch on all my things, and he gave me complete privacy."

"Really? Then how did he know about the sketch of him? And why did he want it? Did you ever stop to consider that maybe there was information in the journal he needed?"

"Like what? A girl's thoughts of her fiancé? Seriously, Michael . . . it's not like he ever even had the opportunity to read it."

Michael looked away and focused on a young Spanish woman entering the nearest café. She was younger than Sophie and beautiful, with thick black hair that fell to the middle of her back. An older gentleman was at her side.

Her escort, no doubt. It's only the proper thing to do.

The young woman paused when she noticed Michael. She spotted Sophie and then, with a furrowed brow, quickly looked away and hurried inside.

"Michael. Who was that?"

"The girl?" His voice was conspicuously casual. "Oh, the sister of a dear friend. Maria is her name." He quickened his pace.

"She seemed displeased to see me with you."

"Honestly, Sophie, you aren't used to this Spanish sun. I believe you're seeing things. Next time, when we're not on an errand, we will stop and I'll introduce you."

"You don't have anything to hide, do you? I mean . . ."

"*Divina*, of course not." His fingers brushed the hair from the nape of her neck. "And you're right about this newspaperman, too. I'm a jealous old man, that's all. I just hate the thought of my girl spending all those hours with someone else. May I see the paperwork you received at the border?"

Sophie pulled it from her handbag and handed it to him.

"The Central Committee of the Anti-fascist Militia of Catalonia authorizes the North American newspaper correspondent, Sophie Grace, to pass freely to the ends of all fronts," Michael read aloud. "Impressive. It seems I have competition." He grinned and handed it back.

Sophie sighed. Her feet ached, and she wondered why she hadn't worn more sensible shoes. "I'm not a newspaper correspondent, and no offense to you news-hungry types, but I don't really ever see myself as one. So why do I have to make this official?"

Michael patted her hand. "You're a smart girl, but your quick talking can't get you out of every bind. If you get stopped for some reason, proper paperwork will help. It will also help get you out of the country. After lunch, I have a small errand, but then you can meet me at the office. Twenty-third floor of the *Telefónica* building. We'll get your paperwork authorized for Madrid, which my boss will do—he owes me more than one favor. Besides, maybe you'll even be put to use. Most correspondents can't speak Spanish."

"Well, then, put me to use as an interpreter. Because I'm not leaving. I want to help these people." She smiled at two young women walking by, arms entwined, chattering away faster than she could translate.

"Which people? The Socialists? Communists? Anarchists? Fascists? Darling, no offense, but I've lived here for years, and sometimes I still question whose side I believe in."

"Not the Fascists. That's for sure."

"Really, it's that clear? You've got the fight between good and evil all figured out, then? Brutality is everywhere, Sophie, on all sides. Here in the city, we hear about the Fascist murderers, but there are many others dead, and not just by the Fascists. The wealthy, Catholics, business owners, landowners."

"It makes no sense. Why landowners?"

"The anarchists favor agricultural communities. They model their system after the Russian *kolchozes*—the people working the land in common. For as long as they can remember, every part of the Spanish people's lives has been controlled by the government, the church, and, yes, the landowners. After the elections, they have tried to find a better way to bring equality with land, with work.

"They say Spain is a Christian nation, but in my opinion, this is more word than deeds. The Christian way, of course, is to give freely. Instead, those with power keep it. Those with land do the same, and the people are tired of it. While I understand the people's Communist tendencies, their desire to keep their country from Fascist control has gotten out of hand. Hundreds and thousands have lost their lives. I have lost friends, close friends. . . . Do you know the Communist Reds have killed priests?"

Sophie shuddered, but though Michael spoke with passion, it was hard to tie his words with reality. Though she'd witnessed many things, parts of Madrid still seemed to go on as if no war existed.

As she listened to Michael's words, she couldn't help but be enraptured by the new sights and sounds on the streets. There was a gentle ebb and flow to the city, an almost peaceful moving of the people. Motion picture theaters were open as usual, with people waiting patiently in orderly lines, chatting and laughing as if it were a typical afternoon's diversion. Posters on the brick walls announced benefit performances for the hospitals and troops. Then, breaking the tranquility as they strolled past another café, the sound of soldiers' singing drifted onto the streets.

"The Catholic church claims to be the church of the poor," Michael continued, gesturing broadly. He moved and spoke as if he were giving a political speech before a Harvard classroom, and not for her alone. "They say riches are not of this world. Then why then do they grasp the treasures of the world? You should see the luxury these 'servants of God' live in. The lavish cathedrals and rectories are evidence of that. That's why the people are so angry. The priests side with the Fascists, because a powerful government means a powerful church."

"So that's why Franco is fighting for power?" Sophie asked. "To gain control over the people once again? And that's why the church is helping him?"

Michael paused and motioned toward a café, then opened the door for her. "Yes, and it's not going as smoothly as planned. Franco's complete failure in Barcelona is one example. The Catalans are not known to be fighters. As history can tell, they usually run at the first shot. Not so this time. I have a feeling this war will be long and drawn out . . . which is exactly why you need to go back to France—at least for a while."

Sophie didn't respond as a friendly waiter seated them at a table by the front window. She wouldn't argue with him, but Michael couldn't *force* her to leave.

"And it's not only the battles outside the city we have to worry about. What will happen when Franco's troops enter Madrid?"

"You mean *if?*" She glanced up from her menu to meet his intense stare.

"I mean when. The people have little organization, few weapons. How can the city hold? It will take a miracle to hold longer than a month. And what a massacre will occur when the city is breeched. The anarchists would rather burn down the whole city than turn it over to Franco. I'm afraid, my love, you've come at the wrong time."

Michael's words came to an end as he studied something outside the window. Sophie turned and followed his gaze. It was Maria again. She strode down the street, this time with a young man at her side. Sophie's throat grew thick and she cleared it loudly, but Michael didn't seem to notice.

She placed her hand on his, and finally he turned to her, his mossy green eyes revealing something Sophie feared even more than talk of armies and battles.

Chapter Seven

Schlafende Hunde soll man nicht wecken.
One should not awaken sleeping dogs.

German proverb

Ritter smoothed the sleeves of his pressed Luftwaffe uniform as he strolled through the large crowds of the Wagner festival. Some people had come because they actually enjoyed the music—or pretended to, hoping to gain Hitler's approval. The majority came to be seen. Ritter had come to see the woman he knew in his nightly dreams.

Twenty-one flags bearing national and Bavarian colors decorated the entrance to the opera house. Double that number of black-and-red Nazi flags also waved in the breeze.

He scanned the crowds and asked himself again why he hadn't insisted on giving Isanna a ride himself. She had no doubt forgotten they were to meet at the entrance of the Festspielhaus, an opera house designed by Wagner. In Ritter's opinion, Wagner should have stuck to arranging music. The Festapielhaus was the only opera house he'd attended where the orchestra pit was hidden from the crowd. At least during most operas he could entertain himself by watching the conductor and musicians. What was Wagner thinking?

Finally a black sedan pulled up, and he spotted Isanna's blonde curls in the back window. Striding to the parked car, he opened the door before the driver had a chance to reach it.

"Isanna, precious, why do you make me wait so long to partake of your beauty?"

She stretched out her hand and placed it in his, her blue eyes peering up at his, full of mischief. "I'm so sorry, dear, but an old friend arrived from out of town. You remember Xavier von Herman, don't you?"

Ritter bent lower to peer into the backseat. His fists balled at his sides as Xavier flashed a brilliant smile.

Isanna climbed out and moved to Ritter's side. "Xavier is a veteran of the Gran Chaco war in South America. He's been telling me wonderful tales of his exploits. They are fascinating, to say the least." She patted Ritter's arm, then reached for Xavier's hand. "I'm awed by men who risk their lives to defend our strongly held beliefs. Aren't you?"

"Of course. So, Xavier, are you meeting someone here?"

Isanna laughed. "Just us. I knew you wouldn't mind. I've already phoned your uncle, and he agreed to switch seats so Xavier could sit with us."

Ritter offered his best practiced smile. "Of course. We're delighted to have you join us."

"Would you believe this is the first time I've attended the festival?" Xavier said.

Isanna slipped an arm through each of theirs and moved them toward the building. But her attention remained on Xavier, who continued his babbling.

"Look at all the people." Xavier gave a low whistle. "I never really wanted to associate myself with the crazed fans that descend on this little Bavarian town. But Isanna encouraged me to come. She said I needed a little culture in my life in order to find a good wife."

"That's right. Good looks, charm, and military honors aren't nearly enough." Isanna chuckled again, and Ritter placed his hand over hers, giving it a firm pat.

"So what did you do in South America?" Ritter asked, raising his voice to be heard above the crowd.

"Trained troops for Bolivia."

"Did you see any action yourself?"

"Of course, but I'm no hero. It takes an army to win a war, not just one man."

"Sometimes." Ritter slid his arm around Isanna's waist, pulling her closer to him. "Sometimes not."

Isanna pulled back slightly and cast him an angry glance. "Excuse us for a moment, Xavier, would you? There's something I must discuss with Ritter before we go in."

"Yes, of course." Xavier slid a cigarette from his pocket, leaning against a lamppost and lighting up.

Isannna took Ritter's hand and pulled him around the corner of the opera house.

With a smile, he pulled her into his arms and snuggled up to her neck. "Really now. You can't wait until later, after the performance? I always knew my uniform did something to you, but—"

She pushed against his chest full force. "Ritter, please, you're embarrassing me."

"That is not what you said last week."

"Last week was different. Last week we were in Berlin and there was news of a mounting war. This week you still wear the uniform, but for what? To parade around town, acting as if . . ." She bit her lip and paused, turning from him.

"Go on." He wrapped his fingers around her upper arm, refusing to let her leave. "Finish. Tell me what you were going to say. Acting as if I were someone of importance like your friend Xavier? You can't seriously be taken by that guy. He's at least ten years older than you and most likely never came under gunfire once, despite whatever tales he tells you."

"And you have?" Her eyes narrowed, and she flipped a handful of curls back over her shoulder. "As if you have a reason to talk."

"What are you saying?"

"I'm saying that I want you to treat Xavier with the dignity he deserves. He is a friend and a war veteran. If you keep up this act, I'll highly reconsider the next time we attend an event together." She tilted her head, cast him the pout she knew he adored, and slowly pulled her arm from his grasp. "Yes?"

"And if the tables were turned? What if I showed up—"

"In a uniform with medals across your chest?" She snuggled up to him and smiled.

"That's not what I was going to say. What if I were to show up with another woman on my arm?"

Isanna ran a finger down Ritter's sideburn, and then brushed a fingernail across his lips. "You know you are madly in love with me and wouldn't consider it. Now be a doll and show some kindness, okay? We have an opera to watch, and I hear this one is especially good."

"Fine, but tell me afterward there will only be two of us riding away together."

"Of course." Isanna strode ahead, but looked back over her shoulder. "Tonight we'll ride away together and catch the moon; how does that sound? You know how Wagner's soaring music and Teutonic legend cause my heart to pound."

Ritter pressed his hand to his forehead and chided himself. How could he have been so foolish . . . and so jealous. Destiny demanded Isanna was his; he knew it. Now if he could only make Xavier aware of that fact.

Ritter slumped in his sedan in a darkened parking lot, waiting for his uncle. The night hadn't gone as planned. Halfway through the opera, Xavier had complained of a headache, and Isanna offered to see him back to his hotel. Ritter pounded his fist into the steering wheel, wishing he'd introduced that headache.

To make matters worse, after the curtain ran down on *Siegfried* at 9:50 p.m., his uncle pulled Ritter aside to inform him that an important matter had developed concerning Spain, and Hitler himself had requested his attendance at an impromptu meeting. So Ritter drove Uncle Oswald to the Wagner family villa nearby where Hitler waited.

Now the clock read after 1:00 a.m. as Uncle Oswald finally exited the villa with his friend Hermann Göring. Ritter drummed his fingers on the steering wheel, then paused their motion as the front door opened and three other men were escorted out by Hitler himself.

Hitler stood on the stoop and waved to the small group of men. "Give General Franco my best wishes for the defeat of Communism!"

As if a weak country like Spain should be of any concern to Germany, Ritter thought.

Ritter knew he should step out of the car and greet the Führer. He knew his uncle would scold him if he didn't, but Ritter didn't care. The only thing that mattered was Isanna. Rubbing his sleepy eyes, he climbed from the car and opened the door for the two men.

"Thank you, my boy," Uncle Oswald said, sliding inside and handing Ritter his hat and cane as though his nephew were a mere servant. Ritter gritted his teeth and nodded, also helping Herr Göring inside.

The balding, overweight general hardly resembled the much-decorated pilot who'd flown in the Red Baron's squadron. The gaudy uniform did nothing to improve his looks—quite the contrary. Ritter's stomach turned at the vain smile on the man's face and the heavy odor of liquor on his breath. He slammed their doors shut, then returned to the driver's seat.

"So, I hear you're having woman problems?" Göring called from the backseat.

Seeing no reason to answer, Ritter's fingers tightened on the key as he started the automobile.

"A pity, isn't it," Uncle Oswald added. "You'd think my fine nephew would have dozens of women vying for his attention, with his uniform and all."

"I care only about the attention of one." He focused his eyes on the roadway, reminding himself that soon such experiences would no longer plague him—if he could only remain patient.

"Well, lad, if you need a place to prove yourself, perhaps I could help." Göring's voice rose in volume. "I've been looking for the opportunity to test the Luftwaffe's men and machines, and it seems my desire will soon be granted."

"To your utmost delight, my friend," Uncle Oswald added. In the rearview mirror Ritter noticed his uncle's pat on Göring's shoulder.

"An opportunity for pilots?" Ritter cocked one eyebrow.

"*Ja*. I cannot reveal more, but may I suggest practicing your Spanish."

"Why should the Duce have all the fun cleaning up Ethiopia?" Uncle Oswald added. "It's time we got to have a little fun, throw ourselves into international affairs. Mussolini is a good man for our Führer to follow. After all, what happens beyond our borders greatly impacts Germany as well."

Ritter pulled up to the hotel and parked the car. He jumped from the vehicle and rushed to the back door to assist the general.

"It should be a short fight—but worth doing. Nothing like seeing if our planes and pilots can maneuver as well as we hope in combat." Göring heaved his massive frame from the automobile. "And most likely, son, you'll be home by Christmas. With a hero's welcome, I may add."

Though Göring hadn't been ready to share details of the news of Spain, it didn't take much coaxing from Ritter to get Uncle Oswald to spill the facts. Orphaned as a young teen, Ritter had not only enjoyed the pleasantries of living in the old man's home, he also became a student of his uncle. Ritter studied his moods and watched for the right moment to present his requests. He knew the more Uncle Oswald talked with his friends, the looser his tongue would develop toward his nephew. Talking with Göring had primed the pump.

At breakfast the next morning, Ritter watched his uncle pore over the newspaper, pausing to read an in-depth report on Spain. Soon he'd learn what he wanted to know.

"You should have seen the look on Hitler's face when the three delegates from Spanish Morocco pleaded for assistance. He was ready to explode when he heard about the Reds trying to gain control of Spain. Though he has not said so publicly, his eyes are set on Moscow; and if he doesn't help control the situation in Spain he's, in effect, allowing a new enemy to rise." Uncle Oswald ran a hand over his bald head.

"I care little about the politics, Uncle. Tell me more about the conflict. Do I have a chance of being one of the pilots chosen?"

Uncle Oswald nodded slowly as he meticulously spread

blackberry jam on his toast. "My friend Göring has hinted as much. And his hints are as good as sealed."

Ritter stirred cream into his coffee.

"General Franco's men already control one-third of the country, you know. But the Republicans hold Madrid and the rich mining and industrial centers along the north and east coasts. The Nationalists need more troops—especially the regiments of the Foreign Legion and Moroccan soldiers stationed in North Africa under Franco. The problem is getting the soldiers to Spain."

"Ferry pilots? Is that all? I'd rather stay in Germany." Ritter dropped his spoon onto the polished tabletop.

"Oh, that's just the beginning." His uncle took a bite of toast, then slowly chewed. "If I know Göring, he will be as displeased with mere ferrying duties as you. I guarantee in a few months the Germans will control the air over Spain. In fact, Göring has named the project Operation Magic Fire. That's the code name representing the circle of fire that Wagner's Siegfried penetrates to rescue the captive Brunhild. Now, does that sound like a mere taxiing effort to you?"

The old man brushed crumbs from his face but missed half.

Ritter smiled, rose, and patted his uncle's shoulder. "As your friend suggested, Uncle, it's time for me to practice up on my Spanish."

Chapter Eight

Tanto te quiero, perrito, pero pa' pan muy poquito.
I love you, puppy, but not enough to feed you.

Spanish proverb

As the sun inched across the brilliant Spanish sky, Sophie tried to convince herself that she'd misread Michael's look. She was imagining things. The young Spanish girl meant nothing to him.

By that evening, she believed it. *He loves me. Of course he does.*

After lunch Michael had left for a short errand, then escorted her to the twentieth floor of the Telefónica building. The elevator girl was all smiles as they rode up, asking Sophie about the United States and her new role in Madrid. Sophie gave a convincing performance concerning her work as a translator. The girl had honored Sophie's bravery and joked about her own work in the "safest place in all Madrid."

Sophie knew exactly what the girl meant. Earlier, Michael had told her that every phone line in Madrid traveled through the Telefónica building—lines that provided communication with pro-fascist cells hiding inside the city.

"Which is a reminder, you never know who's listening," he'd said, leading her to his office.

She entered the news office, catching the scent of ink, alcohol, and tobacco—similar to Michael's old bureau in Boston. And within a few minutes a white armband stamped with the American flag, a number, and the embassy seal was fastened around her sleeve with a strict warning to wear it on the street at all times.

With business done, Michael whisked her away to a friend's villa overlooking downtown Madrid. Though well kept, the house was old and small. Sophie followed him through a metal archway leading to a small patio. The faded tiles had been scrubbed clean and glimmered in the evening light. A few empty flowerpots and a cushioned bench welcomed them.

Michael approached the bench and brushed off the cushions, though they appeared spotless, extending a hand to her. He sat and patted the spot beside him.

Sophie curled up to Michael's side, taking in the second-story view overlooking the downtown sector of Madrid. Below her, the city appeared as a maze of streets, with people moving in all directions. She was beginning to love this city.

Yet it was good to view it from a distance. She'd grown weary of watching soldiers trudge their way to the front and forever listening to the war news over the radio.

Michael ran his fingers down Sophie's arms, and she nearly pulled away from his touch. The intimacy seemed shocking after keeping herself at bay for so long. During their time apart, she'd guarded her heart, diverted her eyes from male temptation. She'd even stayed away from the wing of Greek and Roman art at the Museum of Fine Arts, to avoid the sight of all those male nudes. *But now . . .*

His hands moved to her face, as if studying the curve of her jaw with his fingertips.

She closed her eyes and let out an uneasy sigh. "So, uh . . ." she started, "what do you do when you're not taking pictures?" Her voice quivered. "Do you have friends? Have you traveled much?"

"Dear, dear Sofía," Michael said, using her Spanish name

and clucking his tongue. "You always ramble when you're nervous." He placed a kiss on her cheek, and she opened her eyes. She scooted closer and prepared to place her cheek against his shoulder, when he gently pushed her upright again.

"But wait, your hair."

"What do you mean?" Sophie touched the back of her neck where she'd knotted her dark locks into a French twist.

"Take it out." He tugged at a bobby pin. "It's pretty, but not you at all, sweetheart. Show me the girl I fell in love with."

Sophie pursed her lips, then pulled a few pins and shook her head to free the twist. With her fingers she combed through her hair from the base of her neck to the ends of her hair, until it smoothed over her shoulders and fell slightly into her face.

Then she looked shyly at Michael, and—for the first time since she'd arrived—saw in his eyes the same love she'd seen in Boston.

He pulled her close, wrapping her in an embrace. "I wish . . . ," he whispered. "If only you didn't have to leave."

The sun had set just enough for the red-tiled roofs below her to glisten like the city lights of Boston reflecting on the harbor. And like the small boats in the harbor, the locals moved within the sea of reflection, going about their daily routines despite the turmoil.

Michael pulled her closer, as if not wanting to let her go. "*Te amo, mi Divina*. You are the girl I have thought about every night since our parting, and although my logic tells me that you must leave, everything within me wants to keep you close."

The image of the raven-haired girl filled her mind, but she brushed it away and relaxed in his embrace.

After a moment, he slowly let her go, and she sat back on the cushioned bench. She watched as he motioned to a servant for some wine, for the first time realizing they were no longer alone.

"To you," he said after the wine was served. "And to our being together. I only wonder how I survived without you for so long."

Sophie brushed her hair behind her ear. "Well, you don't have to think about that, because I'm here, and we are together—just as we planned." She snuggled closer.

"Do you like Spain, then? I haven't had a chance to ask."

"It's more amazing than I'd imagined. It has a terrific sun for painting. The trees and buildings are silhouetted not only in black and white, but in blue, red, and violet. It's lovely."

"Once an artist, always an artist." He kissed the top of her head. "That's what I loved about you first, you know. I saw your heart in your work. Especially those landscapes of the sky and sea. Maybe it is their limitlessness. Is that a word?"

"I understood it." She leaned back and studied his face. His soft smile. That knowing look in his eyes. She closed hers and leaned forward for a kiss. His lips met hers—warm, tender.

With a sigh, she returned her head to his shoulder. "I had a teacher once who said that painting gives shape to sensations and perceptions. He said great art is only created when you discover the truth of what lies before you, and the truth found within, and you express it on the canvas. That's why I think I'd paint more beautifully here than anywhere else. I've found my heart." She slid her fingers down his arm and wrapped her hand over his. "Despite the war."

He raised her hand to his lips. "War?"

As if in a dream, she watched a flock of yellow birds swoop from behind them and land upon an olive tree making it look as though it had suddenly bloomed with orchids.

"So you're happy to be here?" he asked.

"Almost."

Michael leaned his head back to get a better look at her face, his eyebrow cocked in question.

"Picasso claimed he'd rather go without food than paint. My tummy's full, but . . . well, I left my paints and brushes behind."

"*Divina*, of course. I'll see what I can do."

"Michael, also, do you think I can visit the Paseo del Prado? I'd love to see some of the work of Diego Velázquez and Goya. Things have settled down enough for a little tour, don't you think?"

"Well . . ." He studied her face for a second, then sighed. "Unfortunately, I have to work tomorrow. But I have a dear friend from childhood, José, who I'm sure would be happy to escort you. I met him years ago when visiting my mother's family here, and I trust him completely, as he is deeply in love with a nurse in a small northern village. Although any other Spaniard, beware . . . This is a country of admirers and lovers. *Madrilenos* are the worst. I witnessed for myself men turning their eyes from the fighting to take a second glance at some of the women fighters dressed in the *monos*. Even though the women looked like house painters, those overalls accentuate every curve and have a dazing effect on the men who aren't used to seeing women in pants."

Sophie chuckled. "No wonder I received so much attention on the train. I'd changed into trousers for the journey over the border."

Michael pointed his finger into the air. "See, I told you who really helped whom. You, my dear, were a lovely distraction. And you just thought your quick wit impressed the committee leader."

Sophie stood and leaned against the balcony to catch the evening breeze. "And after the Paseo," she resumed, "may I spend a day painting near the Puerta de Alcalá? I read it's so similar to the Arc de Triomphe in Paris. The Alcalá is something I've always wanted to see. . . ."

"Sophie, you never know your limits, do you?"

"Is that a bad thing?"

"I will allow this, but you must return to France by the end of the week."

She returned to the bench. "But you just said you're glad I've come. . . ."

He moved beside her, smiled, and brushed her hair with his hand. "But you know it's not safe. Just until things calm down. You can wait for me in France—"

She rested her head on the cushion on the back of the bench and pulled her legs to her chest, wrapping her arms around them and tucking her skirt around her legs.

"Sophie." Michael sighed. "You don't understand. You missed the worst of the fighting, but I fear it's only the beginning. If you were here when the government recaptured the *Curatel*—that large barrack that overlooks Madrid—you wouldn't think it is so safe."

He pointed, and she saw the building in the distance. It stood like a fortress overlooking the city.

"On the day the revolution broke out, most of the soldiers mutinied to the Rebel side and took control of the barracks. At first, the people acted as if nothing had changed. In the city, one minute it seemed as if everything was normal. Everyone went about his business. Friends met at cafés. Lovers walked hand in hand through the streets. Then, at ten to four, men from every station of life rose and joined together. I think they only had one heavy gun, two fieldpieces, and some rifles. The people against a trained army. Yet they marched toward the Curatel as if they were led by Napoleon himself."

"That was happening *here*, in Madrid?" Her eyes widened. "Who was inside?"

"Militia, police, cadets, and officers—all those who sided with the Rebels. The anti-fascists marched up the steep ascent under full gunfire. The men walked over the bodies of their fallen comrades right into the barracks. Over two thousand were killed. And that was just days before you came."

She shielded her eyes from the setting sun and studied the hillside below the barracks, trying to imagine the bodies of two thousand men strewn there, their blood seeping into the hillside.

"These poor people. Someone should step in to help them. It almost makes me want to write President—"

Michael held up his hands. "I have one last piece of advice for you, *Divina*. During the time you are here, make sure you don't get too involved."

"Involved?"

"From first appearances, it may seem that this war is a clear fight between good and evil. The people against the Fascists. Democracy against dictatorship. I wish it were that easy."

"Well, the people *did* elect a government."

Michael's brows furrowed. "Yes, well, this government calls themselves 'The Popular Front,' but as I said before, they don't even agree among themselves. If you ask me, most of the people are too simple and untutored to govern themselves. Like little children, they need discipline, and Franco and his Fascists could provide just that." He shrugged. "And so their whole world is at war."

"Of course, I'm not here for war," Sophie said, leaning into his chest and wrapping her arms around him. "I've come for love, remember?"

Philip and Attis lined up with the other Americans to board the small Spanish boat, *Ciudad di Ibiẓa*. They were just two of the five hundred being evacuated from Barcelona at the order of the Catalonian government. Fading sunlight sparkled orange across the water, and Hungarian and Belgian voices radiated over the dock. These foreigners had chartered the ship, and those from the Workers' Games were lucky enough to catch a ride. The destination of all was Sète, the first port in France.

Attis shuffled from one foot to the other and glanced at the guards lining the docks.

Philip noted a familiar look in his friend's eye—one he'd first witnessed when they were thirteen and saw an open window to the girls' locker room. As they hoisted each other up to peek, Philip had learned more in that day than his science class taught him all through junior high. He knew that look meant trouble if he didn't put a stop to whatever crazy notion was brewing in his friend's head.

Attis bounced his duffel bag in his hand as if measuring its weight. "If we toss these aside, we can run faster." He leaned close to Philip's ear and spoke low. "We just need something to distract the guards."

Attis's scheming was no surprise. He had mentioned staying on in Spain at least once a day—as they left Barcelona, on the train, last night at the small hotel on the water's edge.

"We'll be thrown in prison if we're caught. And you may never see your wife again." Philip shuffled his feet as the line moved slightly forward. Mentioning Louise always brought Attis back to his senses.

"Yeah, but if I don't do this thing—don't fight for what's

right—then who will? I'll make it home. I know I will. I just have this gut—"

Shouting interrupted Attis's words. A fight had broken out between members of the Belgian and French wrestling teams. The pent-up frustrations of the week's events, added to the inability to meet in the ring, must have reached a head.

"Ouch, you'd think they'd move to the grass or something." Philip winced as he watched one man plow another man's head into the hard wooden dock.

Attis made no response.

"Attis?" Philip turned. Attis's duffel bag was abandoned at Philip's feet. "Why, that—"

Scanning the perimeter of the dock, Philip noticed a flash of red and blue scaling a brick wall. Without hesitation, he hoisted both bags to his shoulders and sprinted toward the wall. With each pounding of his feet upon the pavement, he expected the sound of gunfire to erupt.

"I'm gonna kill him," Philip panted, as he wove through the crowd. "He's dead now. He's . . ."

In a matter of seconds he reached the brick wall. With all his strength, he tossed one bag over, then the other. Then, using every bit of the muscle in his arms, he hoisted himself over. He landed unevenly on the other side and felt his body crashing toward the ground. Two hands encircled his waist from behind and pulled him upright.

Philip let out a slow breath. He lifted his hands high in the air. "I'm sorry. I wasn't planning to leave, honest. I was just—"

"Rescuing a wayward friend?" The familiar voice shook with laughter.

Philip spun around, and with an open hand struck Attis's shoulder. "What are you thinking? Are you loony? You could've gotten us killed."

Attis leaned down and pulled civilian clothes out of his duffel, stuffing his track jacket inside. He quickly changed, then snatched up his bag. "Yeah, but we're not dead, are we?" He turned toward town and began strolling down the narrow alleyway.

"Not yet!"

"Keep shouting like that and you'll draw the guards."

"Ugh." Philip removed his jacket, pulled out a white shirt and pulled it on, then hurried after Attis.

"I should've let you go."

"Without my bag? What would I wear?"

"That's not my concern."

Attis cocked his head toward Philip. "Obviously, you've made it so."

"You knew I'd follow, didn't you?"

"You're here, aren't you?"

"Louise is going to kill me."

"She can't if you're in Spain with me."

His cocksure attitude made Philip want to turn and head back to the docks—to leave Attis to his own devices—that would show him.

The alleyway opened to a wide street. Attis pulled some money from his pocket and hailed a horse carriage. Philip sighed. He shook his head and tossed his bag inside.

"To the train station, please," Attis said.

The carriage moved toward the station with the driver humming in time to the clomping of the horse's hooves.

"Then where, after that?" Philip glanced around, checking to be sure they weren't being followed.

"Madrid."

"Why there?"

"Because I've heard they're organizing international volunteers."

"All two of us?"

"I don't think we'll be the only ones."

Philip lowered his forehead into his hands, wondering how he'd gotten into this mess and how long it would take to talk some sense into his friend. *Too long. Never. I know him too well.* . . .

"And what if we are the only ones? What if no one else is stupid enough to answer the call?"

Attis leaned back and crossed his arms over his chest. "Then I'm ready to die anyway. The people should have a right to control the land, to work together for their common good. Their alternative is no better than enslavement . . . and who wants to live in a world like that?"

83

Chapter Nine

De musico, poeta y loco
Todo tenemos un poco.

Of music, poetry and madness
We all have a little.

Spanish folklore

Sophie waited near the hotel's front desk for José the next morning. She watched a young Spanish woman walk past the glass doors and admired her soft, smooth skin and deep eyes. Sophie touched the low simple knot of hair at the base of her head—the same style as that of the woman walking by. She took in a deep breath of the already warm air and grinned down at her new dress. *Just like yours,* she silently said to the woman, who had disappeared around a corner.

Before long a wiry man, about her height, entered the hotel lobby. He approached with a proud stride, gently but firmly grasping both her shoulders and placing a kiss on each of Sophie's cheeks.

"*Buenos dias, señorita.*"

"*Buenos dias, José. Soy Sofía.*"

"Nice to meet you." José pointed toward the door. "Shall we walk? We could call a carriage, but it is not far." He extended his elbow. "And we can acquaint ourselves as we go."

Sophie slid her hand into the crook of his arm.

He opened the door for her, and they stepped onto the Gran Via.

"*Nuestro amigo*—our friend, Miguel, has asked me to escort you to see some of our country's finest artwork. It is good you are in Madrid and not Barcelona. Here, the churches are closed, but not burned."

A group of soldiers dressed in dark blue *monos* passed, each nodding a greeting. Sophie returned their glances with a smile.

"If the churches are closed, how will we get in?"

"*Sí,* your Miguel, this man has many friends. And those he doesn't know, thankfully, I do. First we will stop at San Antonio de la Florida. I know you will be pleased to see the Goya frescoes. Beautiful. The door is kept locked by the keeper, but he promised to open it on your behalf."

"I'm honored."

"It is not every day an American artist visits."

"It's not like I'm Picasso or something." Sophie chuckled. She took in the sight of the people moving along the streets. Businessmen in suits. Women carrying baskets of food from the market. Mothers strolling with their children in carriages.

"Picasso is a master, *sí*, one of our own sons. But painters of all stations are much honored here, as are photographers. You will see. Much more appreciated than in the United States. The Germans, they are thinkers," he continued, shaking his head. "They think this and that, and how to make what belongs to everyone else to be theirs. Have you heard that German planes have been seen in the Spanish skies? Bombers delivering Moorish troops from Africa."

His pace was as quick as his words as he led her through the crowds. "But mark my words, that will not be the last we see of them."

José pointed to a small, simple church ahead. "This church has been out of service for some time. Yet this is good. Another church close by has been requisitioned for the use of a district militia committee. We would not be able to go there today or anytime soon."

He said something in Spanish she didn't understand. Perhaps a curse or a statement of disbelief.

"Can you believe that holy places are being used by the militia? Incredible!"

Sophie tried to catch her breath, urging herself to keep up with the pace of his legs . . . and his words. *If he continues at this rate, I doubt I'll last the day.*

They approached the small building, and even before they knocked, an old man, bent with years, opened the door and motioned them inside. Then, just as quickly, he disappeared.

A dozen candles attempted to illuminate the dusty room, with negligible results. Sophie covered her mouth and sneezed from the scent of smoke, incense, and dust. When her eyes finally adjusted to the dim interior, she was disappointed by the room's shabbiness—until she looked up.

"Goya," she said in quiet reverence. She slid her hand into José's and squeezed. "Oh, look at those rosy-cheeked angels."

She turned to one side and noticed a marker and a large marble coffin. In Boston the graves of important men could be found in old cemeteries, but for some reason Sophie couldn't get used to the idea of final resting places being inside the church. "Is that Goya?"

"*Sí.*"

Trying not to shudder, she returned her attention to the mural painting adorning the walls, cupola, and bows of the building.

José pointed to the cupola. "*Mira, señorita.* Goya represents the miracle of San Antonio. Have you heard of it?"

"I can't say I have."

"According to legend, San Antonio was transported from his own Padova to Lisbon with the help of an angel after a dead man prayed for his help. There he resuscitated a slain person, who was then able to testify who murdered him, thus saving the father of the dead man, who was wrongly accused of the murder."

Wonder filled Sophie as she scanned the mosaic, taking in the small details that caused the legend to come to life within its parameters. "Yes, I see it now. The angels are rejoicing over the miracle. Look at their joyful faces. And the people whisper and gawk at the scene. Do you believe it's true?"

José shrugged. "Perhaps there was a time for miracles in our country, but no longer. Darkness has fallen over this land of vivid light and distant vistas."

"You speak like a poet."

"Then you have judged well."

"I'd love to read your work sometime."

"Perhaps." José shrugged. "Poets are appreciated here, but not as much as artists. Sixty percent of Spain is illiterate, you see. I knew an artist once, who unfortunately lived in Seville, which is now under Rebel control. He designed some of the first posters to grace our fine city during the elections. Just days ago, I heard, he was targeted by a bullet, not long after the revolt started. He never once even held a gun, yet he was one of the first sought out."

"For painting? That makes no sense."

"*Señorita*, if it were only painting, there would be no problem. Yet he was one who painted *ideas*. For a country in which most can't read, he communicated in the way the people know best."

José spread his arms, returning her attention to the display before them. "Do you think the churches are only filled with art for art's sake? They speak the stories without saying a word. They remind the people of the saints of God. Of Christ. Of sacrifice. Of eternity. My friend—the painter who is no more—did the same. And if you look closely at the political posters that cover our city, you'll see stories in the images, and hopes, and pleas. Spaniards, as you may have realized, are visual people. The eyes are the most important of all senses." He opened his hands as if holding a book. "The ears—not so, unless they can create images in the minds of the people."

"In New England, where I grew up, I noticed that most people walk around with their eyes down. Here, I feel as if eyes are on me everywhere I go."

"Yes, Spaniards appreciate beauty. But it's not just you, *señorita*. We look at everything, take it in, and then pour it out in canvas, prose, and song. Sometimes an artist seeks to involve viewers." He pointed to the frescos. "Other times, the art created is the result of a private experience. If you could only see the place . . ." José paused, then shook his head.

"What place?"

"I'm sorry, *señorita*, but I have made a promise to Miguel. No political talk. No introductions."

"Introductions?"

"*Sí*, to the artists' community of Madrid. For they are as radical about their freedom as their art."

"And you, José. Do you feel the same?"

"I do not think of myself as radical. In fact, I hardly know what that word means. Instead, I think only of a liberal government, whatever the form. I wish only for freedom in place of submission, and this is the reason worthy of the fight. Yet my friends, they would have much to share."

He shook his finger at her. "But see here, *señorita*. Look at what you have done. Like a spider you have entangled me in your web of questions, and now I have a war raging in my own soul." He stroked his chin. After a few seconds, he sighed. "Maybe, I believe, just a short visit won't hurt."

Less than an hour later, Sophie felt the weight of the past few weeks fall from her shoulders as she entered a small studio. Though many of the artists had returned home for the afternoon siesta, a few remained, working at easels set up around the room.

The large warehouse-type room was a chaos of painted canvases. Collected objects lined the shelves. Drawings and sketches were pinned on walls haphazardly. Sophie strode along one wall noticing landscapes, portraits, and modern art reminiscent of Picasso's most recent work.

The smell of oil paint and turpentine brought a smile. Energy stirred the air, and with every breath she felt as if creativity and life flowed into her.

"Thank you, José. This is just what I needed. I feel like I'm home again." She lifted a clean brush, feeling its weight, remembering its sensation.

"Yes, well, I still question if it is worth losing the trust of a friend. Miguel will not be happy if he finds out."

Sophie crossed the room to where a man worked on an image of the Curatel overlooking Madrid. He painted the event Michael had spoken about, the storming of the hill. Though a few men at the top of the hill lifted their hands in victory, the hillside below them consisted of black and red shapes. It was only as she studied the abstract images more closely that Sophie realized they were disjointed body parts sprouting among the blood-red stones. Her mood changed instantly, as if the emotions of the piece had bounced from the canvas to her heart.

"We don't have to tell him, do we—that we've come?" She turned to José, noting the serious look in his dark eyes. "After all, I'll be gone in a week or two, and what Michael doesn't know won't hurt him."

"Unfortunately, *mimo*," José said with a shrug, "the man you have come to marry has recently said the same thing about you."

Chapter Ten

Camarón que se duerme se lo lleva la corriente.

Shrimp that sleep, the current takes.

Spanish proverb

José must have noted Sophie's brooding attitude as they exited the studio and then strode down the Gran Via toward her hotel.

"I spoke out of turn. Forgive me, *señorita*. Miguel is my friend, yes, but we disagree on many things. And in one afternoon, you've discovered at least two." José shrugged. "I should not say as much, but I can see the worry heavy on your face." He paused and turned to her, lowering his voice. "It is his work, you see. So dangerous. He doesn't want to bother you with it, but I tell him you deserve the truth. There are many who wish to silence his voice."

"His voice?"

"*Sí, señorita*. His photos speak volumes, and though he has tried to publish them under an alias, they know. His work is as a fingerprint, you see. It is quite unique, the way he can choose one object to tell the story of a battle or one face to represent throngs of soldiers."

"So, that thing . . . what he's been hiding from me—it has to do with his work?"

"*Sí*. Now let me see those bright eyes. I do not wish to ruin your afternoon or your *relación*. Whether your *señor* knows it or not, he needs you here. In fact, we must hurry, or we will miss meeting Michael for the bullfight."

"Bullfight!"

"Did he not tell you? It is something to look forward to, indeed." José rubbed his hands together in anticipation. "It must have been a surprise, *no*?"

They hurried down the last block, and José opened the glass door to the hotel. "See, there he waits for you."

Michael's green, smiling eyes caught hers, and her heart did a flip. His grin communicated volumes as he strode toward her, holding a bouquet of red carnations.

Sophie smiled, noticing a grace in his walk he hadn't exhibited in Boston. It was as if he'd taken in the essence of the people, just as one absorbed the hot Spanish sun.

Michael swept her into his arms. "For you, my dear." He handed her the flowers, then twirled her around, causing her Spanish dress to flare whimsically. "*Mi amor bonita*. You look like a true *Española*."

Sophie bowed her head as she'd seen the young women do. "*Gracias, señor.*" She leaned close to let him kiss her cheek.

"Now go put these in water and hurry back. I have a treat for you."

Sophie studied his face. His green eyes gazed adoringly at her; yet despite José's explanation, uneasiness still gnawed in her gut. She lifted the blossoms to her face, breathing in their sweet scent. "They're beautiful. Where are we going? Do I need to change?"

A sparkle lit up Michael's eyes. "Yes, there is another dress in your room. Hurry now; we don't want to be late."

Opening the door to her room, Sophie sucked in her breath as she discovered a black dress laid out on her bed. Red poppies decorated the fabric that was as light as silk. A ruffled, V-necked collar matched the ruffles on the hem of the skirt.

She quickly dressed, buckled on the large, black suede belt, fixed her hair in a loose braid, and tucked a carnation behind her ear. She spun in front of the mirror. With her dark hair and new style, she felt as if she fit in. She dared even to call herself pretty.

She grabbed her sketchbook and gave one final glance in the mirror before hurrying down to the lobby.

Michael showed his appreciation with a low whistle.

"You like?" Sophie twisted her torso just enough for the layers of fabric to swoosh around her legs.

"Very much." He stepped forward and placed a kiss on each of her cheeks. "Just as I'd imagined. Now for the surprise. We have tickets for the one event that reveals, above all else, the true heart of Spain."

"A bullfight?"

Michael nodded and extended his elbow.

On the carriage ride to the arena, Sophie marveled at the number of people heading for an afternoon of entertainment in the middle of a workday. The carriage drove them down wide, tree-lined avenues and twisting narrow streets. Polite men tipped their hats as they passed, and women waved as if Sophie had been a friend for life. Handsome children laughed and played in a grassy park, and a few danced in a spouting fountain.

"For the Spaniards, everything comes before business—especially pleasure." Michael laughed, pointing to a group of young women walking through the park arm in arm. "On any given day, the talk around town usually centers on which café a favorite dancer will appear at, or which fighter will be in his best form at the bullfight. Many Spaniards never go to bed before five o'clock in the morning—and then only because they've had their fill of drink." A huge grin filled Michael's face as he spotted a man waving to him from the street.

"Miguel! ¿Como estas, mi amigo?"

"Bien, Paulo. ¿Donde esta su espousa? Where is your wife?"

Paulo just grinned back and strolled toward a young woman waiting up ahead.

Michael turned back to Sophie. "You see why my Spanish friends will meet me day or night to discuss anything I like, but won't take me home to their family? I'm more likely to meet a friend's mistress than his wife."

Sophie glanced at Michael to see if he was joking.

He sighed. "Unfortunately for me, I have deadlines, and for some odd reason New York won't hold up production because I stayed up to the wee hours at Café Miami."

"Café Miami?"

"Oh, not a place you would like, *mimo*—it's a seedy bar. A woman of culture and class like you—someone who appreciates fine art, not chrome tables, leather armchairs, and loud music—wouldn't feel comfortable."

"So you think I've never been to a seedy bar, my love?" She threw him a sassy glance, then told herself she'd have to stroll by this café—and perhaps peek inside.

They arrived at the Plaza de Toro a few minutes before four o'clock.

"The only thing that begins on time in Spain is the bull-fight," Michael said, helping her from the carriage.

Excitement stirred in the air as he led her to their seats in a shaded spot four rows up from the arena.

"I can't believe this. The closest I've come to a bullfight is learning the steps to the Paso Dobles your mother taught me."

"You're in luck. Today they're raising money to support the Republican troops, so you'll see twice the number of matadors."

Michael waved to someone behind her, and Sophie turned. She spied Maria with an older, gray-haired man at her side.

Michael touched her back. "I hope you don't mind that we are meeting my friends." Michael stood as they approached. "Paco, Maria Donita, may I introduce Sophie?"

Paco grinned broadly. "Welcome, Sofía."

"We've heard so much about you," Maria added.

Both honored her with a quick kiss on the cheek before sitting by Michael's side.

Sophie fanned her sketchbook in front of her face, attempting to follow Paco's story about the influx of refugees entering the city. She commented at all the right times, then turned her attention to the flushed faces across the stadium. Their stirring told her that the event was about to begin.

"Is it true that sometimes the matadors are killed?" Sophie asked.

Michael patted her hand. "The daily possibility of death is what makes Spaniards passionate about living."

Paco nodded, his hands moving excitedly as he spoke. "The sport of bullfighting celebrates the strength of the human spirit. Against all odds, the little man faces the monster. *Sí*, it makes perfect sense that the bullfight is our *fiesta nacional*."

"I am not in complete agreement, cousin." Maria flipped a brightly colored fan from her pocket and fanned her face as gently and gracefully as a butterfly in flight. "It is not sport, but art. Some say the bullfighter has taken his gestures from the traditional dances of Spain, but I believe the opposite is true. The dancer is only as beautiful as the bullfighter. And some of the greatest, world-renowned dancers, such as La Argentina, found fame in bullfighting passes set to music."

Paco flipped his arms as if holding a cape, then winked at Sophie. "Perhaps I will show you a few moves later, *señorita?*"

"Or maybe I will." Michael pulled her close, snuggling her to his neck and placing a soft kiss on her forehead.

Maria stiffened on the seat beside them.

With a loud cheer from the crowd, the gates opened, and Michael grasped Sophie's arm. A military band marched forward, playing the Spanish national anthem.

Sophie rose with the others, setting her sketch pad on the bench and mimicking their clenched-fist salute. Passion radiated from the crowd's voices, and Sophie's heart swelled. As tears flowed down the cheeks of those seated around her, Sophie remembered—for the first time since entering the arena—that war raged just outside the city. Something *the people* had not forgotten.

One thousand voices rose in perfect harmony. Though she understood the words, every time Sophie attempted to sing, she stumbled over them. Michael sang heartily, as if he'd been born and raised in Madrid. Beside him, Maria Donita's voice rose above the rest, not due to her strong presence, but rather because the crowd around her seemed to soften their own voices in appreciation of her beautiful refrain.

The song came to an end, and cheers erupted again as eight matadors entered the arena. They marched, straight-backed, to blaring trumpets and the cheers of the adoring crowd.

Sophie scanned their faces, attempting to remember each one, wondering if they would all exit as triumphantly. "I imagined the bullfighters to be tall and brawny like football players, but that is not the case."

"Their strength is in their agility," Michael answered. "Besides, wait until you see the fight. I couldn't imagine a football player moving with such form and grace—it would be like an elephant in a ballet."

The matadors' black hair glistened in the sun. She'd heard of the fine costumes typically worn, *suits of light* as they were called. Yet today the *mantillas* and fine satin suits were put away, and matadors wore only the *monos* of the militia fighters, reminding the people again of the purpose of today's fight.

The procession through the arena included *banderilleros* and *picadors*, in addition to the matadors. Paco took great care explaining their role to Sophie as they entered the arena. Once the procession was over, only two matadors remained.

Sophie followed the gaze of the others and turned her attention to the bull in the closed stall. He snorted and pawed the ground.

"The foreordained death of the bull is as sacred as the Mass," Michael explained. "And the possibility of death of the matador displays passion, tension, and truth. You're right, Maria." He patted Maria's hand. "It is much more than sport."

The gate lifted, and the bull rushed out. The creature's squinted eyes attempted to adjust to the light of the arena. It seemed so alone and angry, and Sophie winced as she saw that it was already wounded by tiny lances in its neck.

As if chasing the bull, two assistants ran into the ring.

"What are they doing?" Sophie watched as they waved their capes, and the bull made a few passes.

"They're testing the bull to see if he's brave or treacherous." Paco leaned forward and pointed into the ring. "See how he's watching every movement? Each bull enters the ring only once. If for some reason he leaves alive, he never returns. They are too clever, too quick to learn the weaknesses of the matadors."

"Every bullfighter prefers a brave bull," Michael added, lifting his camera and snapping a few shots.

"A brave bull will charge every time," Maria said, the movement of her fan speeding up as she looked at Sophie. Sophie noted a warning in the young woman's voice, something the men hadn't seemed to pick up.

"Yet a coward is hard to read. It is far more dangerous, to be sure," Paco added.

"That bull looks very brave." Maria scooted closer to Michael's side. "That matador best be on his guard."

Ignoring Maria, Sophie turned her attention to the arena. Her pounding heart quickened even more, and she held her breath as the matador stood balanced on his toes with the bull racing toward him. He stretched the cape at arm's length in front of him, making an arch with his lean body. The bull raged past, and the matador's stomach drew in so tightly Sophie was sure there was no room for him to even take a small breath of air.

"There are four parts to every fight," Michael said. "The cape play by the matador, the thrusts by the *picadors* on their mounts, and then the placing of the *banderillas*, which are those long wooden shafts. Only then does the death blow come with the *muleta*."

"*Muleta?*"

"Yes, it's a sword concealed behind that beautiful cape," Maria Donita said.

Feeling tension building in her limbs, Sophie lifted her sketchbook and began to draw. She noted the lumpy flesh on the bull's back—the way it quivered as he propelled his body down the length of the arena. His vain charges to the broad and beautiful capes wielded by the *toreros* brought cheers from the crowd.

Next a horse and *picador*, its mounted rider, entered the ring and stood fixed like a statue. Revulsion at the thought of bleeding horses caused Sophie to pause, her pencil in midair.

"Is that bull really going to charge that blindfolded horse?" A sick feeling washed over her, and she looked away.

Michael patted her cheek. "Yes, he's free to gore it as the *picador* attempts to drive his long lance deep into the bull's neck muscles. The lance will weaken the bull and make him vulnerable to the *torero's* sword."

Sophie continued to watch, but not with the passion of the

crowd. Instead, she focused on the page, attempting to catch every small detail on the dramatic stage set before her.

When the first matador finished, one of the officials offered him the ears and tail of the bull he'd slain.

"Is that some type of trophy?"

"Exactly. It proves that it was a clean kill and perfect cape work."

The sun slipped lower in the sky as, one by one, the bulls were downed and dragged out of the arena. Eventually, only trails of blood and one matador remained.

"There is no middle ground when it comes to bullfighting. People either think it's crude and barbaric or a great art," Michael said as he snapped a shot of the last matador entering the arena.

Sophie gave no answer.

When the last matador approached, the crowd rose to their feet with wild applause even before the bull was released. Though the matador's dark hair and light eyes made him wickedly handsome, the dejected look on his face nearly brought tears to Sophie's eyes.

"His brother was killed yesterday on the Guadarrama front," Paco explained. "He would not be here today if this weren't a charity event."

Sophie snatched up her notebook and continued her sketch. With quick strokes she hoped to relate the tense excitement of the event. Yet she could not capture the spirit of patriotism that ignited the air, and the image seemed flat and lifeless on the paper.

She started to tear the page from her notebook when Michael's hand covered hers. "Leave it there. It's not perfect, but it's a memory just the same. . . ."

She lifted her eyes just in time to see the matador march across the sand, his boots moving in time to the music. A black hat sat straight just above his eyebrows.

As the music crescendoed, a gigantic red bull roared into the ring. Sophie held her breath, her eyes fixed on the man who appeared so alone in the center. As the bull circled the perimeter, the matador lifted his bright red cape high in the air, swaying it to catch the bull's attention. The bull snorted and sped up, closing the gap between it and the man.

Yet the matador stood motionless, and Sophie gasped as he pulled the cape even closer to his body. "What is he doing?"

Michael held up his hand, silencing her.

Just as the animal reached the cloth, the man spun, twisting the cape around himself, and the bull plowed into empty air. He repeated the dance three more times—the bull's horns just grazing his body. And it wasn't until Michael's laughter broke through her consciousness that Sophie realized she was on her feet as the matador killed the bull with one perfect thrust. She was both horrified and enthralled. The rest of the audience joined her, standing, then they tossed bouquets of carnations into the ring. Some men even tossed their hats.

Then over the gates jumped many *milicianos*, lifting the man to their shoulders . . . yet the matador's face was not one of triumph. Even with his hands covering his face, Sophie noted his trembling shoulders and tears dripping from his chin. She sat down again at the sight of the bull being dragged away. Her stomach felt queasy.

"Someday, I will bring you back for the display of the gypsy bullfighters," Michael said. "Though cowards, their style and elegance cannot be matched."

"I can appreciate the fight, but I'm not sure I want to come back anytime soon. It just seems so unfair." Sophie closed her sketchbook. "The bull didn't seem to have much of a chance."

"Now *that* sounds very American. And I'm sure a slaughterhouse would make a better end?" Michael's voice was terse, and he released her hand. "Besides, the matadors only make it look like they have the upper hand. Many are killed each season."

"Oh, Michael, be kind to the girl. She is a foreigner, after all. She knows no different."

"I'm a foreigner too, remember?" Michael's voice calmed, and he offered his arms to both Sophie and Maria as they rose.

Maria patted his chest. "Did you forget Spain's blood is in your veins? It brought you home. And only true sons and daughters of Spain are destined to remain here."

Chapter Eleven

No hay mal que por bien no venga.

There is nothing bad that does not bring some good.

Spanish proverb

Flower arrangements of red carnations covered every available surface of the chapel. Faces of family and friends smiled back as Sophie stepped down the aisle to the wedding march, her powder blue dress swishing around her legs as she walked.

Her glance passed over the admiring audience and back to the front, where the groom waited. Yet she paused midstep as she noticed a bride already at his side.

First the groom turned to look at her—Michael. Then the bride turned—Maria Donita—divinely beautiful in a black dress with red poppies. Maria opened her mouth and laughter spilled out, but as Sophie rushed toward the woman, the laughter was replaced by a bloodcurdling wail.

As the wail continued, Maria's mouth widened, covering her whole face with a black, yawning cavern. Sophie bolted upright in the darkness of her hotel room, perspiration—or tears—stinging her eyes and wetting her face. She placed a hand over her pounding heart while trying to shake off the horrid nightmare, then jumped out of bed.

After taking a calming breath, she again heard the wailing sound and rushed to the open window to scan the street below. The only one occupying the street—lit by the first pink rays of dawn—was an old man yanking a gray donkey's halter rope, attempting to urge it forward. The donkey, rump plastered to the pavement, held his head high despite the old man's best efforts to drag it down so he could lead the animal. In frustration, the farmer picked up a large straw broom from the cobblestone street and swung it wide and hard, striking the side of the donkey's head, and it shrieked again. If Sophie hadn't seen it for herself, she'd never have believed a woman's screech could come out of a donkey's mouth. She fanned her face, trying to calm her frayed nerves.

She returned to the large, overstuffed bed, found the residual warmth of her body, pulled the feather comforter back over herself, and burrowed her cheek into the massive feather pillow. Hoping to avoid her interrupted nightmare, she concentrated instead on her favorite dream since she was ten. The one where she was a bride in a flowing gown, step, step, stepping down the aisle of a church filled with flowers toward an adoring groom. Family and friends were gathered with joyful and expectant faces.

For many years the face of the groom had eluded her, until the day she met Michael. He was so different from Boston's homegrown guys. Growing up in Washington, D.C., and Spain, Michael had an air of classiness mixed with Spanish charm. Even the fellow artists at the museum seemed boring compared to the international journalist. Michael's ruggedly handsome features would have been enough to capture her interest, but he was also smart and sophisticated.

She smiled and sighed as she remembered their first date. Instead of offering her the typical dinner and theater tickets, Michael had chartered a small speedboat and whisked her off to Little Brewster Island in Boston Harbor, where they picnicked on the sandy beach, then walked the trails to the crest of the hill. There he photographed the harbor and the city beyond while she sketched, appreciating him as much as the landscape before her.

Five years her senior, he'd traveled the world and seen his photos published in some of the country's top magazines. At the time Sophie met him, Michael was taking six months to catch his breath and spend time with his parents, who'd recently moved to Boston. Yet even during this breather, he worked for the local paper. And even around Boston, his camera had seemed an extension of his arm. He babied it and spoke to it lovingly, as one would a cherished child, as he snapped the photos. As the sun began to set, she watched as he took an almost transparent piece of cloth and placed it over the lens of his camera.

Sophie had leaned in close, breathing in his scent of soap and fresh air. "What's that for?"

"This silk will make the photo appear hazy, as if capturing the ocean mist. Except for this one part, you see." He showed her where the cloth had been cut away, leaving a small opening over the center of the lens. "I'll center this clear spot on that boat in the distance. Only the boat will be in focus, and it will make it seem as if it is sailing through a dream." He wrapped his arm around her shoulder. "After all, being with you is like a dream come true."

"How's that?" Sophie had rested her head on his shoulder. Her heart pounded and she couldn't hide her slight smile.

"I always pictured myself with someone like you. Someone in love with art and life. I think, Sophie, that this day is just the start of something beautiful."

They had talked and laughed as if they'd always been friends, capturing the scenery around them on film and paper until the fading sunlight made that impossible. Then, after the sun had slipped away, they'd explored Boston Light, the oldest lighthouse in the country, sitting atop the rocky cliff. In the distance, the glow from the lighthouse danced on the water in circular swirls, and her heart mimicked the dancing within her chest.

Late that night, after Michael had dropped her off back home, grinning and smelling of saltwater spray, she had the dream again. Only it was his smiling face awaiting her at the end of the aisle. And his engagement ring six months later brought that dream one step closer to coming true.

Sophie withdrew her left hand from under her comforter, extending it in the pink predawn light to study appreciatively the thin platinum band with seven small European-cut diamonds.

Then she stretched and kicked the covers off, padding to the closet where the dress for her wedding hung. She removed it from the hanger and pressed it to her, turning to the full-length mirror. It was all she'd ever wanted. Yet since being here she questioned if Michael still wanted the same. Maria's face came to mind, followed by the image of soldiers marching down the street—their faces set with determination as they headed to the front. The war compromised their safety; that was certain. But Sophie knew, deep down, this other woman posed an even greater threat.

She walked to the small desk with the phone, considering calling Michael's apartment to ask him to meet her—to get everything out in the open. Then she remembered he'd left the city last night on assignment and wouldn't be back until later that afternoon.

A longing to see the former tenderness and love in his eyes filled her chest until she couldn't stand the ache. With heavy steps, she returned the dress to the closet and wondered if the nightmare had been a harbinger of what lay ahead.

Sophie gently set her sketchbook and pencils on the shaded, grassy area near a cluster of trees in the small city park near her hotel. The building beside her had a window cracked open, and she heard the rattle of typewriter keys pounding like the distant machine guns she imagined on the front lines. She settled on the grass, trying to determine what she should sketch.

An old man and woman sat on a bench at the street corner, with a small suitcase set between them like a table and two white teacups steaming with what she assumed was tea. The man's jowls hung from his jaw, and after taking a sip from his cup, he let out a long sigh. A faded blue scarf covered the woman's head tightly, pressing down on her forehead as if creating a permanent scowl.

Sophie tried to imagine them as a young couple in love. Had they danced in fields of flowers together? Had she, with a child on her hip, watched him from the window of their small cottage as he chopped wood for their fire?

As she sat there, Sophie watched washerwomen transform the landscape around her. It was as if the clothes they pinned to their lines were the strokes of a brush, adding color to the gray landscape. Red socks, a blue blanket, crisp white nightshirts. A small blue dress. Grey trousers. Another woman added to the color until colors fluttered across the grey brick buildings like ornaments on a Christmas tree.

Sophie heard her name called and looked up to see José strolling up the sidewalk, a broad smile filling his face.

"*Mimo*, guess what? My mission, it has been accomplished." He squatted before her, took both her hands in his, and squeezed. "I have a gift for you. Something you want more than anything."

"A gift?"

"Sofía, you wished for an apartment, and one has opened up with dear friends. You'll love Benita and Luis. They are like a second family to me here in Madrid. Although in my opinion, Benita spends far too much time with those foreign Baptist missionaries."

"Please don't tease me like that, José. You know what Michael said. I only have a few days left until I return to France."

He pointed a finger into the air. "And this, Sofía, is my second gift. Michael has agreed for you to stay."

She cocked her head and studied his face, sure this was some type of joke. "José, I don't believe you."

He removed his grasp, stood, and placed a hand over his heart. "Lady, I am shocked you think a noble Spaniard such as I would misrepresent the truth. Your Michael is meeting us for dinner tonight to discuss the new situation, but before that we must move your things."

Sophie jumped to her feet and snagged her arms around José's neck. He stiffened, and she pulled back, chiding herself for obviously crossing some type of boundary.

She cleared her throat, noticing his reddening cheeks. "Well, tell me about it, then. What did you say to convince him?"

José motioned to a park bench, and they sat. He rested elbows on knees and leaned forward. "First, I told him he needs you here. You are the woman of his heart, and he must be reminded of this daily, *sí*? Not only that, but your press pass will help him greatly."

"My pass? How so?" She closed her sketchbook.

"He captures images for one publication, you see. But you have an open pass, which gives you much more leniency. Photos that he cannot get out of the country under his name can be transported under yours."

An uneasy feeling came over her. "Yes, but is that legal?"

"Of course not, but neither is lying to get such a pass in the first place. But I told you I would help you, remember? I'm surprised you are not more excited."

She rubbed her sweaty palms across her skirt. "Of course I am. I'm sorry. So when do I get to see this new place?"

"At this moment. It is just a short walk from here. We will send later for your things if you so approve." José stood and led her away with quickened steps.

Dark rain clouds had gathered over the city, blocking the sun and making the heat more bearable. They'd gone no more than a block when a misty rain began to fall. The crowds around her didn't even pause. They strolled through the streets as if unaware of the water falling from the sky.

"José, do you know somewhere I can purchase an umbrella?" She tucked her sketchbook close to her chest to protect it.

"You're not serious, are you? Look around, *mimo*. Spaniards believe water falling from the sky is a sign of wealth and luck. Rain is also supposed to be good for the skin. This is a good sign, yes? Evidence of good things to come."

Sophie tilted her chin slightly as she continued walking, eager for those *good things* José spoke of, and trying to ignore the nagging in her mind concerning the use of her press pass. Hadn't José been the one to tell her that there were those who didn't want Michael's photos to get out? Hadn't he been the first to warn her of the danger in Michael's work?

The streets beyond the main thoroughfare gave Sophie the impression she'd stepped into another world. Peasant carts jammed the roadways. Family groups with their sheep and goats carried the odor and poverty of the countryside into the city. The drabness of the peasant women even caused the simple sidewalk cafés and ornate churches to appear formal and stiff in comparison.

They walked by a small park, and Sophie saw a group of

women washing their children in a fountain. Though they had no soap, their bare hands scrubbed at the faces and full heads of hair with vigor. Sophie smiled, noticing the children's clothes already washed and spread out on the sidewalk to dry.

Ten minutes later, they approached a small apartment on the lower level of a three-story building. The door opened to them before José had a chance to knock. A tall, thin man with a bushy moustache and large, round eyes greeted them with a smile.

José patted the man's shoulder. "Sofía, this is Luis."

"Sof-ia," Luis said, drawing out her name. "We have heard much about you. I am certain you will consider us close friends, as we do you."

"I would like that." She allowed him to kiss her cheek and followed him inside to a small, but clean, apartment. The painted walls seemed to bring the reds and oranges of the city inside. A large window at street level provided a perfect view of the busy street, packed with people in motion. A table and two chairs sat before the window, and she imagined all the wonderful afternoons she could spend there sketching the quaint neighborhood.

"My wife has gone to the market, but she will return shortly. Of course, you will notice that we live in no luxury, but we are comfortable. It is also good to be with others when the difficult times come."

"Well, maybe the revolt will be over soon. Surely, it can't last more than a few weeks, can it?" She turned to study José's face, but he only shrugged. She glanced back at Luis.

Luis's eyes fell to the floor. "*Sí Dios quiere, So-fi-ia.* If God so wishes. I suppose we will only have to wait and see."

A soft knock sounded on the open door, and Sophie turned to see Michael standing there.

"It will be a safe place until we make arrangements for you to return to France." Michael's voice was quiet, controlled, without inflection.

She attempted to mimic his demeanor and crossed her arms. "Do you mean, until *we* return?"

Luis's eyes darted between them, and the look on Michael's face told her she had overstepped.

José spread his arms wide as if to smooth over the situation. "Until we all experience the goodwill of God and—"

The sound of gunshots split the air, followed by women's screams on the street.

Sophie froze, and José ran to the window. He cursed. "Two soldiers, shot in the street!"

More gunfire exploded. A shot rang out against the apartment wall. Michael grasped Sophie's arm, pulling her down the hall. Shattering glass met her ears.

"José!"

Chapter Twelve

De árbol caído todos hacen leña.

Everyone gets firewood from a fallen tree.

Spanish proverb

Sophie's stomach turned at the sight of a shard of glass protruding from José's shoulder. She covered her mouth with her hand, as much to retain her stomach's contents as to suppress a cry.

His face had drained of color, yet his expression said he worried about *her*. "Do not worry, *señorita*. I have faced much worse. We can be glad the rebel was a bad shot, yes?"

"Sophie, hurry. Start some water on the cookstove. And see if you can find some clean dishcloths for bandages," Michael urged, helping to ease José down the hall and onto the narrow bed in the first room.

She returned to the main room. The shards from the window glistened like a creek of glass on the tile floor. The wind had picked up, blowing in damp air through the gaping hole. Without a barrier between the street and apartment, the cries and shouts of those on the street overwhelmed her. A crowd had gathered, tending to the injured men while crying children searched for their mothers. Didn't the people worry there would be more shots? Why didn't they escape into the safety of their homes?

With trembling hands, she turned to the cookstove. At home her mother did the cooking—that is, when they weren't dining at the hotel where her father worked. She looked at the black, wood-burning monster and wondered what to do first. Then she heard the crunch of footsteps over broken glass behind her.

"I'm sorry," Michael said. "I forgot. This is all new to you." He made quick work of lighting the stove. "I'll take care of this. Why don't you see if you can find Benita and tell her what happened. There is a market a few blocks away, down the same street you came. Just ask at any of the stalls. Everyone knows who she is."

He must have seen the panic on her face. "Don't worry, the shooters are gone. They've been doing this all over the city—shooting from the rooftops, picking their targets, then escaping before they are discovered." He placed a hand on her shoulder and brushed a lock of hair from her cheek. "Do you think you can do it?"

Her mind raced, trying to remember the streets José had led her along. They all looked the same; how would her fragmented mind find the way? Her stomach clenched at the thought of walking past the men lying in pools of blood on the street.

She glanced toward the street and back to Michael, noticing his eyes narrow, as if in challenge. She knew him well enough to read his look. *So you say you want to stay . . . show me you can handle it.*

She planted her sweaty palms on her hips and let out a low breath. "Benita. Okay. I'll be right back."

With determined steps she hurried out the door and moved through the crowd. Sucking in a breath and letting it out slowly, she placed a hand over her quivering stomach and hurried past the downed men, past the ambulance rumbling toward them, to the market, which seemed to be emptying of people who'd surely heard the shots. With halting steps she approached a woman sorting a basket of oranges.

"Pardon me, can you point out Benita . . . Luis's wife? There has been an incident."

"Benita is not here. She is delivering food."

"To whom, where?"

The woman's mouth opened to speak, but another interrupted. "I'll show you."

Sophie turned and noticed Maria Donita with another young woman at her side.

"Many people have taken refugees into their homes, but most are housed at the school. Come."

Maria squeezed the hand of the young woman beside her. "Tell Mama I'll meet her at home." Then Maria turned, the rustling of her long skirt brushing against Sophie's leg.

Sophie had no choice but to follow.

Maria walked straight-backed and graceful, despite her quickened pace. "How do you know Benita?"

"I am staying there. And there has been an accident. A shooting. Their window was shot. Michael—"

Maria interrupted. "He's hurt?"

"No. A piece of glass injured José. Michael sent me for help."

Maria nodded, then led her into a more depressed area of town. Alongside the dilapidated buildings, small hovels had been built, and the people used oxcarts, blankets, anything to keep out the elements. Animals filled the streets, and Sophie held her breath as she pushed through a small flock of sheep. Their baaing rang in her ears, and they nuzzled her legs as if searching for food.

"We are trying to find homes for all the people. And helping family members to find each other—so many were separated in the fighting."

Maria paused before a small primary school. An older woman with a round face and equally robust frame exited as Sophie waited for Maria.

"Señora Sanchez, you must come." Maria rushed the older woman to Sophie's side. "We have been sent—there is a horrible incident at your home."

As Maria related the events, Sophie peered into the windows of the primitive school and noticed scores of children, some staring back at her. They huddled in small groups, eating with vigor from dented tins, scooping some type of mush with their cupped fingers.

"You!" Benita pointed to Maria. "Hurry to Francisco the glassmaker and tell him we need a new window by nightfall."

Maria scampered away without a word.

"And you." She placed a hand on Sophie's arm. "Do you know how to sew?"

"No, I—"

"*Bueno*. This will be a perfect opportunity to learn. The days of war will force all of us to find new ways to help our fellow man." Benita started out with slow, plodding steps, and Sophie followed by her side.

Though she wasn't tall herself, Sophie seemed to tower over the older woman as they walked, yet she'd never witnessed such strength emanating from one person. Sophie immediately respected this woman. And it wasn't until they turned onto the street with their apartment and spotted the pools of blood on the street that she remembered she should feel afraid.

Sophie followed Benita into the small apartment and watched with amusement as Michael and Luis snapped to attention.

"You." She pointed to Michael. "The broom is in the corner. Clean up the shards before someone injures himself further. And, Luis, will you fetch my sewing basket? Sofía is going to patch José's arm."

José, who had been lying quietly on the bed, opened his eyes wide and attempted to sit.

Benita pushed against his chest, sinking him back onto the bed. "What, you ask, am I doing? You asked me to take her in, as one would a daughter. And I tell you, if the good Lord had blessed me with a daughter she would be useful and skilled in all things. *Señorita*, scrub your hands, please, with hot water. I will clean the wound."

When Sophie returned, her hands hot and itchy, she watched as Benita cut away the fabric from the bloody mass of flesh and gingerly worked the shard of glass from José's shoulder.

José winced, and Benita clucked her tongue. "Oh, please, *señor*, what is this? Just today I watched a soldier's leg amputated. He made less of a fuss than you."

"That is because *they* give medications for the pain. Unlike you." A bead of sweat rolled down José's brow.

Sophie held her red hands out for Benita's inspection.

Benita lifted her nose and nodded her approval.

"Are there many injured soldiers from the front?" Sophie inquired.

"Yes, many."

"Is there some way I can help them? Or maybe work with the children?"

"And what kind of help would that be? What skills do you have—no offense meant, of course, *señorita.*"

"I know how to paint, and I've taught classes in Boston. It is not much, but it can help to occupy the children's minds for a time—to help them forget what they've seen."

"Not to forget, Sofía, but to explore it with art. Haven't the great painters done the same—to let their emotions reveal themselves on the paper?"

The shard slid completely from the shoulder, and Sophie grimaced as Benita plunged her fingers into the wound to check for fragments.

"Luis, do you have that needle sterilized yet?" she called.

"Coming. Coming!" Luis's voice answered from the front room.

Benita looked to Sophie, then pulled her fingers from the wound. "Yes, very well. Good. The children need someone like you. But do not believe this"—she moved her fingers like a paintbrush—"will get you out of this." She swooped them in the air like a needle rising and plunging, then wiped her bloody fingers on José's shirt.

Finally, she patted his chest with a smile. "Do not worry, José. She knows how to hold a paintbrush; how different can a needle be?"

The congregation squirmed in their seats as they waited for the last words of the Mass. With Father Manuel's final "Amen," they rose.

"Wait!" Father Manuel raised his hands. "Let us sing together our anthem. And let it remind us of our great God and His power even during times like these."

Lowering his hands, he lifted his eyes to the rough-hewn lumber of the church's ceiling and began.

"Hay un roble en Bizkaya."

The congregation's voice joined his.

"Viejo, fuerte y fiel, commo ella y como su ley.
Encima del árbol tenemos la Santa Cruz,
Siempre nuestro lema . . ."

Without a pause he led them through a second time, smiling at the devotion clear in the bright eyes of men, women, and children —young and old before him.

"There's an oak in Biscay,
Old strong and true, like her and her law.
Above the tree is the Holy Cross,
Ever our guide . . ."

Their voices faded, and Father Manuel spread his hand to the door. Near the back sat his childhood friend, Armando, with his wife, Nerea, at his side. While most of the other successful businessmen attended the larger cathedral in town—the fifteenth-century Santa Maria—Armando remained one of his most faithful parishioners.

Armando lifted his hand to wave, then must have thought twice and lowered it again. Father Manuel cast him a smile, then turned to Señora Vega, helping her to stand from the hard wooden bench.

"Bless you, Padre." The white-haired widow patted his hand. "May God bless you and keep you, and your beautiful voice, in his safekeeping until we meet again." It was the same parting every week, but her eyes sparkled as if it were the first time.

Father Manuel smiled. "But no voice is finer than yours. And no heart as gentle." He patted her hand in return, causing her to blush.

He led her to the back door and noticed Armando had slipped out. No matter. He would see him later that afternoon, when his friend dropped off a week's worth of produce, a gift from his wife's abundant garden. Nerea always sent over the best of her crop, and the visit from Armando was the highlight of the week.

Sure enough, not two hours later, neither the bounty of fresh vegetables or conversation disappointed him. As he sipped a cup of tea, Father Manuel shuffled his sandals along the paving stones of his small patio.

"You are keeping the place well, better than the old priest." Armando settled in one of the willow chairs and scanned the tree branches, laughing at the two bluebirds that flitted from limb to limb.

"The man was old."

"He was from the south. He cared more for himself than his people. More for himself than the Lord's church. The stones look nice."

Father Manuel wished he could share how he'd hauled them there himself, one each morning just before dawn. He enjoyed scouring the hills for the flat, wide rocks. And, as remembrance of his Savior's passion, he carried each one home by hoisting it on his shoulder, prayerfully reminding himself of the heaviness of the cross.

"Yes, just a few more and the patio will be done."

Armando lifted a large tomato from Nerea's basket, turning it over in his hands. "They say the Generalissimo Franco fights against atheism. Did you hear him last night over the radio, stating God has marked him for glory?"

Father Manuel reached across the small table and placed a hand on Armando's shoulder. "*Sí*, my son, but I wonder what our Lord has to say about that?"

Though his tone was playful, he knew Armando grasped the seriousness of his words.

"He fights the constitution. It is what all *generalissimos* fight, only this one holds a crucifix in his hands." Father Manuel sighed. "And wasn't it the men in their fine robes and religious claims whom Christ rebuked? Our Lord is not found here"—he pointed to Armando's forehead—"but here." He moved his hand to his heart.

Armando nodded and then crossed his arms over his chest, casting Manuel a boyish grin. "*Sí*, you are correct. I just wonder how the troublemaking *mutiko* I knew has become so wise. I am thankful, as are the others, for you to guide us."

"Only the Lord grants wisdom, and you must realize I ask for it plenty."

He gazed at the distant mountain, his brow furrowing at the thought of the war crossing over it into their land. Needing to talk to someone, Father Manuel lowered his guard to confess what he hadn't dared speak aloud.

"We are in God's hands, and He will dispose of us as He wills. Yet if we must die, then now is the time to prepare our hearts. But I fear it is in the living where the battle truly is." He lowered his voice as he peered into his friend's eyes. "My only comfort is that God, whose eye is on the sparrow, watches over us all."

Even as Father Manuel spoke the words, Armando shifted in his chair and tapped his foot against the patio stones. Maybe Armando was uneasy at the talk of death, of war. It was that way with this people. For they somehow believed if it wasn't discussed, such things would not come to pass.

"Yes, well, I must go. Nerea has dinner." With a quick embrace, Armando patted his back and left.

As he watched Armando amble down the road, Father Manuel clasped his hands under his wide sleeves, as if in prayer. Yet his thoughts refused to still. Fear filled his mind. Worry that he would not stand in time of trial, or be able to offer hope to the people who looked to him for guidance. At times like this he questioned the call. Surely God could use another—someone more capable.

Dedicating one's life to serving a God of love was easy. Yet God's people? They were another matter entirely. Their needs overwhelmed him, and he only prayed that one day he could help to meet them in even the smallest manner.

Father Manuel dropped to his knees, as if the heaviness of his heart weighed him down too much to stand. "Lord, make me an instrument of Thy Peace. Where there is hatred, let me sow love. Where there is injury, pardon. Where there is discord, unity. Where there is despair, hope."

He continued the prayer as an utterance of his breath, then lifted his voice as his shoulders trembled under the impact of the prayer's final words. "It is in the forgetting oneself that one finds oneself. It is in the forgiving that one obtains forgiveness. It is in dying that one is resurrected to eternal life. Amen."

Chapter Thirteen

Viel Feind, viel Ehr.
Many enemies, much honor.

German proverb

*B*elow the sea-sprayed deck a cot awaited him, yet Ritter knew he wouldn't be able to sleep. For days the idea of war had echoed as a distant dream. Now, as the SS *Usaramo* slipped out of Hamburg with eighty-five German flyers and ground crew, the idea had become reality.

He ran his fingers through his hair, then slipped his hands deep into the pockets of his civilian trousers, leaning back against the cabin wall for support.

A half-smirk, half-smile broke through his calm demeanor as Maj. Gen. Hugo Sperrle, a veteran of the Great War, who had fought in Africa and also in the South American Chaco War, strolled by with a young woman at his side. To any outsider, the officer appeared to be a doting father on vacation. Of course, appearances could be deceiving.

Ritter had arrived at the docks ahead of schedule to watch as dockworkers loaded hundreds of crates with SEVILLE stamped on their sides into the hold and onto the deck. Inside the crates, components of Ju.52 bombers and Heinkel He.51 fighter planes hid, ready to be assembled on Spanish soil.

Turning up the collar of his jacket against the cold ocean spray, he imagined other Ju.52s, commandeered from Lufthansa, being shuttled to Morocco or to a Nationalist-controlled Seville to start the airlift of troops from Africa into Spain. With his uncle's influence, Ritter knew he could have joined the bomber crews, but he'd requested the He.51 fighters instead. One man. One machine. Solo glory.

Posing as an ersatz tour group, other pilots gathered on the crowded deck. They spoke little, lest they reveal their cover. Yet, glancing around even in the moonlight, Ritter noted anticipation on their faces.

Above him the stars shone brightly in a pale sky. He looked into the horizon, knowing that by tomorrow the sky above him would be the Spanish firmament he would fly above on his "volunteer" mission. Ritter only hoped the adventure, the status, and Isanna's excitement would hold out. It was because of her he'd ventured beyond the German border in the first place—resigning his commission, being classified officially as a reserve, and exchanging his uniform for civilian clothing—all of which were required for travel to Spain.

A young pilot Ritter recognized from training approached, his light brown hair blowing in the wind.

"Magic Fire." Ritter patted the side of one of the crates, ensuring his voice was low enough for only the pilot to hear. "Hard to believe this box will allow us to soar over Spain in a few days."

"It's about time." The kid grinned, and his youthful face and easygoing manner reminded Ritter of the popular student in school who always hogged the center of attention, making everyone laugh. In fact, Ritter felt his guard fall as he stood in the kid's presence.

"The world may have kept Germany from building an army for the last twenty years, but no peace treaty could remove the inner warrior." He lifted his finger as if shooting at a passing airplane, then extended his hand. "I'm Eduard, by the way. That was some send-off they gave us, wasn't it?"

With a smile Ritter thought back to his last day in Berlin,

where civilians greeted the Wehrmacht's arrival with signs of joyous celebration. Their steel-helmeted battalions marched through crowds, who surged into the streets to greet them. As each rank passed, they had snapped their heads smartly to the right—on command—to face Hitler.

Eduard hummed the song they had sung with vigor.

"Our enemies are the Reds, the Bolsheviks of the world!" Ritter mouthed to the tune.

Eduard placed a hand over his heart. "I thought I'd found paradise. Young frauleins handing me those red carnations. Dancing, cheering, singing patriotic anthems. I don't know about you, but I felt like *we* were the display of strength and skill everyone's hoped for all along."

"You sound like a dreamer, Eduard. Are you sure you can fly?"

"And you sound like you didn't get quite as many kisses as you'd hoped for. . . . Are you jealous, old man?"

"Not at all. I've discovered in my years that the love of one woman—true, dedicated love—exceeds that of a hundred admirers." He recalled the look on Isanna's face as she spotted him among the other uniformed men. She'd waved her arms wildly, throwing kisses his direction. And after the ceremony, as they returned to his uncle's house together, her passionate excitement over his Spanish adventure made it all worth it.

"Good point. Yet, truthfully, the knowledge of the war awaiting brought me as much of a thrill as the women. What boy hasn't played with swords and tanks, or imagined himself in dogfights in the sky? I can't wait to get up there."

Eduard's wide smile was contagious, and a chuckle escaped Ritter's lips.

"So, you leaving anyone special behind?" Ritter gripped his hands on the rail as the sway of the ship increased, evidence of their movement into deeper waters.

"My wife and two sons . . ." Eduard sighed.

Ritter frowned.

"Just kidding! No woman pining over me, unless you count my mother. She's just sure I'll never come home, but I reminded her that our country's military freedom and national honor are at stake."

Ritter placed a hand on Eduard's shoulder. "More nice words, but what you're really saying is you like flying those planes."

A twinkle lit Eduard's eye. "Yeah, and I'll like it even more if I can shoot down some Reds."

Ritter nodded, then looked to the open sea as Hamburg disappeared in the distance. "You heading down to the bunks?"

"Nah, I was waiting to spot the naval escorts—not something one sees every day."

"Good, I'll wait with you. That was my plan too." Ritter crossed his arms over his chest. "I've always wanted to see what one of those big ships looks like. It will somehow make this whole business real. Until I can claim my own kill, that is."

Sophie took a deep breath as she followed Benita through the streets toward the school. With donations from a few of José's artist friends, Sophie carried a small wooden box filled with paints, scraps of paper, and brushes. She focused on the wide black braid that swung like a pendulum on Benita's back.

Sophie swore that despite her round shape, Benita moved with the elegance of a queen. She even carried the loaves of bread she'd baked on a tray like one carrying a crown for coronation. And she hummed as she walked—some quick, Spanish tune that Sophie knew she'd heard before.

It had only been one day since Michael left, and she missed him already. They hadn't talked much after she'd arrived back at the apartment with her things. He'd said good-bye with a quick kiss and news that he'd be out of town for a week covering the front.

"Will you be okay?" he'd asked, running his hand down her cheek. Her chest had filled with warmth, and a sweet peace had settled over her.

"I'll be fine." She pointed to Benita and Luis. "Do you think these two will let anything happen to me?"

It was true that she found strength in their presence, but it was more than that. The shooting of the two militiamen had the opposite effect from what Sophie had anticipated. Sitting around the small wooden table with her hosts that evening, she realized life was fleeting. Resolve replaced the fear that had pounced on her—goring into her as if with a bull's horns. She also had a determination *not* to let the unknown scare her into living in a dark hole, afraid to step outside the apartment. To give in and run away would be the same as letting the enemy win.

And as she strode along behind Benita, Sophie wondered if the matadors felt the same empowerment when they faced death in the arena. Did their face-off with their own weak humanity make them understand the joy of truly living?

They reached the school, and Benita directed her inside to the first room on the right. Then Benita stopped a woman in the hall, rattling off the story of yesterday's events, and only slightly embellishing José's injury and the damage to her apartment.

Sophie strode into the room without her. A dozen children sat in a circle, waiting. She pulled up a chair and sat before them, setting her box to the side. "*Hola*, children."

"*Hola*, Teacher." Their excited eyes fixed on her, and one would never know they'd faced so many horrors in recent days —of being forced from their homes, some losing family members, all finding refuge in a strange, unfamiliar place.

"Would you like to paint? What should we work on today? A flower? A cow?"

One boy's hand shot into the air. "How about an aeroplane, like the ones that flew over our village?"

Sophie thought about Benita's words, remembering how the wise woman had told her that what the children needed even more than fun was a release from their own fears and questions.

"That is a wonderful idea. How many would like to paint aeroplanes?"

All hands shot into the air.

Sophie saw Benita peek into the room, holding the tray of bread at her hip. The scent of bread mixed with the smells of children's feet and the pungent soap used to wash their tattered clothes.

"You are well, then?"

"Yes, I think we will do fine."

Warmth and a sense of peace spread through Sophie as she rose and handed out paper to the children. She paused before one girl who clenched her hands on her lap. Tears rimmed the child's dark eyes.

Sophie knelt before her. "Don't you want to paint?"

The girl shook her head then sighed. "No, well, yes, I do . . . but, Teacher, I do not know how."

"What is your name?"

"Rosita."

Sophie placed a hand on her hip. "Rosita, do you know how to walk?"

The young girl scowled. *"Sí."*

"What about run or tumble in the grass?"

"Sí."

Sophie took Rosita's hand. "Those are things you did not learn in one day. And you do not even think about them now. They are simply a part of you. We will start slow, okay? First with the body and wings, then we will worry about the rest."

She placed a piece of paper in front of Rosita, then handed her a brush, wrapping her fingers around the girl's. Her small dark hand trembled slightly as Sophie swooped it on the page.

"First, the body, then the wings." Sophie formed imaginary ovals on the paper. "Do you think you can do that?"

"Sí." A smile filled Rosita's face, brightening her eyes and revealing a hint of dimples in her cheeks. Then the joy in the girl's eyes dimmed immediately, as if a harsh memory resurfaced. "And after that, can you show me how to draw a soldier?" the girl asked.

"Did you see a soldier, Rosita?"

She nodded. "Oh. Many."

"I will show you how to draw one, but you must promise me one thing."

Rosita looked at her questioningly.

"That if you paint him, you must leave him there. On the page. You cannot let him bother you in your dreams anymore."

Rosita's eyes widened. "How did you know he visits my dreams?"

"Because I'm an artist, remember? And what is in our hearts comes out on the page . . . and in our sleep."

"I promise, *señorita*." She lifted the brush in the air. "Can we paint him first?"

Chapter Fourteen

Aller Anfang ist schwer.
Every beginning is difficult.

German proverb

*R*itter stood at the sink with his hands in the stream of cool water. The gashes on his fingers had nearly healed. Though years of flying for the military had trained him to expertly pilot the aircraft, he realized this trip to Spain had given him new insight into the inner workings of fighter planes. Over the last few weeks, together with the Heinkel mechanics, the volunteer pilots had put together the fighters. As the pieces were uncrated, they assembled the airplanes in makeshift workshops around the airfield. Ritter had walked away with a few cuts and bruises and a deeper appreciation for the men who kept him in the air. The mechanics beamed like proud papas that August 12th, staring into the sky as Ritter led the first Kette of He.51s over Seville.

Ritter patted his hands dry, then dressed in the cursed white uniform and cap he was required to wear in Spain. The clothes had been worn by the security forces of the Berlin Olympics a few months prior. Some officer in Berlin thought these clothes would downplay their military presence and help the German pilots blend in, but the Spanish population could not fail to notice the similar white clothes. Soon word leaked about their duties in Spain, and they received much ovation in Seville and later in Escalona de Prado, after their move.

Today, the gusts outside his window made the palm trees bend and dance like the Spanish ladies at the dance hall the flyers frequented. Even the beautiful *señoritas* could not distract his heart. No matter how late he returned to his quarters after laboring all day, Ritter spent a few minutes writing to Isanna. He sent a letter at least twice a week and received the same. Her letters were short and flighty . . . just as he'd expected them to be. Isanna never sat still for more than a few minutes, but as long as she kept writing, confessing her love, Ritter didn't mind. Besides, he had no need to hear the details of her life, especially if they included her family and news of her friends. What a bore.

Noting the wind again, Ritter pulled the hat tighter on his head and slid the letter into his jacket and zipped it up. The first envelope containing the letter was addressed to Isanna, then placed in a larger envelope for Max Winkler, Berlin W8, Post Schliessfach 81—the special mail drop through which all correspondence to and from the Condor Legion in Spain was processed. He stepped outside exactly on schedule, and a few doors down Eduard did the same.

"How is my favorite soap salesman doing?" Eduard chuckled, slapping Ritter's back. "So much elegance and virginal white." He gave a low whistle. "For some reason, my jackets never come that clean. I'll take three bars."

"Oh, such a comedian. They should put you on stage, since you aren't doing much flying."

"Advise and abet." Eduard sighed. "Foolishness, in my opinion. I don't understand. Our Junkers fly with blacked-out markings; what difference does it make who drives?"

"Did you hear about Schwartz? He flew recon yesterday and drew fire from a Republican cruiser in Malaga Bay. It made him so mad he rigged a bomb bay in the floor of his Ju.52 and bombed the cusses. They're out of commission, from what I've heard."

"Lucky sap."

"You got that right." Ritter waved to a group of women passing by, flashing them a smile.

"That's a better story than mine." The brightness in Eduard's eyes faded. "Did you hear? Last night another crazy Spaniard crashed on landing. The fighter is damaged real good."

"Mechanical trouble, I suppose?" Ritter scoffed.

"You kidding? I hear the offender's Latin temperament got the better of him."

"How many lost planes does that make now? Five? How hard is it flying escort missions for General Mola? Sperrle's out of his mind asking us to train the Spaniards . . . for what purpose? To see the aircraft we worked so hard on crash out of commission?"

"Perhaps we should be glad the Spanish air force remained loyal to Madrid." Eduard chuckled. "It will be easier to shoot them down than it would have been to train them."

The throaty roar of the aircraft's twelve-cylinder engine filled his ears as Ritter glanced at his He.51's instrument panel. Before Spain, he'd seen numbers on the gauges, but now his mind took in so much more—steel, aluminum and wire, oil and glass, chrome and glycerin—the parts that made up the whole.

And as he flew through the sun-drenched Spanish air, he realized his perceptions had shifted here too. Sky and clouds above; land, rivers, villages below. And equally separated in his mind, those people he sided with and many more whom he longed to diminish or destroy.

To destroy those with Bolshevik, Communist leanings would only make Germany's job of facing Russia easier in the days to come. Each of the small parts played its role in his larger dreams for his life. *War hero* had a nice ring to it.

Eduard's news at dawn had been just what Ritter had hoped for.

"He did it! Sperrle held discussions with Berlin," Eduard had shouted in Ritter's open window, waking him. "They're going to let German pilots fly the last three He.51s. And we're up today."

Ritter played down his own excitement for appearance's sake.

Now, his hands maneuvered the aircraft expertly toward his target. On the horizon a jagged ripple interrupted the Spanish plain. He smiled as he spotted it ahead. Madrid. The Bolshevik citadel. Through his propeller, it appeared to grow till it resembled a crop of bricks and cement rising up from the brown earth.

Though Ritter had never been there, he recognized the major landmarks from the maps he'd studied in the quiet of his quarters. He flew nearer until Madrid's buildings appeared close enough to touch—and soon he would leave his mark.

Two thin rail lines led into the city to the Atocha station. A perfect target.

The half-dozen bombers ahead of Ritter released their bombs, lurching upward as the weight fell away. Slivers of steel floated downward, and plumes of smoke rose as the gray stones of Madrid splintered like water droplets bouncing into the air.

Fire, smoke, and airborne debris partially obstructed his view of the railroad station as more bombers found their mark.

"Ja . . . ja . . . ja!" Ritter shouted. "Right on target!"

Ritter noted the signal from the lead bomber and grinned as he turned and dove toward downtown Madrid. Just as he prepared to release his fury on the people scurrying from the main square, a spot in the sky grabbed his attention. A Red Breguet XIX reconnaissance aircraft flew about two kilometers in front of him and slightly above. Sucking in a breath, Ritter aborted his attack and maneuvered his gun sight onto the Nationalist aircraft. He anticipated an easy kill, until two Russian aircraft came into view on his left. His hand trembled as they turned in his direction. Thankfully, Ritter had two other German pilots flying his wing.

"Good boys," he whispered, noting their turns to bear down on the Russians.

"The first is mine," Ritter called into the radio. His stomach tensed as he saw the Russian plane bearing toward him. The muzzle lit up, yet Ritter knew the distance was too great. Moving his right hand to the machine guns, he aimed and waited. Sixty meters. Fifty. Thirty.

Ritter fired a short burst, watching the tracers hit their mark, then jerked his aircraft upward. His plane skimmed over the top of the Russian bomber, missing it by mere feet. Turning, Ritter watched as smoke and flame burst from the right engine. The aircraft dove, then rolled over, spinning to the ground like a dead leaf on the wind.

With a wide grin, Ritter circled the area and watched as Eduard attacked a second bomber from a steep climb. "That's a lad."

Ritter turned to back up his friend, but by the time he circled, flame had already erupted from the second Russian plane as it plunged toward the earth. The third backed away, rejoining the formation of Reds returning to their base somewhere north of Madrid, where the Nationalist troops had not yet penetrated the territory.

Laughter filled Ritter's throat, and he knew the first thing he'd do when he returned was write to Isanna. And as the others relived the experience over their radios, Ritter wrote and rewrote the letter in his mind.

Dear Isanna, Today I tasted the first blood of the hunt. Now that we are officially killers, we must have a new name. Perhaps the Hunters of Guadarrama? That is perfect, don't you think?

Later that evening, Ritter found Eduard sitting on his balcony blinking at an empty wine bottle, a cigarette smoldering between his fingers. The youth looked dazed by the wine and the taste of victory.

"Operation Magic Fire." Eduard patted Ritter's back. "Yes, my friend, that was magic, all right. And just think, those other fools are still ferrying Moorish soldiers to the mainland. Poor saps."

"I think my uncle was right." Ritter sighed, focusing on the bright stars filling the sky. "He believes we'll be home by Christmas. And in my opinion, a winter wedding is always nice."

Only a few coins jingled in Deion's pocket as he walked along the ditch with a dozen hoboes waiting to jump a train to New York. Two men huddled around a fire, though the warm sun still hung high in the air. A few more seemed to be napping, yet every once in a while they lifted their heads, cocking their ears toward the tracks as if picking up a distant rumble. Deion kept quiet as two men jabbered on about how cheap everything was in New York, compared to Chicago. They talked about their next destination—maybe D.C. or Miami, wherever they could find a little work and some new scenery.

Deion felt their eyes on him, and he wanted to tell them he wasn't a hobo. He simply needed a way to get to New York to join up with Party members. He heard the Reds accomplished great things for people of the city. He also wanted to see if there were plans to aid Spain. He'd missed out helping in Ethiopia and wouldn't live with the same regrets again.

"Here it comes!" a man called, jumping to his feet.

Deion's knees trembled to see the roaring machine bearing down on them. Tension knotted his stomach at the thought of what he planned to do. He'd jumped trains not ten times in his life—mostly getting himself from Mississippi to Chicago.

He tucked his small satchel under his arm, stretched his legs, and joined in the pursuit. Spotting an open freight car door, he reached out his arms and grasped the edge. With a swing of his legs, he was through the door and inside the car.

A dozen set of eyes turned to him as he found a spot in the corner. Using his satchel for a seat, he made himself comfortable for the ride ahead. The man sitting next to him pulled out a thick book and tilted it to catch the light from the open door.

"We're reading Dickens. You don't mind, do you?" The man cleared his throat. Though filthy and smelling sour, he had a presence about him that reminded Deion of the friendly white banker back home—the one who slipped his mama a few coins whenever he saw her shopping at the corner grocery.

"No, sir, I happen to like that story. I'm lookin' forward to reading it again someday."

"You can read?"

"Sure can."

"Good, then." The man handed him the book. "My eyes are getting tired, since my glasses broke somewhere near Kansas City."

And so Deion began to read, a smile on his face, realizing it was the first time he'd talked to a white man without feeling like trash, without feeling his skin color was the sole reflection of his worth.

The next morning, Deion awoke to the whistle of the train and a half-empty freight car. The book, which had been tucked next to his side as he slept, was gone, as was the friendly white man, who he'd learned was named Rich. Rich had told him about the Empire State Building and the best places to find work around town—or at least where the best places had been five years ago when times weren't quite as bad economic wise. Grabbing his things, Deion jumped from the slowing train and focused his eyes on the large buildings in the center of the city.

Two blocks from the train station, he found a soup line and joined in—the growls of his stomach increasing in volume the nearer he drew to the front.

He got within ten men of the front of the line when a small parade passed.

"Down with Hitler and Mussolini! Defend the Spanish people. End discrimination against Negroes and Jews!" a small group of men, both white and black, called out as they marched along. They carried megaphones and banners, and unlike those in the soup line, their clothes were clean, and they were all shaven.

"Hey, wait!" Deion called as they passed. "Where you headed?" He looked to the bowl of steaming soup only a few feet away, and then turned back to the marchers. They must not have heard him, for they continued on, repeating their same chants, moving forward, for the most part ignored by the people in the streets. Deion placed a hand over his stomach, then bolted from the line.

"Aren't ya hungry?" a voice called from behind him. Deion didn't have time to explain that the soup could wait. There were some things in life far more important than a full stomach.

FALL

The harvest is past, the summer is ended, and we are not saved.
—Jeremiah 8:20

Chapter Fifteen

SEPTEMBER 21, 1936

En casa del herrero, cuchillo de palo.
At the blacksmith's home, there's a wooden knife.

Spanish proverb

*S*ophie wearily kicked off her shoes and settled at the table by the front window, her mind too tired to focus on the faces of the people who passed. Yet she knew they were not too different from the ones she'd helped care for over the past couple of months. Tired faces. Hungry faces. Fearful ones.

"Coffee, Sofía?"

"Please."

Luis shuffled around the kitchen, reminding Sophie of the chef in the restaurant attached to the hotel where her father worked in Boston. Luis used half as much energy as anyone else in the kitchen, but somehow he managed to accomplish twice the work. He seemed to plan his every move for maximum efficiency.

He blew life into the fire and placed two stale *churros* in the oven to heat.

Within a few moments he brought a large cup of steaming *café con leche* and a *churro*, and set them before her. He readjusted the three forks that had been laid out for dinner, and Sophie knew his idling meant he wished to talk.

"Have you heard from Miguel?" he finally asked.

She motioned to the empty chair and sighed. "No, all I know is he's at the front."

Luis sat, shaking his head. "This is not good. On the radio I hear reprisals are being carried out. In the towns and villages once held by the Republic, men and women are lined up and shot. I even heard of one whole town that was dragged into a bullfighting arena, yet instead of a savage bull being released . . ." Luis's eyes grew wide as he spoke. "Rebels armed with machine guns slaughtered them all. The blood. The screams." He shuddered and paused. "I can't imagine."

Sophie sipped her coffee. The horror in her mind's eye turned her stomach, and she glanced out the window, hoping to see Benita approaching. Luis never spoke like this when she was around, unless he wished for a tongue-lashing.

"Do you not think the Lord Himself will protect us?" Benita often proclaimed. "Do you believe our prayers fall on deaf ears?"

While Sophie had not grown up around such open religious discussion, she found comfort in the woman's words. Benita's confidence might not be as realistic as Luis's fears, but it sure helped her to sleep at night.

"Poor, poor man," Luis proclaimed, fingering a postcard of the great Spanish poet, Federico García Lorca. "Even the greatest of men is not above being shot in a ravine. And we think we have a chance to survive the terror?"

Sophie absently stared at the crowd outside until something caught her attention. A man strolling through the crowd moved like Michael—or maybe she'd just imagined it. She lost sight of the figure among the others.

No, there he was again. Yes, it was Michael's walk. As the face came into view, Sophie sprang from her chair, knocking it over as she lunged for the front door. She swung it wide open, stretched to her tiptoes, and scanned the throng.

"Michael!" In ten steps she was in his arms. The long weeks since she'd seen him had passed so slowly. She let out a sigh of relief as she peered into his face and saw for herself that he was well, safe, alive.

"Darling, you look wonderful. I saw Benita as I passed the

market, and she told me about your work with the children." He rapped her chin with his soft knuckle. "That's my girl. I want to hear all about it, and I'm sure you will not get bored by my experiences. Come. Let's celebrate. I hear that one of the finest Spanish dancers is in town, raising money for the troops in training. Hurry now; I have the whole night planned."

Two hours later, after a fine dinner and a romantic stroll through the streets, Michael led her to a villa not far from the center of town. People of all ages and stations in life pooled in front of the large home, and men dressed in white suits escorted them inside.

Men and women filled the large room, seated among the granite columns, with their attention focused on the center stage. Women of all ages wore high combs and delicate lace mantillas. Even the older women looked ravishing with carnations in their salt-and-pepper hair and fringed shawls draped over their voluptuous curves. The women's dresses splashed color about the room and contrasted with the handsome men's dark suits.

As they entered, Sophie's eyes were drawn to a beautiful gypsy on stage. Her thick, black curls cascaded down her back. Her large, enchanting eyes radiated green, like the first blades of spring's new grass. Her curvaceous body swirled as her dancing shoes clacked and her hands clapped a rapid staccato with the guitar player's flawless flamenco. The guitarist sat in the corner with a wide-brimmed hat pulled low on his brow, his dark eyes fixed on the twirling woman while his fingers danced over the strings. The air between them was electric.

The wild, lusty dance caused heat to rise in Sophie's cheeks till she felt compelled to look away, but couldn't. Yet instead of calming, the dancer's passionate fury grew with the rhythm's crescendo.

When the dance abruptly ended, a curtain fell over the stage, and the crowd erupted in wild applause. Sophie's heart skipped and heat again rose to her cheeks as she spotted Maria Donita across the room wearing an incredible blue satin dress that accentuated her . . . everything. Her dark hair was tied back in a neat chignon under a wide-brimmed hat.

Her stunning beauty, her graceful presence, and the admiring looks the men sent in Maria's direction made Sophie feel frumpy, clumsy, and annoyed. Even the young woman's simple gesture of sliding one hand up and down her arm while she spoke to her escort appeared innocent, but Sophie could tell from the interest in the man's eyes he considered it extremely sensuous.

"What did you think of the dance?" Michael turned to her, his eyes sparkling.

"I liked it. It was very good."

"Good?" He frowned. "It was the most stunning thing I've ever witnessed." Then his expression softened as he tucked a strand of her dark hair behind her ear. "Except for you, of course. You, Sofía, look truly stunning tonight."

Sophie relaxed and slid her hand into Michael's.

"Come." Michael rose, glancing ever so slightly in Maria's direction. "The party will continue for hours, but there is something we must discuss."

Sophie followed Michael from the crowded room, outside and down marble stairs, which led to a private garden behind the residence. Michael whistled along as the melody started up again. The music rose in volume, its quick, urgent beats causing Sophie's heart to pound.

Michael released her hand and turned to her with a wink. "Wait here."

She clung to the lamppost illuminating the garden, suddenly feeling weak at the knees. When he returned after a brief moment, the flushed look on Michael's face reminded her of the night he'd proposed. He grinned widely and reached into the inside lapel pocket of his jacket and withdrew a folded newspaper clipping, handing it to Sophie.

She took it, her brow furrowed. It was a photo of the Duke and Duchess of Windsor strolling, arms linked, down the street.

"And you're excited because . . . ?" Sophie cast him a questioning glance.

"Look beyond the people, and see the small cottage behind them. I bought it, Sophie." He took her hands in his. "For you. For us."

Though she couldn't make out the words, Sophie knew the text was French.

"You bought us a house in . . . France? We're leaving, together as man and wife?"

Michael rubbed his chin. "Not quite. The man and wife part, yes. But until this war is over . . . well, I can promise to visit once a month."

"You're joking, right? Once a month?" The music swirling around her suddenly caused her head to pound. "That's not a marriage. Two people facing life's obstacles together is what a marriage is."

An image of Maria in the blue dress flashed in Sophie's mind. The picture of Maria's adoring face when she looked at Michael, and Michael's attempt to hide any evidence that he cared for the young Spanish woman. Sophie had ignored it for long enough, and she had to know the truth—no matter how much it hurt.

"And that's not the only thing," she said. "I'm still uncertain—"

"About what? My love?" Michael spouted. "Just because I'm not willing to leave Spain, my career, and move away, you question my love?"

"Michael, I know you care for me, I really do." She looked at him intently, hoping that even if his words didn't tell her the truth, she would read it in his eyes. "It's . . . it's Maria. I want to know what's going on between the two of you. And don't tell me nothing, because I can see it. Women can always tell these things."

Michael let out a sigh. "You are right, Sophie. I should have been more honest from the beginning. It's Maria, you see, and her family too. For a while they were determined to get us together. I've told them she's too young. I told them I was in love with someone else. But they continued to push us together. She's a beautiful girl, and I suppose they thought that I would eventually give in."

"And that's all? That's the truth?" She studied his green eyes, searching for any hint that he had more to hide. But she saw only tenderness in his gaze.

"Yes, *Divina*. That is the truth. No matter how she pursues me, it is you I love. It is you I long to spend my life with. Of course, unless you are determined not to make that the case—a long life, that is."

The smile on Michael's face faded. "You are the most stubborn woman I know. What type of husband would I be if I allowed the woman I love to remain in danger? I'm sorry, but I can't be at peace with you here in this war-torn country. I see the worst, Sophie. I photograph it. I know the dangers as no one else does."

"But if I leave Spain, I leave you. I don't want to live that way."

"So what is your solution? For me to leave Spain, as well?"

Sophie could see how much even saying those words pained him.

"No, you're right. And what type of wife would I be if I forced the man I love to leave the country of his heart?" she murmured, more to herself that him. "Maybe we should just spend time apart, reconsider—"

"Wait." Michael lifted a finger to her lips. "Don't say anything else. Think about what should happen next. Sleep on it." He leaned close, his nose only inches from hers. "And, *Divina*, I promise to do the same. Love conquers all. Isn't that the popular saying? We'll figure something out. I know we will."

The music continued at its frenzied pace, but Sophie's attention was focused on the green eyes of the man before her. They'd find a solution. Besides, it wasn't him against her. This was *their* battle. And they would face it together.

Michael placed a soft kiss on her lips, then her cheek and ear. "I love you, Sophie. No matter what happens, I want you to remember that."

"I will remember." She wrapped her arms tight around his neck. "I don't know why I doubted. If there is one thing we can trust in, it is our love," she whispered, and she returned his kisses with fervor.

It always saddened Father Manuel how an institutionalized religion could matter so little to the people forced to join in. In fact, he often pictured the people's union to their church like an awkward, arranged marriage—the vow mattering more than the relationship. And tragically, to those caught in such a struggle, the time often came when the only way to truly feel free was to kill the one you swore to love.

The voices on the radio, ever fervent and passionate, were evidence of this as the Nationalist Rebels fought to save the church by slaughtering the people. And the Popular Front, consisting mostly of Communists and Socialists, aimed a knife at the throat of the church, seeking its demise.

"I think too much," Father Manuel told himself as he walked behind Armando on the familiar trek through the mountains. "And for what good? These eternal, internal conversations lead nowhere."

He swung his arms as he planted his feet on the roots of trees that over the years had formed a natural stairway up the mountain. The air was crisp on his cheeks, causing a shiver to travel down his spine. But the cold mattered little. In fact, it felt good. It reminded him of the natural cycle of the earth. The dying of green life, of long days, which paralleled the slow death taking place in his country.

From the moment Cardinal Segura, Archbishop of Toledo and Primate of the Spanish Roman Catholic Church, recommended violence and self-sacrifice in order to defend the national religion of Spain five years before, Father Manuel had replayed the eulogy in his mind. Sometimes he pictured the state religion smoldering like the first Jesuit parish, burned to the ground in the province of Andalusia. Other times he imagined rows of coffins, cradling within them the remains of anarchists, Socialists, and Communists who opposed both formal government and institutionalized religion.

Yet in both cases, he never wept at their funerals. Instead, he tried to revive them, to bring them to common ground, to hope in their impossible union.

"I still think a relationship with God is far more important than religion," Manuel declared an hour later as he perched on a fallen log, partly decayed and smelling earthy and sweet. "Where is the heart to devote itself if we focus too much on ritual? Not the essence of what these things stand for, but rather the mindless, meaningless acting—the people playing the same roles their ancestors have followed for a hundred years?" He kneaded his hands in his lap as he watched Armando tirelessly swinging an ax, the blade chipping at a trembling oak that would provide warmth during the long winter.

"Do you hear yourself?" Armando paused, leaning the ax handle against the tree and reaching for the jar of cool water Nerea had prepared. "It's the same as saying we should have no laws against murder or theft. The people live best when they are given clear guidelines to follow. If we based all our actions on relationship, there would be no boundaries for men's actions."

Manuel rose and moved to the tree, fingering the ax's wooden handle. He'd give anything to shed his heavy garment and give the ax a swing. To work unhindered with his hands. Instead, his work of late seemed to entail sifting through numerous ideologies and duties that accompanied the Lord's work. The lessons he'd been taught for the priesthood replayed in his mind. The truths seared him, like cattle brands imprinting his brain. Yet these dogmas never quite stuck.

"Besides," Armando continued, "the state of the church in Spain is not our concern. Madrid declared Basque an independent state, remember? We will neither die for the church, nor for those who strive to disestablish the church." His arms swept to the hills. "Does not God's Word say something about lifting your eyes to the hills? These mountains hold us in, and others out. Do they not? We will be safe here."

"Dreamer." Manuel found he had been grasping the ax handle with a death grip. He released it and wiped the sweat of his palm on his smock. He shook his head slightly. In his mind's eye he thought of the fine statuette perched on the mantel of Armando's home. The white ceramic image of the suffering Christ, with cuts of red glass cascading down the Lord's face as drops of blood.

"Do you not realize the statue-like image of God you pray to does not exist? Armando, do you not see? He is not a frozen figure to dust off. He isn't a benevolent king who protects us with hills, for the mere fact we are a people of honor. And believe it or not, His greatest concern isn't that this small cut of land regain the freedom it has always honored above all else. God, He—"

"Are you, Padre, stating my devotion is false? Or my concern for the land of my father's father is in vain?" Armando replaced the jar with a clunk on the stump so hard Manuel was sure the glass would break.

Manuel shuddered at the poisonous spouting of Armando's words. "No, I——" He placed a hand on Armando's shoulder, only to have it pushed away.

"So my faith is weak? Or worse yet, false?" Armando ran his hand through his sweaty hair, then turned and pointed a finger into Manuel's face. "I thought we understood each other. I thought we could be ourselves without that . . . that piece of fabric coming between us."

He flicked Manuel's white collar, although Manuel was sure he would have rather punched his jaw.

"You say you want to remain friends. You claim you are the same man inside you've always been. Yet we can't spend one hour together without your words turning to religious babble." Armando lifted the ax with one hand, holding it high over his head as if to emphasize his point. "If you aren't content with the manner in which the church teaches her followers to approach our Lord, then why have you devoted your life to her? If you truly believe in a Lord who desires to speak to us all hours of the day —as you so say—then why do you set yourself up as the one we must turn to, to reach Him?"

A strong wind came up, and the tree Armando chopped shuddered as if agreeing with his words. Manuel knew that with one firm push, he could topple the tree. He also knew the words he prepared to confess could as easily topple their friendship.

"These are questions I ask myself, Armando. Truly they are. But in the end it comes down to one thing. When you close your eyes at night, do you sense Him there? When you pray, do you know He hears? If not, then how can you claim you are His follower? For how can we follow One—"

Armando's curses interrupted Manuel's words, and Armando swung the ax to his shoulder. "I'm through with you, Manuel. Do you understand? Through with all this manner of talk you share even outside church walls. In fact, thank you for helping me, my friend."

Armando kicked at the wavering tree, severing the wood

fibers and propelling it to the forest floor with a crash. "I used to question how the Communists could say that all men are equal and reject the notion of God. Well, thanks to you, I believe their ideals more by the day. Because I, of all people, know what's inside that robe. I know the weakling who chooses his *own* way because he has neither the moral fiber to stand behind the church, nor the courage to turn his back on it."

Armando crossed his hands over his chest and jutted out his chin. "In fact, maybe that's why you've chosen to hide behind the robe. Without it, all the world would see you have no backbone."

Chapter Sixteen

The lines of my policy have not been to create an offensive
air arm that might constitute a threat to other nations,
but to provide Germany with a military air force strong
enough to defend her at any time against aerial attack.

—Hermann Göring on
March 8, 1935, following
the announcement that
the *Luftwaffe* was
already in existence.

*R*itter strode across the airfield with a grin and punched
the air with his fist, spotting new He.51 fighters that had arrived
at Caceres, their third airfield in Spain in as many months. This
time he didn't mind the move, since there were now enough aircraft to form the complete Staffel. More planes meant more air-
power and greater victories.

From the first scramble in the morning to collapsing in bed at
night, Ritter flew as many as four sorties a day. There was enough
action—dogfights, bombing runs, reconnaissance missions—to
keep them in the air. Only the limited fuel supply brought them
home every two hours for the Spanish ground crews to repair, refuel, and rearm the planes.

On days with a lull in the flight schedule, most of the other
pilots visited the notorious German-approved, red-light district
where men marched up in formation, ready to advance in single
file on orders from the commander inside. The thought of

overused and overtired Spanish harlots sickened Ritter, especially knowing Isanna waited at home, thinking of his return.

Instead, Ritter used his free time to visit with the Spanish mechanics, helping them communicate with the other pilots who, when he wasn't around, often resorted to tourist phrase books or tried snatches of their schoolboy Latin to bridge the language gap. Together crewmen and pilots worked to update the planes and experiment with new devices, such as incendiary bombs. And in these moments, when grease covered his hands and arms, and his back ached from bending to work on engines, Ritter found solving intricate mechanical problems nearly as thrilling as soaring through the clouds.

The only thing that truly bothered him about Spain was the religious babble of the Nationalist commanders assigned to them. Their talks of "this new Crusade of sincere faith" caused a rush of nausea to Ritter's stomach. In addition, Franco insisted that all Spaniards, the mechanics included, cease work on Sundays whenever possible. No tinkering allowed.

So after a day of writing letters and studying the maps of Spain, Ritter welcomed Monday, which dawned bright and clear with a chill of winter on the air. He strode into the ready room of the airfield and let out a low moan. The Spanish general they'd labeled "Little Britches," due to his small frame and high-pitched voice, waited for them. Some high-ups had labeled him the morale officer of the group, yet Ritter found the man's religious babble nothing less than ridiculous—as if the Germans cared about the state of Spain's soul.

"Today, my friends, we prepare for the victory of God," the Spanish general stated after the last pilot of the J/88 fighter group entered the room and sat down. "It is a crusade for what is holy. The men we fight are the fallen angels of Beelzebub, the prince of the demons. And before we fly today, let us gather together and lift up a prayer for our chosen protector, General Franco. It is he who will ensure that Christ's reign never ends in our great country of Spain!"

Ritter cleared his throat and coughed. The flyer next to him did the same, as did the rest of the German pilots. Soon the clearing of their throats overtook the sound of the man's declarations.

"What keeps us here sure ain't ideals," one pilot said under his breath in German.

"More like youthful enthusiasm, lust for adventure, and the 1,200 marks combat pay," Eduard chimed in.

"Yes, and if our exploits were publicized, we'd be toasted as heroes throughout Germany!" Ritter added louder, drawing the applause of the other pilots in the room.

The Spanish general, unable to understand their words, turned to the German general with a confused look on his face.

Sperrle raised his hand, silencing them. His piercing eyes scanned the room. "After we win the war—or maybe if our exploits are so grand as to draw national attention—only then will the newspapermen be allowed to hear of the *true* saviors of Spain. Until then, you'll have to satisfy yourself with the case of beer for each kill."

"Is that a promise?" Ritter asked, rising and folding his arms over his uniformed chest. "And I'm not talking about the beer."

"Of course. But now, men—let's get back to the task at hand. With the new Bf.109s coming in, your team will take over ground support. Which means you'll fly at low altitudes."

"Which also means we face the danger of our planes being blown up by our own bombs," Eduard spouted. His brows narrowed with concern.

"That's the risk you take, men," Sperrle said. "You knew the dangers coming into this mission. Just make sure you have your papers on you, in case you end up behind enemy lines."

Ritter patted his shirt pocket, ensuring his civilian papers were in order. If caught, the papers stated he was Ritter Lindemann, German volunteer for the Communist-sponsored International Brigades. He shook his head in disbelief, not understanding how his own countrymen could defy their Fatherland in such a manner to fight for the other side. Hadn't Hitler pounded into all Germans' minds a hatred for those who, like sly foxes, infiltrated German soil with their lies and anti-German customs?

"Now that we got all that out in the air, men, let's turn our attention to today's mission," Sperrle said. "We will try a new technique—one I'm sure you'll appreciate."

Ritter could not ignore the twinkle in his commander's eye as Sperrle lowered a large-scale map of Madrid.

"You will head out in three waves." The general moved his pointer across the map of the city. "First will come the 2,000-pound bombs, which will smash the concrete buildings. Then the 220-pound bombs to break up the rubble into smaller pieces. Followed by incendiary and antipersonnel 22-pound bombs designed to kill the men who arrive to put out the fires."

"Not to mention our machine guns that will mow down those who dare show their faces to care for the wounded," Ritter said with a smirk.

"Of course." Maj. Gen. Sperrle cast Ritter a smile. "I see you think the same as I. Now do us proud. We are named after the giant birds of the South American Andes, after all. It is the role of the condor to make its presence known in the sky. And whether we receive glory or not, that is not our concern. Instead, think of every battle won in Spain as one less Germany will have to fight."

Before they headed out for the day's missions, "Little Britches" led them in a Nationalist tune. While most pilots followed along, singing the Spanish words with gusto while understanding little of their meaning, Ritter stood with his fists balled at his side.

"My comrades who went to fight with happy and firm attitude, they died in the name of the Spanish way of life," they sang. "Honor and glory to the fallen of Spain. Our redemption rests in you. The blood that spilled from the fallen marks the road of resurrection."

The general dismissed them, and Ritter tucked his leather flight helmet into his belt and strode to his aircraft. *Only one problem,* he thought, offering one last wave to Eduard. *I have no plans to die for Spain. And the only blood to be spilled as far as I'm concerned will be that of those saps on the ground, fighting for a cause that will only bring them imprisonment and death.*

Father Manuel's prayers seemed to hang in the fog of the chill, gray air, yet he refused to return to the warmth and security of his small rectory. Weeks had passed since Armando's outburst on the mountain, and while the words replayed in his mind as if they were spoken only moments before, Manuel understood for the first time what it meant to feel truly alone in the world.

A shiver ran down his arms, and he pulled them tighter to his chest, remembering the biblical account of Jesus' last day on earth. In the darkness of the garden He had prayed, wanting more than anything to have a friend to hold His hands, to pray with Him, to warm Him with a concerned look—but no one remained.

Of course, the Lord chose His path to further God's plan, unlike I, who despite good intentions, fail miserably at the task given to me by God.

Of that he had no doubt. Not only did he struggle in leading the Mass and sharing messages of hope in a time of war, but his own heart leaked like a cistern. No matter how he prayed, and no matter the sweet peace that filled his heart for a time, as soon as he rose from his knees or began the simplest tasks of daily living, fear and doubt pounced upon him like scavengers on a dead carcass. Having no one to talk to about these things didn't help.

The population of Guernica grew by the day as hundreds of refugees fled aerial bombing on a scale their country had not experienced before. The people in the outlying areas realized that once the planes dropped their death-loads, ground troops followed. And the horror of what those troops imparted upon the people caused Father Manuel's skin to crawl.

Men were shot after surrendering, and women faced worse. Not only were they raped, they were condemned to live and carry that memory always. Yet out of those people fleeing such horrors —or the town's citizens taking them in—there was not one he could turn to who understood. Even Father Sebastian of the Church of Santa Maria did not have time to talk about their common concerns. He had his own parish to oversee, his own people with numerous needs. Not to mention the ceremony to occur in a few hours.

With so much unrest, the Basque people had decided they must care for their own, even with Spain treading with uncertainty.

Though Guernica's famous Parliament Building hadn't been used for fifty year, preparations were being made even now for the *Procuradores*, Basque leaders, to assemble together. They would elect a president, and Father Sebastian would hold a Mass, leading them in prayer for divine guidance.

And while Father Manuel was thankful that the leaders considered God at such a time, his heart turned again to the common people, his congregation, mostly made up of the working class who, living among the cobbled streets between the Rentería Bridge and the railway station, also lived their lives as they always had, deciding that an hour-long Mass once a week was enough to secure their souls.

Father Manuel rose and walked slowly toward the church to view the plaster statue of the Virgin in the niche. She, to him, was a reminder that God desired not part of our week—or our heart—but all.

"May it be unto myself, your servant, as you desire," had been the Virgin's prayer before the angel of the Lord. And because of that, the Christ grew in her first—in her womb, then in her heart.

Father Manuel's desire to feel the Presence of Christ caused his chest to ache even more than the biting cold at the darkest time of night. For only then could he offer the common people what they needed most, even if they didn't realize it—peace in their souls despite the war and terror around them.

Chapter Seventeen

NOVEMBER 6, 1936

It ought to be inconceivable that in this modern era, and in the face of experience, any nation could be so foolish and ruthless to run the risk of plunging the whole world into war by invading and violating, in contravention of solemn treaties, the territory of other nations that have done them no real harm and which are too weak to protect themselves adequately. Yet the peace of the world and the welfare and security of every nation is today being threatened by that very thing. . . . If civilization is to survive, the principles of the Prince of Peace must be restored. Shattered truth between nations must be revived . . . America hates war. America hopes for peace. Therefore, America actively engages in the search for peace.

Franklin D. Roosevelt
1936

The planes overhead, flying through the sky dimpled with clouds, had become as common as the sound of armored vehicles roaring through the streets. Cold, fall-scented rains forced Sophie to pull her scarf tight around her head as she hurried back from the school. She was already late for dinner, and she knew she'd receive a tongue-lashing from Luis—the same thing she heard every evening if she were even a minute later than he expected.

"We are a besieged town, with enemies in our midst. Did you hear, *señorita*? Just yesterday masked assassins drove down our very street, spraying the crowds with bullets. One of my old friends, my *amigo* from childhood, was killed. Poor, poor Jorge."

Yet Jorge was only one of thousands. *Thousands gone.* Her mind refused to absorb the numbers.

As she hurried along, the cold, damp air hung heavy with fog and with the wails of mourners burying their dead. Then there were those unaccounted for—caught in an air raid most likely. Sophie's favorite waiter at the local café, the daughter of the corner butcher, in the wrong place at the wrong time. Seen one day and gone the next. Never to be heard from again.

Taking her cue from the Spaniards around her, Sophie lifted her weary head and focused on the people, the shops lining the narrow streets, the aching heartbeat of the city. Bullet holes flecked the walls, and every shop window was punctured or shattered.

Even the streets seemed to decay before her eyes. The fires in the buildings around the city dripped soot, causing thick, black liquid to stick to the soles of her shoes. Dyes from the posters ran down the walls like tears of red, blue, gold. Even her clothes were ruined, stained black from brushing against the rubble.

She scooted off the road onto the sidewalk as assault guards drove by in open-sided vehicles that offered no protection for the men perched inside on benches.

At one café, a doctor attended to the wounds of a guest stretched across an outside café table. *Not that it's needed for food. They're lucky to have coffee,* she thought, hurrying past. Poor man, most likely hit by a sniper's bullet—every day a more common occurrence.

As she walked by one apartment building, she shuddered at the sight of walls peeled away, revealing the shattered contents. It reminded Sophie of the open-faced dollhouse she had played with as a child, the one her grandfather had crafted, adding pieces every birthday and Christmas. Once or twice, as she planned her trip to Spain, she imagined returning home with Michael and starting a family. She even pictured a daughter playing with the dollhouse in the corner of her studio as she painted. It was a dream that had faded in the face of Spain's reality.

Even the open-faced apartments before her did not remain untouched. As soon as a house was destroyed by enemy bombs, propaganda agencies affixed posters on the ruins. Colorful posters denouncing the enemy—their purpose to stir rage. Yet, didn't they realize, the piles of rubble and lost lives needed no propaganda to incite the fighting spirit?

But most curious of all, in the midst of conflict, were the people themselves. Around her they sauntered amidst the shell holes and barricades as if they were stage props. Even after a bombing, the people returned to the streets, gazing at the destruction with curiosity and wonder. And then, in less than an hour, they went on with their daily activities as if they'd been interrupted by a bad turn of the weather and nothing more.

For the most part, tall buildings suppressed sounds of the battle. The crack of hand grenades exploding and the splutter of machine guns could be heard in the distance now and then. Sometimes screeching sirens caused her to jump as officers roared by on motorcycles. But worst of all was the drone of bombers. Even now the sound of them grew louder as they closed in on the city.

"Not again," she moaned, hurrying down the last street. She paused only slightly, reaching the door to Luis and Benita's home. More hisses and explosions sounded behind her. Red, green, blue flares lit the fading sky; and she cocked her ear, listening. Sadly, she—as well as all of Madrid—had become expert at distinguishing between the sounds of artillery shells, anti-aircraft, and shrapnel.

As Luis had told her more than once, "When you hear the shrill whistle, throw yourself to the ground. Shrapnel always explodes upward after the strike."

Sophie breathed a sigh of relief, realizing their target was further north.

How horrible, she thought, *to be relieved that others face those horrors tonight and not us.*

At least for now . . .

In her dreams, she ran from the twisting shadows falling from the sky. In her nightmares, she covered her ears against the fire bells, policemen's whistles, cries and shouts from the people. And instead of strolling down a church aisle to meet her groom, she now dreamt of walking through the streets over broken glass, the tinkling of it reminding her of the tiny bells her mother hung around the house at Christmas.

The worst part was that even when she awoke, the war continued.

Sophie entered the doorway and paused, noting a third person sitting at the table with Luis and Benita.

Michael. He turned to her with a nostalgic expression and melancholy eyes. "There you are, beautiful," he said with a gentle voice, standing.

"Michael, you're here. You're safe!" She rushed toward him and buried herself in his arms.

It wasn't until he placed a finger over her lips she realized the radio was on.

"Fernando Valera is speaking." He pulled out a chair for her and offered a tired smile. "He's a Republican deputy, very popular with the people."

Sophie sat, then rested her head on Michael's shoulder, as they listened to the voice over the radio.

"Here in Madrid is the universal frontier that separates liberty and slavery," Valera's voice echoed through the radio. "It is here in Madrid that two incompatible civilizations undertake their great struggle: love against hate, peace against war, the fraternity of Christ against the tyranny of the Church. . . . This is Madrid. It is fighting for Spain, for humanity, for justice, and with the mantle of its blood, it shelters all human beings! Madrid! Madrid!"

Leaning forward, Michael switched off the radio.

Luis let out a low sigh. "This is not good."

Benita rose and moved to the stove. "You do not know this. Maybe he simply offers encouragement."

Michael shook his head. "I have to agree with Luis. Back in the States we call that giving a pep talk. This means he knows great hardship is coming. He's preparing the people for the fight ahead."

A knock sounded at the door. Benita opened it and welcomed José in.

"So you heard?" Michael asked.

"Valera? I heard enough in the first two minutes." He turned to Michael, registering no surprise at seeing him there. "You have a smoke?"

Michael handed a cigar to José, lighting it for him, and Sophie felt a knot in her stomach. *Can't we get alone to talk?* she wanted to say. She hadn't seen Michael in weeks, and now he wanted to talk politics with friends?

José smiled as he took a long drag. "Then again, perhaps it is not as bad as we imagine. "

"Thank you, José. Finally, someone who talks sense. Listen to him, Luis." Benita firmly patted Luis's back with an open hand. "Go on, José."

José lifted his cigar as if making a point. "*Sí*, maybe it will not be that bad. The Fascists have used up their energy, yet ours is just arriving. From what I hear, tomorrow we will open up on our enemy at its most vulnerable spots."

"Is that why you've been going door to door distributing instructions for hand-to-hand fighting?" Luis asked. "If you do not fear our city will be taken over, why are you working so hard to prepare the people for that very thing?"

José's face reddened. He lowered his voice and leaned in close. "It is not that. Do you not know? That is only part of my job with the *elected* government. The small part. Mostly I work behind the scenes to search out those who fight against our cause. I'm on the lookout for Fascists among us."

"The newspapers call them the fifth column," Michael said, holding Sophie's hand.

"The what?" She peered into his green eyes, searching for emotion, any type of emotion, but saw only weariness.

José answered. "A month ago, the Fascist pig General Mola declared there were five columns acting against Madrid. Four from the front, surrounding the city, and the fifth, underground within the city itself."

Sophie turned to their friend. "So have you found any of these men—these Fascist rebels?"

"*Sí, señorita*. I have found many. Yet, please do not let this talk leave these walls. We each do our part, yes, even if it is not on the front lines." He turned to Michael, locking his eyes on his friend's. "Sometimes we fight with weapons, sometimes by befriending people who are in fact enemies, and other times with images caught by the camera."

"And if this isn't enough? What then?" Luis crossed his arms over his chest.

José closed his eyes, drew deeply from his cigar, and then opened his eyes. "The Fascists may win this battle. They may invade our land with foreign ideals, but they cannot hold the people. Spaniards will rise to the occasion as they have before. It cannot remain this way." He cleared his throat. "They call us stupid, yet do not school us. They call us simple, yet we must live according to our meager existence. If you are born poor, poor you will remain all the days of your life. If you are born wealthy, the whole earth is handed to you on a silver platter. . . . Is that fair? Is equality worth fighting for?"

José sighed and turned to Sophie. "Your Roosevelt has been reelected, sí? If only we could choose one man and know he will serve his term. How many lives would be saved?"

Sophie nodded. "I knew things would be different here, or at least I had a hint of that. But I have to admit that once I crossed those borders, it was as if my whole world turned on end. I was so naïve." She looked at Michael. "You tried to tell me. . . ."

"You are mistaken. The boundaries that matter most aren't the country borders that separate people and languages." Michael stood and turned to look out the window.

An old woman hobbled by, clutching a small bag to her chest—most likely her food for the week. Three young boys walked side by side, and despite the rain, wore no shoes or hats.

"Yes, he speaks truth," José said, running his fingers through his dark hair. "If that were the case, there would be no war here. It is the invisible barriers—economic, political, religious—that oppress. They prevent the poor man from ever making something of his life, ever providing for his children. They keep rich men in power, and the church in control. This is what people fight against. In that system there is no hope. And without hope, what's the purpose of life? They wouldn't fight if they didn't have a chance to think otherwise.

"The world is getting smaller, and other ideals are seeping into their minds and hearts. The people now understand there are other ways to live. Ways worth fighting and dying for. That's why many are Communist. Or Socialist. Or anarchists. They've learned these new ways, which tell them they can shed oppression and fight for equality and freedom. *That* is something worth dying for—if not for themselves, for their children."

"José, you never cease to surprise me. You, my friend, are

someone I'd love to take home to meet my mother." Sophie patted his hand and looked into his dark, soulful eyes.

"Your mother?"

"She writes speeches for causes—some of which she has a passion for, and some whose passion she attempts to absorb. She spends hours writing and rewriting, yet you say so much with so few words. Promise me that after this is over, you will find a way to travel to Boston. The city is called the Cradle of Freedom, because that is where the men who formed our nation first formed their thoughts."

José's grin stretched until his white teeth contrasted against his dark skin. "I think I would like that. The Cradle of Freedom? Yes, I believe I should like that very much."

"Of course, we have to win here first, right?" Sophie rose and wrapped her arms around Michael's waist. "When this is over, sweetheart, I want to see all of Spain. But until that time, I consider whatever little I can do here worth the fight."

Before she could read his expression, Michael looked away, turning his focus back to the street and the plumes of smoke in the distance where the enemy's bombs dropped more destruction.

Tanks bore down on early morning Madrid, yet to Philip the whole scene seemed far removed from reality. It had taken over a month for Attis and him to reach the capital. On foot and by cart, they'd traveled mostly on small country roads to avoid the fighting. And it appeared they reached their destination just in time. With only a few days to acquaint themselves with the other Internationals who volunteered for Spain's cause, they were given a weapon to share, directed to a ditch near one of the main roadways leading into Madrid, and told to hold the line at all costs.

Never mind the fact that Philip had never held a rifle before in his life. Unless you count those popguns at the Washington State Fair. He studied the weapon in his hand, replaying in his mind the directions for how to reload.

"Wake up, friend. Snap to it. We're really here. No time to be sluggish about your work." Attis cocked back a hand grenade, waiting for the perfect time to hoist it toward an approaching tank.

The lead tank shuddered and rumbled forward, its turret gun tilted downward, aiming at the mines in the road. Men and women swarmed around Philip like ants in a crazed dance—at least the ones still able to move. Others lay dead or dying.

A woman next to him grabbed the gun from Philip's trembling fingers and cast him a look of disgust. With a determined set of her chin she lifted it to her shoulder and fired. "*No pasaran! No pasaran!* They shall not pass," she cried.

Other women in the barricade screamed out the same. Women militia. Fighting for their very survival.

With the perfect form of a baseball player in centerfield, Attis cocked back his arm toward a group of Moorish horsemen following the tanks. It hit in the middle of the group, exploding in bright white. Men's screams and the trampling of hooves filled the air. Scents of blood and cordite stung Philip's nose. The horsemen retreated, and soon small sounds of gunfire were lost in louder explosions from old cannons—outdated weaponry pulled from military museums, no doubt, suddenly dragged from retirement.

Just as it seemed the lead tank would make it to a bridge, a deafening blast tore through one of the tracks and the hull's underside. Shards of steel flew through the air. Thick, black smoke rolled from its still-quivering body. A human torch piled out of one of the hatches, and Philip turned, pressing his face into his hands at the sight. Women around him cheered.

A voice erupted from the loudspeaker overhead. "Men and women of Madrid, this is *La Pasionaria*. The glorious victory of Madrid can be ours. . . . They shall not pass. It is better to die on your feet than to live on your knees!"

Chapter Eighteen

Espana prefiere morir de pie que vivir de rodilla.
Spain prefers to die on her feet rather than live on bended knees.

La Pasionaria

*S*ophie awoke, remembering that Michael had been there. And remembering next that he had already left—with no more than a quick hug and a few words, and not a mention of the cottage in France.

"I'm sorry, *Divina*. I must get back to my office. There are reports I still need to write and send out tonight."

In the darkness of the alcove just outside the door, she couldn't see the expression on his face, but the caress of his hand on her cheek made her ache with missing his touch. "But I wanted time to talk. We—"

"Shhh, I understand. But now is not the time." He leaned down and placed a kiss on her forehead. Then he moved his lips to her ear. "Just remember, no matter what happens, I love you, Sophie. I always will."

"Michael, that's the second time—"

"Shh, just remember." And with one last kiss, he was gone.

"Sofía!" Benita's voice broke Sophie from her memory. "Hurry, *señorita.* There is something happening downtown. Something we do not wish to miss."

Thirty minutes later, Sophie caught her breath as she noted the Gran Via shimmering under a frosting of ice. She pulled her sweater tighter and followed Benita to the edge of the street where a line of people had gathered, as if preparing to view a parade. Above them, the loudspeaker blared *El Himno de Riego.*

The people lining the street sang along. "Soldiers, the country calls us to the fight. We swear to her to conquer or to die."

Others hurried out of the stores and buildings, mobbing the streets. Old men filled the sidewalks, with children lifted on their shoulders. And down the center of the avenue a wide column of men moved west toward the river. Toward the front lines. The men's faces against the wind appeared like a religious procession. The first group to pass wore dark blue overalls like the militia, making them appear all the same, like a sepia portrait.

Sophie's heart swelled at their handsome faces, jaws set with determination. She glanced at the crowd, wishing Michael were here to capture this on film. "Who are they?" She tucked her hands into her sleeves, attempting to warm them.

"Volunteers from everywhere. They are being trained. They've all come across the Pyrenees in the night. Some call them the Internationals. Mostly, they are the answer to our prayers." Benita made the sign of the cross.

"Son of the people, your chains oppress you," the men marching past sang. "This injustice cannot go on. In your life is a world of grief. Instead of being a slave, it is better to die!"

A shudder traveled down Sophie's spine as the last phrase replayed in her mind.

The voices rose again:

"We are the young guard.
Noble is our cause of liberating
Man from his slavery.
Maybe the road there will have to be strewn
With the blood of our youth."

Sophie turned to Benita. "Why do they say such things? Why don't they sing of victory instead of death?"

"Sometimes they do. But these songs are messages to the people. They are reminding us of their sacrifice, of the things worth dying for."

Their voices faded on the last refrain, and Sophie's cheers joined in with those of the crowd. Then she paused, her cries catching in her throat. She pointed to a group of men nearing. "I recognize those men. They are José's friends."

"*Sí.*" Benita waved to them, and a few noticed and waved back. "After the last fund-raising benefit, the artists signed up to fight. They put down their brushes and took up weapons. They realize, as we all do, there is no need for art in a time of war."

"Yet look at them. They don't look like soldiers, or even march like them."

Sophie's eyes focused on one man she recognized from the studio the first day José had taken her there. His blue mono hung on his thin frame, and his spectacles and thin moustache seemed out of place next to the rugged young men marching on either side of him.

"Oh, Benita. We should pray. Pray they remain safe."

Benita wrapped an arm around Sophie's shoulders and offered a slight smile. "*Sí*, child. We will do this as soon as we return home. Now you are understanding, are you not, where our true hope lies?"

The parade continued for what seemed like hours. Each regiment had its own flag, and the men reveled in throwing salutes to the crowd. There were only a few rifles scattered among them and very little heavy artillery. Most groups had no uniforms, but all marched proudly. Each man's gaze held intense passion as the cry rippled through the ranks. "*Viva la Republica!*"

The parade had barely cleared when bombers descended upon the city like vultures, scattering the crowd in all directions. As Sophie and Benita hurried to their quarter of town, people on the streets cheered at the sight of an enemy plane spiraling out of the air. Then they cried in horror as it crashed into the Puerta del Sol, undoubtedly costing numerous lives.

"Oh, look." Benita paused as they made their way down the street. "Is that not our neighborhood?"

Sophie's stomach lurched at the sight of airplanes swooping over their district. The first bomber reached it, dropping its bombs at random. Plumes of smoke and fire rose before them, and the ground quaked under their feet.

"Luis!" Benita lifted the hem of her skirt and quickened her pace.

"Benita, no. We must wait. Wait until the planes leave."

Benita tugged forward, attempting to pull away from Sophie's grasp. "My husband, my Luis, Luis . . ."

"Listen to me." Sophie grasped Benita's shoulders and turned the woman toward her. "You know Luis. He's the most cautious man we know, always the first in the bomb shelter. I'm sure that's where he is now. He's safe. And he'll be very upset if we do not take cover."

Benita blinked slowly and let out a sigh. The shrill whistle of a fire engine passing forced her to cover her ears. "*Sí*, you are right." She scanned the street as if attempting to get her bearings. "Come, come."

Then she took Sophie's hand and pulled her in the direction of the nearest air-raid shelter. They hurried down a set of wooden stairs to the basement of an apartment building. Children cried as they curled onto their mothers' laps. Young men helped old women find a place in the musty room to sit, to rest, to wait.

Sophie helped Benita settle onto a bench, then sat beside her, holding the older woman as Benita lifted her voice in prayer.

"Eternal God, in whose perfect kingdom no sword is drawn but the sword of righteousness, no strength known but the strength of love," Benita said, reciting the familiar prayer.

"So mightily spread abroad your Spirit . . ." Sophie joined in, having memorized it from hearing Benita daily.

The older woman smiled, hearing her.

"That all peoples may be gathered under the banner of the Prince of Peace." They raised their voices together, causing a stillness to spread through the room. "As children of one Father; to whom be dominion and glory, now and forever. . . . Amen."

Hours passed, and just as the first stars blinked in the twilight sky, Sophie and Benita trudged back to their apartment. Signs of destruction met them at every block. They turned the corner to their own street. Sophie paused, grasping Benita's arm. The apartment building next to theirs had taken a direct hit. And there, in the middle of the rubble, was Luis, sorting through their things that spilled from the half-crumbled wall onto the sidewalk.

Tears streamed down his face. "The vendor at the market needed help taking down his stall. He needed the wood to patch holes in his home. So I went with him, Benita. Today of all days. But so many others, our neighbors . . . I do not think they even had time to reach the shelter."

Together they entered the apartment. The wooden table and chairs set near the window had splintered into hundreds of pieces, like oversized toothpicks scattered around the room. The walls stood, but brick had been exposed under the plaster. In her room, Sophie's bed frame had twisted like a spring.

Sophie hurried to the small wardrobe where her clothes hung. She brushed aside the rubble and pulled out the garment bag with the dress for her wedding, the only thing untouched. She pulled it to her chest, and her shoulders quivered. *What now?* Numbness spread through her mind, and she couldn't comprehend the destruction around her.

Then she remembered her sketchbook. Lifting the mattress, she found it too was safe.

"Sofía! Someone to see you," Luis's voice called to her.

She turned to find José standing in the doorway.

"They ask for you at the newspaper office. It seems in the morning they are evacuating all their correspondents to Valencia."

"Evacuating? But what about Luis and Benita? What will happen to them?"

José reached a hand toward her. "We will worry about that later, yes? Why don't you come with me for now?"

Grabbing up her satchel, she stuffed the dress inside and a

few more of her things. "I'll follow. But I'm not leaving—not yet. My friends . . . I need to make sure they are safe first."

"You think so? Well, you'll have to tell the office that. Remember, *señorita*, you are here at their allowance. It is their paperwork, after all, that gives you permission to stay."

"I understand, José, but what about Michael? I can't leave without telling him. How will he find me?" She sighed. "Can't we go in the morning?"

The weight of the satchel pulled at her shoulder, and she mouthed *gracias* as José took it from her. "I'm so very weary tonight. Tomorrow, my friend, I'm sure things will be better."

José wore a sad expression. "We can only hope, *señorita*. We can only hope."

After staying the night with Benita and Luis in José's small apartment, Sophie set off with determined steps toward the tallest building in Madrid, the Telefónica. A line of cars waited outside, but she ignored them.

"Evacuation," one reporter muttered to the other as they climbed into the car.

Inside, the windows were blocked with mattresses. Only a few office workers remained, packing up their things, preparing for the journey ahead.

The editor to whom Michael had introduced her now sat behind his desk, staring at piles of prints spread before him. Sophie's muddled mind couldn't even focus on the photographs, yet she wondered if they were Michael's.

"Miss Grace. Good to see that you're okay. I hope you have brought your things." He spoke in English, with a pronounced New York accent.

"Where is Michael?"

"He is somewhere at the front—just outside the city." The man shrugged. "Who knows exactly? He's a hard man to keep up with. But he'll be happy to know you've come. Things in Madrid are no longer safe."

"I do not argue." Sophie crossed her arms over her chest and sighed. "But must I go today? I want to help my friends move their things; they have so little left. And no"—she opened her arms—"I don't have my satchel. I'll have to go back and get it either way."

"We're evacuating to Valencia. If you want to live to see next year, here's your chance."

"I will think about it."

"Think about it?" He leaned forward. "You're not sure?"

"Can you give me a couple of hours to make a decision? I wish to see my friends one last time. And maybe, if you knew where I could find Michael . . ."

"If I hear from him, I'll send him to you. Does he know where to find you?"

"Tell him we'll be at José's house. For the time being." Sophie jotted down the address and handed it to the man. "If you need to reach me . . ."

"Yes, Miss Grace. I will tell him. But we are leaving this afternoon. If you are not with us, I cannot guarantee your safe travel out of the city."

"I understand."

There was a look in his eyes Sophie couldn't quite trust. She didn't know this man—or any of the other workers. How did they know Valencia would be any safer? If she faced danger, she'd rather do so with friends. And what about the children at the school? If she could be of any help to them, it would be worth staying.

By the time she reached the street, planes were again roaring overhead.

"German bombers," a man behind her on the street said in English. "Junkers. They even wear the swastikas. It seems Franco is becoming bold with his strong arm. And it looks as if things will only get worse. An enemy lurks—"

The boom of antiaircraft fire interrupted his words.

Sophie covered her ears; then she paused, suddenly recognizing the voice. She turned and saw the black hat pulled low over the speaker's eyes. "Walt?"

The whistle-whine-scream-roar filled the air. Sophie covered her ears, wondering how close it would hit. Not more than a hundred yards from her, a geyser of cobblestones erupted into the air. The ground shook, and violent air beat against her. Tall buildings around her trembled, then settled again. Excited, high-pitched voices called out. Pained cries met her ears.

She turned again to the spot where Walt had stood, but he was gone. Had she imagined him? Pillars of smoke rose around her, and she coughed, attempting to expel its heaviness from her lungs. The continual roar assaulted her body and mind with vibrating concussions. Sophie ran for cover, noting people darting across the square. She followed them, knowing they'd lead her to the closest bomb shelter.

Another blast, closer this time. A window shattered, tinkling like an off-key music box, sprinkling glass shards at her shoes. She stumbled, and frantic movements of the crowd behind knocked her off her feet. A woman landed on top of her, the weight of her body pressing Sophie into the ground.

She tried to turn, to breathe. The woman moaned and rolled off her. Sophie crawled to the closest wall, leaning against it for support and trying to catch her breath, wiping blood from her nose.

A scream pierced the air, and Sophie turned to see another woman leaning over a man's body. He lay on the ground covered in chunks of brick and debris. The side of his head had been crushed in, and he stared into the sky with wide, unseeing eyes.

"Carlos!" the woman cried, touching his face as if trying to wake him.

Sophie knew it was no use.

The ground trembled around her, yet fear froze her legs. She stared into the sky, watching the planes above twist and dive. Those running for cover paused slightly and went wild with joy as more planes appeared. Russian planes—there to save them. The screams of engines and propellers overhead replaced the roar of explosions.

Sophie began to cry. Then, as the droning faded, she stood and sprinted, skirt hoisted to her knees, toward the basement of a nearby apartment building. Like a rabbit running to its burrow, she joined other equally frightened rabbits.

After an hour of their quivering bodies pressed together, their attention focused on the sounds of aircraft overhead; the rumbling of airplane engines and boom of bombs began to fade.

She had tried to remember the words of one of Benita's prayers, but they eluded her. *Why can't I think of them? Why won't they come?*

Instead, she'd mumbled one phrase over and over, barely loud enough to hear herself, "Be merciful, O Lord. Be merciful, O Lord."

Finally, only the sound of fire engines filled the air outside. "Certainly they will not return today. They have done enough damage," said a young mother, clutching her baby to her chest.

"They are leaving, all right. Returning to reload," an old man replied, rising and brushing himself off.

"By now they are landing at their base," another added, offering a hand to help Sophie up from her place on a hard bench. "And tonight they will join their friends for a drink at the bar."

"Humans who have made themselves into demons, leaving the rest of us to take cover and wonder why," Sophie said, following them out of the musty room. "Sometimes it's hard to believe this is really happening." She shielded her eyes as she climbed up the stairs into the smoke- and dust-filled sky of midafternoon.

It took Sophie less than twenty minutes to make her way to José's apartment. As she rounded the block, she noticed a small crowd gathered on the street. She hurried forward, wondering if someone was hurt. Sophie paused in her quickened steps as she saw the crumpled body of a man lying facedown. The clothes, the hair, the camera bag at the man's side.

Michael . . .

José knelt beside the limp body lying in a pool of blood. He glanced up and spotted Sophie. The color drained from his face, and he sadly shook his head. "A sniper." He cursed under his breath.

Sophie's knees grew weak, and a sob caught in her throat. She rushed toward him, but someone grabbed her arms, holding her back. "Michael!"

"No, *señorita*. It is not good," one of the men said in her ear. "Remember him as he was."

She longed to look into Michael's face, to see him one more time, but couldn't bring herself to do it. The fixed eyes of the dead man she'd passed on the street earlier that day, staring lifeless into the sky, came to mind. Blood had oozed from his temple. Her stomach lurched, and she felt her knees grow weak.

Sophie held her stomach, and then lifted her face toward the windows in the apartment above, wondering if the demon who'd shot Michael still watched. Watched her naked grief.

José hurried to her and grasped her arm with bloody hands. He turned her away from the sight of Michael. "We must go. It is not safe. He is the third American correspondent shot today." He yanked the armband from her blouse.

"We can't just leave him . . . I'm not going to leave him!" She turned to look back at his body. *Michael's body.*

"Why doesn't the sniper just kill me too?" She yanked her arms from José's grasp and lifted her fist to the sky. "Kill me. I want to die!" she shouted, sobs overtaking her.

José's arms embraced her, and she sank into his chest.

"I want to die. Just let them kill me. . . ."

Another shot rang out, and Sophie screamed.

"Come." José yanked her hand and pulled her along down the street. More shots, more screams.

Her legs propelled her forward. And as they turned the corner she paused, glancing back over her shoulder one last time. The image of Michael's body being dragged off by two men shattered her heart like the storefront glass, falling to a million pieces at her feet.

Chapter Nineteen

Dime con quién andas y te diré quién eres
Tell me who is by your side, and I'll tell you who you are.

Spanish proverb

The dim Spanish sun attempted to shine through the haze as Sophie unzipped the garment bag, realizing she would wear her blue dress to Michael's funeral instead of their wedding.

The sound of an automobile pulling to a stop filtered through the open window on a cold breeze. Sophie squared her shoulders, knowing what she had to do. The door was slightly ajar, and she heard José in the living area, welcoming a man inside. She left the dress in the wardrobe and sat upon the bed, her back to the door.

The men's footsteps and hushed voices approached. José knocked on the door to his bedroom—the one he'd turned over to her and Benita to share for the time being.

"Sofía?" Though he attempted to be all business for the stranger's benefit, she sensed the gentleness in José's voice.

When she didn't respond, he knocked louder.

"Miss Grace. It's time." The man spoke in English—most

likely one of the office workers sent to fetch her. "The train to Valencia is due to arrive in thirty minutes."

The hinges squeaked as the door opened, but she refused to turn. Sophie knew that one look at the urgency on the man's face would cause her to second-guess her decision.

"I'm not going."

"But, Miss Grace, Michael is gone. And the train. We do not know if it will come again anytime soon."

"I'm not going until I say good-bye." Sophie ran her finger along her lace collar.

"Sofía. Really, your safety—it's what Michael worried about most." José placed his hands on her shoulders, and she trembled under his touch.

"It's a chance I'm willing to take. I'll find a way to Valencia next week. Or to France. I'll hire a driver if I must. Just don't question me, José."

English shouts from the automobile outside, pleas—urging the man to hurry—allowed no chance for him to argue.

"Good-bye." Her voice was stern as she turned to the office worker. "I'll see you on the other side. Go before you make everyone else late."

The man cursed under his breath, then hurried away.

José's hand remained on her shoulder. "I'll drive you. After the funeral, I'll take you and . . ."

Planes roaring overheard muffled his words. She didn't need to look out the window to distinguish the black swastikas on their wings. From the sound of their engines, they were Rebel recon planes—most likely sent ahead to discover which areas of Madrid still stood, in order to effectively plan today's bombing raid.

She glanced into his dark eyes and saw there the same sorrow she felt. "And the funeral?"

"It's in two hours. If the bombers don't arrive, that is. . . . Curse this war." José strode from the room and shut the door.

"I'll see you on the other side," she repeated, returning to the garment bag and bunching the light blue fabric of the dress tight in her fist. "Oh, Michael, how could you go ahead without me?"

She'd traveled all this way. Thousands of miles. She'd found a way to illegally cross the closed borders into Spain, and for what? To lose the only man she'd ever loved?

During her time with Benita, Sophie had learned many things—to stitch wounds, to use art to bring healing to children, to trust that God was present always, listening to the prayers and concerns of the needy. Only problem was, Sophie wasn't sure He wanted to hear what she had to say.

God, is this some type of trick? To bring me so close to everything I've ever desired, only to take it away? First the war, then the bombings —now this?

Sophie slowly unbuttoned her blouse, listening to José's heavy footsteps as he moved around the small house. Then the voices of Benita and Luis joined his. Though she couldn't make out their words, knowing they had arrived safely comforted her.

Just as she slipped on the dress, a knock sounded at the door.

"I'll be out in a minute."

"Please hurry, *señorita*." Luis's voice was low. "We don't have much time. We worry about the bombers coming and have changed the time of the funeral. If we don't pay our respects now, who knows what else the rest of the day will hold. . . ."

Sophie walked through the small group of mourners, drawing nearer to the closed coffin, her blue dress the only spot of color in a sea of black. Upon spotting her, women's heads leaned close together and whispers rippled through the crowd. Sophie ignored them and wove her way to the front.

Only one row of women stood between her and the plain pine coffin. Maria Donita, dressed in black from head to toe, leaned her head on the coffin and sobbed, her wails rising as her shoulders shook.

Sophie lifted her hand, preparing to touch the shoulder of the woman in front of her and ask to pass, when the woman spoke.

"Poor thing. She should not have to deal with such a thing in her condition."

"Her condition?" The second woman patted the tears on her cheeks, then loudly blew her nose in her handkerchief.

"*Sí*, she is expecting his child. First the American woman arrives, now this. Such tragedy for one so young."

Sophie felt her knees weaken, and she reached out for support, grasping the woman's shoulder. The woman turned, eyes wide, and Sophie immediately recognized her as Maria's sister— the one she had met in the market.

Tears sprang to Sophie's eyes, and she turned and hurried back the way she'd come.

"Sofía!" It was José's voice.

She continued on with staggering steps. Her eyes scanned the road for the carriage José had borrowed for the day. Realizing what she needed even more, she looked around to see if Benita and Luis had arrived. *Where are they?* She wanted nothing more than to fold herself in Benita's arms, to hear her friend's prayers and know someone cared. Panic clawed at her chest when they were nowhere to be seen.

"Sofía! Wait." José's voice called out to her again, but she knew if she stopped, she'd collapse. She spotted the carriage and moved toward it, tears blurring the cobblestones before her. She tripped, nearly fell, then righted herself again.

"Sofía." His voice was closer now.

Stomping her foot, she turned and pointed a finger at him. "You knew, didn't you?" She swallowed hard and felt her breath coming quicker. "Have I been played for a fool this whole time? If *this* was the reason he wanted me to leave so badly, why didn't he tell me? The war. The bombings. What a good excuse. If only I had known the truth—" She peered into José's face and saw tears streaming from his eyes too.

"The truth?" His brow furrowed. "What is this you speak of?"

"That woman . . . Maria . . . is pregnant with . . . by . . ." Sophie shook her head and covered her mouth with her hands, unable to say the words or even imagine them.

José opened his arms to her, and she collapsed into his embrace. "I did not know," he whispered in her ear. "I promise I did not."

Sophie let out a shuddering breath. "If someone would have told me the truth, I would have left," she whispered, wiping her face with her hand. "A child . . . Michael's child? Oh, God, what have I done to deserve such a thing? I can't face this, José. It's too much. Too much for me to bear. The bombings. The fighting, anything but this . . ."

"Oh, dear Sofía. I am so sorry. If it is any consolation, I would have spoken the truth if I had known. Once or twice I watched them dance. And maybe noticed them leaving a party together, but that was before you arrived. I had my concerns, but . . . yes, it is my fault. I should have asked. I should have been so bold as—"

"No." She shook her head. "Don't blame yourself. I—I can't think of this. Let's go far away, shall we? Is there any way we can make it to the French border?"

"Leave Madrid?"

"Yes, José. I want to be anywhere but Madrid."

"Sofíia, are you awake?" José's voice was urgent.

She attempted to open her eyes, but they were thick and sticky from her tears. Even worse than her nightmares of late was the image in her mind of Maria in Michael's arms.

Finally her eyes opened, and the room around her was dim. Somehow, dusk had gathered without Sophie perceiving it.

"Benita and Luis have gone to stay with his sister across town. They didn't want to wake you, but they were needed to help care for their nieces and nephews—some who have lost everything. They would offer you room there, until we leave . . ." He shrugged. "But there is no space. I told them not to worry;you will be well cared for."

"Thank you, José. You are too kind."

José's eyes darted toward the bedroom door as if expecting someone to walk in at any moment. He dug his hands deeper in his pockets. "But there is a problem—a few actually, but one we must discuss first. I have a fiancée, you see. She lives in the north. Ramona is a wonderful and understanding woman, but I'm sure you can agree—it would not be good for us to stay here alone."

Sophie sat up and ran her fingers through her tangled hair. "I'm so sorry. Of course, you're right. I'll find a place. Maybe a hotel?"

José cocked an eyebrow. "The hotels are full. They are orphanages now, homes for widows. As you know, there are many refugees from the villages. My neighbor, he is on the front lines. His place is small, but I can stay—"

"No, José. You stay here; this is your home. And I'll go there until we leave." She studied the concerned look on his face. "We can leave soon, can't we?"

An ache filled Sophie's gut. All the desire that just days ago had made her long to remain in Spain had turned into a need to leave that was equally great.

He let out a low sigh. "I am looking at the possibilities. The front has moved, even in the last few days. The trick will be seeing *who* is fighting *where*, who has control of which piece of land, and finding a safe passage."

Sophie's head throbbed. Yet she rose and lifted her satchel from the floor onto the bed, then took the blue dress from the peg on the wall. "I sure have made a mess of things, haven't I? The whole idea of traveling to Spain was a horrible mistake, and staying, even worse."

"Yet somehow we must trust, Sofía, that you are here for a purpose. This turn of events did not surprise our Maker. I, for one, feel honored to have you as a friend."

"Now you're starting to talk like Benita. God this—God that." She tossed the dress onto the bed, considering leaving it. Yet her anger toward Michael and shame over the situation with Maria hadn't completely replaced the love that still lingered. The two feelings formed a jagged edge that parted her heart, and she couldn't wipe away the pain as easily as her tears. "In my opinion, God has a sadistic sense of humor."

"*Madre María!*" José touched his forehead, chest, and shoulders in the sign of the cross. "I would not go that far. Though I do not believe as strongly as Benita does, I still show my respect. I believe." He extended his hands in a gesture of appeal. "But at least you know the truth. No matter what happens from here, you know you've done all you could—loved all that was possible."

"Unfortunately, that's the problem. It seems I have more questions than answers. And with Michael de—" The word caught in her throat. "With Michael gone, there are some things I'll never know."

Chapter Twenty

Workers and anti-Fascists of all lands! We the workers of Spain are poor, but we are pursuing a noble ideal. Our fight is your fight. Our victory is the victory of liberty. We are the vanguard of the international proletariat in our fight against fascism. Men and women of all lands! Come to our aid! Arms for Spain!

Republican appeal

*O*ne bare, dusty lightbulb fought to illuminate the room packed with men. *No wonder the Communist cause is so strong in this country,* Philip thought as he stepped lightly through the group to where Attis sat in the far corner.

The prevalence of poverty humbled him. Though the main avenues of Barcelona and Madrid displayed extravagance, the common people lived in small shacks and had a few tattered garments and meager food—barely enough to survive.

No wonder they're willing to fight and die for the hope of something better for their children. Philip was glad he could help with their efforts.

Attis rested against the wall with no blanket or pillow, reclining in a half lying, half sitting position. As of late, they slept in shifts, mostly to protect the front lines surrounding Madrid, but also because there was no room for all of them to lie side by side in the cramped warehouse.

Philip reached Attis and squeezed himself between two other sound-asleep soldiers, wedging himself by Attis's feet.

"Weird dreams last night," Attis mumbled, opening one eye. "You should have woken me up."

Philip laughed, trying to forget the imprinted images of shredded bodies and the haunting memories of pained cries on the front lines—anything to forget. "As if your dream was my fault? What'd you dream about?"

"Dreamt I was back in school, and I showed up to find everyone waiting on stage for me—I was supposed to be the drummer in some type of band performance. Only problem was, I didn't know the rhythm. The beat kept changing in my ear until I threw down the sticks and ran from the stage."

As if on cue, the concussion of ground artillery shook the brick building, flaking a layer of ceiling plaster that fell like snow. The machine guns' *rat-a-tat-tat* soon followed.

Philip yawned and rubbed his eyes. "Yeah, that *is* a confusing beat to follow. I had a few dreams too."

"Any pretty girls?"

"Now that would have been nice. A caring American girl with dark eyes and a sweet smile. If I could have ordered up that dream, you know I would have."

The man next to Philip coughed and rolled onto his side.

Philip lowered his voice. "Actually, we were back in Barcelona, and both of us were racing. We lined up, preparing to start, and my dad showed up with his big, black Bible. He told me he had some encouragement for the race, but I pushed him away, telling him I didn't have time." Philip's voice caught in his throat. "It made me miss him, even if it was only in a dream. Surely, he and Mom received my letter by now, telling them where we are and why we're staying. I wonder what they said. They must think I've lost my mind."

The man on Philip's left side stirred, accidentally kicking Philip's shin. Philip rubbed the sore spot and nudged Attis, urging him to scoot closer to the wall.

"I was anxious for Louise's letter too, hoping she'd agree with my decision to stay. I told her as an anti-fascist, I saw this as my opportunity to stop aggression before another world war

176

erupted. She's a Communist too, you know. She embraced the cause after seeing how the Party has helped the unemployed and homeless."

"You said you *were* anxious. Does that mean you've heard from her?"

Attis straightened and slid a letter from his pocket. "Arrived yesterday."

"And you didn't tell me?" Philip playfully slugged Attis's socked foot.

Attis shrugged. "I just needed time to read it alone, think about it. Wanna hear?"

"Of course."

Attis cleared his throat.

Dear Attis,

> *Darling, though I miss you greatly, I truly understand your desire to fight for this cause in Spain. Though my heart wishes you were home again, my mind knows full well the importance of your fight. I consider you a liberator, my dear—giving your time, your spunk, and mostly your hope. During our three years together, I have seen your desire to do your part in opposing social, financial, and racial injustic. And, deep down, I see this as a new birth of who you were truly meant to be. . . .*

Attis paused. "It goes on from there, personal stuff—married stuff, you know."

Philip glanced to the high, lone window, but it gave no hint dawn would arrive anytime soon. "Actually, I don't—wish I did."

Attis refolded the letter and stuffed it back into his pocket. "In that case—it probably *would* interest you, but I'm still not gonna let you read it."

The man next to Philip turned and sat up, resting on his elbow. "Hope you don't mind me butting in, ol' chap, but that letter sounds like a Take Three to me."

"Take three?" Attis rubbed his jaw and cocked one eyebrow.

"Don't you know how they do it in Hollywood? Being Americans and all, you should. When they're filming those movies, they usually don't like the first thing they capture on film. So the next time, they say 'Take Two' and try again. They keep on going until they get it right."

"So what are you trying to tell me?"

The red-haired man pulled out a pipe and lit it, pressing it between his lips and speaking out of the side of his mouth. "My pappy, he was after fightin' in the Great War. I'm Breck O'Malley, by the way; nice to meet yer."

Breck didn't give them time to respond before he continued, puffing with each sentence. "My mother, bless her departed soul, she'd pull out a piece of paper, cursin' and mumblin', complainin' about all the things going wrong on the farm and yellin' at Pappy for leavin' her to deal with so much. Then she'd crumble that letter and toss it aside and write a second. Sometimes she'd mail that one; other times she'd rewrite it again, leavin' out everything but her undyin' love and support."

He pulled his pipe from his mouth and pointed toward Attis. "Yessir, that's a Take Three, and you should be glad of it. I'd say that your rubbish pail was after dealin' with the first two drafts. Like my pappy said, there is nothing worse than a woman's scorn."

"Or as my father used to say," Philip added, "it's better to live in the corner of an attic than in a fine home with a contentious woman. Then again . . ." He scanned the sleeping men. "An attic would be moving up in the world."

The two men laughed, and Philip joined them.

Philip cocked his head and studied the man with a mischievous grin. "I'm after thinkin' you might be Irish, O'Malley. Am I right?"

"Yes, lad, but don't be spreadin' that rumor. I'm tryin' to keep up on my English; otherwise, they might send me to the Germans."

"Germans? You mean the ones fighting for Franco?"

"No, sir. There are German volunteers in the International Brigades. Most of the Irishmen have been teamed up with them for the fight. *Those* Germans are as anti-fascist as the rest of us. A few welcomed us with food, wine, and women after our hike over the Pyrenees. Most were born and raised there—as German as they come. One man was even a Berliner, in fact."

"Is that so? I assumed all Germans would be on the other side," Attis said.

"Not quite. One in the group told me he'd been in Spain over three years now. As members of the Party, the chaps fled when Hitler took office." He spread his hand around the room. "There's quite a crew collectin'. They're callin' themselves the Thaelmann Battalion, in honor of Ernst Thaelmann, leader of the German Communist party. Thaelmann got a good number of votes when he ran against Hitler, you know. But not near enough."

"Wasn't he arrested after the Reichstag fire?" Attis sat up straighter. "Remember me telling you about that, Philip? He's still in prison."

Philip nodded, though he had to admit that too often it was easier to let his mind wander than to keep straight all of Attis's political concerns.

"Those Thaelmanns are a good group, really they are, but I speak better English than German. . . ." Breck lowered his voice and leaned close. "Besides, I've heard rumors of spies among them. Pro-Nazi soldiers sent in to infiltrate our lines." Breck shrugged. "Then again, lad, that could be said of any of us. It all comes down to trust, doesn't it now. Trustin' that the man watchin' your back is truly on your side."

Deion nearly pinched himself to make sure he wasn't dreaming. He finished his dinner and then jingled the coins in his pockets, realizing he had enough money left over to visit the Savoy Ballroom on Lenox Avenue. As he strode the streets of Harlem, he recognized one of the guys he'd first met marching through the streets of New York shouting anti-fascist slogans. The man, Jeb was his name, immediately recognized him and paused in the street, offering Deion a pat on the back. Jeb was slightly shorter and quite a bit wider than Deion, with skin so dark it made Deion's look pale in comparison.

"You looking good; glad to see you. I assume you found yourself a job?"

"Sure enough, I got one at Father Divine's where you introduced me around."

"Good, good." Jeb rocked back on his feet. "Good people, they are. Hey, what are you doing tonight? There's a speaker over at one of the local clubs talking about Spain."

"Is that right? I'm in."

They strode through the streets of Harlem, and though the sky had already darkened, it seemed as if the people were just getting wound up for the long night ahead. Crowds were lined up at the Apollo for a movie. More people, spit-shined and gussied up in their finest, made their way over to the Savoy where two bands played nightly.

"So you like it better here than in Chicagee?" Jeb flashed a smile as they passed a group of young ladies.

"You kidding? I feel like I found my own. Finally, some folks who don't think I'm nuts for my political leanings."

"I know what you mean. I read Hitler's book myself, and I figured that if those things are happening to the Jews, the Negroes won't be too far behind."

Deion let out a sigh. "You got that right. It's the same enemy I been fightin' all my life. I saw babies starve to death, and men—boys, really—lynched for being black." Deion shook his head as if trying to dislodge the memory that was never too far away.

They neared a tall, brick building that looked like hundreds of others on the New York streets. Jeb took the front steps two at a time and opened the door for Deion.

"That's why I talk to others wherever I go. I'm sure if our colored community knew more, they'd be willing to help. The only problem is, they're living hand to mouth, working hard just to fill their stomachs. They don't have time to consider world events."

Before they entered the room, already filled with men, Jeb stopped him. "Have you joined officially? For fifty cents you can get a red card."

Deion turned his near-empty pockets inside out. "Heck, alls

I got is three dimes. I'm not even sure where I'll be sleeping tonight."

Jeb slipped a crisp dollar bill from his pocket and handed it to Deion. The edges were sharp as if it had just rolled off the press that morning.

"What's this for?"

"Oh, just one comrade helping another. And I'm offering you a place to stay, if you don't mind sleeping on the floor."

"Mind? I nearly froze on a bench in Central Park last night."

"Good, that's settled." Jeb waved to one of the men at the door. "Your brothers will take care of you, you'll see."

Deion had barely stepped over the threshold of the small meeting room when a white man with skin leathery and tanned from the sun, light blue eyes, and a wide smile approached with his hand outstretched. He wore some type of uniform. Deion stepped aside, sure someone far more important stood behind him. But the man moved toward him, reaching Deion's side and taking his hand with a firm grasp.

"Welcome, comrade. Thiz is first time you are com-ink here, cor-rect?"

The r's rolled off the man's tongue, and Deion recognized the Russian accent. A true Russian Communist, welcoming him.

"Yessir." Deion lowered his eyes. "Thank you, sir."

"*Nyet.* No yessir-r, no sir-r, or any other sir-r." The man patted Deion's arm. "You, my comrade, are an asset to our cause. Who better to speak of equality and unity than one who his whole life has lived under the power of others?"

"Did Jeb tell you that?" Deion dared look into the man's blue eyes and was surprised to find acceptance there—more than that, admiration.

"Jeb? *Nyet.* I do not know thiz Jeb. I see it in your eyes, comrade. Thiz is gaze of one who fears to stir the waters, to speak his mind. But let me say, the time for silence is past. Your voice is as important as any other in our new fight. *Nyet.* More important. Come."

The man took Deion's elbow and guided him to the front of the room, offering him a seat in the front row.

"Here?" Deion asked, still unsure. He felt almost certain it was some type of trick.

"Yes, here." The man sat beside him. "We wait."

Only a minute passed, and a hush fell over the room. After a round of welcoming applause, the man at Deion's side was introduced as General Bogdan Kralka. With a set of his chin and erect stance, he strode to the front of the room.

"Comrades, before I tell you about new developments in Spain, I must warn you." His jaw jutted out and his eyes grew serious. "A great need has arisen, and we are call-ink comrades to arms. I do not look for mercenaries or soldiers of fortune. *Nyet.* You will earn nothing for effort—nothing but pride. If chosen, the trip will be long—into southern France and across the Pyrenees by foot into Spain. You will face thirst and hunger, loss of friends. Perhaps your life."

He pointed to a large map of Spain on the wall. Pins marked major points of interest, and lines of red yarn marked the current front.

A tremble traveled through Deion's body at the thought of actually traveling there. Could he, the grandson of a slave from Mississippi, actually find himself in Spain walking the land and fighting for the people?

"Yet there will be great reward. For the rest of your days you will have satisfaction of know-ink you had a part in stop-pink the spread of Fascism!"

Out of the corner of his eye, Deion spotted Jeb raising his hand. Deion did the same.

"Do you have question?" The general pointed to Jeb.

"Yes, sir. I was wondering about fund-raising efforts. How will the cost of transporting men be covered?"

"I am sorry. For se-cur-rity, small information can be given at thiz time. Only after recruits pass the interviews will they receive instructions about such things as funds and passports." He pointed to Deion. "And you, comrade. Do you have question?"

Deion stood. He removed his cap from his head, twisting it in his hands. "No, sir, I did not. . . . I just didn't want to miss signing up."

Chapter Twenty-One

Vámonos que nos vamos a mojar.
Let's go, we're getting wet.

Spanish proverb

Sophie waved good-bye to José and shut the door. She let her smile drop as she surveyed the large room divided into a bedroom, bathroom, and kitchen. Dust particles danced in the light that filtered through the door and single barred window, which looked into the weed-strewn courtyard.

Her smile flitted back slightly when she noted the cluster of candles on the table and the small bunch of flowers arranged in a jar next to the flickering light. *José . . . what a friend.*

Sophie put down her satchel and set to work sweeping up the dirt her shoes had carried in. She folded the rug in half and laughed out loud, noticing that the wooden floor had been recently repainted—except under the rug. She moved to the next rug, by the small sink basin, and noticed the same.

Returning the broom to the corner, she plopped onto a spindly chair, causing it to nearly flip onto its side. A burst of laughter spouted, and tears came too. But those tears opened the floodgate for more, and she gulped them back so loudly she was sure it was heard at the market next door.

With the tears came a sudden weariness, and though her stomach rumbled, she blew out the candles and found her way to the bed, climbing under a soft blanket that smelled of José's shaving soap.

What did she have to look forward to? She'd lost Michael. Not only that, she didn't know if he ever had loved her. He'd lied to her about Maria. Even when she confronted him, he'd looked into her eyes and lied. With the passing hours since his death, she had lost every feeling of being loved herself.

And where did that leave her? Alone in a foreign country. Forced to return to Boston with everyone knowing how big a fool she had been.

I'd rather die than face them.

The siren bellowed over the rooftops of the city, stirring Sophie from her troubled sleep. She was surprised when she opened her eyes and noticed the morning sun shining through the windows.

"Air raid!" she heard the old man upstairs call to his wife. "Air raid!"

Doors slammed as people moved toward the shelter in the basement.

"The morning song, waking us again." She sighed. And with the siren the thoughts that had replayed in her mind returned. *I might as well be dead. I have nothing to live for.*

Following the siren came the faint rumble of aircraft engines in the clouds. And everything within Sophie told her not to run. Only then would the pain stop.

She sat up, retrieved a comb from her satchel, and ran it through her hair.

The whistle came first, then a pause, followed by a deep thud.

Another bomb hit, close enough to cause the apartment to shiver. Flecks of whitewash drifted from the ceiling, and incongruously, she wondered if it was snowing in Boston. The next bomb hit, and the whole building shook. The lamp on the side table tipped, shattering, spilling its precious oil on the floor. With slow steps she retrieved some rags she found near the sink and cleaned up the glass and oil.

The bombs fell so steadily, it was as if the dark blue sky above them had shattered. She imagined it falling like shards of glass all around, blades of destruction slicing through anything in their path.

Sophie didn't know how long it was before the sounds of motors faded away. The smell of smoke and scorched stone drifted in through her front door that had somehow been knocked open.

She thought about rising and forcing herself to the Hotel Palace, now a home for orphaned children. If the bombs didn't kill her, at least it would be something to live for. Maybe they would need art lessons there too. Anything to keep her mind busy. She tried to picture the hotel as it was when she first arrived. It was so different now from the exquisite showplace Michael had first squired her to.

Michael . . .

Had it only been four months since she arrived in the city? What a different place Madrid was then. Now, twice a day Fascist planes attacked, and somehow that seemed normal. Was it only weeks ago that the cafés were full, music filled the clean streets, flowers bloomed in the plazas, and children danced in the fountains? Last night she'd dreamed of what life must have been *antes de la Guerra* . . . before the war. If she'd arrived even two months earlier. The wedding, the groom. Maybe she would have arrived before Michael and Maria . . . she shook her head, banishing that thought.

Many laughed away the shortages, the hunger, the confusion. But the air raids cut to the core. The loss of life pained the city the most.

Sophie snatched up José's blanket and the broom and made her way to the courtyard. Sweeping the dead leaves into a pile, she spread out her blanket and lay down on her back, feeling the sun warm her face. She stayed there until the sun dropped behind the tall buildings and the planes came again. Like a string of dots from the south, they grew in her view like sponges soaking up the sky, growing and changing before her eyes.

The ground shook once more, and she went back inside, taking in the view from her window. She was certain this time the slithering snakes falling from the sky hit the stone buildings of the Gran Via. The street beyond the apartment building moved like waves from the sea. Then, as she watched, a voice broke through her consciousness.

"*Nuestros! Nuestros!* Ours!"

Sophie sat up straighter, noting the small "hummingbirds," as the small Russian planes were called, that attacked the large German bombers. Right overhead now, the clatter of machine guns caused her heart to pound. Men, women, and children rushed into the street to watch. At least six of the Russian fighters darted and jabbed at the flying beasts. A roar rose from the crowd as the first of the German aircraft stalled, rolled over, and plummeted to the ground somewhere beyond the Manzanares River.

"Beautiful! *Estupendo!* Our saviors!" Men and women alike waved red handkerchiefs in the air.

Another German bomber burst into flames, and pieces of metal broke loose, glimmering as they fell to the earth. Sophie then noticed a small German Bf.109, a slender monoplane. It swung over the city low, then turned and attacked the hummingbirds. One of Benita's prayers filled her mind, and she repeated it from memory.

"Teach Your people to rely on Your strength and to accept their responsibilities to their fellow citizens, that we may serve You faithfully in our generation and honor Your holy name."

And with those words, she thought of the people, their divisions, their desire for peace. She also thought of the peace she so desperately needed for her soul. The strength she needed. The faith.

Sophie took a deep breath and finished the prayer, realizing more than anything she desired it to mean the same to her as it did to Benita.

"For Yours is the kingdom, O Lord, and You are exalted above all."

And as if the clouds in her foggy mind cleared, she looked to the hummingbirds in the sky that fought so worthily against the enemy. *If they, so small, can fight, I can too.* She straightened her shoulders. *To live. To love again.*

The smaller German plane shuddered and drifted away, wounded. The hummingbird had hit its mark, and Sophie found herself wiping tears from her face. Tears she didn't know had trickled down her cheek.

The bells of a fire vehicle rang out in the distance, and a deeper, more sacred ringing stirred in her soul. Like the emotion evoked by the church bells she'd first heard around town, the reminder of God's loving presence sounded in her soul.

He is near. Come, the church bells used to say. *Come.*

Philip scanned the crowd, trying to remember the names of the volunteers he'd already met. *Breck, Henry, Richard* . . . and many more whose names had slipped his mind.

Philip had lost track of how many days they'd waited for additional weapons and instructions—three, maybe four. Beside him, Attis shivered and complained about "sunny Spain." A man walked through the lines handing out oranges and cigarettes. Most of the volunteers were British, a few French, and even some Poles and Germans made up their ranks. Some men curled back-to-back against a stone wall, like kittens nestled up to their mother. They were the newest arrivals, catching up on sleep from their journey to Madrid, and Philip wished he were among them. At least sleep made the time go faster.

The loudspeakers crackled, but the news was the same as it had been. More volunteers were soon to arrive. With them, food and weapons.

"Oh, joy, more welcome speeches," Attis muttered. "I've heard them often enough to give them myself."

The fighting had died down slightly, and now their commanders filled their time with political speeches, encouraging them to continue their fight. *Preaching to the choir.* It was one of his father's favorite sayings.

Finally, as afternoon rolled around, the courtyard came alive with calisthenics and drills. Philip chuckled at the sight of Attis running in place.

"Gee, I hope you don't tire yourself out, old boy. You haven't been on your running legs for a while."

Attis shrugged and pumped his legs harder, not even winded. "It's like riding a bicycle, ol' chap," he answered, mimicking the British volunteers. "It all comes back once you start."

One of the commanders approached, calling out the names of those heading back to the front lines. Philip's gaze met Attis's, and he could tell his friend hoped their names would be called. Sitting in ditches and hearing the sounds of bullets whizzing over-head was far more exciting than sitting around doing nothing.

Finally Philip's name was called, but Attis's was not.

"Excuse me, comrade. My name wasn't on the list, but if I could, I'd like to join my friend."

"Name?" The man cocked his head to look into Attis's face.

"Attis Brody, sir."

The balding man slipped a pencil from behind his ear and jotted the name on the list. "Fine, but hustle now, lad. The truck is leaving in a few minutes."

"Yes, sir." Attis threw the man a salute, then reached out a hand to help Philip to his feet.

Attis's hand was warm and big, as was his smile, and Philip couldn't help but chuckle. For though the crisp air brought a chill to his bones, Attis helped him forget the cold, the hunger. Crazy Attis somehow made him feel as if Spain was one great big ad-venture, after all, like the camping trips they took as kids or the war games they played with sticks and shouts. War games in which the good guys always won.

Someone knocked on the door. Sophie opened it to find José, but it was a different José from the one she knew. His face was ruggedly handsome as always, but his eyes seemed weary—older than the old men with gray hair and wrinkled skin who sat on the benches in the plaza.

"I was downtown today, inquiring about the best route for leaving the country. To see if we could not travel a slightly different route and see my future bride. Communication has been scarce over the past month, and I worry she is not well—perhaps she is busy as a nurse? Or maybe there is more danger in the area than the radio suggests."

José looked at Sophie, but she could tell he was not seeing her face. It was another woman who invaded his thoughts. "I'm going to talk to a few more men at the tavern—perhaps new information has come in."

"Tavern?"

"*Sí, señorita.* Around here, the taverns are more like universities. If you want to know anything about everything of importance, you will hear it there." He pointed a finger in the air. "Or, depending on whom you choose to listen to, you might learn everything about that which has no importance at all."

"May I go with you?"

"To the tavern?"

"Yes, anything to get out of this place for a while. As wonderful as it is," she quickly added, "some fresh air will do me good."

A short walk brought them to the small tavern located on the corner of the market district. The door was ajar and the room was filled with people, despite the fact that both windows had been boarded up, and nothing remained of the building on the opposite corner except a pile of rubble.

José led her to a table of men, and they all stood as she approached, tipping their hats. Sophie glanced around the room. Only a few other women were present, and those were the waitresses, all older women, who carried glasses of wine to the tables with a sway of their wide hips.

"We've been discussing your venture, and we think we've found a route." A man with a scarred face, yet soft and gentle eyes, spread a small map before them. "If you can make it to Albacete, we believe there is a train from there."

"Albacete? That is the opposite direction of France. Why Albacete?"

"The path through Albacete is the safest way out of the country. It's there they have a training camp for the International Brigades. From there, my *amiga*, you can catch a train to France . . . safely. They have to keep the line open, you see. Volunteers are crossing the Pyrenees by foot. Then they travel by rail to be trained at the barracks before being sent to the front lines. But do not worry." He leaned back in his chair and folded his hands behind his head. "You do not have to go alone. Alejandro will drive you."

"Oh, no." A gray-haired man with big ears and small darting eyes stood. "I can't do this. Don't you understand? They're going to kill us. They're going to kill us all."

The men laughed, and Sophie frowned. It was clear they knew they'd get this response. When the laughter died down, José took a sip from the drink before him, the smile fading. It was also clear that though they joked with their friends, they too felt the same.

"So is no one willing to risk his life for the sake of a beautiful maiden?" José motioned for the waitress to bring another flask of wine. "Anyone care to join us on our journey?"

No one responded.

"As if protecting our lives matters!" someone in the back shouted—his words slightly slurred. "Tell me one man who has cheated death! Show me one body that will not someday become the very dust you walk on. The question isn't how we will die, but how we will live!"

"Well said!" José lifted his glass, sloshing the red wine over the rim onto his arm. It dribbled down to his sleeve, looking like blood, thick and red.

Sophie forced herself to look away, remembering the blood pooled under Michael. Despite their laughter and joking, she saw the same fear in their eyes that gnawed at her own insides when she allowed it to. It was easy to talk of death as a noun, but rather impossible to truly understand it—until the verb of death cut your soul like a knife.

"Fine then, friends." José tossed a coin onto the table and rose. "We will travel alone, and we will not fail!"

Chapter Twenty-Two

Al buen entendedor, pocas palabras.
To him who understands, few words are needed.

Spanish proverb

The outer defensive line around Madrid surprised Philip. He wasn't sure what he'd expected, but this wasn't it. The raw, red earth heaped along the side of the trenches. The ragged soldiers huddled with one gun for every three men—one steel helmet per ten. And though the sun shone overhead, it did little to warm them.

Trenches ran from house to house, empty rivers containing only six men each, sitting on the cold ground shoulder to shoulder. Sandbags and loose wire looped at the top offered their only protection.

Some of the International volunteers shouted toward the Fascist lines, taunting them. The men on the other side of the line grew tired of their voices, and bullets whacked against the sandbags. The foul names intensified, volleyed back and forth.

Attis stood and fired back, a grin curling up the end of his lips. He fired because he could, Philip knew, not because he expected to hit anything or anyone. But only one bullet every thirty minutes or so—there weren't that many to go around.

"This is foolishness," one Spanish soldier said, cleaning his Spanish Mauser for the second time that hour. Philip remembered his name was Rico; and his baby face and wide, curious eyes fit the name.

"For all I know, it could be my uncle on the other side, my cousin. Our country has gone mad. Like Cain, we hunt down our brother." Rico lowered his eyes to his hands. "And I am certain it is due to the fight over the church. God has left our country, *amigos*. And I don't blame Him. If I were Him I'd do the same." He made the sign of the cross.

"That's why I don't believe in God," another soldier spat. "Believing only brings disappointment. Don't you agree?" He nudged Philip's arm.

"No, I don't agree. I don't think God has left Spain. If what the Bible says is true, then that's not the case at all." As Philip spoke the words, he thought of his dream of his father. He also remembered the big, black Bible that had seemed useless to him for many years. *But here.* He glanced at the red dirt and the barbed wire. *Here things are different.*

"Show me this God. Let me see His face. You say God is true, but you have no proof, which means this *truth* can equally be untrue, can it not?"

Attis turned to Philip, cocking one eyebrow as if waiting for his response.

Philip knew that Attis's ideology matched the stranger's more than his own—yet, as a friend Attis would never admit it . . . until they were alone again.

"Yes, I suppose it can be equally untrue, but as one who's read many of the Holy Scriptures describing man's purpose on earth, I find it makes the most sense. The Bible doesn't try to excuse human behavior, but instead explains it. And if you view Spain in light of the words of Scripture—of men wanting to become God, to have the knowledge of God, to live as gods themselves, in control of their own destinies—then what we see around us also makes sense."

"It sounds as if you've been thinking about this for a while."

Rico shivered and pulled his cap lower over his ears.

"Before a few nights ago, it was something I hadn't thought about for years. But being here, facing this—" Philip pointed toward the enemy lines. "Well, my mind has taken me back to what I learned in my youth, and I've considered that perhaps my old man isn't as foolish as I once thought. Of course, don't tell him I've said that." Philip chuckled. "It would be like the prodigal son coming home, and there is no way I'm going back just yet."

A Frenchman, wearing the uniform of an officer in the International Brigades, hurriedly jumped from the next trench into theirs, interrupting their conversation and causing all of them to squeeze in tighter. "I need someone to deliver a message to the university."

Attis raised his hand, and Philip did the same. Attis must have lifted his fingers too high, because an eruption of gunfire followed, showering sand across their heads and shoulders. Attis cursed, then lowered his hand.

"I only need one—you." He pointed to Philip.

Attis slugged Philip's arm, and Philip smiled.

"Be careful. I hear some of the buildings have been captured by the Fascists," the French officer explained. "Others are ours, held by the 5th Regiment and the Internationals." The officer took a few minutes to explain the safest route and to hand Philip the note.

Philip sprinted down the line, darting between blocks of brick buildings. An eruption of gunfire sounded as those in the trenches provided cover. Soon he was out of range of the guns, and he slowed his pace slightly, noticing some buildings still stood, others only partly so. He moved past the Casa de Velazquez, remembering the lecture in the courtyard about how the battle over that building cost the Internationals 122 Polish volunteers. Yet passing it, one would never know. It stood so innocently among the rest of the buildings—the red tiles of its roof scattered over the ground where Philip jogged.

He found the correct building and delivered the sealed note. He hardly looked around the dim room, heavy with the scent of smoke and body odor. Rifles were piled on the tables. Mattresses of lounging men filled one corner. The man at the desk thanked him, and tossed Philip an orange for his effort.

In less than half an hour, he was back at the trenches. But just as he jumped inside the first trench to tell the Frenchman he'd succeeded at his mission, two men grabbed his arms.

"Philip, no, you don't want to go any farther. Come with us." The men tugged against his arms. A third man joined them, jumping between the trenches.

"Let go. What are you doing?" He struggled against them, realizing they were covered with blood.

Philip looked into Rico's eyes, and the sadness he witnessed there sent a lightning bolt of pain shooting through his chest. Immediately he understood.

"Attis . . ." Philip mumbled the name first, then shouted. "Attis!"

"Your friend stood to shoot, just like always, but they got him first. One bullet, clean in the center of the forehead." A sob escaped with Rico's explanation.

Philip tugged harder. "Let me go. Let me see him." He jumped into the next trench and saw four men huddled around the body, preparing to hoist it out. A fifth man vomited in the corner.

"Attis. Let him go. Put him down. Attis."

The men obeyed, and Philip knelt at his friend's side. His eyes were open, yet unseeing. A single bullet hole dimpled his forehead, and a stream of drying blood trickled down into his eye.

"He didn't know what hit him. Look, he's still smiling."

Philip looked at his friend's lips, curled up slightly, so happy to be included in this. Thankful to be doing his part.

Philip sank to the ground, laying his head on his friend's still-warm chest. It neither rose nor fell.

"Why did I go? I should have stayed." He shook his fist in the air. "One of you should have volunteered." He pointed at a face blurred by his tears. "How come you didn't go?"

"Quiet now. No one is to blame. He was our friend," Rico said. "A brave example to all of us . . . he was so kind."

"I should have made him get on that ship." Philip's throat was tight and achy. "He'd be alive now." He entwined his fingers with Attis's larger ones. "He'd still be alive. What am I going to tell Louise?"

Ritter had stayed up until 3 a.m. dancing, talking, drinking champagne, and watching the girls perform their Spanish dances, yet he could not forget. He knew there was a problem when Major General Sperrle met him on the runway after the last bombing raid over Madrid.

The day's events played and replayed in Ritter's mind, and sleep evaded him.

"Eduard's plane is missing." They'd been the first words out of the general's mouth. "A few others witnessed it going down in a spin with a lot of smoke near the Red lines. I know you were close."

"Close? He was a fellow pilot, and nothing more. True soldiers know better than to make friends." Yet even as Ritter spouted the words, he knew it was a lie. He'd taken the kid under his wing, like a younger brother. Ritter had even shared about his feelings for Isanna, after Eduard had teased him about not starting a romance with a Spanish maiden.

"Do they know the cause of the crash?"

"Shrapnel from the ground, most likely. They believe his right engine blew up. Smoke billowed from it."

"He could still have made it." Ritter turned and strode across the landing strip.

Sperrle followed close to his side. "Yes, of course." When they reached the pilots' quarters, the general paused. "You okay?"

"Of course. See you in the morning."

Entering the room, Ritter spotted a group of the other pilots circled around the radio. He could tell from the excited voice of the host that they were listening to Radio Libertad, the Red station broadcasting in German.

Felix, one of the other pilots, spotted Ritter and immediately switched it off.

Ritter paused in his tracks. "Is there a problem?"

"Red lies, all of them," spouted Niklas, another pilot.

Ritter noted the bead of perspiration on Niklas's brow and went closer. "Really? Well, what do these lies say?"

Instead of answering, Felix turned the radio knob, and the announcer's voice blared.

"Today, comrades, a German He.51 was discovered behind enemy lines. The young pilot was still alive, but not for long. The Reds not only made quick work of the foreign enemy, but as a symbol to others like him, the body was crated up and dropped over enemy lines. I pity the Fascist pig who opens the crate to discover a body wrapped in a bag—one of their own!"

The man's voice continued on about new tanks arriving daily, when Ritter reached over and turned the switch.

"You are correct. Lies, all of it. Eduard is alive; wait and see. They only *wish* they could do such a thing . . . they only dream . . ." Ritter's voice caught in his throat and he turned, high-stepping his way to his quarters. His hand shook as he opened the door, and he cursed at the sound of flamenco drifting through his open window.

He shut the window, then noticed a piece of paper stuck in the frame. He unfolded it, recognizing Eduard's handwriting. As of yesterday, some of the pilots had been writing a song for the Condor Legion, and Eduard was lending a hand. He must have slipped the note inside the window frame before heading out for the day.

"Hey, maybe my name will go down in history," Eduard had said the previous day. "I can be known as one of the men who gave voice to our fight."

Ritter had laughed at him. "*Ja*, well, I'd rather be known as one of the men who provided more fight than words, more caskets than silly songs."

Eduard had shrugged it off with a smile, but Ritter could not help noticing the pained look in the young man's eyes.

With a tightening of his chest, Ritter read the words, first in Spanish. Then in German.

Die Jungfrau Maria ist unsere Legion
Franco, ber Azana.
Arriba Espana . . .

Es ist so schoen
In der Condor A.G.

Jetze sind wir Legionäre
RLM ade . . .

Es kommt kein Fein duns in die Quer
Wo unser Banner weht
Wir sind die Condor legion
Der niemand wiedersteht.

The Virgin Mary is our Legion.
Franco over Azana.
Upward Spain . . .

It is so beautiful
In the Condor Company
Now we are Legionnaires
Reich Air Ministry, Good-bye . . .
We will meet no enemy on the square
Where our banner flies.
We are the Condor Legion
That no man can hold back.

Anger coursed through Ritter's chest, and he crumbled the paper, hoping the news report was indeed a lie. Hoping that tomorrow they'd receive a call from Eduard, telling them it had been a mistake and he waited on another base, safe and needing a ride back.

Ritter poured himself a drink, then sank into his chair by the window. He sipped his whisky, enjoying the burn in his throat and the heat that traveled through him—numbing heat.

Outside, a shepherd's campfire glowed on a distant hill, and that glow gave him solace. It reminded him of the fires that raged in Madrid. The ones started by the bombers . . . and the ones that continued to burn—drawing them in and marking the best targets to destroy the mortally wounded.

Then, for the first time since he'd been in Spain, the sound of the flamenco called him, inviting him to join in the laughter, the party. And promising he'd forget.

WINTER

And pray ye that your flight be not in the winter.
—Mark 13:18

Chapter Twenty-Three

DECEMBER 25, 1936

Saliste de Guatemala y te metiste en Guatepeor
Out of the pot, into the fire.

Spanish proverb

Sophie couldn't help grinning as she heard the step-step-thump of José walking up to her front door. She opened it before the knock and caught him standing there with a wide-eyed look of surprise.

She pointed to the crutch he'd been using for the past month. "How's your leg feeling?"

"It would be doing much better if Franco would stop the bombing. One building falling around me was enough."

She welcomed him in and noted the dark circles under his eyes and the worry lines on his forehead. She also noticed a canvas bag hanging from his shoulder, swinging with his every step across the wooden floor.

A strong wind blustered through the doorway, blowing dust and debris in from the street. Sophie quickly shut the door.

"Winter is upon us, and you are still here, Sofía. This was not the plan. . . ." He turned to sit on her spindly chair; then, thinking better of it, he hobbled to the bed.

Sophie sat beside him. "Honestly, I understand. It's not as though you planned to get caught in a building that took a direct hit." She patted his knee. "I'm just thankful you fared as well as you did."

"*Sí, señorita,* but the plan was to take you to safety as soon as possible. The city is far too dangerous." He shrugged his shoulders. "But as Benita would say, that was not God's plan."

"I miss Benita. Are they well?" Sophie had only seen her friend three times since Michael's death, as Benita had rushed around caring for her three nieces and two nephews who'd lost their mother to the bombs and their father to the front lines.

Sophie stood and walked to the table, retrieving the book Benita had brought over during her last visit. She had apologized that it wasn't a complete Bible, but Sophie had been thrilled with the devotional book, in English no less, which included the Psalms. She reread them on many lonely nights, using the biblical songs as her own prayers for safety, courage, hope.

She caressed the leather cover. "I thought I'd read a prayer, and then we'd exchange presents."

José's brow furrowed. "Christmas, *sí,* I almost forgot. But I'm sorry, I . . ." He followed her gaze to the canvas bag. "Oh, I suppose I do have a gift, after all."

Sophie opened the book and read. "The Nativity of Our Lord: Christmas Day. Almighty God, You have given Your only begotten Son to take our nature upon Him, and to be born this day of a pure virgin: Grant that we, who have been born again and made Your children by adoption and grace, may daily be renewed by Your Holy Spirit; through our Lord Jesus Christ, to whom with You and the same Spirit be honor and glory, now and forever. Amen."

"That is beautiful, Sofía, truly it us. The daily renewal—*sí,* a good reminder."

"So." She returned the book to the table. "Do you want to go first, or should I?"

"I think you'd better." He leaned back against the wall, closed his eyes, and opened his hand expectantly.

Sophie bent down and pulled a small canvas from under the bed, placing it in his hand. "Okay, you can open it."

José's eyes brightened as he took in the angelic form on the canvas.

"Do you recognize it?"

"*Sí*, the cherub from San Antonio de la Florida. It's as if Goya painted it himself."

Sophie chuckled. "Not quite. But it was the best I could do, under the circumstances. My time lately has been filled with trying to find food for the displaced persons, and . . ." She shook her head. "You don't want to hear about those things. Today is our time of celebration."

José nodded, then dropped his eyes to the bag. "First, I must explain. My plan was to give you this when you arrived in France. You should have been there by now—safe." With a sigh, he held it out to her.

Sophie took it from him, the weight of the object inside the canvas startling her. She untied the cords and looked inside, sucking in a breath. Tears soon followed. Gingerly she pulled a large camera from the bag.

"It's Michael's. . . ." A sob caught in her throat, and she could almost feel his presence in the room. Anger stirred within her at the sight of it, rage at what he'd done to both her and Maria. But also the deep ache that comes from losing someone cherished for so long.

"I knew he'd want you to have it. But even more than that, Michael wished for your safety. We will leave in the morning."

"Leave?"

"*Sí*, to France. I still need to find a good map, but I've already gathered our supplies."

Sophie fingered the camera, lifting it to look through the viewfinder to the street outside her window. The street was nearly empty, but even the emptiness was comfortable to her now. Was there life beyond war? Did people really go to bed at night in safety or wake up without questioning where the day's meal would come from? She returned the camera to the bag, uncertain what it would feel like to be safely across the border. "Are you sure? Do you feel well enough?"

José rubbed his leg where it had been broken. "I am still on the mend, yes. But I hear that Franco is repositioning his troops outside Madrid. If we are leaving, now is the time. Who knows how long the city will stand? The people have already faced so much."

"Fine. I'll be ready in the morning." Sophie glanced across the room and realized there wasn't much to prepare. She had only a few items, including her blue dress. Though it was her last clean item of clothing and the only thing not suited for the rubbish heap, she didn't know why she'd held on to it.

She looked down at the camera once again, her conflicting emotions still waging a war inside her. "Yes, I'll be ready at dawn, José." She took his hands in hers. "Thank you, my friend."

But instead of answering, José glanced away, letting his eyes follow two young women who hurried down the street. His mind was someplace else entirely. Sophie had a feeling the camera wasn't the only thing he'd withheld from her . . . but in time, she was sure, he would tell all.

Deion laid back and idly stared at the ceiling, hoping that the ship's gentle rocking would lull him to sleep. Yesterday he'd celebrated Christmas with Jeb and their other comrades. And today he was deep within the belly of the French luxury liner *Normandie*. If he dared to venture outside in the biting cold, he imagined their ship was moving past the Statue of Liberty about now. But he was looking to the future rather than the past. For Deion and the other eighty-five Americans aboard, the next destination was Le Havre, France.

Most of the other volunteers aboard the ship were members of the New York Artists' Union. They had stood in line with one suitcase each, waiting to board, chatting about the Armageddon ahead—where Fascists attempted to control all freethinkers and threatened the essence of independent creativity. To these writers, artists, and musicians, Spain was a place where their blood would redeem art and liberty, or those ideals would vanish forever. And though Deion knew nothing about art, he did identify with their passionate drive for freedom.

Another volunteer approached, his walk swaying with the ship's motion, and sat on the floor next to Deion's bunk. The man, who looked to be nearly forty, wrapped his arms around his long, thin legs and pushed his steel-rimmed glasses back on his nose. "I met you before, at Jeb's house, right? I'm Clark. And you're Deion, right?"

He extended his hand, and Deion sat up on his bed and shook it firmly. "So where is old Jeb now?"

"Back in the city, raising funds. He says he could be a better help there, making sure we can get the supplies we need."

Deion looked away, hoping Clark didn't see the disappointment on his face. Over the months, as he worked with some of the other men, he'd come to the growing realization that some people, Jeb included, were more talk than bite.

"And what about you?" Clark removed his glasses and wiped them with the corner of his shirt. "I assume you got the paperwork you needed, after all. I know you were worried about that."

"My birth certificate. Yessir, I got that straightened out. My mama had to sign an affidavit giving the day I was born. In Mississippi they didn't pay no mind to the birth of Negro babies. Or their death either, for that matter. According to the family Bible, I'll be twenty-three in April."

"And she signed it without question?"

"Nah, my mama's like any mama. She worries 'bout everything. I had to spin her a tale. I told her up north you need a birth certificate to get a marriage license. She was so happy I found me a woman." Deion lowered his voice, ashamed at the memory of his deceit. "I'll be sorry when she discovers the truth. . . ."

Deion slid his passport from his pocket, glancing at the large, red print—*Not Valid for Travel in Spain*. His story to his mother was simply the first of many lies.

"So what made you decide, you know, to go to Spain and all?"

Deion smiled, then slowly nodded. "It's like this. The little guy finally won out against these big landowners. The peasants, workers, unions, Socialists, and Communists beat out the monarchy, right-wingers, and military. Can you imagine that? It would be like my uncle in Mississippi becoming mayor, and my mama and aunts being the ones to get the good union jobs—not having to wash the floors for those white women no more. Then, imagine all the whiteys going and taking it back, with nobody stepping in to say a word—" He paused, remembering the color of Clark's skin. "No offense and all."

Clark pushed his glasses farther up on his nose. "None taken." He waited, and Deion continued.

"I imagined these Spanish people facing the same oppression I'd seen growing up. Both in Chicago and New York, I'd leave work, walking those busy streets and feelin' small and insignificant. I always knew if I walked out, there'd be a hundred more just like me in line to take my job. But in Spain . . . that's a different matter. There I can fight to hold onto what people like me worked so hard to achieve. In Spain I'll make a difference."

"You're right. The Negro people suffer doubly. Why shouldn't you get equal pay for equal work? Or the right to organize, vote, serve on juries, and hold public office? Doesn't the constitution say it should be so?"

Deion studied the man before him and figured he was a writer. The artists he knew studied his face. His large nose and ears. His black eyes. But the writers looked at his mouth, waiting for the words and the story behind them.

Deion pressed his lips together and narrowed his eyes. Seeing the eagerness in Clark's face for what might come next, he decided it was worth sharing a little more of his story.

"Even more than that, I grew up with a mama and grandma tellin' me I could do anything I set my mind to. That color didn't matter one bit. This was saying a lot, since my grandma lived near a quarter of her life as a slave. She remembers the day she heard she was finally free. The Yanks come down the road, and all those in the field started hootin' and hollerin'. Their master had left the day before, runnin' for his life, you see. But she really didn't believe it till the Yanks showed up."

Clark yawned and rose, his legs unfolding, bringing him to his full height. "I want to be a Yank for these people. A Yank for Spain. Hey, I like that." He turned to leave, then paused, glancing back over his shoulder. "Can you read, Deion?"

"Shore can, better'n most. My mama got together with some other folks and hired us a tutor at the church. We ate potatoes for breakfast, lunch, and dinner, but I've read Dickens. Shakespeare too. Not that I understood much of it." Deion grinned.

"Then take a look at this." Clark withdrew a newspaper from under his shirt and pushed it into Deion's hands. The headline read "Republican Spain Under Attack."

Deion studied the photographs of Spain, of Moroccan soldiers, and General Francisco Franco himself observing the course of the battle through binoculars. In another photograph, children were presenting flowers to the Rebel general.

"I hope we make it in time," Deion said, looking up.

But the tall man was already gone.

"I hope we make it," he repeated to himself.

Chapter Twenty-Four

Cuando te toca, te toca.

When it's your time, it's your time.

Spanish proverb

Philip shivered under the wool poncho as he rested on his haunches and listened to his trench mate whistle a catchy jazz tune, just loud enough for Philip to enjoy too. In the past month he'd moved from place to place with the International Brigades in a half daze, as if watching someone else complete the drills, fire the weapons, and shout the Communist slogans with a fisted, straight-armed salute.

They were back on the Madrid front with *La Marsellaise,* the French-British battalion. He did his part, obeying orders and trying to join in small talk with friends, but sometimes he marveled that he was still in Spain. The fact that those who deserted were hunted down and killed was a pretty good reason to stay, he supposed. But staying meant something more than that. Attis's body lay in a grave in Spain.

He'd want it that way. No one can make him go back. . . .

Now, when Philip fought, he battled for his friend. And as

the days passed, the cause in which Attis had believed so strongly became Philip's own.

"Hey, chap, got any smokes?" the man in the trench next to Philip asked. "I lost the last of mine in Albacete."

What was the fellow's name? *Charles,* Philip reminded himself. *His name is Charles.*

Philip felt his pocket and pulled out a cigarette. Though he didn't smoke himself, he bought the best cigarettes possible with the few pesos he received each week. It was his way of keeping connected, of not walling himself off completely.

Charles lit the cigarette, took a long drag, then let the cigarette hang from his lips as he spoke. "I have to use the slit trench. I'll be right back." He slapped Philip on the back and climbed from the foxhole. Then he tightened the strap on his steel helmet, hiding his blond hair.

It was the same color as Philip's. In fact, many commented they could be brothers. Philip only nodded when they said that. He didn't want to burst their bubble, but over the last few months he'd learned one thing—brotherhood had little to do with similar appearance, and everything to do with heart. Philip also knew that he'd have to start opening his heart back up again, before it turned as dry and impenetrable as the hard-packed dirt he sat on.

The sound of an approaching automobile stirred him from his thoughts. He listened, holding his breath. Gunfire erupted from the opposite direction of where Charles had just run. Then he heard the crunch of metal and something that sounded like a woman's scream. He lifted his rifle and peered over the edge of the trench. More gunfire sounded, closer this time. And then he saw movement in the trees between his location and the road.

He peeked out to get a closer look, and a few enemy bullets thudded into the ground next to his head. He knew he'd been hit —maybe shot dead—when he saw the angel of light coming toward him. A dark-haired beauty with fair skin, wearing a light blue dress. The angel's hair blew in her face, and her hands tried to brush it away, as if she fought against the very breath of life escaping his lungs.

She hurried to him, her eyes locked with his, and leaned down. Her hands touched his face. She spoke to him in Spanish.

"Sir, can you understand me? My friend—he needs help. We got lost. Made the wrong turn. We ended up—oh, can you please come quick?"

He could tell Spanish wasn't her native tongue. The tears in her eyes pulled him to his senses and woke him up completely, causing him to stand up with a start.

"Who are you?" It wasn't until the words were out that he realized he'd spoken in English.

"Sophie. I'm—oh, it would take too long to explain why I'm here, but can you please come help my friend? There was blood everywhere, and . . ." Her voice trailed off as a sob caught in her throat.

He heard a distant rumble, and an instinct to protect her kicked in. Philip pulled her down on him. Her mouth opened to scream, but he clamped his hand tight over it. She smelled of clean skin and lilacs. Her hair wrapped around his hand like silk, and her dress was thin and soft under his fingers. She trembled, from the cold and from fear, then tugged against him, struggling. Grasping her more firmly, Philip pulled her ear closer to his mouth. "Shhh . . . they'll think we're injured and come for us. You must be quiet."

Gunfire sounded; then a flurry of fire was returned. It was farther away than he thought, which was good.

The skin of her cheek brushed his lips, and he pulled his head back, still unsure if this fleshly being were real or a wayward angel come to his rescue.

"If I move my hand, will you promise not to scream?"

She nodded slightly.

"Okay. Now who are you, and what are you doing here?" He released his grasp, and she sucked in a great breath.

"Sophie. My name is Sophie. I'm an American . . . news correspondent. My friend was trying to drive me to the French border. Obviously he took a wrong turn, and our automobile came under fire." Her body trembled under his grasp, and Philip released his hold. "I think he might be dead."

"And you got out and came for help? How did you know where to go? You could have ended up on the wrong side."

More trembling. "I didn't know, but I knew I couldn't stay there and watch José die." She lowered her head. "I prayed."

"We can't go yet; we have to wait till dark. I still don't know how you made it across that field."

"But . . . José. We can't just leave him. I'll go back alone if I have to."

"Where was he hit?"

She wrapped her arms around herself. "His head."

"Was he moving?"

She shook her head. "No."

"Then most likely he's dead. Or will be when the Fascists find him. I'm sorry." He didn't know what else to say. He didn't know what to do, and he hoped Charles would return soon. What was taking him so long? "But I can go back after dark."

He took his blanket, dirty and smelling of sweat and campfire, and wrapped it around her shoulders. "I'm sorry this is all I have."

"Thank you."

"Can I ask you something? Why are you wearing that?"

"Oh, it's . . . it's my wedding dress. I had this crazy notion this morning . . . as a final good-bye." She brushed her hair from her face. "It was stupid, I know. But I can't . . . I can't wait."

Before he could stop her, the woman climbed from the trench and darted back the way she came. The blanket flapped from her shoulders—making the biggest target possible.

Philip had no choice but to follow.

The automobile's motor still ran. The back wheels remained on the road, but the front had slid off the side into a sheared-off tree. The woman had climbed back into the passenger seat and scrunched low, attempting to stay out of line of the shooter— wherever he happened to be hiding.

Philip repositioned his rifle on his shoulder and scanned the rolling field across the roadway. Though no sign indicated it was any different from the opposite side, Philip knew it was enemy territory. He reached the automobile and opened the driver's door, the bottom of it catching in the stony ground. Reaching his hand around to turn off the engine, he let his eyes fall on the driver. A Spanish man, about Philip's own age. His face had turned powder gray, and blood trickled down his forehead. But that was only a flesh wound. A larger gash beneath the spot was already swelling, and Philip guessed he'd hit the steering wheel hard. The worst wound, however, was a gaping hole in the man's neck, seeping blood down his shoulder. That was the bullet that killed him.

"We've gotta go. There's nothing I can do for him." Shots rang out up the road, and Philip scanned the hills. Whoever shot this fellow had moved on—though it made no sense why he would.

The woman held the man's hand between her own. "No, he's still alive; I can feel his pulse."

"That's not possible, ma'am." Philip took the man's other limp hand from his side. He search for the vein, then closed his eyes. There was a slight pulse.

"See? I told you."

Philip quickly slid his poncho off and covered the man. Then he took off his outer shirt, ripped it into the strips, and wrapped it around the wound to help with the bleeding. With a loud sigh, he slung the rifle over his shoulder and crouched, sliding his arms under the man's legs and around his back. Thankfully, the man was light.

His eyes locked on the woman's. "Go on ahead—back to the trenches. Wait there."

"No, I'm staying with you."

"Ma'am." He tugged on the man, feeling the full weight of his body, and winced. "Go back . . . and tell Charles to send for a medic."

With a look of resignation she obeyed, lifting her dress to her knees and sprinting ahead, the blanket again flapping behind her like a cape.

Philip moved as fast as he could, despite the heaviness of the limp body in his arms. He tried to imagine the man as the medicine ball he used to run with . . . imagine he raced on the track toward the finish line . . . picture Attis running beside him, and his father on the sidelines cheering him on.

He also tried to pretend the sound of gunfire echoing in his ears was the starter gun in a race. Only this one sounded again and again and again.

Two medics ran to the man's side in a matter of minutes, hoisting him out of the trench and rushing him back, away from the front lines.

"Where are they taking him?" The woman shivered beside him, and Philip again wished he had more than his dirty blanket to offer her.

"Back to the ambulance waiting behind the lines, then to the field hospital. Don't worry, miss, he'll be well taken care of. Now . . . we just need to figure out what to do with you."

Charles blew in his hands and smiled at the lady. "So again . . . what are you doing here?"

The woman's eyes darted from Charles's face to Philip's. "I'm a war correspondent. A . . . photographer." She clutched her satchel closer to her chest. "We were headed for France and took the wrong turn."

"I'll say." Charles snorted, then his face softened. "You're a photographer? Why, you are the prettiest one I know."

Philip wanted to slug him, to tell him to leave the poor woman alone. He shoved Charles's shoulder, putting some space between him and the woman, and hoping Charles got the message to shut his trap.

"And you, sir, are quite charming for someone who looks as if he hasn't seen the light of day in weeks."

She turned to Philip, and he noted fear in her eyes despite her brave front. "You're coming with me . . . taking me back . . . to wherever it's safe, right?"

"Yes, ma'am—"

"Sofía . . . Sophie, actually."

"Yes, Sophie. I promise to stay by your side until you're safe." Then he took her hand in his own and said a silent prayer.

212

Sophie pulled the blanket tighter around her shoulders and focused her attention on keeping up with the tall soldier before her. An American soldier, no less. How God had managed that one didn't cease to amaze her.

It was dark when they reached the small cottage, which appeared more like a boulder on the sloping hillside. A young boy in a long, dingy nightshirt opened the door and held a lantern to Sophie's face. The glow warmed her cheeks.

"Hola, amigo," the tall, blond soldier said. "I found this lady in a broken-down jeep. A driver was taking her to the French border. He's been taken to the field hospital. Tomorrow we can think of how to help her. For tonight, can you give her a place to sleep?"

The Spanish family welcomed them inside. To her surprise, the scent of Gauloises—expensive French cigarettes—met her as she entered. The smell reminded her of burning tar, and she noted a short, wide stub bouncing in the lips of a white-haired gentleman sitting before a crackling fire. The cigarettes must have been a gift, no doubt from a patriotic Frenchman passing through.

When Sophie first arrived in France, she'd adored the French shade of blue on the cigarette's package. It was the perfect shade to paint the Atlantic Ocean at sunset. How odd then, to discover the scent here, of all places. Wherever here was. How odd to think about painting and about her trip across the sea into France. It seemed like another lifetime. Like a fine coat she used to wear and admire but that no longer fit.

The soldier who'd rescued her talked with the woman in the kitchen. Sophie was too weary to follow their conversation. She watched as he reached into his pocket and pulled out some cigarettes, offering them to the woman. She took them and nodded.

Sophie felt the eyes of the family on her. She smiled, then turned her attention to the rolling hills outside the window. In the fading sunlight, the frozen world outside reminded her of Cézanne's chromatic art, in which the trees and sky outside the window had been muted and shaped with structural firmness and order.

"Sí, she can stay," Sophie heard the woman saying. "Poor

dear, so much has happened. Look at her, like a puppy thrown out in the cold."

The woman approached and lifted Sophie's satchel. Her eyebrows rose at its weight. "Come, *señorita*. Let's get you settled for the night."

"Yes, thank you." Sophie rose, glancing out the window one last time. Even the sky appeared muted and lifeless. The view beyond the glass reflected how she felt inside.

A warm hand touched her arm, and she turned her head to see the soldier's kind eyes studying her.

"I'll be back to check on you tomorrow. Then we'll make a plan."

"Thank you." She took her hand in his. "If you hadn't been there to help . . ."

He shrugged. "I'm glad I was. Will you be okay until I return?"

"Yes, I'm sure they'll take good care of me." She squeezed his hand and released it.

The handsome soldier turned to leave.

"Wait." She reached her hand toward him. "I never asked your name."

"Philip."

Though he smiled, she saw a deep sadness in his eyes that made her heart ache even more.

"My name, ma'am, is Philip."

Chapter Twenty-Five

Gott Mit Uns.
God with us.

Nazi slogan

Steam rose from the tin cup of coffee given to each of the men who prepared for the night hike over the Pyrenees. Deion took a sip and wrinkled his nose, deciding the only thing it offered was warmth. His thoughts drifted back to Paris.

From the moment members of the French committee met them, it was as if he were playing a part in one of those Hollywood pictures. Staying in a hotel room overlooking the Seine. Heading out with the men to find girls to dance with in the fancy French clubs. Walking by the Cathedral of Notre Dame and Place de la Concorde.

Yet while those memories were of exotic Paris, other things made even more of an impression—sharing a suite with men from four different countries. And the Parisians who greeted him with a smile and didn't seem to notice the color of his skin.

The coffee finished, he blew on his hands, warming them, remembering his fear at entering a café and seeing only white faces. His heart pounding, he'd taken three quick steps backward, out the door—only to have the waiter come after him and welcome him inside.

In the glow of the moon, Deion looked at the white faces of the other men and realized none of them knew how much their acceptance warmed him—even more than the coffee had.

Though the voices around him spoke in hushed tones, Deion could make out numerous different languages. And somehow, being on this side of the ocean—receiving this type of welcome—he suddenly believed anything was possible. Though he'd personally never set foot in Germany, Jesse Owens had won four gold medals on this continent—a black man winning in Nazi territory. Deion looked forward to achieving something even greater—freedom for a class of people who'd been oppressed far too long.

"Methinks this is a bigger deal than I first imagined," said a man with light hair and a thick moustache, tossing a knapsack over his shoulders.

Deion cocked his head back and peered up at the dark mountains. "Yup, it's gonna be some sorta night of climbing, all right."

"Not that, lad. The other day I caught up with the latest in the headlines. Twenty thousand Moroccans, Spanish legionnaires, German and Italian Fascist forces—all putting in their best fight. They have Madrid under siege day and night. On our side, citizens building barricades and volunteers filling the front lines. There's not enough equipment to go around, so they take up the rifles of the dead. . . ."

The man's voice trailed off, and Deion noticed three men in dark trousers, black jackets, and berets approaching. Most likely their hiking guides.

Deion turned to his companion. "Which means the people needs us more than ever, don't they? Because how I see it, they face an even bigger mountain than we do tonight. One that can't be tackled with climbin' shoes and rope."

One guide stepped forward, motioning them to circle around. "Men, this is a great obstacle that already has cost us many lives. You will precede upward, two abreast. Keep track of the man in front of you. If you stop for some reason and lose sight of him, consider yourself dead. And if for some reason you are stopped, we are a group on holiday, on a night hike. Whatever you do, don't lose the trail. Two wrong steps in any direction, and you'll find yourself taking your first—and last—Spanish flight."

With those encouraging words, the line moved upward. The first incline was a soft rolling hill, and despite the fact he'd done mostly sitting on a ship during the last few weeks, Deion didn't even get winded. The next hill rose sharper, into the night sky. His legs ached. *At least Spain will be on the other side,* he reminded himself.

Yet as he crested the hill, Spain was yet to be seen. Instead another, even steeper, incline rose before them. Rocks tumbled down on his head, kicked off by the men ahead of him. Deion's own feet cast more onto the men below.

As they climbed, Deion and his new Scottish friend—whose name, he learned, was Ian—chatted about their lives, their families back home, and their involvement in the Party. But as the night wore on, and the hills never seemed to end, their words became few. Soon, their only interaction involved lifting each other up when one stumbled, and pausing just long enough to brush the other off and prod him on.

To keep his aching legs moving forward, Deion replayed the talks he'd heard at the various meetings.

"Two people cannot occupy the same space. Two beliefs the same mind. Two armies the same victory," the speaker had said the night before Deion sailed away. "As one rival becomes more powerful, his advantage grows over his competitor. And the other rival moves down the same curve."

As Deion took note of the men around them, giving their energy and forcing their bodies forward with sheer will, he felt as if their advantage grew with each step. The people of Spain had given the call, and the world responded. With dedicated volunteers like these entering the country night after night, how could they not win?

As Ritter strode from the briefing room toward the airfield, he glanced at the Spanish pilots lounging in their wrinkled uniforms and scoffed.

"¡*Buenos dias, senor!*" one pilot said.

Ritter tipped his chin in response. Another bearded man searched his pockets for a cigarette, then motioned to Ritter, as if asking for a smoke. Ritter ignored his unspoken request and continued on.

Even after months of working with the Germans, these men —who called themselves pilots—still had no inclination for regimentation. Some were simply ungovernable. The more he worked around the Spaniards, the more Ritter believed that having Franco control the lot would be in the best interest of the whole accursed country.

If these are the educated pilots, what is the rest of Spain like?

Ritter didn't even want to consider the peasants who fought for their right to govern themselves. Poor saps. Did the people of Spain not realize it was his duty to save them from themselves? Authority, power, and a centralized identity made Germany great. The Spanish people needed the same.

Thankfully, the Germans worked to provide just that. Even this morning, in the operations room, brilliant strategists had sat in their leather-covered armchairs, studying maps on the wall and piles of information that dealt with everything from weather and intelligence summaries to updates on the planes and pilots. Only then, with all the information before them, did they mark their plans on the blackboard. Spain should be thankful for such diligence.

Ritter strode past the fat-bellied Junkers bearing black-red-and-white swastikas on their wings, toward his bi-plane fighter. Glancing up, he noted the perfect "bomber's sky"—a sky cleaned by a slight enough breeze to clear smoke from the target and a thin splattering of clouds to provide the right mix of visibility and cover.

Within a matter of minutes Ritter was in the air, gazing down at the mountains that loomed into view and the symmetrical stripes of farmland beyond them. Though the land appeared tame, the same could not be said of the people.

Rebels, the whole lot of them, who fight for freedom yet don't realize their own lack of self-regimentation will bring them anything but.

After a short flight, he circled in a birdlike arc around the bombing area and thought of what he'd heard last night on Red radio. It still made his face burn with anger. The excited announcer had claimed German fighters were losing air superiority over the Spanish capital as new Russian planes filled the skies. While Ritter didn't deny the Russian planes were faster, he instead turned his focus on the Germans' superior tactics.

Any man can maneuver a great plane, but it takes a great man to use an ordinary plane for greatness.

Last week, the general's order had been to engage the enemy fighters until the Reds were low on fuel. Then, as the Russian aircraft landed at their bases to refuel, Sperrle's bombers—which had been circling the battle at a high altitude—dove in on the Red bases. The plan had been a success, and more enemy planes were lost that day than in all the prior weeks in air combat.

But today the Germans fought a different war. On the Loas Rozas de Madrid, a major supply route to the north, panzer tanks rolled toward the Red-held lines. A two-hour artillery barrage had already pounded the enemy; now it would be Ritter's He.51—and the others with him—that would strafe key points of resistance. And when Ritter and the others were done, the panzers would roll in, followed by the infantry marching in to secure the ground the tanks had already taken.

So far, so good.

Ritter swept closer to the ground, preparing to strafe the troops scurrying to help those injured in the bombing. His hand wrapped around the machine gun trigger.

Just then an explosion sounded in his ears. His plane rocked wildly. He scanned the gauges as the left engine sputtered and the plane dropped fast. He'd been hit . . . by antiaircraft most likely.

With quick movements, Ritter swung around, determined to make it back across the lines to safety . . . but he patted his pocket for his false papers, just in case.

Father Manuel raised his hands to welcome the small congregation of the faithful. He'd thought about his words. Rehearsed them. Yet seeing the faces before him, he wondered again if they should be spoken at all. He glanced to the place were Armando used to sit. Many other faces were missing from the pews as well. Manuel lowered his head, pausing, questioning if what he'd heard in the early hours of morning had truly been from God. Then again, who was he to question? He opened his mouth and drew a deep breath.

"As you know, friends, Spain is a land of deep religious belief. We have as many saints as olive groves. Churches rise from the ashes of cathedrals. Then they are burned as disillusionment blinds the people again. This should not be the case, my brothers."

His voice grew in volume as an inner strength prodded him on. "I urge you to stop and look around. How can you trust in the idea of a better Basque nation if you act just like those you fight against? Consider again if what we wish to uphold so dear to us is the tradition of men? Or rather, do you fight for the living God?"

The people listened intently, yet he could not tell if his words made any difference. Even as the Mass finished and they filed out of the sanctuary, he questioned his motives.

After the room had nearly emptied, Sister Joséfina approached him with a smile. "Hello, Padre." Her voice was as singsong when she spoke as it was the moments he found himself privileged to hear the daybreak chant of Lauds or the nuns' worship hymns during the traditional Mass.

"Father, I appreciate your words. As we both know, during times like these we must serve God in ways we had not known before . . . which brings me to the nature of my request."

Her eyes locked on his with steadfastness, but he also noticed the quick way her hands moved over the rosary beads she held close to her heart.

"Padre, I wonder if you know where we could get more help? The hospital is overflowing. There are more dead than people to bury them, and—while the nuns would never say so— they are becoming weary from their labors, especially our older Sisters."

Something stirred within Father Manuel's chest, and he gazed up at the image on the wall. An image of Jesus on His knees before His disciples. And another painting of Christ walking among the crowds. Father Manuel appreciated the large paintings far more than the statue of the gaunt Christ suspended on the Cross hanging before the altar. Viewing the paintings representing Christ's care for the people, Father Manuel felt an inner confirmation that it *was* God's voice that had spoken to him during the morning hours. He also knew *he* was the one to fill the Sister's request.

"I'll come, Sister. Tonight."

Surprise registered on Sister Joséfina's face. "Oh, Padre, I did not mean you. If there is another . . ."

"Sister, if the Lord rolled up His sleeves to wash the feet of His disciples, if He—though weary and misunderstood—reached out a hand toward the sick and dying, I should do no less. I'll be there tonight. Do not question me."

"Yes, Padre. I understand." A soft smile filled her face. "I'll tell the Sisters whom to expect."

Dusk had gathered without Father Manuel perceiving it. Outside, snow had transformed their town into a white, frozen world.

As he approached the Carmelite convent, he realized it bustled with noise so different from the months and years prior. The private world of the nuns was now limited to the chapel and small wings where they slept, but the ground and two upper floors were filled with beds. And the beds overflowed with injured men.

Father Manuel knocked at the door, and Sister Joséfina welcomed him in. Her face appeared pale, even in the glow of the lantern in her hand.

"Sister, what is wrong?"

"There are too many to care for . . . they come too fast."

"Injured soldiers?"

"No, dead ones. Mother Superior refuses to let them be put into the ground without being washed. Without prayer. But the task—" She shivered. "The worse ones are those who expire during an operation. When they come, their bodies are still warm . . . and to touch them . . ."

Father Manuel followed the woman down the narrow hallway, and while he knew a few hundred wounded men had been brought to the convent, he hadn't thought much about those who died in the care of the two dozen nuns, five surgeons, and lay nurses.

"What other duties do you have?"

"Oh, I don't mind the cleaning, or even caring for the men. It's just the dead—not knowing the state of their souls when they passed. My favorite task has been sitting on the roof scanning the sky for enemy planes. Even though it has been cold lately, it is a great time to talk with the Lord as I watch."

"And have you seen any planes?"

"No. Well, once I saw a speck in the distance, but later realized it must have been a bird. But the fighting has picked up around our Basque front lines. And though I know we are not supposed to hate, Padre, I do feel those emotions rising within. Witnessing the shredded bodies and knowing someone caused that on purpose—I just can't imagine the type of demon who would do such a thing."

Without waiting for a response, Sister Joséfina opened the door and swept her hand across the room, as if emphasizing her point. Bodies of men, shrouded with white sheets, crowded the floor of the room.

"And my task?" Father Manuel swallowed hard, trying to hold back the emotion filling his chest.

"To prepare them for burial. Wash away the dirt and blood from the battlefield; fold the arms. I will hurry back with warm water and a towel."

Father Manuel nodded, seeing relief in the woman's face. Tonight the task would not be hers.

She hurried away, and Manuel fell to his knees, lifting his

hands in the air. "Oh, God of mercy, how You desire to rescue the people from their sin. When will we learn, O Lord, to end our destructive ways? When will we fight for Your cause and not our own? When will we strive to save lives of our brothers instead of destroy them?"

He opened his eyes and dared to pull back the sheet, revealing the face of the young man beneath. He was younger than Manuel expected—no more than a boy. His peaceful face looked as if he slept, and the only sign of injury was the jagged scar that crossed his abdomen. It had been an attempt at mending the lad. A failed attempt. A reminder to Father Manuel that though men fight their wars, and others try to mend those broken in the process, it was the Lord who determined the span of their lives.

And the end of their days.

Chapter Twenty-Six

No por mucho madrugar amanece más temprano.

Waking up earlier won't make the sun rise any quicker.

Spanish proverb

Sophie awoke to the sound of knocking at the door of the small cottage and the tall American soldier's voice speaking her name. She could hear the Spanish woman welcoming him, offering the seat by the fire for him to warm himself.

Sophie dressed quickly and hurried into the kitchen, pleased to be greeted by his smiling face.

"You look well. Uh, better than yesterday." The solider removed his helmet, revealing his light hair.

"Oh, I hope so." She studied the man's features, surprised at how different he looked. He'd bathed—and smelled much better than yesterday—and the bearded shadow had disappeared, revealing a small cleft in his chin.

"My friend, José. Have you heard? Is he doing okay?"

"I checked this morning. He made it to the first-aid center. I assume they performed surgery there. But I'm sorry; I know little else." The soldier accepted a tin cup of coffee handed to him by the Spanish woman. She glanced back and forth as they spoke, seemingly confused by their English. She watched as Philip drank.

"*Gracias, señora.*" He took another sip and smiled. Then he turned back to Sophie. "If it's okay with you, we need to leave soon. Our commander has asked to see you."

"Your commander?"

"Yes, ma'am. American press isn't seen too much in these parts."

Sophie ran her fingers through her hair. "Yes, of course. Give me a few minutes."

She returned to the small room and took a deep breath, wondering what to expect. Surely, they'd kick her out of the country if they discovered her lie. Could people be hanged for such trickery? Maybe they'd even accuse her of being a spy.

"Dang you, Walt," she muttered under her breath as she repacked the last of her things. "Just look what you've gotten me into."

A small gray truck pulled to a stop in front of the cottage and beeped its horn. Sophie thanked the Spanish woman and smiled as Philip graciously opened the truck door for her and helped her inside.

Once on the road, there were few other vehicles in sight. Motor-lorries passed with provisions for the troops on the front lines. Smoke and flames from the distant fighting tinted the air with an eerie haze. Every now and then she heard an explosion in the distance, but so far no planes had flown overhead, dropping their bombs. She'd be thankful if she never saw another plane in her life.

Sophie noticed that the villages they passed were heavily guarded by men who appeared to have stepped out of Goya paintings. She pulled out her sketchbook, jotting shaky notes about their white billowing shirts with red neckties and bandoliers full of cartridges. Most militiamen also sported red badges with the name of a local committee. All lounged on the road or leaned against their sandbag barricades, perking up as the car approached.

After about ten minutes, the driver stopped the car at a roadblock. Sophie's heart pounded as she noted the Spanish guard on the side of the road with a rifle swung over his shoulder.

He looked past the driver to her, and his pencil-thin moustache twitched slightly as he eyed her.

"Where is your pass?" His dark eyes showed no friendliness.

She handed her press card to the guard. The driver also produced his papers. With a grunt, the Spaniard handed them both back. Without warning, his face cracked in a grin.

"Comrades, it is not easy to find dinner. All meals are rationed. But you are in luck. My family owns a small café inside this village. I welcome you as our guests."

The driver pulled into town.

"Are you sure this is safe?" Philip questioned.

"*Sí*, the people's houses are used for the militia, as are their food and wine," the driver said, passing in front of the café. "Although I have to admit this is the first time I've been welcomed inside. You must have impressed them, *señorita*."

Sophie's gut knotted with nervousness about facing the commander, and she longed to ask if they could just continue on when she spotted the group sitting in front of a café eating tortillas. Steam from the warm bread rose in the biting air. Her knotted stomach relaxed enough to growl.

They entered the café, and she noticed another group of soldiers inside. Sophie thought their accents sounded Russian.

Many peasants lined the bar, and their eyes turned to Sophie when they entered.

The driver leaned close to Sophie's ear. "It's a big event to have foreigners in their midst, especially women . . . and especially women who have come to help their cause."

"But I . . ."

Her words were cut off by a man hurrying toward her. "*Señorita*, come; I must tell you my story. My brother and I have killed twenty Fascists ourselves from this small village." He slid his fingers across his throat. "The priest and lawyer. The rich landowners." He beamed. "Well, of course, we did not do it ourselves. We assisted the soldiers when they came here. We showed them where our enemies hid, and they arrested them, then killed them."

Sophie's stomach lurched. *A priest? They killed their priest?*

She turned to Philip. "Why are they telling me this?"

He placed a hand on Sophie's back. "Your press badge. They believe you will put them in the American newspapers. They feel they are heroes for rooting out the Fascists in their midst." Sophie could see in Philip's eyes that he too was troubled.

They ate as quickly as possible, then left, to the disappointment of the villagers who continued to fill the small café to overflowing. Soon the truck pulled in to the farmhouse that served as the commander's headquarters.

Philip led Sophie inside. She crossed her arms before her, hoping to hide her trembling hands.

The commander sat in the farmhouse kitchen. The scarred wooden table before him held a radio and stacks of papers. He rose as she approached. "Miss Grace, welcome. It is not every day we have an American journalist in our midst. Do you plan to stay long?"

"Actually, I was leaving the country—heading back to France —when we had a most unfortunate accident. Philip, here"—she swept an arm in his direction—"saved my life, and that of my friend, José. Do you know how he is?"

"*Sí*, last I heard he was taken from the first-aid station to a hospital farther back in the lines. He's still alive."

Sophie blew out a breath she didn't realize she'd been holding.

"But back to you, Miss Grace. The International Brigades are wondering if you'd reconsider. We have volunteers, you see, from all over the world, coming to fight for our cause. Yet . . ." He leaned forward, resting his elbows on the table before him, looking intensely into her gaze. "We need so much more—funds, weapons, volunteers. Perhaps your photography could be used to draw sympathy to our cause."

"My photography . . . yes, of course."

"Good, we will start with the field hospital. Once we get the photos we need, we will be happy to help you find a way out of Spain."

"Photos at the field hospital?" Sophie strode forward and extended her hand, feigning confidence. "Yes, sir. That is something I can do." She glanced toward the soldier standing beside her. "And what about Philip?"

The commander stood and stretched a hand toward the tall, blond soldier, giving him a firm pat on his back. "You've read my mind. I wish for him to stay, of course. For your protection. You can be sure that anyone offering help to our cause in such a public way is sure to be a target of the enemy."

Sophie shivered slightly at his words, but the thought of Philip by her side was reassuring. Still, she wondered what he thought about it. After all, he hadn't planned on leaving the front lines.

She looked to see his reaction, and noted his slightly furrowed eyebrows. For a second she thought he was going to decline the request.

Instead he offered the commander a quick nod. "If it's helping the war effort, sir, I'd be glad to stay. Just as long as I know I'm doing my part."

"That you are, son," the commander said, leading them into the fading light. "That goes for both of you."

As delicately as if she were pulling out a Ming vase, Sophie removed Michael's camera from its bag. The Leica was Michael's treasure. Holding it was like holding his hand once more. At night when she drifted off to sleep, she dreamed that it wasn't truly Michael who'd lain dead on the pavement. But now, with this camera in her hand, her doubt evaporated. Michael had journeyed to the one place where he wasn't allowed to take it with him. Though, Sophie guessed, he most likely put up quite an argument with Saint Peter about that fact.

Thankfully, she'd taken a few photography classes and had learned enough from watching Michael that she hoped for a few exceptional photos—or at least some good enough for the commander to find her a ride to France. There she'd retrieve her things, and maybe even look up the small cottage Michael had purchased for her. After that, she'd decide how to live next.

As Sophie gently cleaned the camera's lens, she realized she was doing it again—remembering Michael without including thoughts of Maria or their relationship. It was easier that way. The grief felt cleaner, though, she'd be the first to admit, it was built on lies.

Sophie lifted the viewfinder to her eye and looked through it at the young man in the bed closest to her. She focused on his bandaged face, keeping the rows of beds beyond him out of focus. When developed, she hoped the image would appear as surreal as she felt. As if the pain of one man stood alone, no matter how many others suffered with him.

Having Philip beside her brought her a sense of comfort. Maybe it was the peace she sensed in the American soldier's eyes, despite the conflict all around them.

"How did so many foreigners end up here?" she asked him, referring to Spain as well as to the makeshift hospital. She'd come for love, and her mind couldn't even begin to fathom another purpose strong enough to compete with that.

Not that love had made any difference for her.

"These guys are volunteers. Americans from New York, Chicago. All over, I suppose. Others are from all over the globe —Poland, Germany, Holland, Scotland, you name it. They've come to help the people hold their country from the Fascists."

Sophie moved to the next bed and focused on the man's bandaged hand. Blood seeped through, the crimson flow refusing to be stanched. She tried to talk to the man in Spanish and English, but the injured man shook his head, understanding neither.

"Abraham Lincoln," Philip stated flatly.

"What was that?" She snapped the picture, wound the film, then turned to face him, realizing for the first time how very dark his blue eyes appeared. As deep as the moonless sky had appeared the first night she'd seen the Pyrenees Mountains from the train window.

"The name of our English-speaking battalion. Symbolic of our freedom fight."

"The Abraham Lincoln Battalion. Interesting." Though a thousand questions filled her mind about the quest of these Americans, Sophie snapped the photos in silence, then hastily retreated to the bathroom where red cellophane had been taped around the sole lightbulb for her use.

Would they turn out? Or would these prints prove her deception?

When the photos were developed, Sophie's tears came. Tears

she'd managed to hold at bay since yesterday's accident. Tears for José and for the danger she'd been in. Then old, bottled-up tears for Michael. And for his stupidity. And for the realization that if he were here he'd be able to accomplish what she'd failed to do.

Philip must have heard her sobs through the solid wooden door, because he knocked, then entered cautiously.

"I'm sorry. I tried." She motioned to the prints strung across the room, drying. "But it's no use. These black-and-white pictures take the blood out of the pain. They seem flat, lifeless." *Just like my soul . . .* she wanted to add.

"Sophie, these will work." Philip leaned closer to take a better look. "Surely, people will see the pain in these images. Their hearts will be able to see the color their eyes cannot."

"That's it." Sophie rose and moved toward the door, and she motioned for Philip to follow. "Red paint. Blue. Black. And a green as sharp as the new grass in spring. All the colors. I need canvases, too."

"What are you talking about?" Philip scratched his head.

"I don't know why I didn't think of it before." She looked at Michael's camera again, understanding that he could have captured the drama of the hospital, even in black-and-white. Yet she was a painter. And in order to earn her ride out of the country, she'd paint images that would bring the most uncaring Wall Street businessman to tears.

Excitement built in her as she remembered the images plastered all over Madrid. The posters called out to the illiterate nation, urging them to resist Fascism and defend the Republic. They encouraged international solidarity.

In her mind's eye, she remembered one of the last posters she'd spotted on the door of a factory shop—an image of a war-impoverished family standing against the backdrop of their burning village. The woman leaned against her husband's frame. He wore no shirt and his hands were open, palms forward, reminding Sophie of Paul Gauguin's yellow-skinned Christ. If illustrations could do that for the common people of Spain, what about the common people in New York? or Boston? Would they rally to help the cause?

She returned the camera to her satchel, not understanding why this idea hadn't come to her sooner. She had dozens of pencil sketches from Madrid that she could bring to life . . . and these men . . . maybe even the battlefield.

Sophie laughed and gave Philip a quick embrace. "Seriously, I need paint and canvas. I need your help. I know a way to stir help for our cause. . . ."

Chapter Twenty-Seven

If you don't have a plan for yourself,
you'll be part of someone else's.

American proverb

The fierce shivering of Ritter's body woke him from a troubled sleep. How many days and nights had he been exposed to the elements? He tried to sit, but pain shot up his leg. He glanced down and cringed, noticing the bruising and swelling around his ankle. It was broken, he knew it. Just his luck.

The plane had fallen quicker than he ever imagined it could, hitting a steep hillside and sliding down, finally catching in the trees. Though smoke had poured from the engine, there was no fire. He'd managed to climb from the wreckage, nearly passing out from the pain. Not only did his leg throb, but pains shooting through his chest made it hard to breathe. His fingers gently prodded his ribs; then he pulled them back as the pain increased with the slightest touch. Broken ribs too . . . what a fine mess.

After climbing down to solid ground, he half-crawled toward a small cluster of trees, planning to use his knife to cut down a branch for a splint. Halfway there, he'd come upon a small cave opening, just large enough for one or two men and offering a wide view of the valley below. A filthy knapsack, mess tin, a cartridge belt of ammunition, even a rifle, proved it was used for such a lookout. Or at least it had been. A thin layer of snow told Ritter no one had used it for at least a few days. Most likely, someone had gone out for the day and been injured or killed, never to return. Maybe Ritter's plane had delivered the fatal wound. Despite the pain, he grinned at the thought.

Too weary and overcome with pain to make it to the trees, he crawled inside and waited to be captured. Or rescued, depending on which side of the lines he'd gone down. Surely someone had seen the plane crash. Or maybe the cold would take him before his injuries did. . . .

In his fitful sleep, Ritter dreamt he was back in Berlin, marrying Isanna in a winter wedding as he'd planned. He awoke to a clacking jaw and numb fingers. Curse the fool who'd told him he'd be home by Christmas.

Yet one, two, maybe three days had passed and nobody had come, which only meant one thing. He needed to find a way out. Struggling, he took off his outer shirt, then removed the undershirt underneath and tore it into strips. Then he half-crawled, half-dragged himself to the closest tree. Removing his knife from his belt, he sawed away at a small yet sturdy sapling. His numb fingers made the job slow and tedious, but it gave him something to focus on—to forget the cold and pain for a time.

With the cloth from his undershirt, Ritter tied the branches tightly to either side of his leg, forming a strong splint. With that secure, he cut a larger branch with a wide fork and measured it for a crutch. He used the remainder of the undershirt to pad the spot where his armpit rested.

Satisfied with his work, but exhausted, Ritter hobbled back to the cave, the pain nearly causing him to black out. Despite the crisp air, beads of sweat formed on his brow. *Have to get inside . . . have to find food, water.* Especially since the small canteen of water he'd brought from the cockpit was now empty.

Eventually he managed to build a small fire with the supplies the man before him had left. But before he could scrounge around for some type of food, the warmth of the fire caused him to drift off into another fitful sleep.

Dim red light, reminiscent of her favorite Rembrandts, spread over the valley outside the cottage window. It was a lonely view, but lovely just the same. Olive trees and loose stone walls as far as the eye could see.

Sophie watched as a young woman strolled down the street toward a well, a bucket swinging in her hand. A soldier was already there, washing his feet in the cold running water. They chatted briefly, and the girl blushed; then they both turned as the sounds of an aerial dogfight overhead drew their attention. The planes were close enough that watchers on the ground could appreciate their battle—but far enough away to still feel safe.

She sighed, appreciating the contours of the Spanish countryside. Sad that they had no place in her painting of Madrid's dark, sharp images after an aerial attack—slightly muted as if a layer of dust still hung in the air.

Sophie dabbed her brush on the palette and stroked it across the canvas, satisfied she'd mixed the correct shade of brown-red, reminiscent of the bricks that made up the structures of Madrid. Most were whitewashed, of course, a way to reflect the heat of the sun. Yet when they were broken open—torn apart from the bombs—only then was their true color revealed.

Outside, only a stone's throw from the well, a group of soldiers huddled around a fire that burned with a cherry-colored flame, and Sophie realized the hue of the flame would make a lovely tinge for the scarf wrapped around the woman's head in her painting. Excited by her discovery, she set to work on the woman's form—a small, timid creature caught up in something much greater.

Sophie paused to light the small oil lamp on the side table and glance out the window. Though the front lines were only a few miles away, she hadn't known such peace since arriving in Spain. Painting had something to do with that. She had worked with the children, of course. And had painted one small canvas for José. Yet here she could escape into her thoughts and emotions, allowing the images that had been simmering in her heart to work their magic with her brush.

Yes, Benita was right. Painting is therapy for the soul. . . .

She turned back to the half-finished painting, wondering what the people who saw it would say of her work. Or more important, what they would do. Would her painting cause someone to care a little more deeply about the fight in Spain?

She returned to the stool and picked up her brush once again, taking a deep breath. She loved everything about painting—the smell, the feel, the emotions.

The only thing was, she wondered if Commander Johnson would think her work was worth the risk when she asked if she could stay. . . .

❦

Ritter found two important things as he scrounged around in the dead man's abandoned knapsack. First were canned food rations, which filled his stomach and kept his mind off the pain for a time. Second, the man's journal. Ritter could hardly believe his eyes when he opened it and found it was written in German by a Communist who had escaped a concentration camp and crossed the border to fight in Spain.

"The Thaelmann Battalion," Ritter spat. Then he tucked the journal and the rest of the man's things into the knapsack and stood. His only shot at making it back to Isanna was to climb down this mountain.

He hopped out of the cave, using the crutch to support his weight, and gazed down at the valley below. A cloud of dust caught his attention, and he used the binoculars in the knapsack to take a closer look.

Yes, there was a road . . . and what looked like a small encampment in a cluster of trees. A cold chill rushed over his body as he noted the small flag waving from the camp. A red flag with a white hammer-and-sickle. He had come down on the wrong side. Worse yet, he didn't know which way or how far away the Nationalist lines were.

Ritter slumped against his crutch in defeat, and then a new idea hit him. He already had the paperwork of a German soldier fighting for the Internationals.

He turned and settled back into the cave, removing the journal from the knapsack. One week ago, he would have never thought he'd care so much about knowing the heart of a German Communist. Now his life depended on not only knowing it, but living it.

Four days after receiving art supplies, Sophie presented her first painting to the English commander, along with the photographs she'd taken.

He first looked at the photographs, then turned his eyes to the painting. "The pictures are fine, but this . . ." He held the canvas at arm's length to get a complete view. "This is amazing." He cleared his throat.

The painting wasn't what the commander had asked for, but rather an image imprinted in Sophie's mind from the first bombing she'd witnessed in Madrid. A crumbled building filled the left corner of the canvas, its outer wall peeled away. Clothes and furniture inside the structure were scattered about, looking as if a tornado had hit. Only it wasn't a tornado, but something far worse.

Partly cloudy skies, gloomy and ominous, revealed just a hint of a bomber flying away from the destruction. Almost hidden among the rubble and smoke, two figures huddled in the lower right corner—a young mother with a child limp in her arms. The mother's head tilted upward, peering into the menacing sky—her mouth open, as if a cry of horror had caught in her throat.

Footsteps approached from behind Sophie, and Commander Johnson turned the canvas toward Philip.

"Amazing, I know," Philip said. "She hid away for a few days in a quiet room and emerged with this. Unfortunately, sir, I'm afraid I haven't been of much help in the matter. I question how my friends are doing, and wonder if I might return to the front lines."

His eyes darted to Sophie's. She nodded her head in agreement, and Philip's eyebrow cocked, obviously with surprise.

"Yes, I agree. Philip has done a fine job protecting me, and now he should get his opportunity to serve in the capacity he volunteered for . . . and I should go with him," she said.

"To the front lines?" The commander lowered the canvas onto the table.

"I can use my sketches, paint more of the things that happened in Madrid, but don't you think it would be more effective if the paintings represented what was happening now?" She stood straighter, setting her face with determination. "I wish to stay, Commander. I desire to do this. To bring the war to life, to give it meaning—for those who don't understand."

Commander Johnson leaned back in his chair and stroked his chin. "Yes, I've heard the pen is mightier than the sword, Miss Grace. I suppose the same could be said of the paintbrush."

Sophie turned to Philip.

Instead of smiling, fear radiated from his eyes. "Sophie, I don't think—"

The commander's voice interrupted. "Pack your things, Miss Grace. Philip will escort you on the front. But be warned; it is a dangerous place—even roadways are roamed by snipers. And you can be sure of one thing. If word gets out concerning your work, you too will become a target. The Nationalists have killed many who fight against their cause with the pen and the brush. The fact that you're a woman will not hinder them . . . if anything, it will draw more attention. And attention is the last thing you want on the front lines of war."

Chapter Twenty-Eight

Siembra vientos y recogerás tormentas.
Sow winds and you will reap storms.

Spanish proverb

*T*hough weary from the climb and the train ride across Spain, Deion could hardly sleep more than a few hours without waking to the sound of voices around him. They'd finally arrived at the Albacete base, or what the men referred to as the Grand Hotel, where they would train. Albacete was situated ninety miles southwest of Valencia, the provisional capital of Republican Spain and one hundred miles southeast of Madrid. In addition to all the International volunteers, streams of refugees also entered the city, hoping to find a safe haven.

Deion rolled to his side and rubbed his eyes. The men closest to him were speaking French. He could make out only a few words. Their dress was similar to that of the farmers they'd passed in the fields during their journey through France—also very similar to the field hands back in Mississippi with their white cotton shirts, baggy pants, and suspenders.

Noticing this, Deion jotted down notes to himself about the way they spoke with their hands and leaned close, nearly touching noses as they jabbered. He had never kept a journal in his life, but during the climb, men ahead of him had thrown out their possessions in an effort to lighten their load—blankets, coats, knapsacks, and a journal with a few pages written in a language he couldn't read. Instead of tossing it to the side, Deion kept the man's pages intact and added his own memories and thoughts. Maybe someday he'd find someone who could read the other man's words to him.

Already he'd filled pages with his first memories of Spain. The monastery halfway down the Pyrenees where they'd found refuge, a bed, and a warm meal after the seemingly never-ending hike. The celebration at their arrival. Two Hungarians had kissed each other on the cheeks. An Italian and a Pole had each taken one of Deion's hands and swung him around in a jig.

The truck ride down the narrow donkey trail. Their first days housed in a military barracks at Castillo de San Fernando in Figueras—a small town with hilly streets and white houses and buildings.

The numerous slogans and appeals on the walls.

Spanish men with rifles, who welcomed them with the salute of clenched fists—the People's Front salute. *"Salud, Camaradas!"*

And, of course, the real reason he came—Deion took special note of the refugees escaping the regions occupied by Rebels, glad he could be there to help these people. Their small carts harnessed with mules or donkeys, transporting their meager household goods.

And now, ten days later, their arrival at Albacete, headquarters of the International Brigades of Volunteers.

Fire crackled in the fire pit, causing the men's faces to glow a warm orange color. Two Germans spoke to a group of American Jews in broken English, sharing stories of concentration camps in Germany that sounded bloodier than the stockyards in Chicago. The men had been imprisoned there because of their anti-fascist beliefs, and they displayed their scars like medals.

"Not all Germans are friends with Hitler," one man stated in a heavy accent, as his friend nodded his agreement. "Ve know the cost of going against him. Vat is it you say, conquer or die? *Ja, ja,* ve have approached death. Now ve try to conquer."

"We are on the right side; we'll win for sure," one American stated.

Deion recognized him from the ship, and watched as he gave the German a firm handshake.

"The right side uf the hill?" The German cracked a grin.

"That too, but I meant the right side of the war," the American replied.

"I do not know, lads." A man with a heavy Irish accent approached the small group. "I hear Madrid has fallen, but the officers are afraid to tell us."

"That's a lie." The American planted his hands on his hips. "Franco has claimed that a few times before. In November the newspapers even reported that he rode down the Gran Via on a white stallion." He nudged Deion. "What do you think?"

"Me?" Deion straightened his shoulders, realizing again things were different here. "They've said the same thing before. All lies. And not only that. Once we secure Republican Spain, we can go on to fight other battles. Maybe even back home! Look at us. I never knew so many would volunteer for the same fight."

"I hear there are twenty thousand volunteers now. Four thousand through these gates between Christmas and New Year alone," one of the Germans stated.

The numbers passed down the lines, in various languages, and excitement stirred among the men. Soon the Germans took it upon themselves to display their commitment and gathered into a long line, breaking out in song. "We do not fear the thunder of the cannon! We do not fear the Nazi police!" they sang.

Not to be outdone, a Frenchman called to the others, "Let's sing 'Le Jeune Garde'!"

Deion couldn't understand the words, but one of the other Americans translated. "We are the young guard. We are the bodyguard of the future," they sang.

Finally the British followed with one of their popular labor songs, a song Deion knew well.

We meet today in Freedom's cause,
And raise our voices high;

We'll battle here in union strong
To conquer or to die.

Deion had sung it many times himself at union meetings, and he felt more at home as he heard it. With a smile, he added those words to his journal too. Just as he finished writing, the men were asked to line up.

"Cooks?" an officer called.

A few men raised their hands.

"Riders?" he called next.

A few more did the same.

Deion leaned close to a dark-haired man beside him. "I don't understand. What is he doing?"

"Typists?" the clerk called, jotting down the names of men who stepped forward.

"They are identifying the recruits and registering them," the Jewish man answered.

"Officers?"

"But I have no training in these things. They told me we'd be trained." Deion felt his heartbeat quicken, wondering if he'd misunderstood all along.

"Do not worry, my friend." The man patted his back. "Most reply according to their ambitions rather than ability."

"Machine gunners?" the clerk called.

"In that case, I've always wanted to learn how to drive a truck. . . ."

And when the clerk called for drivers, Deion lifted his hand high.

Large bomb craters, pieces of scattered equipment, even a burned-out tank littered the sides of the road as the truck carried Sophie and Philip to the front lines. Yet as the truck slowly rumbled through a rough spot in the roadway, something about the pile of rags on the side didn't seem right to Sophie.

"Wait!" she called to the driver. "It's a soldier, over there to the left."

"You're right." Philip leaned closer to her side, peering out the window to get a better look.

The driver slowed, and the man's face lifted. Under his light hair, his face seemed to be drained of color. With wide eyes, he lifted his hand and waved some type of crutch.

The driver's hands tightened around the steering wheel. "I don't know. It could be a trap. I see a rifle."

As if hearing the driver's words, the soldier lifted the rifle and tossed it before him. Then, reaching into his jacket pocket, he waved a small red armband in the air, similar to those worn by Party members on the streets of Madrid.

The driver stopped the truck and stepped out. Philip opened the passenger side door. His eyes focused on Sophie's. "You stay here. And if anything happens, you leave us and drive until you get to safety, understand?"

Sophie nodded, though she had no intention of leaving them . . . even if she *did* know how to drive.

The driver and Philip leaned over the man, who removed some type of identification from his pocket and showed it to them. They conversed for a minute longer, then moved to either side, carrying him to the vehicle. Sophie scooted closer to where the driver sat to make room.

"*Gracias, señorita.*" His eyes appeared weary.

Sophie could tell by his accent and his features that he was German.

The driver climbed in, and Philip did the same. Philip turned sideways on his seat, partly against the door, to give the man as much room as possible.

"He was on lookout in the hills when the bombers hit days ago. The blast from a stray bomb knocked him down a small cliff. He's been struggling to make it to the road ever since." Philip shook his head in awe, refocusing the conversation from Sophie to the man between them.

"I'm not sure how you made it this long, *comrade*. Ritter, right? It appears you had quite the break."

"During the climb over the Pyrenees, one of our companions

had a similar break after a fall. I—" He paused as the driver started to turn the truck around. "Wait, you have supplies you are delivering to the lines, correct? You must do this first, and then take me back. The men, they are in need of these things."

"Are you kidding? The road's too rough. Besides, the supplies are few." The driver glanced at Sophie. "These two are my main delivery, and I'm sure they don't mind."

"Of course we don't mind. What's another day?" she said, hoping they couldn't sense her disappointment. More than anything, she longed to take in the men and activity on the front lines. Though she was sure she'd never be allowed in the heat of battle, she itched to get out her paints and capture some of the soldiers' world just the same.

"*Gracias,*" the injured man said again. "And can you tell me, friends, how are we holding? Last I heard the enemy tanks had taken a lot of ground."

The driver scoffed. "Then you heard wrong, my friend." His voice rose with excitement. "They thought they had us, they did! The German tanks don't stand a chance with the Russian T-26s. It's like a dolphin facing a shark—they both look the same, but only one has bite."

The truck hit a bump, and the man grasped his leg and let out a low moan. "They are really that impressive?" he asked, as if trying to take his mind off the pain.

"Oh, yes," Philip said, jumping into the conversation. "I saw one up close—you should see the 45-mm cannon mounted on the turret. It can pivot 360 degrees. I've never seen anything like it."

The man drifted off in a fitful, pain-induced sleep as they drove back the way they'd come. As he slept, his head lolled back and forth until Sophie sat up straighter and moved it to her shoulder. With a sigh, the man nestled in, for the first time a gentle peace crossing his face.

"So are you this kind to all strangers?" Philip asked with a cocked eyebrow.

"Only tall, blond men who risk their lives on the front line. . . ."

Philip let out a low whistle and ran his fingers through his hair.

"And only when they've been injured and are in so much pain that they don't take it as a flirtation."

"In that case . . ." Philip shook his head and turned his attention out the side window. "I'd rather wait for the out-and-out flirtation. . . ."

From the slight reflection of the window, Sophie was sure she saw a grin cross Philip's face—a first since they'd crossed paths. And something she hoped to see more of in the future.

Reports of a second wave of intense fighting made Commander Johnson second-guess his permission for Sophie to visit the front lines.

"Do a painting of the injured men, *señorita*. At least until we know the tide of the battle. You are no use to our war effort if you are dead."

Again, Sophie feigned enthusiasm for the changed plan.

The next morning Philip waited for her in the small hospital ward. She smiled when she noticed he'd already set up her easel in front of the large window and next to the stove that warmed the room.

He offered a slight grin as she entered, then dug his hands into his pockets. "Chilly out there. Why don't I see if I can find us something warm?"

"Thank you, Philip. That would be wonderful."

And with a small good-bye wave he strode from the room.

The German soldier they had picked up the day before lay in the cot closest to her. "I am very sorry to have caused such trouble. Your friend, he has told me about your mission to paint canvases—to gather sympathy of your . . . our cause," the man said.

"Ritter, right?" She settled onto the stool and slid an old uniform shirt over her own clothes—a makeshift painter's frock. "I suppose God had a purpose for my being here instead. Maybe to paint you?"

His eye's widened with fear, and she laughed. "Oh, do not worry, *comrade*. You look better today . . . not so gray and pasty."

Ritter shook his head. "No, I do not think that is such a good idea. . . ." He glanced over at the journal. "I escaped a camp inside Germany, you see. There are many who would like to know where I am. Who would kill me where I lie if they only knew where that was."

Sophie turned the easel slightly and cocked her head, taking in the light of the room, the sensation of battle anxiety—even though they were a distance from the front lines. Taking in the many voices that spoke to each other in soft tones and in words she couldn't understand.

"Fine then. I don't do very well with faces anyway, truth be told. I'm much better with landscapes. Besides . . ." She nodded toward a man in the next cot. White bandages circled his head, and red seeped through from a head wound. "That guy has a far more interesting injury. Blood stirs more interest than an old cast."

A spurt of laughter erupted from the German, seeming to surprise even him.

"Ouch," he moaned, holding his ribs. "Please warn me if you attempt humor again."

Just then Philip entered the room, balancing three tins of coffee in his hands. He handed one to Sophie. Placing his on the windowsill, he turned to the German. "It's not very tasty, but it's warm."

Surprise registered again on Ritter's face, and he sat up slightly, taking the cup from Philip's hand. *"Danke."*

Noticing the unnatural tilt of his head, Sophie placed her own cup on the sill next to Philip's and moved toward the German. "Here, let me help you with your pillow. If you could scoot up a little more, we can fix this." He did as he was told, and she adjusted the pillow, setting it behind his shoulder blades. "There, is that better?"

The man nodded, but his attention was on a small plane taxiing into the field just beyond the makeshift hospital.

"Is that some type of airfield?" He sipped his coffee, trying to appear only vaguely interested, but Sophie noted the spark of fascination in his gaze.

"Hardly." Philip settled down on a chair next to the man's bed, also turning his attention to the window. "There's usually only one plane out there. Two if you count the one with some type of mechanical problem. They're mostly used for reconnaissance work—keeping the commanders up to date on the fighting. From what I overheard, they're looking for a mechanic to assist them." Philip cracked a grin. "You wouldn't happen to know anything about planes, would you?"

The German shrugged and sighed. "No, only a former appreciation that has turned into fear. Even as I slept last night, they filled my dreams. After all, what would it be like to have the bombs fall with this thing weighing me down?" He softly knocked on his plaster cast.

"Not to worry." Philip leaned closer to the man, resting his elbows on knees. "If I've learned one thing in the war, it's this . . . deep, close friendships may be rare, but a helping hand is never too far away. We're all in this together, and we didn't volunteer because we're watching out for ourselves."

"No, I suppose not." Ritter quickly lowered his gaze. "I never thought of it that way before." Then he closed his eyes.

And whether it was weariness that overwhelmed him, or a distant memory that stirred his thoughts, Sophie couldn't help but notice the man's features soften . . . as if realizing for the first time that he could rest in safety, far from the front lines.

Chapter Twenty-Nine

A quien madruga, Dios le ayuda.
God helps those who get up early.

Spanish proverb

As Ritter lay in the dark hospital room, his mind considered every possibility for escape. One of the airplanes, he knew, would provide the easiest route once he fled into the air. The problem, of course, was making it onto the field without being discovered. Not only that, but getting into the aircraft unassisted while wearing the heavy cast and feeling so weak was a major problem. He grew tired after sitting too long. He couldn't imagine finding the energy to make it out to the plane.

He also replayed in his mind the best way to hurt the enemy. Could he sabotage their weapons? Spy on their commander's office? Or maybe he should think ahead to their efforts to gain support from the war effort.

That woman artist . . . she is a greater threat than the simple soldiers. As someone who had followed Germany's propaganda efforts, Ritter knew all too well how a speech, a song, an image could move the hearts of the people.

Maybe it would be better to wait. To heal. To discover his

enemies' weakness. To befriend the woman and the American soldier. To use them for his escape. And then to make sure their plans to recruit for their cause died with them.

Philip scooted his chair closer to the woodstove—closer to Sophie, actually—to get a better look at the painting. It was an image of the hospital room, the beds lined up, the men displayed in their various forms of brokenness—without Ritter, as promised. Ritter, who slept peacefully not four feet from them and seemed to be healing well.

It was one of three paintings she had completed in the past four weeks. The others were images of Madrid—skies filled with enemy bombers while rows of men marched out to battle. Another of a lone man lying in the street, cut down by a sniper's bullet.

A soft smile rested on Sophie's lips, despite the pain and anguish Philip noted in the hospital painting.

"You seem content, Sophie. Each day, it's as if you transform the canvas with the pictures in your mind, and the canvas does its own transformation within you."

"I've painted as long as I can remember. The colors and shapes come together in my mind, and I give them life on the canvas. It's more like I'm relating a message than creating it. And though I question many things about my life, I never have questioned my art."

"I can see why."

"And what about you, Philip? You ask so many questions about me, my life. What's going on inside there?" She pointed to his heart.

"Oh, I don't know. I guess you could say I'm a work in progress. Only instead of holding a brush in my hand, I suppose my ideals are expressed by my involvement in this war." He patted his rifle, set in the corner of the room, but never farther than arm's reach.

"You can't compare war with art." Sophie picked at the paint under her nails, then cocked her head and studied the canvas before her.

"I couldn't disagree more. Each morning when a soldier wakes up, there's an image in his mind he's trying to capture. For me it's an image passed on by my friend. A picture of poor people having the same respect, the same freedom, as the rich. We're both idyllic dreamers, Sophie. Only I know that for my picture to come to pass, it requires many shades of red."

"It's a good picture—the equality part, that is. And I think I understand what you're saying. I paint with brushes; you, on the other hand, lace up your boots and clean your rifle for the day's battle. I never thought about it that way."

"Nor did I when I waited on the front line. Lately, I feel as if I'm falling behind on my responsibilities."

"I'm not so sure." She chuckled. "It might be easier facing those Moroccan soldiers than dealing with me."

Commander Johnson strode into the room, and Philip noticed Sophie's face brighten as the commander nodded appreciatively at the painting on the easel.

"Good work. I already have word that as soon as it is finished and shipped, it will appear in the *Daily Worker* . . . and perhaps a few other, more well-known magazines."

"Thank you." Sophie smiled at the compliment and turned to Philip, who nodded his agreement.

Out of the corner of his eye, he saw Ritter awaken, yawn, and stretch.

"Then we're heading out to the front lines?" Philip asked as much for himself as for Sophie's sake.

"Yes, there's a battle mounting near the river Jarama. The Nationalists are attempting to push the line forward."

Ritter sat up straighter in his bed, his eyes bright. "I would like to go too, if possible. My strength has returned, and surely it is time for the cast to be removed."

Commander Johnson crossed his arms over his chest, and Ritter seemed to cower slightly under the man's gaze. "I will check with your doctor and see what can be done. I appreciate those who are eager to get back on the lines."

He turned to leave, then paused, reaching for the newspaper tucked under his arm. "Oh, I almost forgot."

Philip noted a twinkle in the commander's eyes.

"Your first painting—the one we sent by courier last month—has already made the press." He handed the newspaper to Sophie.

She opened it and gasped. A black-and-white print of her Madrid bombing scene had made the front page. "Is this a French paper?"

"Yes. The story talks about the bombings themselves. More than that, copies of your painting have been made into colored posters and now hang around the city. You should be proud, Sophie. I cannot tell you how much this helps our cause."

With only faint light rays seeping through the window to light the twelve beds in the room, Ritter listened as the nurse's footsteps padded down the hall. Then he quietly slid off the covers. She had been later tonight than usual, caring for a new batch of wounded soldiers from the front lines. With every injured man carried through the doors, Ritter inwardly cheered, knowing his teammates performed their job well.

Now only a few hours separated the night nurse from the early morning shift. He had to move quickly. He looked to his knapsack, then decided to leave it all except his knife. He slid it into its sheath.

Four days had passed since he first saw the French newspaper with Sophie's painting on the front page. Four days of sneaking out to work on the airplane in the hangar. Four nights to convince himself he could do what needed to be done . . . finish off the biggest threat to their cause.

He climbed from the bed, thankful there would be no sleep tonight. Last night, after returning from his work on the plane, he'd dropped into bed exhausted, only to dream about his winter wedding again. Only this time, instead of Isanna walking down the aisle to him, it was Sophie. Beautiful dark-haired Sophie, whose wit and charm tempted him not to follow through with what he knew he had to do.

Ritter slid on the mechanics overalls he'd hidden under his mattress and quietly shuffled out of the hospital ward into the crisp night air. He'd been caught only once, peering at the plane with his stolen flashlight. Thankfully his mumbled excuse about how Commander Johnson needed the plane by morning had worked. The guard hadn't even noted anything odd about Ritter's outstretched right leg.

One more connection between the ignition wires, and he'd be on his way. But first he had to deal with Sophie.

He crept along to the small cluster of cottages not far from the hospital. Earlier in the day, the window near his hospital cot had afforded a view of Philip carrying the easel to the third cottage, setting it up for her to paint by the window, peering out at the fading sun as she worked.

Ritter made his way to the door and paused with his hand on the knob. He took a deep breath. The image of her walking down the aisle wouldn't leave him.

But her paintings . . .

He turned the knob, and the door opened slightly. Just then, the sound of an approaching truck startled him. Its headlights bounced over the road, and he knew in a matter of seconds they'd see him. Releasing the knob, he moved around the corner of the building, squatting behind some overgrown shrubs the best he could.

The truck stopped outside the cottages, and he heard the sound of a man's footsteps approaching. Then an urgent knock pounded on the cottage door. The unlatched door creaked open.

"Sophie?" It was Philip's voice. "Are you in there? Is there a reason why your door is open?"

Ritter cursed under his breath, then wondered if he could kill them both and still have time to make it to the plane. Already a thin layer of light promised the new dawn.

The driver. There's a truck driver out there too . . . it would be too noisy. And then I'd have to give up my escape.

Sliding the knife into the sheath, he turned and scurried toward the airplane.

He hobbled the best he could, removed the chocks from the wheels, and climbed into the plane. He'd be in the sky before he knew it. Heading back to the Nationalist side of the lines. And then he could forget any of this had ever happened.

Ritter waited until Philip and Sophie jumped into the truck and the headlights slid out of view, then started the engine. He smiled, noting how it purred like a kitten, and he realized that perhaps their planes arriving in boxes hadn't been such a bad thing, after all.

Ritter taxied onto the field and aligned the plane with the barely visible ruts that defined the runway. A glance toward the cottages revealed lights coming on and two doors open, showing the profiles of men investigating the noise.

He shoved the throttle lever all the way forward, and soon he was in the air, forcing himself to ignore his conflicted soul.

Though many of the volunteers had previously served in the military, the Americans, Deion discovered, were the least trained soldiers of the International Brigades. They made a pact among themselves that they'd prove their worth by excelling at the front. And today they'd get their chance.

Their task was to hold the lines in the valley surrounding the river Jarama. It was a land of rough scrub and gentle slopes, covered with leafy olive trees.

Deion stepped lightly, just one of a small group of men walking through the river valley. Their leader, twenty yards ahead, raised his hand and signaled them to stop. The pounding of Nationalist artillery was evident. Every now and then—hearing an approaching shell—the leader motioned for them to hit the ground. But there was no guarantee of safety.

As Deion walked, he spotted evidence of the previous bombardments—bodies scattered in the fields or leaning up against the base of trees. Many images of the trip to the valley filled his mind as he moved along—the square with the Baroque church, the road with many hairpin turns, the gray village on the hill. He'd come to the front after an unpleasant ride in the back of a van, only to wish he could return—to experience the countryside they'd passed through so quickly. Maybe he'd get that chance, for when Deion received his rifle and helmet, a promise followed that when he returned he'd be transferred to the drivers' pool.

As they prepared to climb into the vans and trucks to take them to the front lines, their commander had offered these parting words.

"Men, before you head to the lines, there is one thing you need to understand. The Fascists came to suppress the people, yet we are here to do the people's will. The People's Front contains various parties, and we are not to prefer one party more than another. Hitler and Mussolini have sent hundreds of planes, hundreds of thousands of men, and a vast quantity of machines to conquer the people. Our purpose is to make sure they don't succeed. If we have come to fight for our own agenda, then we will do so in vain. What sort of government the Spanish people decide to have is up to them, not to us. For that reason we will wear no party insignia."

Hearing that, Deion had removed his Party armband. For the first time he wondered if he'd come with the right motives, after all. No, he didn't want to impose his views on anyone else . . . but what about those who'd sent him?

A shout broke his reverie. "Everyone get down!"

Gunfire broke out, and a man only ten yards in front of Deion crumbled to the ground. Deion dropped facedown, hands on his helmet, pulling it tighter on his head. Then he heard another cry off to his left. On a bridge in the distance, a large colored man held a knife to the throat of a Brigade member. With one quick motion he slit the man's throat, then pushed the convulsing body over the side of the bridge. It tumbled like a limp rag doll, splashing into the river below.

The colored man signaled to the cavalry unit on the other side of the bridge, and uncountable men on horses thundered across, their gray cloaks flowing in the wind.

"The Moors," cried a man next to Deion.

"The Moroccan Calvary." The blood in Deion's veins turned ice cold. "Paid killers."

They'd heard and even passed on rumors of the Moors the way young boys shared ghost stories around the campfire. Deion had thought of them more as imaginary monsters than actual men. Yet they were real men, colored men, just the same as him.

When the cavalry were halfway across the bridge, an explosion filled the air, nearly bursting Deion's eardrums. Republican mines, laid on the bridge for just such an emergency. The bridge rose a few feet in the air, only to drop back into place. In less than a minute the dark cavalry poured into the unprepared Republican positions.

The commander rose, waving his hands and shouting. "Forward and smash 'em!" he cried, leading his men in a charge.

Deion had no choice but to follow. With his rifle to his shoulder, he ran forward. His heart pounded as he saw the Moors pouring into the orchards, firing their rifles from their hips.

Deion ignored them all and focused his eyes on one—the first man who had slit the throat of the guard. His back was to Deion as he faced his approaching troops, guiding them to the best paths. Deion propelled himself forward until he stood within twenty yards of the man's back; then he pulled the trigger. The shot missed, and the man turned.

His dark, sweaty skin glinted in the sun. His eyes narrowed with blood-thirst, and he plunged toward Deion, extending his bloody knife like a sword. Deion reached forward to eject the spent shell, jacked another into the chamber, took more careful aim, and fired again, this time hitting his mark. The man jerked and winced, then looked down at his stomach, where blood seeped through his shirt. His wild eyes widened in fear. As if surprised, he pressed his hand to his stomach, pulling it out bloody.

Deion steadied the rifle again and shot one more time, hitting the man's shoulder. The force of the bullet jerked him back, and he tumbled to the ground, rolling down a slight hill until he stopped at the bottom.

Deion moved to the nearest tree and squatted down behind it for protection. And there he remained, taking shots at the hundred of Moors streaming across the bridge. Hitting some, missing most. As he reloaded, he glanced at the black man dying before his eyes, crying out words Deion didn't understand.

The battle raged around him unabated, men dropping; some crying out in agony, some lying still. The dark horsemen rode through the Republican line almost at will, alternately shooting their guns and slashing with their scimitars. Some fell, but most continued to kill Deion's comrades.

Deion did his best to fight against the men on horseback, and somehow he survived. As darkness descended, he looked again at the first man he had killed, and realized how easily their roles could have been reversed. They were both colored men fighting on foreign soil for causes not their own.

Chapter Thirty

Fue por lana y salió trasquilado.
She went looking for wool and came back shorn.

Spanish proverb

It wasn't until the night turned pitch-black that the fighting stopped. With a shiver that caused his whole body to tremble, Deion dared to crawl back to the safety of the trenches. Moving past the dead horses and dead men on both sides of the fight, he found a group of men from the Abraham Lincoln Brigade—men he'd trained with and those who, like him, had somehow survived.

The night was cold, yet his numb limbs mattered little to his exhausted mind. More than anything, he longed for sleep and warmth. All his senses peaked, waiting for the next explosion and the hail of earth and shrapnel.

"I feel betrayed," one man said, warming his hands by the fire. The hands were covered with blood, as was the man's clothing.

Deion didn't ask what happened. He didn't want to know.

"They led us into that . . . led us into the slaughter. I'm not sure how I made it. How any of us did."

"I think I know why I survived." Deion sipped from his water jug. "My mama must have been prayin'. She's likely figured out where I am by now. Not married, but off fighting in some foreign war." He wrapped his arms around himself and rocked back and forth, attempting to stop the shaking, though he couldn't tell if it came from cold or fear.

"Not that I believe like she does," he added. "I grew up wondering not *if* one of ours would be killed in a lynchin', but *when*. I'd say, 'Mama, if the Lord loves us like you says He does, why does He allow white folks to treat us like they do?' I still don't know why bad things have to happen. Things like today."

"My mum is one of those religious types too, lad."

Deion recognized his climbing partner over the Pyrenees. Ian. His hair was shorter, nearly shaved to his head, and a thick red beard covered the lower half of his face.

He nodded to Deion with a deep sadness in his gaze. "Of course," he added, "it's hard to see if it's done much good in her life, though she tried to convince me it did. Mum could retell most every Bible story from history, but then she cried her eyes out when I told her I was heading to Spain."

Ian puffed on a cigar, pulling it out to finish his story. "At first, it bothered me to leave her like that. Then I got to thinking—what difference was there between me and the fights of those characters in her Bible book? Weren't it David who dared to step out against a giant, and Joshua who led the people, even though there were giants in the land? So I told her that, and she cried even harder."

"Because she knew you were leaving no matter what?" Deion asked.

"No, I think it were tears of joy, because I actually had paid attention to her stories all those years! After that she still cried, but she did it when she thought I wasna lookin'. I'm supposin' we've come to a truce of sorts. An unspoken agreement that if I did come, then I'd win, just like David and Joshua. Of course, then days like today come." He folded his hands behind his head and leaned back, gazing into the starry night. "What about you? Are you thinking we'll win, Deion?"

"Wouldn't be here if I didn't. But even today, when I was near sure it was my last day on earth, I'd rather be here than back home."

"Why's that?" another voice asked.

Deion didn't know who spoke, for the exhausted gestures of the men around him seemed to meld as one.

"Here I feel like a human being. A man. It's something you can't understand unless you've been treated worse than people treat their dogs."

"Equality?" another man said. "Yer right 'bout that. Those Fascists send equal bullets all around."

"Makes sense to me." Ian shivered and pulled his blanket tight over his shoulders. "When it comes to real fightin', phrases like 'volunteer for liberty' aren't meaning a thing. Truth be told, war isn't you against the other guy. It's you against yerself. All your past demons. All your fears and worries visit you there."

His words made Deion think of the Moroccan soldier. He shook the thought away, not wanting to let himself go there. Because for him to feel like a human being, he'd killed like an animal. And that made no sense at all.

The sun was just cresting the distant hills as the truck drove Philip and Sophie toward the front lines. Eagerness stirred within Sophie, causing her leg to bounce with built-up tension at the thought of painting the battlefield—tanks facing off, planes soaring overhead, men in their trenches holding the line.

"After this painting, do you think we can visit José?" She turned to Philip. "Commander Johnson said he's in a hospital beyond the war zone, and he's recovering well."

Philip didn't seem nearly as excited about approaching the battlefield. Fear filled his gaze, and without saying a word, he wrapped his left arm around Sophie's shoulders, as if that gesture alone would protect her from whatever lay ahead. "It would be good to visit your friend. Did you know him before you came to Spain?"

"Oh, no." The truck rumbled over a bump, jarring her, and her head hit against Philip's jaw. "I came for other reasons—but

261

José was one of the first people I met. He helped me to not miss home as much."

"You said home is Boston, right? I've been meaning to ask you; how come you don't have an accent?"

"You think people from Baw-stin should tawk about wheah we pahk our cahs?" She grinned. "I've worked to hide my accent all my life. My mom is from California, and she always felt that the best accent is none at all. She wrote speeches for a living, you see, and hated it when no one could understand the speaker."

"Speeches? What kind?"

"Women's issues mostly. Women's right to vote. Safety in the workplace. Things like that."

"So that's where you get your fighting spirit."

Though Sophie couldn't see his face, she was sure he was grinning. "Fighting spirit, eh?"

"You're a young, single woman traveling alone in Spain, aren't you? And now you're a combat artist."

"Combat artist? Why, I guess I am."

Out of the corner of her eye, Sophie watched the driver. Either he didn't understand English very well, or he was a man of few words. His gaze stayed fixed on the road ahead.

"So what's Boston like?" Philip asked. "I bet there's a historical monument every mile or so."

"Make that every block. My father was an assistant manager of one of the finest hotels in the city," she continued. "When I wasn't in school, I was there with him. The Old City Hall was across the street next to King's Hall. Boston Common, just around the corner. It's a small city, actually. Nothing like New York. I walked everywhere. Chinatown, Little Italy, up to Cambridge . . . it's all real close. Of course, I visited the Museum of Fine Arts practically every day."

Her eyes focused on the rolling hills ahead, but in her mind she walked the narrow cobblestone streets, looking at the boats in the harbor and the old cemeteries where the names on the weathered headstones were no longer distinguishable—the identity of those they honored lost in history.

"Home to me is the whistle of the traffic cops, the street performer with the trumpets or juggling balls," she continued. "Police officers on horseback, and lines of children on school trips following guides dressed as Benjamin Franklin or Paul Revere. Women pose by the historic meeting halls, and they'll let you have a picture taken with them for a coin. And in the midst of it all are homeless men and women in unemployment lines looking longingly at the businessmen who hustle back and forth between the office buildings. Tall skyscrapers overshadow the historic churches, making both appear out of place."

Philip smiled. "I think you're a writer as well as an artist. Tell me more."

Sophie sighed and smiled. If Philip was trying to take her mind, as well as his, off the battlefield that awaited them, it was working.

"Well, there are carriage rides and big cemeteries that haven't added new bones in dozens of years. There's Boston cream pie, and Boston baked beans, and tea sold at every family restaurant. Not to mention lobster and fish—so much so that I keep away from the restaurants near the docks at dinner, because the scent is so overpowering.

"I've never appreciated it until now," she whispered. "I mean, I've heard the tour guides give the same speeches time and again. This battle started here. This man died on these steps. This document was signed within these doors. . . . It was so familiar it became commonplace, like knowing the color of your mother's eyes or the feel of your father's hand on your own. You don't appreciate those things until you no longer have them."

"So have you written home to tell your parents about your paintings or the French newspaper?"

"Not yet. I've been so busy I barely glanced at it myself."

"Do you still have a copy?"

"Yeah, sure." Sophie dug in her satchel and pulled out the paper. Together they looked again at her painting on the front page; then Philip opened it to a spread of photographs from the front lines just outside Madrid.

Sophie studied them. She looked at one image of a soldier's body caught in the line of gunfire. His body was arched in an awkward angle. And the edges around him were hazy . . . as if a piece of silk had been placed around the edge of the lens. . . .

Beside her Philip chuckled. "Did you see the photographer's name? If I were the guy, I'd change my name. Who would name their kid Arnold Benedict? Then again, if your last name is Benedict I'm sure you get tied in with the historical figure no matter what."

"Arnold Benedict . . . like Benedict Arnold . . . the traitor." Sophie's hands began to tremble, and she moved them to her mouth. "Philip. How recent are those photos?"

"A week, I suppose. Maybe a little longer."

She reached across Philip for the door handle. "Driver, please pull over. I'm going to be sick."

He did as asked, and Philip jumped from the vehicle. Sophie followed, retching in the ditch on the side of the road. She felt Philip's hands holding back her hair. She retched again, and he rubbed her back.

"Sophie, are you okay? What is it?"

She lowered her face in her hands. "He's alive," she whispered. She lowered herself onto her hands and knees and crawled close to a small tree, leaning against it for support.

Philip crouched in front of her. "Who's alive? What are you talking about?"

"Michael. He's the reason I came to Spain. We were going to get married. Then—" Her voice caught in her throat. "Then he was killed by a sniper's bullet. At least I thought he was."

Sophie looked into Philip's face. His eyes radiated concern.

"Was he the man in the painting?" he said softly. "The one gunned down in the street?"

"Yes." She wiped her eyes with trembling hands. "I thought he died, but I didn't see him up close."

"But what makes you think he's alive now?"

Sophie pointed to the photograph. "I need to talk to José," she said. "He was there. He can tell me the truth."

"Yes," Philip said. He took both of her hands in his. "But first, you need to go to the front lines. They're counting on you, remember?"

Sophie shook her head. "I don't know. I don't think I can. Philip, I don't want to do it. . . . Please, can we just turn back?"

"Sophie, you can do this, and you will. We don't need to stay for long. Just take some photographs. Do some sketches. Then we'll leave." He lifted her face toward him and looked her in the eyes. "I'll be there with you, every step of the way, okay?"

"Okay." She wiped her face. "But then we can go see José?"

"Yes, Sophie. Then, together, we will see José and get to the bottom of this."

The truck moved slowly, and Sophie felt Philip's arm tighten around her shoulders.

"Driver. This is close enough," he said.

In the distance, the whole bank of the river was pitted with craters from the bombing. The river shimmered with a million flecks of light, giving a false sense of peacefulness.

Sophie jumped from the truck.

Philip placed both hands on her shoulders and looked intently into her eyes. "We're about four hundred meters behind the front lines. If anything happens, you run back here. Understand?"

She nodded.

A black velvet shadow fell over the grove of olive trees, the sun's rays not quite reaching that spot. In the field closest to the bridge, bodies could be seen sprawled on the packed earth. In the distance, machine guns crackled like popcorn. And beyond that came the sound of grenades bursting.

Next to the road sat a burnt-out farmhouse and a carved stone gate. Sophie wondered who had lived there before war came to their part of the world.

"Philip, we need to find our soldiers. Can we get closer?"

"I suppose we can." He lifted his rifle to his shoulder. "I'll lead, but if I tell you to hit the ground, you drop. Do you understand?"

She nodded. "Yes."

Philip turned to the driver. "Wait here. We'll be back shortly."

Sophie grabbed her satchel and walked behind Philip toward the closest grove of trees.

"Halt!" A man in a blue mono stepped from behind the tree and pointed his rifle at Philip's chest.

"I'm with the Abraham Lincoln Brigade."

"Password?"

"Delores."

The man nodded, then turned his gun to Sophie. "What about her?"

"She's with the newspaper," Philip said. "I'm her escort. Sophie, show the man your camera."

She removed it from the satchel and hung it around her neck.

The man stepped aside. "Proceed."

The first group they came upon contained a cluster of injured soldiers. Philip leaned his mouth close to her ear. "They're waiting for the ambulance. From the looks of things, the fight's been bad."

One soldier, lying under a blood-soaked blanket, cried out in pain. His eyes were open and wild, and his hands clawed the air in front of him as if he were climbing a hill. "Did we take the hill?" he cried. "Did we take it?"

"Sure we did, buddy." Another soldier held the man's arms. "We won."

Philip and Sophie tried to go closer, but the sounds of the battle pushed them back. The cries of men. The smell of dead bodies. The ground pulsing beneath their feet.

Yet Sophie saw enough to imprint her mind for a lifetime. Men scurrying around the valley below stumbled from tree to tree, desperate for cover. Others sprawled on the ground, using their hands to dig deep into the earth. Sophie snapped through one roll of film, then two.

Philip turned to her. "We need to head back. There will only be more of the same. Did you want to do any sketching?"

"No. Only the dead and dying will stay still enough for me to draw. And I can't do that. . . ."

They quickly moved back to their truck, only to find that it was being filled with injured men.

"Can we still get a ride?" Philip asked the driver.

The driver pointed to Philip, and another man stepped forward and spoke. "Philip Stanford?"

"Yes?"

He placed a hand on Philip's shoulder. "She can go, but you're coming with me." His gaze narrowed, and he pulled a pair of handcuffs from his jacket.

"What is this about?"

Another soldier stepped forward and took Philip's rifle from him, pointing it at his back. "We have reason to believe you assisted a German spy."

"What?"

"Ritter Lindemann escaped this morning in a Republican plane. You were the one who found him, and the morning you left, he escaped."

"You've got to be kidding!" Sophie stepped up to the officer. "Ritter was a spy? But— but even if he was, Philip had nothing to do with it—"

The officer pointed to the cab of the truck. "Ma'am, I suggest you get inside before you are questioned too."

Philip placed a hand on her shoulder. "Sophie, this is just a misunderstanding. Don't worry. We'll have it all straightened out soon. Just do as the man says."

Sophie turned to him. "You don't understand. I don't want to be alone. Not again."

The officer pulled Philip's hands behind his back and cuffed him.

"What about God, Sophie?" Philip said.

"What about Him?" She crossed her arms over her chest.

"You're *not* alone. God is watching over you. And when we get this thing cleared up, I'll be back, you understand?"

The truck driver approached. "Ma'am, the injured men are loaded. We need to head out."

Sophie clutched her satchel to her and climbed into the cab. A colored man sat there already, gripping his leg, and he moved over to make room for her.

"I'm sorry, ma'am. There's no more room in back."

"It's okay," she said. She slammed the truck door and turned in the seat, watching the soldiers put Philip in another car. But the truth was, it wasn't okay. Nothing was okay.

Sophie didn't know what to believe anymore. Or whom to believe. "Arnold Benedict . . . Benedict Arnold, the traitor . . ."

"Pardon, miss? Did you say somethin'?"

"Nothing . . . I was thinking out loud. Only thinking out loud."

Chapter Thirty-One

No hay mal que por bien no venga.

There is no misfortune that doesn't come with good.

Spanish proverb

The Spanish village's natural colors changed only slightly as Sophie looked through the viewfinder on her camera. Brown roofs seemed a little darker, richer, grayish-white stucco walls a little less gray. Undulating, green hills with craggy granite outcroppings filled the background. The sound of distant cows lowing soon yielded to desperate cries, as workers lined the stucco-walled school with injured men.

Sophie snapped photographs as they unloaded the soldiers. It helped somehow, to have the camera filter the images for her. To separate herself from the blood, the pain. If only she could block out the stench of burnt flesh and the screams of agony.

"Can you help me, *señorita?*" a man asked in Spanish. He knelt beside an injured soldier with a stomach wound. His bloody fingers pressed a piece of gauze into the hole, but it did little good as the seeping red quickly soaked the gauze. "I need you to hold this. Don't let go. I must help unload the rest of these brave men."

Sophie tucked her camera back into the satchel and knelt before the man. It was hard to distinguish the bloody gauze from the torn skin, and her stomach lurched. Bile rose in the back of her throat, and she swallowed it down.

The man took her hand and shoved it into the wound. "Just hold it tight."

The gauze was already soaked, the blood warm and sticky. A sense of aloneness overwhelmed her, and she wished Philip were there to help. To comfort her.

How could they accuse him of such a thing? Not Philip . . .

Then again, she would have never guessed Ritter had been an enemy soldier, or that Michael would betray her. She had trusted her emotions and his words. A heaviness settled on her shoulders, and she wondered if anyone was trustworthy.

As she looked around at the broken bodies, Michael's words came back to her, and she was suddenly hit with a horrible foreboding. What if he had been right? What if she'd allowed her ignorance of Spanish politics to sway her sympathies to the wrong side? After all, the dead Nationalist soldiers on the side of the road looked no different from the ones she'd met on her train ride to Madrid. What if the train had carried her into *their* territory? Would she be fighting as diligently for their side?

These questions unnerved her. Yet they also turned her thoughts to what Philip had said. Like him, she was here for a reason. It was not fate or destiny that had brought her here, but something more. Sophie thought she'd come for Michael, and imagined she'd stayed to paint—to make a difference for the cause. But perhaps something more kept her here. Maybe it was enough simply to comfort a dying man. She pushed harder on the bandage, and with her free hand took the man's hand. She caressed his fingers with her own.

A medic rushed past and glanced down at the injured soldier in her care. "Don't worry no more, *señorita*. He's dead."

"He's not talking about me, is he?" The man's eyes popped open, and he squeezed Sophie's hand. "Tell them I'm not dead."

She turned to the medic, amazed by the strength in the man's grip. "He's not dead. Now will you please do something?"

The medic called to a nurse, and they carried the man away.

Sophie looked around for someplace to wash her bloody hand. She found a pump and let the cool water flow over her hand to cleanse the blood—the red staining the white rocks at the base of the pump. Even after the blood washed away, she allowed the cool water to flow, stinging her fingers, numbing them just like her emotions.

Another ambulance arrived from Jarama. More men were unloaded, then laid upon the ground.

Sophie rushed to the ambulance as the driver climbed back inside. "What are you doing?" She waved her hand toward the rows of injured bodies. "You just can't leave them there."

"No choice, lady. There's ten times that waiting for a ride. Men are dying by the second. . . ." And with that the ambulance roared off.

She turned back to the scene before her. Removing her camera from the satchel, she took one shot, then returned it. One photo was all she had time for.

Sophie knelt down beside the man at the end of the row. He reached for his leg, screaming like a young child who'd been torn away from his mother. Yet his hands met only air, and Sophie's stomach lurched when she saw the mangled stump that remained.

"The pain, the pain, do something for the pain. Get the bullet out!" He tried to sit up, reaching for a leg that wasn't there.

She tried to hold him down, pressing against his shoulders, but his movements grew more frantic. *Dear God, help me please. If You're here, I need help.* . . . It wasn't one of Benita's recited prayers, but it was all she could manage at the moment.

"Doctor, someone, please, get the bullet out!" the man screamed.

Sophie moved her hands to the man's face, stroking his sweaty brow and looking into his eyes. "It's out, I promise you. There is no bullet."

The man's screams calmed.

Her tears joined his. "It's gone. It's gone," she whispered.

Finally, a nurse rushed over and held a cloth over his nose, and the powerful drug forced him into a listless sleep. The nurse hurriedly checked the wound.

"Have mercy." Sophie pressed her hand to her chest and sank

onto the ground, watching the nurse. "There's no leg. How can you treat something that doesn't exist?"

"Phantom pain," the nurse said hurriedly, moving to the next patient. "We see it all the time. The feeling is as real as if the wound were still there fresh and aching. The pain of what you have lost. It's the worst pain you can get."

The pain of what you have lost. Sophie's mind couldn't wrap around all she'd lost since coming to Spain. Then she chided herself. How could she even compare her losses to the sacrifices of these men?

"Can you come with me?" the nurse asked. "I know you're not here for this, but we need help inside."

Sophie cringed from the stench in the schoolroom, now transformed into a first-aid hospital. Cots lined the narrow room. White-faced men filled the space on beds and floor, moaning with pain and crying out words that knotted her heart. Some words were in languages she couldn't understand. And those she could were dying words.

The soldiers' faces reminded her of the Christs El Greco drew. Pale, thin, heavily bearded. Except this one. She recognized the colored man she'd ridden beside in the truck, yet his eyes were wild, as if he were caught in the middle of a waking nightmare.

"Ian!" he called, trying to sit up. "Where's Ian? He was right next to me before the explosion."

"Listen to me. He's safe. He made it." Sophie grasped the man's hand, refusing to look at the wound on his leg. She had no idea who Ian was, or if he still lived, but she knew these were the words this man needed. If he was going to make it, he needed hope more than anything. "You can rest now. You can rest."

His features softened. "Thank you. Thank you for telling me." His eyes fluttered shut. "Ian remembered his mama's Bible stories," he mumbled. Then he fell into a fitful sleep, his heavy, shuddering breaths evidence of his pain.

The *poupinelle*, a French copper sterilizer, was loaded with surgical instruments. Though she had awakened this morning not even knowing what one was, let alone how to run it, Sophie now worked the machine with skill. Bottles and boxes of medical supplies lined the shelves that previously had held children's schoolbooks. There were donations from America, Holland, France, even Poland—but no bandages. No matter where she looked, she couldn't find one clean bandage.

Sophie had been gathering, cleaning, and delivering supplies for the nurses and doctors for hours. Her clothes were black. Her hands were rough and swollen, her face dusty. Her hair dirty and tangled. And still those around her worked by the light of oil lamps. Sophie had never witnessed a more dedicated group of people.

Most of the men in this section had been cared for, except for one new soldier. His face was ashen, the color faded like the Spanish tiles that lose their color in the sun. Bright red seeped through the bandaged wound in his shoulder.

The other nurses were assisting in surgery and had asked Sophie to watch the bleeding. And there were no bandages. No clean sheets. Nothing to stop the flow of blood.

Sophie thought of her satchel in the corner and what it contained. She released the pressure on the wound and hurried to the tray of medical instruments, snatching up the scissors. In a few steps, she was at her satchel, quickly unbuckling the latch.

"Nurse . . ." The soldier's voice was desperate, and she glanced back to see the bleeding had increased.

"I'm not a nurse," she called back, the knot in her neck tightening with each passing second. "I'm not supposed to be here." She dug through the last of her things. "I had a different plan," she said under her breath. "Don't you understand? This is not what it was supposed to be about."

But I am here, God. I'm here for some reason. Give me strength.

She yanked the light blue dress from her bag and immediately set to work cutting two long, wide strips from the skirt. Without hesitating, she hurried back to the soldier and folded one strip into a small square, pressing it into the wound. Then she quickly wrapped the other strip to hold it in place.

She held her breath and waited. Waited for the deep, red fluid to seep through the cloth, proving her efforts had been in vain.

But after ten minutes, there was still no blood seeping through. Only then did she let out a sigh of relief.

The soldier's eyes were wide. "Why did you do that? Cut up your dress like that?"

"I don't need it anymore," she said flatly. Then Sophie glanced down at her bloodied hands and stained clothes. "And now that you're taken care of, I really need a shower." She smiled and winked at him. "And because a shower was out of the question as long as I had to watch over you."

The man offered a slight grin.

She set the scissors on the tray of items needing to be sterilized and crossed the room. Gingerly she picked up the dress, determined to finish what she'd started. But for now, she *did* need a shower, and she was determined to get one before the next wave of injured men came in.

"If the nurse returns, tell her I'll be back in fifteen minutes. You're doing great, my friend." She put the rest of the dress into the satchel and snatched up clean clothes, then plodded wearily to the back of the building where a manual shower stall had been rigged.

Sophie undressed and gently tipped the bucket of lukewarm water, letting its coolness wash over her. She started to lather her body when a new sound flowed from the hospital. A deep male voice rose in song, and it seemed the moans of the other men lessened.

As she listened to the Negro spiritual, sung with a low Southern accent, Sophie knew who the singer was. The colored man's leg had been stitched up hours ago, and now he had awakened. He sang with a voice so full of emotion that her heart seemed to double in size.

She finished washing, dressed, and returned inside. Many of the nurses had gathered, their weary faces reflecting a moment of peace. The looks on the faces of the men in the room had also brightened, and they seemed to forget for a moment their tattered bodies and lost friends. It was like balm for their souls.

He was now singing "Amazing Grace," and as she stood and listened, Sophie remembered Philip's words. Philip was right. God was with her—and would be with her, in spite of the war that raged on every side.

SPRING

And they arose early:
and it came to pass about the spring of the day. . . .
—1 Samuel 9:26

Chapter Thirty-Two

APRIL 24, 1937

Lo que no mata, engorda.
What does not kill, fattens.

Spanish proverb

The sun hung in the air, and evidence of spring's return could be seen wherever Father Manuel looked. The streets filled with people enjoying the sunshine and flowers budding in window boxes or the leafy grapevines that trailed up many of the town's stone buildings. Some sat outside at the Arrién Restaurant's sidewalk tables, enjoying a leisurely lunch. Others ambled through the marketplace or strolled through the Plaza Las Escuelas, the town's main square. And in their joy of life, most were not aware of the numerous ambulances passing through the outskirts of town, laden with the human toll of battle.

When he looked at the people, Father Manuel couldn't help but think of the Scriptures that spoke of sheep without a shepherd. In addition to the familiar faces, thousands of refugees now filled the town, fleeing from aerial bombings in Bilbao and other nearby towns. The refugees knew too well from hearing stories on the radio that once the bombs were dropped, ground troops followed. And if faceless men caused such destruction from the air, what devastation would come from those on the ground?

Only twenty miles now separated the front lines from this town—from the people he'd vowed to shepherd. Rugged terrain and thousands of Basque troops provided protection, but would it be enough?

The injured filled every bed in the convent, and within the yard-thick walls those receiving care felt safe for the first time in months. Only a direct hit from a large aerial bomb or artillery shell could do any real damage. The nuns believed the large red cross painted on the roof would discourage such a blow, but Father Manuel wasn't so sure. If the bombers dropped their load on whole cities filled with innocent people, what would one red cross do to hinder them?

With a long-legged stride, he hurried to the convent. Since waking this morning, he'd felt an urgency to make sure the town and the people were ready . . . for what he did not know. *Is this from You, Lord? Is it possible You speak through an unsettling in the pit of our stomachs too?*

He opened the convent door and noticed Sister Joséfina walking the halls with a man on crutches. The man turned Father Manuel's direction, peering at him with unseeing eyes. *So too are the people of this town, looking without seeing. . . .*

"Sister Joséfina, do you still have that black cloth purchased for the nuns' new habits?"

"Yes, Padre. In the storage room, but I . . ." She glanced down at her own stained garments. "I know these do not honor our Lord, but I have no time to make new ones. . . . "

"You think I wish for you to sew? Oh, dear Sister, I would not ask such a thing of you. It's the windows I'm thinking of. We must black them out. Just hang the cloth the best you can. Do you think you can find enough hands around town to help?"

"Of course, Padre. I'll see what I can do."

"Good. Make sure it is done by Monday at the latest."

Father Manuel strode from the building and ran his fingers through his hair, realizing the curtains would only be a start. They must find a way to hide the ambulances unloading the wounded and camouflage the wash lines strung with white surgical linen. Both would easily catch the attention of those from the sky.

If the bombers came, he wanted to know they'd done all they could.

Before rounding the corner, he turned and waved to the young nun perched on the roof in her habit.

Lord, the end must be nigh. To have women—brides of Christ—giving part of their day to scan the skies for enemy planes. What is this world coming to?

The nun waved back enthusiastically, then lifted the field glasses to her eyes, once more looking to the north, then east. If only it was the Lord's return for which they waited with such eagerness.

Father Manuel continued back to his parish church, walking by the school where he'd served as spiritual advisor for the past few years. Children clad in school uniforms ran around the fenced play yard. He waved to them as he passed, and they cheerfully waved back. Many of the boys in their early teens already spoke of leaving their studies to fight. But out of five hundred pupils, half were girls. Girls whom the Moors would violate unspeakably if they ever reached this peaceful town.

He thought too of the other order of nuns in Guernica, the Sisters of Penance of the Order of Santa Clara. Unlike the nuns who worked among the people and cared for the injured soldiers, the twenty-nine Sisters of Santa Clara lived in cloisters and never stepped beyond their walls.

The order was founded in 1422, and each new nun was given the number of a nun who'd passed away. The sisters were even buried within the walls when they died. For five hundred years outsiders had cared for them by taking the shopping lists the nuns passed through a grill on the convent door. What would happen to them if outsiders broke in? Did they even realize a war raged outside their walls?

Father Manuel knew there was one more thing he needed to do, and that was to speak out. Louder, bolder if necessary. To stir the people from their complacency. To wake them up from their naïve belief that the enemy would not touch their town. Would not touch their souls.

The dead man's face would have appeared to be gently sleeping but for his pasty, translucent skin and utterly still features. Sophie unwrapped the bandage from his arm . . . gingerly, not to avoid hurting the arm, but to avoid tearing the precious bandage.

This was the third hospital at which she'd worked in the last month and a half. During that time, she had followed the troops to photograph the harshest battles, then ridden back with the injured. Only over the course of a month, the situation was getting worse, not better. There were not enough medical workers or supplies. Bandages, in fact, were so scarce that they were forced to remove them from the dead and boil them to sterilize them for reuse.

She turned slightly and noted the familiar eyes on her. She had a new driver, the man who had ridden back with her from the Jarama River Valley. She'd helped care for him in the weeks that followed. And when he was told he could no longer serve on the battlefield due to the disability the injury had caused, he had offered to be her driver instead.

"I got some dinner for you when you're ready, Miss Sophie. They call it *arroz con pollo*, but it shore looks like chicken and rice to me." A wide smile filled his face, and he stretched out his offering. The tin plate seemed small in the man's large hands.

"Thank you, Deion. Let me clean up, and I'll meet you out front in a few minutes. And, Deion—no more 'Miss,' okay? It's just Sophie."

Sophie scrubbed her hands, wishing she could clean away the memories that swirled in her mind so easily.

Confused memories of Michael, as she continued to scan the newspapers for more photographs from "Arnold Benedict," more sure with every one that they were Michael's pictures, and he was out there somewhere, haunting her.

Hopeful memories of Philip, and of his tenderness and kindness to her. Last she'd heard, he was locked in prison somewhere inside Madrid, where the bomb raids had not let up since she'd

280

left. She had replayed all their moments together, testing her memories to see if there was any connection between him and the German spy, Ritter.

Of course, she knew he was innocent, but no one in authority would take two minutes to listen to her side of the story. In fact, their warnings were the same. *If you keep this up, you'll be questioned too. At least they have not killed him. And he's safer locked away than on the front lines.*

She found Deion sitting on the front steps of the small church across the street from the hospital. No matter how small, each Spanish village had a steepled church. And though they were mostly closed, they too reminded her of Philip's words: "God is watching over you, Sophie."

She stretched out her hand, taking the plate from Deion, and smiled as she settled next to him on the worn wooden step. "How are you feeling?"

"If I was doing better, I'd be twins," he said, unconsciously rubbing his leg. "In fact, I was just thinking how you made me take my mind off the pain that day in the hospital, even if it was just for a few seconds, after they noticed my leg taking a turn for the worse. 'Member what you said?"

"Of course." Sophie lowered her voice and cocked an eyebrow. "I said, we're supposed to notify the doctor if the wound begins to turn black, but I don't know what to do about you."

They both laughed, and Sophie took a bite of her food.

"Later, Deion, do you think you can sit for me again . . . for the painting? It shouldn't be much longer."

In the kitchen of the small cottage she shared with the nurses, her easel had stood for two weeks. The nurses had been her eager observers as they watched the colors on the canvas transform themselves into Deion's face. And there was something about his eyes—all the nurses said it. Somehow she'd captured them perfectly.

"Of course I'll sit for you. But I thought you said you was a landscape artist." Deion chuckled. "Are you telling me my face has ridges and valleys like the Spanish countryside?"

Sophie laughed. "No, of course not. Although I sometimes think there's a whole world of stories in your gaze. I think I used 'landscape artist' as an excuse, for my own protection. It's easier painting trees and hills; but as the days go by, I find myself wanting to paint the things that matter most. There's nothing like witnessing death to make you appreciate life . . . and friends."

Footsteps came from around the church and paused. Sophie turned to see who it was, and her fork slipped from her hand to the ground.

"*Hola, señorita.* I thought I recognized that jabbering voice. Never stop talking, do you? I heard you all the way across the wide plains and followed the sound here." The speaker tipped his black hat to her.

"Walt? What in the world are you doing here?" She put down her plate and offered him a quick hug.

"Well, I met a friend of yours who wondered how you were doing. I told him I'd do my best to hunt you down, and with a few phone calls to some news offices, I discovered where you were." He crossed his arms over his chest and jutted out his chin. "I see you've made good use of that press pass. And just think . . . you almost didn't want my help."

"Wait a minute. Someone is . . . is looking for me?" Her heartbeat quickened. "What friend?"

"José. He's recovering up north with the help of his wife. She's a lovely woman and an exceptional nurse."

"Oh, he found her, and they're married!"

"Yes. When he was well enough to speak, he asked for her, and they transported him to the hospital in Guernica. He's been there a few weeks now, and last I heard is now living in their home."

"That's wonderful." She clasped her hands in front of her. "Thank you for telling me."

"Did you think I was talking about someone else who might be looking for you?"

"Yes. I have a dear friend, Philip—"

"Philip. Now I'm confused. I thought you were going to say Michael." He tapped his finger on his lip. "Who is Philip?"

"Wait. What do you know about Michael?"

"You didn't answer my question." Walt's small eyes narrowed, and his gaze was so intense she was forced to look away.

Sophie blew out a sigh. "He's someone I met—someone who saved both me and José on the battlefield. He's been imprisoned . . . oh, I'll tell you the rest later." She stepped closer to him and took his hands in hers. "Now, what do you know about Michael?"

"I think it would be better if José told you that."

"Will you take me to José?"

"No, I figured you'd take me. You're the one with the driver, aren't you?"

"Oh, Deion . . . I'm so sorry. I forgot to introduce you."

Sophie turned, and the large man stood, extending his hand. "Yessir, nice to meet you, Walt. I'd be happy to drive you both where you need to go. Where's that again?"

"Guernica. It's a small town near the Bay of Biscay, and, amazingly, it's one of the few places still untouched by the war. Come inside, and I'll show you on the map."

The prison cells were ankle-deep in water—no better than dugouts with iron bars and heavy wooden doors. There was no part of Philip that was not wet. The man next to him shivered in the dark corner. They took turns sitting in the light. For the next hour it was Philip's turn, and he realized as he sat there that he would never take for granted the sun's rays again.

The bang of the door startled them, and it swung open.

"You." The guard pointed to Philip. "Come with me."

Philip ran a hand through the hair that fell to his collar, then combed his fingers through his beard. Not being able to shower and shave bothered him. Feeling a weakness in his limbs from lack of use did too.

He strode into the commander's office—the fourth commander in as many weeks. Only this one had given him hope. Just a few days ago he'd listened to Philip with a compassionate gaze and promised to check into his story.

Now the man motioned to the empty chair on the other side of the desk. "Philip, have a seat."

Philip's heart pounded at hearing his first name. It had to mean something.

"I've reviewed your story of finding the German on the side of the road. I sent men out to search the area you described and they found an airplane crashed nearby—a German plane."

Philip sat straighter in his chair. "They did? Does that mean you believe me?"

"It helped. There was one other thing that convinced me. These . . ." He opened the top drawer of his desk and pulled out a stack of letters, then handed them to Philip.

The envelopes had been opened. Philip turned them over and saw the return address. Tears sprang to his eyes as he recognized his father's handwriting.

"With volunteers being moved around so much, it's hard to get mail to them. We do the best we can. Some of these were sent months ago."

"May I?" Philip asked, lifting one of the envelopes. His throat felt tight and he swallowed hard.

Dear Son,

Here's another of my favorite passages: Isaiah 42:6–9.

"I the Lord have called thee in righteousness, and will hold thine hand, and will keep thee, and give thee for a covenant of the people, for a light of the Gentiles;

"To open the blind eyes, to bring out the prisoners from the prison, and them that sit in darkness out of the prison house.

"I am the Lord: that is my name: and my glory will I not give to another, neither my praise to graven images.

"Behold, the former things are come to pass, and new things do I declare: before they spring forth I tell you of them."

Your mother and I are keeping you in our prayers. It rained again today, nothing unusual. We were sorry to hear about Attis's death; Louise told us. She has been visiting a lot lately, and we've been praying with her too. Ma's made dinner. Sure smells good. Hope the food isn't too hard to digest there.

Love, Dad

Philip refolded the letter and started to open another when the officer interrupted.

"No need to look at them now. You can take them with you and read them at your leisure."

Philip looked at him in surprise. "I'm free to go?"

"Yes, comrade. I'm sorry for the misunderstanding."

Philip held up the letters. "These letters played a part in changing your mind? I don't understand."

The officer lowered his head. "The fact is, we can't be certain. You could be a spy. I've learned in the few months I've been here not to judge people by what they seem to be. But as I read these letters, I kept coming back to the thought that you could very well be innocent. That you had no involvement with the German, but just happened to be at the wrong place at the wrong time."

He paused, as if weighing his words, then sighed deeply. "And since it seems to be a coin toss, at least by letting you go I'll have a part in helping to answer a father's prayers. . . ."

The officer lifted his head and met Philip's eyes as if seeking the truth with one look. He must have seen his answer there, because he cleared his throat. "We'll find you a bed, give you some good food, and get you back on your feet. I read in one of those letters that you're a runner."

Philip glanced down at his thin legs. "I was."

"And you will be again. We can use men like you on the lines."

"Uh, sir, I don't mean to sound ungrateful, but I was wondering if you could help me with something else too. I need to find someone. . . ."

"From the look in your eyes, I assume this someone is a female?"

For the first time in weeks, Philip smiled. "Yes, sir. She is."

"Of course. Come back tomorrow, after a good night's sleep, and we'll discuss it. And I promise, friend, I'll see what I can do."

Chapter Thirty-Three

APRIL 24, 1937

A donde fueres haz lo que vieres.
Wherever you go, do what you see.

Spanish proverb

The Reverend Mother claimed God had brought these people into their care for a purpose, but Father Manuel only wished God had not trusted him so much. His eyelids weighed heavy as his head pounded. The dead and the dying haunted him even in his dreams. He'd only slept a few hours, but the urgent needs of those in his town prodded him from his bed like black *banderillas* stabbing his heart. Dressing, he took his walking stick and moved through the dark, asking the Lord to guide him to the lost sheep in need of his care.

Thirty minutes later, as he walked the darkened roadway, he spotted retreating soldiers staggering across the Rentería Bridge in the east, coming into the city, their faces downcast in their retreat. Their mud-splattered gray trousers had been cinched tight with pieces of rope, and Father Manuel wondered when they'd last eaten something filling.

He approached them with arms outstretched. "Men, come, you may sleep in my church tonight."

One tall, thin soldier spoke for the rest. "Sorry, Padre, but the men—they've seen a lot. They steer clear of churches, 'cause they're targets for bombers. Did you hear about Durango?"

Before Manuel could reply, the man continued.

"Bombers killed fourteen nuns in the chapel, and the Jesuit church got a direct hit, killing the priest and civilians. These soldiers—they fled the town days before the first bomb fell. They don't even feel safe sleeping in open squares or anywhere near the rail yard."

Father Manuel dug the tip of his stick into the ground, thinking of the nuns who were working so hard at this moment, caring for the injured. Emotion swelled within his chest. First he would care for these men; then he'd figure out what to do to help the Sisters.

"We have air-raid shelters built by some of the men in town," he answered, pointing toward the town square. "They aren't much, but they're reinforced with sandbags and wooden supports."

The soldier nodded, but hardly seemed impressed. "Got any better ideas?"

It occurred to Father Manuel that Father Sebastian might be willing to help, but even after three years he felt uncomfortable in the man's presence. Father Sebastian was highly respected by the people of Guernica. And though he knew it was wrong to compare, Manuel felt as if he never quite measured up in wisdom or influence. And besides, he had heard from others that Father Sebastian had not yet addressed the subject of the war from his pulpit. Who knew his true feelings? Did he inwardly side with the Nationalists? Did he have his eye on a strong state church in hopes of someday being reassigned to the Bishop's Palace in Bilbao?

"I have an idea. Follow me." Manuel turned toward the edge of town, motioning to the soldiers.

The soldiers shuffled behind Father Manuel as he led them to the gardens outside the Carmelite convent at the northern boundary of the town. Manuel retreated and watched from a distance as the men lay down on the soft ground and fell fast asleep, surrounded by the scent of spring flowers and budding trees.

Christ spent his last night in a garden too. Father Manuel quickly banished the unbidden thought, and then he returned home . . . wondering if there was rest for the weary. And if sleep would be a gift given to him that night.

With dawn came the freight trains, lined up to be loaded with supplies from one of the town's armament factories, the Talleres de Guernica. Lines of men carried boxes of hand grenades and mortar shells, followed by disassembled machinery.

Armando stood among the other workers, overseeing the loading.

Though they hadn't spoken in months, Manuel approached him, waving a hand at the commotion. "What is happening here?"

"The war is coming closer, and there is nothing to stop the destruction of our armament factory—the leaders are worried. Everything movable is being shipped out and reassembled behind Bilbao's Ring of Iron. I'm going to help oversee the reassembly."

"Ring of Iron?"

"*Sí*, a ring of antiaircraft guns, field artillery, rifle trenches, and barbed wire. And since I know how to put these machines back together, they're letting me go. Nesera is coming with me."

"The safest place to be is in the center of God's will."

Armando gave a shrug but said nothing. Father Manuel could see from Armando's eyes that he considered such a thought foolishness.

"Have you heard the stories? Some say the Moors have murdered, looted, raped . . . no one is safe. My wife, she is too precious to me. I must do everything possible to protect her."

Father Manuel scanned the crowd. Refugees loaded down with their meager possessions filled the wooden platform. "I am worried." He crossed his arms over his chest.

"About staying?"

"No, about the panic this will cause. Look at the refugees, how they are lined up, hoping to make the train."

As the loading progressed, men inched closer to the train. When the last box was on board, the train door slammed shut and the engine valve hissed.

"Now!" a man cried out. "The train is leaving. Hurry."

In a mass of bodies and swinging clubs, the men rushed the train. The eyes of the soldiers guarding it grew wide with panic.

An officer raised his rifle to his shoulder and cried, "Aim!"

The others obeyed.

"No!" Father Manuel moved in the direction of the soldiers.

The people continued forward.

"Warning volley! Fire."

Shots rang out over the heads of the refugees. Father Manuel stood before two of the closest soldiers, his arms outstretched. "Please, let me talk to the people."

"Reload!" The officer clicked his rifle bolt as he opened, reloaded, and closed his rifle; and the soldiers followed suit.

"Aim. Shoot to kill on command."

All the soldiers except the two in front of Father Manuel lifted their rifles. He moved down the line. "Stop!" He turned to the people. "Throw down your sticks!"

When they didn't listen, he strode to one of the men in the front of the line. "For the love of God, do you see what is happening? You risk being killed for the mere chance of saving your life? Does that make any sense? Stop! Put down your weapons— all of you!"

His voice was joined by two others, pleading with them to put down their weapons. Armando's voice was urgent as he jumped from the train and ran to Manuel's side. Another young officer ran in front of the soldiers, urging them to lower their rifles. They obeyed and stepped back. The refugees in front of Father Manuel also lowered their clubs.

"The train is leaving," Father Manuel said to the crowd. "It is carrying vital materials for the war effort. Even if you were to make it on board, soldiers would be waiting on the other side, prepared to kill you for acting in this manner."

He straightened his cassock as if to remind the people of his authority, and pointed to town. "Go back. All of you. Another train will come."

Within a few minutes, the crowd melted away. Manuel's hands quivered as the realization of the averted slaughter settled in, and he hid them within his long sleeves. The sound of the train pulling out of the station filled his ears, and he turned to search the windows for Armando's face. He saw only Nesera in the window, waving frantically in his direction. Manuel shielded his eyes to get a better look.

"Looking for someone?" a voice behind him asked.

Father Manuel turned to find Armando and smiled. "Yes, I was looking for one last glimpse of my dear friend. He was on that train, traveling to safety."

"Well, things have changed. He now sends his wife to a place he hopes will be safer, but he chooses to stand by his *amigo*. The tension in this town is like a volcano, ready to erupt. So tell me, do you know where I could offer my assistance?"

Manuel clasped Armando's shoulders. "But why, Armando? Why do you stay to help when you hate everything I stand for?"

"I did not know what you truly stood for until you stood between those rifles and the people." Armando interlocked his arm with Manuel's, and they turned to march toward town. "But enough talk, Father. Take me to where the work is."

"Of course."

Armando chuckled as he patted Manuel's shoulder, their steps taking them through the broad plaza. "When you made the vow to feed the Lord's sheep, I had no idea you would take it so seriously."

❧

The truck lurched slowly along the mountain road, with Deion skillfully navigating the hairpin turns.

Sophie was thankful the commanding officer had agreed to let her travel into the Basque country. To her surprise, he had immediately begun writing up the orders.

"Good idea," he had said. "With the Madrid campaign at a stalemate, the Nationalists have shifted their attention there." After scribbling his signature, he'd handed the orders to Deion.

Deion nodded. "Why, sir? What's so important about that place?"

"Mining and industry, for one. And a people who refuse to

291

submit. I heard General Mola state last night over the radio that he planned to throw the Condor Legion their direction. The major seaport and industrial center of Bilbao has been hit every clear day this month. The nearby rail junction at Durango was smashed into rubble. Even less significant targets took terrible punishment." He scratched his head. "Are you sure you want to go?"

Sophie hadn't told him about her search for José—or more accurately, about her search for the truth about Michael. "I'm sure," she said.

When they'd found Walt waiting for them at the truck, he didn't seem surprised by the approval . . . or the warnings.

"Yes, there is danger. But your paintings are making a difference, Sophie. I hear more medical workers are on their way from the States—your images moved them. The democratic people need you to keep painting, sweetheart. . . . Who would have thought? When I met you, you were some hopeless romantic, with only marriage and a happily-ever-after on your mind."

"Yeah, well, reality has a way of changing things, doesn't it?" she said, climbing into the truck. She turned to Deion. "How about some background music? Could you sing 'When the Saints Go Marching In' as a prelude to our journey?"

Deion smiled. "I can do that, Sophie, though we aren't really marching."

"Nor are we saints," Walt quipped.

"No, but it's better than 'Swing Low, Sweet Chariot.' I don't know about you, but I'm not ready for home yet—either the States or the heavenly abode."

They sang for the first few miles, but as the truck wound its way into the mountains, the effects of war were evident even in the countryside. Peasant women led skinny white oxen and sheep along the road in the half-light. Dirty children begged for food from every passing vehicle. They even spotted magnesium flares in purple-yellow and poison-green in the distance, indicating where the battle still raged.

Walt let out a heavy sigh as he stared out the window. "Things are so—" The truck banging through a hole in the road made him grunt. "—so different now. Last April, around this time, I danced at the fair in Seville. It follows Lent and Holy Week. Sometimes the sounds of castanets and dancing feet still occupy my dreams. When this whole mess is over, I'll take you there, Sophie. Take you both there. You can be rich or poor, Gypsies or foreigners. Everyone celebrates together."

"Sounds like my sort of place," Deion said, his eyes fixed on the roadway. His arms moved the steering wheel sharply in his efforts to miss another pothole.

"You never told me, Walt. How long have you been in Spain?" Sophie asked.

"Long enough to watch her die a slow death."

"Have you worked for the newspaper this whole time?"

"Yes, but I'm not one to always be on the hunt for the next headline. Let's just say I have more interest in watching people than keeping up with politics."

"Do you like to photograph them too? The people, I mean."

"That's part of my job. A good photo, after all, can tell a whole story without words."

"I agree. And that's why I have a question for you." Sophie bit her lower lip, turning to him. "I keep seeing photographs in the papers by a man named Arnold Benedict. He has this style that many newspapers seem to like—the edges of his photos look blurry, giving it a dreamy effect and making the clarity of the object in the center more stunning."

"It's called soft focus. Producers have been using it in films for years. Sometimes a special cloth is used, other times Vaseline over the camera lens." He turned to Sophie, his eyes locking with hers. "It's a difficult technique to master. Few do it well. Your Michael was one of them."

"And this Arnold Benedict is another."

"It appears so."

"Which means they could be the same person."

"It could. It very well could." Walt removed his hat, ran his hand over his sweaty brow, and returned it.

"So are you telling me that Michael is alive?"

"I'm not telling you anything. You need to talk to José."

"Walt, you're really starting to annoy me. I don't understand why you have to talk in cir—"

An ear-shattering explosion kicked the rear of the truck into the air, throwing it into a skid that nearly turned it over.

"Out, out!" Deion screamed as he brought the truck to a stop. "Everyone in the ditch!"

Sophie grabbed her satchel and followed Walt out the side door. As soon as she stepped to the ground, an instant of blinding light and a solid wall of pressurized heat ripped the air and pounded her head, quaking the earth beneath her and punching her hard to her knees. The unimaginable roar soon turned into a ringing in her ears, and pain shot through her skull. In the confusion of noise and dark haziness, she wondered if she'd been shot.

She felt hands upon her, yet her eyes wouldn't cooperate. Her lips wouldn't voice the jumble of questions and thoughts that crowded for attention. And as she felt the darkness pulling at her, drawing her inward, she refused to submit. To be counted as one of the dead.

Dear God . . . not my will, but Yours.

She didn't know if it was a dream, but through the intense ringing in her ears she heard singing . . . Deion's voice, carrying her, refusing to let go.

Chapter Thirty-Four

El que se va a la villa pierde su silla.
He who leaves the manor loses his seat.

Spanish proverb

*I*n the Church of San Juan, Father Manuel lit the altar candles. The altar was bare except for the mandatory cushion for the Missal, the two flickering candles, and the crucifix. He cleared his voice as he turned to his congregation, wondering if, after he spoke, they would ever venture through these doors again.

"It is good that you are here, but for the first time ever, I must ask you to leave. Men, you prepare your fields for the harvest, but I worry the enemy will be upon us before you have time to plant, let alone reap from your toil." Father Manuel lifted his fisted hand high in the air. "It is time to rise up, as one, to protect your families, to defend your homeland. Not only our Basque nation, but Spain. Spain needs you at such a time as this!"

A stir rippled through the congregation.

"For months I have hesitated. Failed to be bold with my words. I, like you, have heard of the horrors committed 'in the name of God' by Franco's forces. This is not the God I serve. God would never sanction such wickedness. The God I serve is the God who empowered the children of Israel to fight for the land that was theirs. Some died, yes, risking their lives for the sake of their people. Shall we, because of fear or even denial, accept all the horrors of the wicked to come upon us? If these things are precious to you—our freedom, our land, our families —then we must rise up and protect that which God has entrusted to us."

Father Manuel lowered his voice and bowed his head, opening his arms before them, wondering if he had the strength to follow through with the words he had planned and prayed over. Then he heard shuffling in the back of the room and saw Armando rising to his feet.

"Know that your silence means only one thing—you condone that which should not be done. It is time to step out of complacency and fight the battle God has given us."

Then Father Manuel strode down the aisle to Armando, and together they walked out the door, hoping others would follow. Hoping the congregation of the faithful would not continue to wait until death and destruction rained upon their doorsteps before they took action to save their lives and souls.

The first thing Sophie realized upon waking was that her head was pounding—as was nearly every part of her body. The second thing was Walt's and Deion's voices arguing over whether Babe Ruth would stay in retirement or come out for another season.

Sophie felt for the blood-soaked bandage she knew would be covering her head, but there was none. "Personally, I think the Babe needs to stop while he's ahead," she croaked. "I think I might need to consider doing the same."

"Sophie, you're awake."

She felt Deion's hands take hers, and she squeezed back. "That was a nasty explosion. Am I still in one piece?"

She opened her eyes and winced at the lights shining on her from the ceiling. Shading her eyes, she tried to examine her surroundings. Despite the blurry double vision, she saw that she was in some type of first-aid station, similar to the ones she'd manned.

Walt leaned closer. "Thankfully, yes. Although the doctor says you have a nasty concussion, and he needs to watch you for a while." He stifled a laugh.

"Okay, Walt. What's so funny?"

"I'm sorry, Sophie. I just discovered where the expression 'knocked cross-eyed' comes from."

"Very funny. What hit us?"

"Artillery. It seems the Rebels are closing in. We arrived just in time to find ourselves in the middle of it."

"Lucky us." Deion handed her a cup of water and helped her lift her head to take a sip.

"Did we make it to Guernica?"

"Not quite," Walt replied. "We're in Marquina, and it's been under attack for days. Guernica isn't too far."

"As soon as you feel better, we can move that way." Deion placed the now-empty cup on the floor. "It's a miracle, but the truck got only minor damage. Nothing to stop us now . . . well, almost nothing."

Walt shot Deion a look that Sophie couldn't read.

Deion stood. "Speaking of our truck, I'd better go see if I can round up some fuel. . . ." He limped away faster than Sophie had ever seen him move.

She turned back to Walt. "What was that about? And don't say nothing, because I saw the look you gave him."

"You need to rest, Sophie. We'll talk about it tomorrow."

"Walt, do you really believe I can rest after a statement like that?"

"All right. Remember I told you the Basque country is in the middle of all the action? Well . . . I've received information that it may be too dangerous to go there."

" 'Received information'? From whom? You're a newspaperman. You report the news, not . . ." Sophie sat up, leaning her back against the wall. She cocked her head, studying his face, remembering how they'd met, how he'd fooled her into believing he couldn't speak Spanish. What other things did she not know about him?

"I saw you that day during the bombing near the Telefónica, didn't I? Walt, you're more than a newspaperman, aren't you?"

He glanced away, looking to the doorway as if hoping someone would enter to distract them. "Sophie, to tell you more than you've already guessed would be to put your life in danger."

She pulled her hands away. "So you do know more than you're letting on. More about the war, about Michael, and maybe about me too? When you approached me at the border, that wasn't simply a chance meeting, was it?"

"No, Sophie, but I can't tell you anything more. I want you to talk to José first. He's in Guernica. He . . . well, he knows the whole story concerning Michael even better than I. Let me just say that nothing has been as it's seemed. . . ."

Sophie ignored the pounding in her head, ignored her trembling hands. "Then we have to go. I need to talk to José. I know it's dangerous, but are we safe anywhere in this country?"

Walt grinned. "Not entirely, though you never heard it from me."

"Then can we leave?" Sophie swung her legs over the bed to stand. Suddenly the room began to spin, and a rush of nausea washed over her. She moaned and settled back into the bed.

Walt stood. "We'll leave, Sophie, but maybe not today. You don't have to think of any of this now . . . just rest, sweetheart."

A nurse came in then and handed Sophie a small white pill. Sophie had given them out to injured soldiers many times. She knew it would ease her physical pain and help her sleep. She just wished it could touch the pain in her heart as well.

She took the pill; then she rolled to her side and pulled the blanket over her head. As she drifted off, the memory of Michael's voice broke through her haze. "Oh, *Divina* . . ."

Just two words, but enough for Sophie to question if she'd ever really move on.

When Sophie awoke, the ache in her head was gone and Deion was by her side. "Hey, there, it's you. You're a sight for sore eyes," she mumbled.

"You expecting someone else?" He offered her a cool compress for her head and a cup of water.

"No, not really." She drank deeply from the cup, then handed it back.

"I know you're most likely not up to this, but we need to talk about whether we head to Guernica today or wait until tomorrow. Walt's afraid the bombers will come back, and if we plan to stay here, we need shelter."

The church bells began to chime, warning them that bombers had been spotted in the distance.

Sophie kicked her feet over the bed and stood, reaching her hand to Deion. "I suppose that's our answer. We're not going anywhere yet."

She let Deion lead her away, down to a crowded basement room. Yet even more than Sophie's fear of the bombers was her realization that soon she would know the truth about Michael. But as the bombs fell around them, she found it was Philip she wished were by her side. *Is he still in prison?* she wondered. *Is he alive?*

After an hour, the sounds of the bombing faded, and Sophie and Deion were two of the last to straggle out of the shelter.

"You're sure Walt had someplace safe to go, right? He didn't get caught in that?" She'd asked the question at least a dozen times, but Deion's answer remained the same.

"That's what he said."

They got to the top of the steps, back to ground level, and Sophie let her eyes scan the destruction. Though the bombers hadn't struck their area, smoke and flame filled the sky across town, evidence of the bombers' target. And in the distant mountains, intermittent shelling flashed as if lightning radiated from the ground, followed by deep thuds.

"I have to ask, Sophie. Where do you want to go next? Guernica? Back to Madrid?"

"Honestly? I want to rewind nine months and talk myself out of crossing the border."

She stepped gingerly over the concrete rubble as they walked back to the first-aid station. Around her others walked through the streets, their glazed looks of disbelief bringing an ache to Sophie's soul.

Deion smiled. "Well, if time travel doesn't work, there's one other thing."

"What's that?"

"Listen to that nagging voice in your head. The one that tells you the right thing to do. Some people call it conscience. I call it gut feeling. My mama says for those who believe in God, it's His voice speaking."

"Before I came here, I wouldn't exactly have called myself a woman of faith. But God's given me some wonderful people to lean on, and I've chosen to follow Him." She slid her arm into Deion's. "Though my steps haven't been all too sturdy or sure."

They walked in silence for a few minutes; then Sophie paused and looked up into his face. "Listen to that nagging voice, huh? The one that says maybe I didn't come here for Michael, after all. That maybe that was just the means to get me here to fulfill a greater purpose."

Deion rubbed his chin. "That sounds like the one to me."

"Yeah, well, I hope that small voice sends a telegram to my heart before it breaks in two."

Chapter Thirty-Five

APRIL 26, 1937

Quien con lobos anda a aullar aprende.
Live with wolves, and you learn to howl.

Spanish proverb

*R*itter scanned the skies over the mountains surrounding Vitoria as he strode down the tarmac, attempting to hide his limp the best he could. The wind from the south blew on his face as he crossed the airfield.

As of last month, a new announcement had been pinned to the bulletin board, signed by General von Richthofen himself. It reminded all concerned that the Condor Legion would only attack military targets; however, it should do so without regard for the civilian population.

Of course, it really wasn't anything new. The standing order, oft repeated, was that if ever a target could not be hit because of foul weather, the bombs should be dropped anywhere over enemy territory.

Better to take out future enemies than waste the bombs, Ritter thought, and in his mind he hoped for a roadway filled with fleeing troops—like those the reconnaissance planes had spotted near Guernica.

He saw movement from the corner of his eye and turned toward the large fenced compound surrounded by Spanish soldiers. Inside the fence, like worker ants surrounding a colony, the ground crew were peeling back canvases to reveal mounds of bombs and ammunition. Once they uncovered it, they would sort out the armaments needed for the day's mission and carefully move them out on wagons for loading onto the planes.

He had nearly reached the briefing room when a voice called out to him.

"Herr Agler!" An office worker scurried toward him. "You asked me to find you as soon as mail arrived from Berlin."

Ritter glanced at the first envelope and recognized his uncle's handwriting. Stuffing that into his pocket, he turned his attention to the second envelope, addressed in Isanna's familiar script. The grin lasted only a moment, however, replaced by a different heat. A fire of anger and disbelief coursed through him as the name in the upper left corner registered in his mind: Isanna *von Herman*.

Isanna . . . had married. In the one month he had been out of communication, she had gone and married Xavier von Herman. Fury made it hard for him to breathe.

Another officer approached, matching Ritter's stride as they reached the briefing room. He opened the door for Ritter. "Herr Agler, are you all right? Your eyes are red. Is your sight okay? Maybe you should sit this one out."

"My sight? No, sir. I see better now than ever before. I want to do this. I need to do it, sir."

He needed, more than anything, to feel the power of the plane. To vent his fury. To release the ache in his heart by focusing it on dutiful destruction. He crumbled the letter and stuffed it into his pocket. Someone would pay for his pain. If it weren't for the Reds and their insane fight, he'd be home now. *He'd* be married to Isanna.

How could she have done it? Hadn't she wanted a hero? He'd fought for *her*.

Ritter's gut tightened with frustration.

He saw the same anxiety among the other pilots. Like bulls snorting to get into the arena, the men stalked around him restlessly. Long periods of bad weather had kept them grounded, and even the brothels and strong Spanish wine had lost their appeal.

Ritter envied them their ignorance. They had remained in the skies, a barrier of air and clouds separating them from the people their bombs had destroyed. But he had experienced something they had not. For him, the enemy now had names and faces. Faces that visited him in his dreams as friends. Faces he longed to wipe away forever.

Sometimes in the night, Ritter found himself awake and thinking of those who had carried him, injured and broken, to a warm and safe place. In the morning, he refused to linger on these thoughts. Instead, he kept his body moving, running in place, doing stretching exercises. Movement kept his mind focused, until his wounds ached. Then the memories came again— stabbing him even deeper than the pain in his leg.

He cursed under his breath at the memory of Sophie's face. These women . . . they were demons sent to destroy him.

He found a seat among the other pilots and tried to focus on the map.

"As you can see here, three roads converge into one." The briefing officer held his pointer against a location on the map. "Just outside Guernica. They merge to a point where the Rentería Bridge crosses the river Mundaca." He adjusted his pointer's position. "It has been reported that enemy troops are retreating into—" The pointer circled a spot. "This area. If we let them gain a stronghold here, they will be difficult to dislodge. Do whatever it takes, men, to ensure that doesn't happen."

Sophie kept herself busy assisting with the patients, wrapping bandages, sterilizing instruments—anything to keep her mind off Michael.

As the new morning dawned, Deion brought her a cup of coffee and news from Guernica. "The town is filling with refugees, but it looks safe. I have your things loaded in the truck."

"Thanks, Deion. Maybe I'll catch a few winks on the road. Walt knows too well how soundly I can sleep in a vehicle."

"Oh, Walt isn't coming. Some officer needed him. He says to go on without him, and he'll meet us there." Deion rubbed his forehead. "And he left you a message. He says even after you talk to José, don't make any decisions until he gets back."

Sophie rested her hands on her hips. "He said that, did he?"

Deion laughed at her indignation. "Yes, he did. Can you be ready soon?"

"Yes, Deion." Sophie took off the smock she wore to protect her clothes, refusing to live with lies any longer. "I'm ready now."

Ritter had refused to rub his aching leg in the presence of the commander, lest he question the pilot's ability to fly. He'd hoped this would be the day of his return. Now he needed it to be so.

He quickened his stride toward the airplanes tucked under the trees. Their branches flexed in the wind, confirming what he'd already known from the moment he awoke. The wind came from the south, along the runway—fine weather, flying weather. Killing weather.

He moved through the checks, his jaw clenched. His eyes burned, but he refused to submit to his emotions.

Ritter moved the flaps into position and flipped the mags on. The whine of a starter motor was interrupted by a loud popping as first one cylinder fired, then others in rapid succession. The exhaust's smoke and roar, and a spinning propeller signaled him that his killing machine was coming to life. The plane rocked on its landing gear, and when the engine smoothed out, he motioned for the ground crew to remove the wheel chocks. Finally, he released the brakes and taxied toward the runway. After running a pre-takeoff check, he positioned himself on the runway and advanced the throttle. The plane gained momentum rapidly and lifted gently into the air.

There were three primary missions today, and all three would converge at the Rentería Bridge in Guernica.

From his viewpoint on the mountainside, Father Manuel could see most of the old town, the streets clogged with peasants coming for market day. Tailors, ironworkers, weavers. The same type of craftsmen who had sold their goods during the six hundred years prior—soon after the city's birth—sold their wares today.

He settled on the pine-needle floor, breathing in the new scent of wildflowers poking up at the first hints of spring. His view took in the candy factory, the industrial zone, and the growing residential area where young couples raised their children just as their ancestors had done for hundreds of years. And beyond all that, wide fields where it was said medieval knights had jousted, and where he and Armando had searched for spearheads in the hot summer sun.

He had needed to get away. To think. He knew yesterday's words had little effect when last night he'd heard Guernica's town band warming up for the regular Sunday night dance in the main plaza. To hear the people's laughter and dancing gave him a small hint of the ache Moses must have felt on Mount Sinai as he heard the people's celebrations below. Not that he was comparing himself to the holy prophet, except that he now understood, in a small way, the weight of one's people's needs on one's shoulders. And worse yet, they were needs the people themselves refused to address.

So, as the music played and the people danced, he'd done the only thing he knew to do. Last night at eight-thirty, the door had been unlocked by one of the nuns in the Convent of Santa Clara. Every evening at the same time they opened the door and accepted requests for prayer.

Father Manuel had placed a folded piece of paper on the silver tray in the chapel, wondering how many of the requests for healings, for safety, for hope had been answered over the years— and if his would be one of those.

After that, he'd returned to the hospital area to help Sister Joséfina hang the last of the blackout curtains. He still hadn't slept; and as he sat in the woods to pray, he felt himself drifting off, until he could no longer tell if the prayers running through his head were part of his conscious thought or his dreams.

By the time Father Manuel awoke to the sound of the church bells ringing, warning of incoming planes, the sun had faded on the horizon, filtering through the pine trees. He wasn't sure what time it was, but from the farmers and traders packed into the central marketplace, exchanging their cattle and produce, he assumed it was midafternoon.

He stood and watched the people below heading for cover in cellars, under bridges, and in prepared dugouts. He ran down the hill as fast as his legs would carry him, knowing the Sisters were most likely in a panic, attempting to do the best they could to create a safe place for those in their care.

Before he reached the base of the mountain, the first German bomber passed low as if the airmen inside were locating the targets below. It took only a moment to pass over the town. Then the plane banked wide, circled the town, and made another pass. This time, however, twelve shiny bombs fell from the plane's bomb bay. They fell in a tight cluster toward the railroad station and plaza. Another strike blew the front off the Julian Hotel, exposing four floors. A cry caught in Father's Manuel's throat at the sight.

Fernando Vegal, one of Manuel's most faithful parishioners, stood in the field just outside of town, his head lifted to the sky in disbelief as a plane swooped low toward him.

Father Manuel ran toward the field. "Fernando, get down! To the ground, now!" He waved his arms and ran toward the man, cursing the heavy robe that weighed him down. The patter of machine gun fire stopped Father Manuel in his tracks, and he dove onto the ground as he used to dive into the river as a boy.

His ears echoed from the sound of the explosions and the crumbling houses and buildings. The cries of the people—his people, his Lord's people—seemed to rip his heart from his chest. And the continuous pealing of the church bells warned of more to come.

Chapter Thirty-Six

Quien a buen árbol se arrima buena sombra le cobija.

If you lean against a good tree you will be protected by a good shadow.

Spanish proverb

*R*itter's He.51 seemed to crawl through the sky. He cursed, wanting to get to Guernica and finish the job. Ahead, he finally spotted the target and watched as the first bomber swooped down, dropping six 500-pound bombs. Five minutes later, a second bomber. After that, three Junkers, until finally a steady stream populated the sky.

Ritter nudged his control stick forward. Sweeping down, he eased his plane right until his gun sight bore down on scurrying forms. He squeezed the machine gun's trigger, satisfied with the pounding recoil passing through the airframe. Bullets—synchronized to fire through the propeller—released on them like rain.

The people in the town below—young, old, women, children —ran from dugouts in panic, and he took aim. The way they crumbled to the ground reminded Ritter of hitting pinecones on the back fence.

A cloud of smoke and grit rose so thick over the town that Ritter knew the bombers to follow would have to fly even lower to distinguish the town from the countryside. He flew lower until he was able to make out the people's panicked faces, glancing over their shoulders as they tried to run from his approach.

He laughed as he watched the people suffer indecision, running hither and thither, then back to the dugouts' false security. The targets failed to realize the bombers would come yet again. Like a Wagnerian opera, a certain rhythm would soon be established—one the German officers had thought through with care. First, bombs to draw the targets out. Then, machine guns to drive them below. Finally, incendiary bombs to burn them alive.

Ritter laughed again, but for the first time, with his laughter came tears. Wiping them from his face, he swung alongside the trucks that rumbled on the mountain road toward the town.

Sophie was jerked awake by the truck slamming on its brakes. Her head slammed against the glass window. "Ouch, Deion. What is it?"

As soon as the words were out of her mouth, she recognized the droning of aircraft. The same sounds that filled her ears day and night in Madrid had followed her here.

"An air raid, Sophie. We need to take cover."

They were only a few miles out of town, on a hillside looking into the valley. She gasped as she clearly saw the Nazi insignia on the planes' wings. They filled the sky, bombers and fighter planes too.

"What are they doing? This isn't Madrid. It's just some sleepy village in the middle of nowhere."

"They're destroying it; that's what they're doing."

"We have to do something. Look . . ." Sophie pointed to a large building with a red cross on the roof. A bomb had struck it, crumbling one of the corners. "Even the hospitals! They're bombing the hospitals."

Deion parked the truck as far off the side of the road as he could manage. "I know what we got to do. Get out of the truck."

"What?" Sophie's eyes widened.

"We can't go into the town; that would be crazy. And if we head back, we'll be too big of a target on the road."

"So we're just going to stand here and watch?"

"No, ma'am. You're going to shoot them pictures with whatever film you have left, and then you're goin' to paint."

Sophie's heart pounded, and her hands trembled like the lone leaf left on a branch. "There's no way I can do that."

Deion turned toward her, and she saw tears welling in his eyes.

"I seen some awful things in my time, Sophie—people killed just 'cause they're colored. Killed in the most awful ways you can imagine. And no one listened or cared." His voice caught in his throat. "I saw my own father strung up on the hillside behind our home. He didn't do nothing to nobody. Was just in the wrong place at the wrong time."

Deion took a handkerchief from his pocket and blew his nose. "If we go running down there, Sophie, we can't do a thing, and we'd likely get ourselves killed doin' it. But the people down there—" He pointed to the town that was exploding in flames as they spoke. Even from the distance, people's cries floated up the hillside. "They need you to speak for them. You can tell their stories through your pictures."

Tears streamed down Sophie's face, but she squared her shoulders. She looked through the viewfinder and focused on a church in flames. Then she took another photo of people filling the roads, running out of town. She jumped as an aircraft swooped into her view . . . a fighter plane machine-gunned the people down as they ran.

Dear God . . .

Then the plane banked in a wide arc, turning toward them. It flew so low, Sophie gasped as she spotted the goggled man in the cockpit. Behind the gun sight, his eye aligned perfectly with her, and he grinned. Sophie closed her eyes and waited, fully expecting bullets to rip into her body. But when she opened them again, she saw the plane had turned and continued back toward the town.

"Deion, did you see that? I know that pilot spotted us. Why

didn't he shoot? And look, he's leaving. The other planes are coming in, and he's flying against them, heading back."

"Your job is to paint, Sophie. I decided mine is to pray."

Sophie turned to him. "Pray? I thought you didn't believe in God."

"I didn't know for myself till one minute ago, but how can I deny that? God spared us. It had to be God."

As the bombs fell, injured people filled the reception area of the Carmelite convent. The roar of bombers filled the sky, and Father Manuel knelt before the crowds, praying for them all. If the convent took a hit, then at least he wanted to know they'd meet their Maker together.

Before him, the broken people cried out for help. A woman whose arm had been torn from her body. A man whose legs were riddled with bullets. A child with burns covering her body. Their cries filled his ears.

"Padre, Padre, come . . . I'm dying. Father, bless me."

He also prayed for those still in the center of town, caught in the dense bombing. The thunder of explosions pummeled his ears, split seconds after the flashes of light. The earth trembled continually.

By seven o'clock the droning of the airplanes ceased, and he walked down the street to inspect the damage. Gone were the roof tiles, wooden porches, and half-timbered houses. Slowly, more people emerged from shattered doorways, stupor on their faces, and Father Manuel found it hard to believe anyone had survived.

More people staggered to the convent, seeking medical care, and just when he thought they'd seen the worst, the sound of aircraft came again. Father Manuel glanced up to see another wave of airplanes racing toward the town at a high altitude. From the moment the bombs began falling, he guessed what they were. Incendiary bombs. In seconds, the entire town would erupt like a furnace.

"Dear God," he muttered. "It wasn't enough to destroy the city; now they've chosen to burn the evidence."

An orange glow on the horizon, as bright as the sun's morning rays, lit the path to Guernica. Even the clouds hovering over the distant mountains glowed as they reflected the flames. As the truck approached, it seemed the whole city was alight from end to end.

The fleeing masses clogged the road. Antique farm carts, pulled by oxen, carried their occupants to Bilbao. They'd survived the destruction, but Sophie could tell from their faces they hadn't escaped the horror.

Low hammering sounds in the distance were carried along on the treetops. Sophie knew they were sounds of artillery fire that interrupted the peaceful stillness of the morning. The ground battle neared.

In the town itself hardly a building stood, and not one roof remained. Piles of rubble blocked every road. Trees were now charred stumps. Automobiles had been catapulted and lay scattered on top of the rubble.

But worse than all of that was the Goya-esque scene of bodies. Men, women, and children. Some in coffins, others on stretchers. None of them whole. Some charred corpses were almost completely consumed . . . lying where they'd fallen—with no one to take them away.

The appalling stench and smoke from the fires thickened the air. Sophie covered her nose, but it did little good. After endless detours around fires, debris, and corpses, the truck finally pulled to a stop in front of a convent. A long line of wounded men, women, and children huddled together on the ground, some surrounded by weeping families. Flies covered the faces of the children, but no one had the strength to brush them away.

News traveled quickly, and foreign journalists were already arriving, wanting to hear the story. Sophie looked around at the vehicles that entered the town, searching for Michael's face, just in case, and wishing she'd urged Walt to tell her the truth. Who knew if she'd even be able to find José in this destruction?

And even then, her search for answers seemed so trivial compared to the horror before her. Everywhere she looked, a dazed population sifted through rubble, searching for loved ones and treasured possessions. She wandered through the town, taking it in.

She glanced over at a nearby field and saw a large group of people gathering. She started to walk that direction, but Deion caught her arm.

"Don't do it. I heard two men talking. One correspondent counted six hundred bodies. It's best you not look."

"What were they after?" Sophie wrapped her arms around herself. "I too heard some men talking. There were only two things here that could even be considered threats—the small-arms factory and the highway bridge outside of town. And they're virtually untouched. The Germans missed their mark."

She saw a priest standing before a still-smoldering church, and hurried to his side.

He glanced at her camera and spoke as if reciting a news report. "Hardly anything escaped the flames. This was my church . . . or rather, the church the Lord entrusted to me."

They stood quietly, staring at the rubble; then Sophie spoke. "Excuse me, Father, do you know a José Guezureya? He has married a nurse from this area, and they live here now."

"I'm sorry. There are many new faces in town. Far too many for me to keep track."

Sophie watched as the priest scanned the destruction around him.

"Even now . . . I don't know who still lives." He turned to her. "I'm sorry. I am Father Manuel." He gave a deep sigh, almost a groan. "God knows the days of our lives, and that is not my concern. Before this . . ." He waved a hand toward the rubble that used to be his parish. "It was up to me to do what I could. But now it has become a matter for God."

"We'd like to help, Father, if there's anything we can do."

The priest lifted his gaze and looked into Sophie's face again. For the first time she realized how young he was—not much older than she.

"While his child lay close to death, King David fasted and prayed. But once the child was gone, he rose and dressed and lifted his hands to the Lord. We can plead with the Almighty, but the matter is His."

Father Manuel reached for her hands, and Sophie offered an understanding smile.

"You say you want to help?" he asked. "Good, come with me. There is much to be done."

Chapter Thirty-Seven

Más vale pájaro en mano que cientos volando.
A bird in the hand is better than a hundred flying birds.

Spanish proverb

Sophie heard footsteps and paused, her fingers still clutching the filthy sheet laid over the body of a dead woman. The face stared up at her with an empty gaze, and Sophie quickly covered it again. She'd been given one simple task—to prepare the bodies for burial. She also included a prayer—not for the dead, but for those left behind, forced to live with the loss.

Deion had an even more challenging job, searching for those living and dead—mostly dead—amidst the rubble.

The footsteps neared and Sophie looked up, expecting one of the nurses. Instead, a young man stood there with hat in hand. He was clean and wore a suit, and she knew he must be one of the reporters trickling into town.

"Are you Sophie Grace?"

She turned, surprised. "Yes."

"I've been sent for you, miss."

"By whom?"

"Your news service. They heard you were here, and they're

evacuating the rest of their reporters and photographers. There's a car outside to take you to Bilbao, and from there to France."

"I'm sorry. I'm not leaving."

The man twisted his hat in hand. "Your editor was afraid you would say that. He asked me to wait until evening. I'll be outside."

Sophie continued to work at caring for the bodies until numbness overwhelmed her. The first body had touched the core of her soul, but now . . . she was amazed how easy it was to get used to such things.

A few minutes later, Father Manuel approached. "Sofía, you have worked much too hard. There is some food waiting for you in the kitchen."

"Thank you, Father, but I'm not hungry."

"Well, then, at least take a few minutes for some fresh air."

Sophie picked up her satchel and strode outside, peering at the waiting car and the driver slumped in the seat. Her heart ached. Then the throbbing of her chest spread to her stomach, causing it to knot.

With ten small steps, she could reach the driver. In five minutes, her things could be loaded and she'd be on her way. She could leave this country altogether. Forget Spain. Forget this war. Forget the life she'd planned with Michael.

Sophie closed her eyes and saw his face—his eyes more vivid to her than her own reflection. Then fragmented thoughts came. Memories all jumbled together like a kaleidoscope of *him*.

Their first kiss.

Her hand in his.

Their walks through the streets of Boston.

Her tears at every parting. And the way he lifted her from the ground and twirled her around every time he saw her again.

She was alone now. Truly alone, and living in the middle of heartache. But at least in France she'd be safe. . . .

It was only ten steps.

Ten steps, and I'd lose myself forever. Lose my new mission, forsake the person I've become.

The driver glanced her way, his cocked eyebrow expressing his concern. His fingers tapped the steering wheel.

Sophie swallowed hard, but the tears remained locked tight. And with a firm set of her chin, she waved the driver away.

I choose Spain. I choose God's plan for my life. It was a decision she'd made more than once, and one she most likely would have to reconfirm with each new heartache. But it was the right path, she knew.

She rose and moved to the garden behind the convent. Part of it had burned, but for the most part it appeared untouched. She hurried to a bench near a large oak and crumbled to her knees. "Please, Lord," she mumbled, "in my weakness be strong." A sob caught in her throat. "Take away the memories. The desire. Help me do the right thing."

Again Sophie heard footsteps on the gravel walkway behind her. She turned and saw Walt. His hat was set firmly in place, as usual.

"I talked to the driver from the news service," he said.

She closed her eyes and rested her head on the bench.

"You considering it?"

She looked back at him. "I'd be lying if I said I didn't consider it. But I've made a different choice—one with far more questions than answers. And I'm praying . . . and I'm feeling strengthened."

"Well, I have something that might make it easier to decide. Or rather, someone."

Sophie looked past Walt to the garden gate and saw a tall man with blond hair. Tears trickled down her cheeks as Philip strode to her. From the corner of her eye, she saw Walt disappear around the corner, giving them privacy in their reunion.

"You're alive. You're here," she whispered.

Philip knelt beside her and slid an arm around her shoulders. "May I pray with you?" he asked, his voice quivering.

Sophie nodded, unable to look into his eyes for fear she would begin to sob.

With a gentleness that amazed her, Philip prayed for her heart, for her path, and for José and whatever answers he held.

"And, Lord, I know what's in my heart, but I find it so hard to express. God, if this is Your timing, give us a chance to explore our friendship and care for one another, and discover Your plan for us, whatever that includes."

Wiping her tears, she dared to open her eyes and peer into his.

Tears also rimmed Philip's eyes, yet instead of wiping them away, he held her gaze. "I do, you know. Care for you, that is."

"Me too. That's why I was so worried." She slugged his shoulder. "What took you so long?"

"It's a long story. But I'm serious, Sophie. I have a hard time expressing myself. The words get all jumbled in this thick skull of mine. But I've had a lot of time to think, and I'm sure it was no accident that I happened to be on that battlefield when you needed help. . . ."

Sophie nodded. "I know that meeting you was part of God's plan for me too."

Despite their time apart, there was a look of tenderness in Philip's eyes that she'd never be able to capture if she attempted a thousand portraits.

"Walt said you've decided to stay in Spain. I just wish I could protect you. Keep you safe. Maybe you should reconsider. . . . After all, you didn't come to Spain for this war. You came for—"

Instead of letting her thoughts dwell with what might have been, Sophie leaned against Philip's shoulder. "I came for more than I knew . . . much more. And besides, do you think you'd stop worrying if I went to France?" She brushed a piece of ash from Philip's sleeve. "I'm not sure anyplace is free from conflict these days . . . and besides, isn't the safest place the center of God's will?"

Then she remembered, and sat up straight. "Well, I do have a trip to take. Maybe you could come with me."

"A trip? To where?"

"To Bilbao. Father Manuel has to meet someone at the palace of the bishop or something, and he needs a ride. He's already heard over the radio that the Germans are denying their actions. They say the Reds burned down the city, and some of the newspapers believe it. The bishop asked Father Manuel to travel to Bilbao and tell his story. It is the best thing he can do for his people now—to tell the world of their pain and loss. And he asked me to come because he thinks my photos and paintings will increase the impact of what he has to say. You can come too, can't you?" She lowered her head back to his shoulder.

"I'll have to get that approved . . . I just can't go abandoning my duties now, can I?"

Sophie wasn't sure if by duties he meant the front lines or he meant her. She also thought she felt the softest touch of his lips against her hair, but she couldn't be sure.

"Coming with me isn't abandoning anything," she said. "It's just a different set of plans from what you first thought."

And as she said those words, Sophie sensed the pain of feeling betrayed and unloved crumble like the buildings of Guernica. But instead of smoke, such as had risen from the city's ruins, she felt her own unbounded hope rising to fill her heart, her mind, her spirit. A hope that God wasn't finished with her yet—and wasn't finished with them.

Sophie looked at Philip and smiled. It was a smile that rose from deep within, from a place she hadn't known existed. "I'm learning that when you look back, those plans may turn out to be the reason something happened in the first place. . . ."

Acknowledgments

John, whose eyes shine with more love any wife could imagine possible. And whose ears always listen to my prattle as I go on and on about these stories dear to my heart.

Cory, Leslie, and Nathan. My favorite cheerleaders.

My loving family . . . grandma, dad, mom, Ronnie—who always rejoice with me.

Stacey, Kimberley, Lesley, and Melissa—my unexpected and special gifts from God.

Amy Lathrop, my right-hand-gal. Thanks friend!

My agent, Janet Kobobel Grant. I'm thankful for your wisdom and dedication.

My editor, Andy McGuire. This book is here because of your enthusiasm over my spark of an idea!

The whole Moody team, whose partnership is a true gift from God.

LB Norton. You make me look good. I consider you a friend.

My "unofficial" editors, Cara Putman, Ocieanna Fleiss, Jim Thompson, and Andrea Brunz. You're the best!

Finally, this book wouldn't be written if not for the wonderful men and women who helped with my research:

Alun Menai Williams. February 20, 1913–July 2, 2006. Veteran of the Spanish Civil War. I feel privileged to have met you and to have witnessed your enthusiasm for this project.

Karen Lynn Ginter. Thank you for making Spain real to me!

Norman Goyer. Though we may not be related, I'm thankful for all your expert aviation advice!

Stellan Bojerud for excellent research assistance.

And others from the Abraham Lincoln Brigade Associated who answered all my questions and provided insight.

Thank you!